Ferryl Shayde

Book IV:

Storm and Steel

By
Vance Huxley

© 2018 Vance Huxley

Published by Entrada Publishing.

Printed in the United States of America.

Contents

Dedication
To my Noeline and to the Joy of my life

Acknowledgements

Thank you to my editor Sharon Umbaugh,
for turning my words into a book worth reading.

My thanks to Rachel at Entrada
for all her hard work and encouragement.

The Big Reveal

For those who might wish to refresh their memories, there are comprehensive glossaries at the end of this book. They describe characters, magic, the magical world, magical creatures, glyphs, Bonny's Tavern, and The Accord regulating magic-users. The index lists them as Abel's World, Ferryl's World, Bonny's Tavern and The Rules of the Magical Tavern.

Once the most dangerous magic creatures on earth, such as dragons and giants, were dead, enslaved, or both, religion and sorcery fought for world domination. Since both sides were human, and their forces evenly balanced, fighting to the death would have left very little for the eventual winner. The threat of extinction forced the plethora of faiths, and independent practitioners, to stop fighting. When the less controlled Gods and sorcerous alliances continued the struggle, the dominant players agreed to combine, and eradicated them. Rivalry continued, with sorcery and religion fighting each other, and other members of their own community, but a balance was maintained. Eventually, one God threatened to become dominant. This time the two sides had learned to talk first, which led to the Accord.

Under the Accord, the churches declared there were no witches, and magic did not exist. Most people never realised the truth, that sorcery and religion had agreed to hide all signs of magic. The public declaration signalled an uneasy peace between them. The magically aware witches, warlocks, sorcerers and sorceresses agreed to stay out of the public eye, providing the church restrained its activities to areas where believers were in the majority. Sorcery stopped targeting true believers, and the church agreed that their witch-hunters would stay inside church lands. Sorcery was left to control any areas not protected by prayers.

In effect, the world split into three spheres of influence, one of which was controlled by religions and another by sorcerous rulers. The spheres of influence were split into areas protected by individual religious centres, and areas controlled by individual sorcerers, known as demesnes. Within those areas, the population would be protected from magical pests.

Magical creatures were left to run riot over the rest of the globe, areas with sparse human populations. The majority of non-magical mankind lived on in blissful ignorance, unaware of the ugly, sometimes venomous creatures that swarmed elsewhere.

Unfortunately, as generations passed without magical miracles, belief in magic faded, and so did the revenue for the witches and priests who provided protection. Here and there, then in increasing numbers, small areas were left without either a witch or a priest. The abandoned humans were still considered a part of a sorcerer's domain, or a church parish, but small magical pests began to appear.

All over the world there are now heavily populated areas with no protection, poor areas where few of the inhabitants pay a tithe to a church, and none believe in witches. In the UK the poorer housing estates and small villages are affected the most. The church or sorcerers still hunt down any large magical creatures, such as trolls and ogres, but consider the smaller types insignificant, not worth the cost of hunting them. As a result, the resident humans are now overrun by invisible magical creatures such as globhoblins, hoplins, pictsies, and fae. The sheer numbers of the smaller magical creatures, each one sucking a little magic, are now affecting the health of the unprotected humans. The young, the old and the sick are affected most, sometimes dying when their natural levels of magic drop too far.

The Accord is still in effect, but the remaining sorcerers, non-religious wielders of magical glyphs, are concentrated in the wealthier areas of towns and cities. These days, the most valuable demesnes are those with the most lucrative contracts, held by the strongest magic wielders. Most modern sorcerers live in penthouses or mansions, rather than draughty, remote fortresses with questionable hygiene. Fewer and fewer witches can survive, because those who believe in charms and curses, enough to pay for them, are dying out. Most village churches are closed, while in other places there are barely enough prayers to keep magical creatures at bay. The churches, synagogues, mosques, shrines and altars in wealthier areas can afford magically-aware clergy, to reinforce the prayers of the faithful, while the prayers in very religious areas provide surplus power for the priests to use elsewhere.

With the sorcerers' demesnes, and many churches, only competing for the wealthier humans, they need fewer apprentices or magically-aware priests. Each sorcerer or sorceress only recruits enough teenagers to replace apprentices killed, or reaching the end of their contracts. The church only takes recruits from those who already attend services. Some of the church recruits become part of their network of magically-aware police, news reporters and similar posts used to suppress any reports of magic. The strongest religious recruits, especially those inclined towards violence, join the Church Militant as magical medics or to fight God wars against other religions and heretics. Today, most frontline priests are unaware magic even exists, so they are unable to recognise the signs of awareness in teenage worshippers.

All humans are capable of using magic, they absorb it daily from the air, but only a few become aware of their potential. An increasing number of people now live in areas where neither church nor sorcerers will spot the signs of magical awareness. The result is that some potential magic users grow up almost aware, seeing occasional movements in the shadows. Others become fully aware and can see magical creatures, but don't know why, and often take to drink or drugs to deal with the hallucinations. Worse, if the person doesn't become aware of magic until they are in their mid-twenties, their brain can't adapt. Suddenly seeing all the magical creatures that surround everyone, without any way of driving them away, is bad enough. The changes in their body and mind, as their brain tries to control this new talent, usually drives the person insane.

In the village of Brinsford, tucked up against the Pennines in central England, a small group of teenagers, a faded sorceress, and a puff of wind began to change that. Now their group has spread to the market town of Stourton, and their numbers have grown to over sixty amateur magicians. So far the group has grown up without real rules or control, but now all that must change.

*   *   *

The group, the Taverners because they all play a new board game called Bonny's Tavern, defeated a savage attack by the dominant local sorcerer. He died, as did most of his apprentices, which means that under the magical laws of England the leader of the Taverners inherited the dead man's demesne, and his wealth and power. Nobody else can do so, because unknown to most, their leader is a very distant blood relative to a dead sorcerer, a very powerful one. Two days after the big fight, Abel Bernard Conroy, a seventeen-year-old student, has to explain to his friends and fellow magic users exactly who he has become.

The gathered Taverners are a magical anomaly, trainees who are not tethered and controlled by a sorcerer. Two years ago Abel and his two best friends, Kelis and Rob, invented Bonny's Tavern. When they accidentally learned about magic the trio found it funny to add real creatures, invisible to most people, to their game. They'd even added one magic symbol, known as a glyph, though in a manner that shouldn't lead players into activating it. Unfortunately, the teenage beta players who tested the game, friends from school, had experimented with the instructions.

Among other things, they took to drawing the Tavern sign, hung outside the illustration of Bonny's Tavern, on their arms as a pretend protection. Since the sign was a true hex, designed by mistake when Kelis tried to banish magical slimies from her bedroom, it helped to awaken their magic. Abel, his two friends, and the faded sorceress Ferryl Shayde found themselves dealing with a score, then more, of new magic users from fourteen to twenty-two years old. After some rapid adjustment of the rules, the pre-game optional meditation now only affects those already almost aware of magic.

The gathered magical Taverners, now up to sixty, know about the Tavern sign. They also know that Abel discovered magic by accident, when he'd tripped over a stone slab while running from the local bullies. He'd woken an ancient sorceress, imprisoned in a pit for about two hundred years. Despite being freed, she had faded to where she couldn't survive on her own. Ferryl Shayde, her public name, moved into an anime-style cat-woman tattoo on Abel's left bicep. In return for freedom and protection, Ferryl offered ninety years of training and protection. Abel needed both, because until then he'd had no idea magic, or magical creatures, existed.

Now all the Taverners, teenagers who have found magic through playing the game, have gathered in a house donated by Frederick, a man in his fifties. It's time for Abel to tell the Taverners the rest of the story. He has to explain why a seventeen-year-old now has the power of life and death over the thousands of humans living in the local area, his new demesne. A magical conquest, so only the magically aware would know, but the lives of the rest now depend on his whim. Under the Accord, non-magical humans have no rights except ignorance.

To this group of youngsters, Abel is the boy with a sorceress in his arm who has shared his magic with them. To the sorcerous community, and the church, he is the blood heir to Castle House, an old building heavily protected by magic and containing an ancient, evil and incredibly powerful entity. Abel has also become the Master of Pendragon Enterprises, the business previously run by a local sorcerer, and the big ugly magical cat is out of the bag.

*   *   *

A hand squeezed Abel's and he glanced at his mentor, bodyguard, and now his thousand-year-old girlfriend. Only three other humans in the whole world, Abel's best friends Rob, Kelis and Jenny, had any idea of her true age. They also knew that Ferryl Shayde had never been human. All of them had agreed to the ephemeral being possessing what now looked like a seventeen-year-old girl's body. The host had been a blood leech victim for forty years, driven insane as the creature forced her to kill or drain blood from living victims. Ferryl had wiped the anonymous woman's fragmented memories of pain and terror, then healed and reshaped her body. The sorceress would eventually build the woman a set of new, happy memories before moving to another host. Despite that, after seeing the Taverners' reaction to leech possession, Abel, Rob, Kelis and Jenny knew they couldn't tell anyone else that Ferryl Shayde also possessed human hosts.

To keep the secret, Ferryl and Abel had created a new life, a magical being. Abel's tattoo now held Zephyr, a puff of wind imbued with Abel's magic and some of his nature, and enough of Ferryl's knowledge and magical skill to pretend to be a faded sorceress. A sentient puff of wind, one that had exceeded all expectations by becoming an intelligent, reasoning being with her own personality. The Taverners believed that Zephyr had been the sorceress in the tattoo all along, but hiding under an assumed name.

Right now Zephyr's 'voice' echoed in Abel's head, transmitted down their private link. "You have to go out there and speak to them soon. Unless you want me to tell them?"

"No!" Abel didn't trust Zephyr's developing sense of humour. He spoke aloud so the rest of the small group in the side room could hear. "First we get Ginny tethered, then I'll face the music."

"Now?"

Abel nodded to the apprehensive, impeccably dressed thirty-six-year-old woman stood between two fourteen-year-olds. As the only survivor among the defeated sorcerer's apprentices, Guinevere expected very little mercy. "It's time Ginny." He turned to the youngsters, the younger sisters of two of his closest friends. "Do you both understand? Ginny will not obey you, even after you tether her. She will watch over your magic practice, and protect you from danger, but she'll do it her own way. Ginny will obey Zephyr, who can read her thoughts down the tether so you'll be safe." A magical tether gave the holder access to the victim's thoughts, and allowed them to take control or administer crippling pain if necessary. Ginny would work hard at the protection part, encouraged by the magical imperatives she'd agreed to have imprinted on her mind.

Melanie, one of the fourteen-year-olds, scowled at Ginny. "Rachel explained. This is Guinevere's punishment for attacking the Tavern. I still don't see why we can't give her orders down the tether like other sorceresses do."

Rob, her big brother, butted in. "Because you pair would play with the control, poking around in her head for secrets, or insisting she did something either incredibly embarrassing or dangerous. We don't believe you could resist the temptation. This way it's a lesson for you two as well, in tolerance." His glare fixed each of the youngsters in turn. "If Ginny behaves, she doesn't deserve you two persecuting her. That will be in the new Tavern guidelines about holding grudges and payback."

"Rachel said…."

Jenny cut off Diane, her younger sister. "Rachel has agreed we need the new rules, and understands why. If Ginny accepts her punishment, she gets a second chance with us. We can't run around like vigilantes, every individual using their magic to decide who should be killed or bound. That's how other sorcerers behave, but the Tavern believe this sort of power must have constraints. Now do you want a bodyguard who can help you with learning to use magic, or do we give her to some other beginner?" Neither Jenny or Rob wanted Ginny protecting someone else, because according to Abel's solicitor the magically-aware relatives of sorcerers were sometimes targeted.

Both Melanie and Diane subsided so Abel turned back to Ginny, the captured apprentice. "Still ready for this?"

"Yes, and much happier because you've just confirmed they can't order me about." She gave Abel's arm a cautious look. "I know Zephyr has tethered me properly, and can read my mind or force me to obey orders if she wishes, but that's normal. Or normal for most apprentices, and a good result for an apprentice on the losing side of a battle." The woman, now looking much more confident, turned to each girl in turn. "Who goes first?"

Diane held up her hand. "Me, because I'm five weeks older than Melanie."

Ginny bared her shoulder and touched her skin for a moment. "Just bring magic into your palm, and touch that spot. Don't try to do anything. Zephyr set it all up ready, created your end of the tether and the parameters, so please don't get creative. At worst you'd burn out my mind, and at best Zephyr would have to set the tethers all over again." Diane did as she'd been told, pushing magic down her arm and out of her hand as if casting a glyph, but without forming any shape. "I felt you connect. Your turn Melanie." Moments later the second girl had finished and Ginny covered her shoulder.

"I can't hear you." Diane concentrated. "How can you tell me anything if I can't hear you?" She looked around, puzzled, then swung back towards Ginny. "I heard that! So you have to do it deliberately, like talking? Can you hear...?"

"No, I can't hear you because you haven't felt for your end of the tether. Remember, the tether lets us talk but I can't mind read. Concentrate on wherever Zephyr put it, and then think what you want to say." Ginny turned to Melanie. "Yes Melanie, that was perfect."

"Enough for now. You three can sort out how it works later." A relieved Abel pointed to the door. "Right now we've got a meeting to attend." He'd wondered if the tether would stop Ginny lying to the youngsters, but she just had. It would be best if the pair didn't know Ginny could eavesdrop now and then, deliberately, to make sure they weren't plotting something silly and possibly lethal. Ginny would stick to her instructions, because Zephyr could listen to her thoughts, and Zephyr could be a very unforgiving entity if friends were threatened.

*　　*　　*

Abel led the others across the corridor, into the large front-to-back lounge full of young people. Ginny and her two charges found seats while Jenny, Ferryl, Rob and Kelis followed Abel down the room to the big window at one end. By the time all five were lined up, conversation in the room had stopped and everyone faced Abel.

He took a deep breath and squared his shoulders. "We've called this meeting to explain the attack three days ago, and what it means for the Tavern. I still haven't been completely truthful about how I found magic. The meeting then, with the most adept Taverners, would have given me a chance to come clean. Pendragon attacked before I even got into the house, and we couldn't finish it afterwards. Half of us had to go home or for medical treatment."

"Magically enhanced treatment, in a private clinic." Eric, a twenty-one-year-old with no hair on half his head, raised a hand to almost-touch the pink, tender-looking skin on his scalp. "Two days ago this was red raw where the glyph burned off most of the skin. Now it only itches. I don't care what the treatment cost, it was worth it."

"More to the point, how can we afford it? I'm pretty sure the charitable donations to the Stourton Refuge can't be sidetracked, not legally. You sort of glossed over how you'd pay for the medics, and the damaged cars, unless the gold we took from Pendragon's car will cover it?" Shannon, an eighteen-year-old student at the local church school, had crashed the charity's minibus in an attempt to break Pendragon's magical shield. She had bald patches, and her skin still looked much too red from when she'd chosen being singed rather than shot. "I don't see much of the other Taverners because I go to a different school, but I'm sure someone would have mentioned finding a treasure hoard."

Abel felt relieved that Shannon had recovered her usual confidence, enough to be a spokesperson. Running down and killing Pendragon's spy, while scorched and half-blinded by the glare of magic and shields clashing, had hit her hard. Despite forgiveness from an archbishop, she'd gone through a brief crisis over continuing to use magic. "The gold would cover it, Shannon, but it won't be used for that. I'm sorry, I've been trying to work out how to start, but now all I can do is jump right in." He looked right and left. "I'm sure Kelis, Rob and Jenny will put me right if necessary." Laughter greeted that, because Kelis and Rob were Abel's oldest friends. Jenny had joined their tight group after almost dying, then being saved by Ferryl possessing her.

"And Ferryl, the latest. He needs Claris up there to make up the set." A ripple of laughter answered Warren. The Taverners thought Abel and Zephyr had used magic to heal Jenny through a kiss, a belief bolstered by Jenny becoming Abel's girlfriend for a while. Claris also became Abel's girlfriend, briefly while possessed, so Ferryl could heal her while still guarding Abel. Warren always found it funny how Abel, a scrawny, fairly unprepossessing youth, had captured four pretty girlfriends in the last year. Abel also found it funny, especially now the latest had become the real thing.

"No chance. I'm safer here." Claris looked much happier than she had while recovering from hosting a blood leech, a creature that lived inside humans and forced them to drink blood to feed it. "I'm pleased Abel is going to explain everything properly, because I'm still not totally clear on most of what happened. I know Zephyr did something to fix me, poured magic into me, and I remember feeling her voice in my head. The next few months are sort of hazy, until I woke up properly holding a tree and crying." Claris shook her head in confusion. "I've tried to work it out, but the whole thing seems like a dream. Zephyr lived in that tattoo, I saw her, but her voice in my head called herself Ferryl Shayde. I wondered about that, but it must have been a link, to control the healing. Then the real Ferryl Shayde turned up, and she sure can't fit between my ears."

Fay Shayde, known as Ferryl by everyone because they thought she'd inspired the game character, held Abel's hand so she could talk silently. "I worried about that. Jenny knows the truth, that I possessed her, but I didn't really trust Claris to keep quiet. Her memories of the whole period are deliberately fuzzy, which also helps to dull the remaining memories of the leech inside her. Now, if she gets drunk sometime, Claris can't spill everything and set the church hunting whatever possessed her."

Although she couldn't hear Ferryl, Jenny did her bit to keep up the deception. "That's just how the healing works." She winked at Abel without letting Claris see her. "Zephyr gave me a bit of magic connected back to her, so she could direct my body to heal and help it along. I thought the dreamy bit was being Abel's girlfriend, but now I know better." Abel waited patiently, accepting the teasing about being dreamy and girls waking up to reality. Several Taverners seemed relieved to have the healing explained properly.

Eventually Abel held up his hands for quiet, feeling more relaxed now. The banter about his love life had somehow dissolved that big knot of worry inside him. "If you've finished picking on me, we'll get to the real business. I've got to go right back to the beginning, to when I freed the sorceress from the pit, because there's a bit more to the story. What you never knew is the reason I could break the glyphs holding the sorceress captive. I am distantly related to a dead sorcerer. Celtchar was a powerful, rather unpleasant type, who disappeared over a hundred years ago. He left some very nasty surprises for most visitors, but my bloodline gives me access to Castle House gardens. Unfortunately, using that access brought unwanted and very dangerous attention."

*   *   *

They'd all quietened now, and stayed that way as Abel explained the boundary wards, and the real reason a mystery sorceress sent bound shades, remnants of the dead that had been magically enslaved, to try and bind him. He moved on to why more magical creatures had been sent to spy on his home and village, kalkatrie, trolls, blood leeches and an Aryadne's hound. Several nodded in understanding when Abel explained that he'd raided the blood leech nest to get the key to Castle House, rather than let some stranger open it up. They all understood the other reason, to stop the Firstseed launching any more attacks on Stourton Comprehensive School or the pupils. Now they found out the school attack had been launched by the blood leech Firstseed, to force Abel into opening Castle House and giving her access.

Abel moved on to explain opening the front door of Castle House, and claiming his inheritance, all of Celtchar's estate. He now owned property and land spread out over the UK, Ireland and Scandinavia, but couldn't get into any of the buildings except Castle House. Unfortunately, he didn't have access to the hoard, treasure chest or bank balance that went with the rest. To get full control of the wealth, and all the properties and magical items and creatures, he had to claim the gryphon, a symbol of Celtchar's ownership, hidden in the centre of Castle House.

Admitting he'd solved the first puzzle and moved further inside, and could now give a few other people access, led to the first real questions. After Abel explained the unknown numbers of tests and challenges still facing him, and the dangers, the Taverners agreed that Abel had chosen the right companions. The sorceresses Ferryl Shayde and Zephyr, and Kelis, Rob and Jenny, were the strongest team for facing the magical hurdles.

Several Taverners were disappointed at not being included, but recognised that a crowd of amateurs in a booby-trapped magical house were a bad idea. All the Taverners cheered up when Abel finished with "though once the place is properly open, it's huge, big enough to throw a party for every member of Bonny's Tavern."

Abel's confession raised a good few questions, among them how a seventeen-year-old could inherit but his mother couldn't? Others wondered how Abel could prove this blood link. Most of them accepted that magic explained the blood part but Kathy, Rob's girlfriend, looked a bit lost. She'd been brought here by Pendragon to help him control Rob during the takeover attempt, and until then she'd had no idea magic existed. Despite a magical battle exploding around her, Kathy's scientific mind still had trouble accepting what she'd been shown and told.

"The sorcerer's will stipulated a male who could claim blood relationship." Abel held up his hands to silence all the comments about the male part. "Despite the equality acts that's legal under magical law, set down long before Parliament existed. The sorcerer sets the terms of the will, so maybe some sorceress has stipulated a female heir. Once I'm eighteen I can publicly take possession, but I still need the gryphon to have actual control."

"The woodland is important because of the magic?" Kathy frowned as several people agreed. "That still seems weird. According to Rob we all absorb magic, even me, but we leak some as well. Plants, especially trees, don't leak any so they are giant magic batteries. Dryads, the church or sorcerers claim all the trees, but you give the Taverners extra magic from yours." She still didn't seem convinced. "Go on, tell everyone the rest and

I'll catch up eventually."

Abel didn't mind helping her out a little, because not everyone here would understand why Celtchar had claimed so many trees. "All mature trees are already claimed by someone or something. According to my solicitor, all the senior sorcerers own dryad-free woodland in areas they might visit, to provide extra magic whenever it's needed. They also try to beat the dryads and church to any mature tree. I'll let the Taverners take magic from mine, though first I've got to find a way to get them past the magical protection. Not like we do at Castle House, by filling lead bars and passing them round, but by letting you walk right up to the tree."

A babble of excited voices greeted the idea of unlimited magic, but after a couple of minutes Ferryl quietened them down. "It won't be unlimited, or you'll kill the tree. Giving you access won't be easy, because the protection wasn't meant to be shared. Permission will have to be personal, under your skin, a magical key that can't be lost or stolen. We loan some of you engraved pebbles, to give temporary access to Castle House gardens, but we always take them back. Otherwise someone like Pendragon might copy the glyph, then take a dozen sorcerers in there and bushwhack Abel to get control."

Abel could see that Ferryl had been right. She'd insisted on keeping his access to a whole wood a secret, to avoid jealousy. Now he'd told them, over half those present wanted to go and visit, right now, to use some of the free magic. That could have caused real resentment if Abel hadn't had other woods to offer. It still might. "Remember there's four dryad-free trees here, in the orchard, to help out in an emergency. Treat them gently. Too many taking too much magic will kill them, so you must ask Frederick first."

Whether by accident or design, Rachel drove that part home when she interrupted. "I did that, took too much magic from mum's rhododendron. The leaves drooped and some turned brown. Abel insisted I put some of my daily allowance back in, and used the plant growing glyph to rescue it." Rachel still sounded a little embarrassed about being caught out. "Several of us tried that, getting magic from hedgerows and bushes, but there's only a trickle."

"We've put that in the starter packs for new Taverners, that they can get a trickle of extra magic from a hedgerow but to be gentle. The idea is to fix them all up with limited access to a tree as soon as possible. As yet I'm not sure how many trees are on my new properties, so I'll be visiting the locations to have a look as soon as possible. We're starting with the ones in Sheffield because that's nearest, then I'm buying a 125 motorbike and taking my CBT. As soon as I've passed, I won't need to borrow transport and drivers to check out the rest. In the interim we'll keep filling lead bars to give you all a little extra. We've got the belts some of you saw, so the strongest users can carry more magic, but making the belts is a slow process."

"That's just the trees." Frederick had volunteered this house for the Tavern to use as a charitable refuge. He'd lived for years either suffering from breakdowns or trying to ignore magical creatures, and had been grateful for Tavern help. Now he looked around at the battle damage, which had wiped out months of repairs and decorating in just a few minutes. "But there must be something more if you are paying to fix this."

"At the moment I get a yearly income, from rentals, but it's a limited income and I've already used up a good bit of it. Even when I get the keys to the hoard or treasure chest, I've no idea if that's a bag of pennies or my own Fort Knox. For now I can afford to fix damaged cars, and pay for private, confidential magical doctors, but only because I can use the gold from the Bentley if I run short. I've already been warned about spending too much more. Most of the money we have now comes from selling the antiques we found inside Castle House. There weren't many, and I've already flogged most of them, but they brought good prices. That's the source of the mysterious donations that let us fix up this place as a charitable refuge, and will pay to redecorate. Some of the money has financed the launch of the game, Bonny's Tavern, onto the open market." Abel looked past Ferryl to Jenny. "Or it will when our business expert gives us the final okay."

"After the exams, at the start of the summer holidays. I'll be leaving school then so I'll be able to concentrate on the marketing and any problems that crop up." Jenny looked out over the sea of faces. "But the exams come first. Just remember, magic won't put food on the table, not without stealing. Get a proper education and a job, then magic will provide some fantastic perks. Though I'm hoping you'll all pitch in and help me to sell the game during the summer holidays?" The cheers and waving arms promised she'd get her help.

"What about those who don't do so well at school? I'm useless at maths and stuff like that." The youth shrugged as several pointed out he seemed to be learning glyphs all right. "That's memorising a simple shape, the same one used time after time. If I can't get a job, or I end up as a burger flipper, can I still be a Taverner?"

"Definitely. Kelis told me there's no monetary subscription, but the Tavern will expect us to contribute magical help now and then. All Taverners are equal, so that has to mean our jobs or money don't matter. Lucky, because I still haven't worked out what I want to do with my life." Tobias laughed as a few suggested chasing sorceresses, one tall slim trainee in particular. "We might find more opportunities if Bonny's Tavern sells really well. I'll be happy with a job like packing and posting the game, or sales rep, that sort of thing, providing the whole thing doesn't just fizzle."

"The launch might go better than expected, after the school Easter dance getting on local TV. The link to charity, this refuge, is why I want to leave the launch until the game package is as good as I can get it. If all goes well this place will get a lot of attention, and donations." Jenny held out a hand in Abel's direction. "In the meantime, Abel wants to explain the rest, the magical part."

Abel deliberately tried to look and sound very serious. "Some of you heard what the archbishop, Vicar Creepio, told me after Pendragon died."

The rugby player hugging Claris looked around the room, his face totally serious. "As the Master, by right of conquest, Abel holds the right of High Justice and Low over everyone in Stourton and the surrounding villages. He can kill or imprison anyone, magical or not, for little or no reason." That took some accepting. As long as he didn't use magic in public, Abel now stood above the law of the land. The main objections came down to how that could be kept secret, until Kelis managed to get heard above the arguments.

"It already happened, right here. All the bodies from when Pendragon attacked us disappeared without trace, while a copper sat out front in his car and ignored it. We know Natalie the traitor will spend her life on a church tether. According to Creepio, she allegedly died in a serious motor accident, so her parents will attend a closed-coffin funeral. Magical medics will blur their memories and grief, to make it a little easier on them, but their daughter is gone."

Kathy wasn't accepting that. "What about road traffic police, ambulances, medics, all that? How can they be fooled into seeing a body?"

"Creepio's people will put in the reports and supply a wreck, I assume, so most coppers won't know about the cover-ups. Only a few police are magic users, working for the church or the Magical Council, but it won't take many. The St. John's Ambulance Brigade, or some of them, are God's medics, and Creepio told us there's a few magically aware nurses and doctors in the hospitals. Magical influence is why local TV reported the creature attack at school as a gas leak and hornet swarm, and nobody reported the big fight here." Kelis turned to Abel with a wry smile. "Though any cover-up depends on Abel's ability to pay the church fees. We got a freebie this time, but it won't happen again."

Rachel, even at fifteen, had a better idea of what magic could do than most people here. "If Abel kills some oik, the corpse will disappear and the witnesses will suddenly forget everything. That's if it looks like murder. If he only gets rid of one person, Abel won't need any help. If he sucked the air from someone's lungs, or used water vapour from the air to flood their lungs for a few minutes? I'm pretty sure a compressed air glyph would block a throat without leaving a mark, or he could blow a tyre as their car went round a bend."

"Or drop a chunk of ice on their car, out of a clear sky." Several people looked pointedly at Kelis, who'd done that to a leech, but she ignored Rob's interruption.

Abel raised his voice above the rising babble. "The point is, the right to kill doesn't mean I have to."

"So why bring it up?" Kathy had found another part of the discussion that didn't need magical knowledge.

"So you all know that if you visit someone else's territory, their demesne, and they kill you, it's legal. So is the Tavern returning the favour, as long as we are discreet and pay for any cover-up, which is why you are safer than non-magical people. All that slows sorcerers up is retribution from other sorcerers, or from the church if they're too blatant and break the Accord." Abel noticed Kathy half-raise her hand and decided to show everyone the Accord, the magical rulebook, now instead of later. "Kelis, please hand out the copies of the Accord, because that might give everyone a better idea of the setup."

Kelis glanced at him, startled because she hadn't expected it yet, then dug in her school bag and passed out a sheaf of single printed sheets. "This is the version in modern English. There's a really archaic version in Castle House, all fancy swirls and ye olde weird spellings. That one doesn't have the bit in italics." Silence fell, as the sixty young people and Frederick finally saw the real rules that governed their world.

The Accord
Modern English Version

In this document, Church refers to any organisation using prayers or religious ceremonies as a source of magical power. Sorcery refers to all other methods used by humans to access or control magic.

Magic must remain a secret, hidden from all humans unless they have been awakened. All religions will announce that there have never been any true Witches, Sorcerers, or magical creatures. Any public display of magic must be explained away as natural phenomena or trickery. Magic users or priests advertising that magic still exists, either deliberately or through gross negligence, will die.

Churches and **Sorcery** will not fight each other. Members of one can only kill members of the other in self-defence or because one has broken the Accord. Forcibly taking control of an area is forbidden, though missionaries and heretics are permitted.

If enough of a population is converted, or loses faith, control of an area may change. The changeover, and other disputes, will be negotiated between two Councils, church and sorcery. Each will have one non-voting seat on the other Council, to observe.

Churches automatically hold sway within the areas protected by their places of worship, taking responsibility for protecting the non-magical and policing their priests. Wars between churches must not include areas held by sorcery, though non-magical soldiers can be used.

Sorcery may claim the rest of the world, shared between the strongest magic wielders. Each holder of a demesne has the right of High and Low Justice over both the magical and the non-magical. Sorcery may have wars, but only using non-magical soldiers. Such conflicts will avoid areas controlled by a Church, and hide any use of magic.

Any unclaimed areas are lawless, though Church and Sorcery will combine if necessary to eradicate serious threats to the inhabitants.

Codicils: By Order of the Magical Council:

Non-magical members of a magic-user's family cannot be targeted. Any such attack will result in the Council Members combining to kill the attacker and every blood relative and apprentice.

Unwarded employees cannot be targeted, providing they wear a hex to show their allegiance. Any such attack will result in the Council Members combining to kill the attacker and every apprentice.

From this date, any newly qualifying sorcerer or sorceress is limited to a maximum of eight senior apprentices, those adept with Air, Fire and Water. Any sorcerer already exceeding that number cannot promote any new senior apprentices unless one is released or killed. There is no limit to the number of junior apprentices, providing they only cast Air and Fire and cannot shield. If the restriction is exceeded, all the apprentices will be killed and the offender will be restricted to two apprentices for the next four hundred years.

From this date, all apprentices must be released or killed after seventy-five years, or earlier. This does not apply to apprentices who have already been tethered for over seventy-five years.

*   *   *

Abel didn't answer the first few questions, to give the rest a chance to digest the contents. As the initial uproar died back a little, he started by agreeing the Accord was difficult to accept. "I know, it doesn't seem possible, not without some sort of hint surfacing on the internet at least, but the world really is ruled by magic. Not bombs, tanks, nuclear weapons or the power of the ballot box, just a bunch of really old church and sorcery types with a horrendous armoury of glyphs and forests full of magic."

"There'll be hints, but there'll also be visits in the night, mystery disappearances, accidental deaths and magical memory wipes." Kelis moved on quickly as Claris's eyes narrowed in suspicion. "The likes of Creepio have the whole Church Militant, what I call God's SAS, on speed-dial. Some of us saw the platycroc, but there's also bound ogres and giants, kept as attack dogs."

"You'll all have questions about how it all works. I've got a few myself, but for now accept that what's in the Accord is how it is. From our point of view the important part is that Stourton and the surrounding area are now my demesne. Outside of the broad rules, the Accord, we set the magical laws. As the dominant local sorcerer, because of the blood thing with Castle House, I had the strongest claim so I inherited Pendragon's business. It's a real business with contracts, even if the work is magical. I've no idea how much profit Pendragon made, but we already know that sorcerers charge businesses a fortune for hexes that protect their buildings. Our new business also puts magic in the hexes on some items manufactured here, like the lawn mowers Shawn used to work on. That means we can pay a few Taverners a wage to be full-timers, and maintain several cars to provide transport when needed."

A half hour later everyone seemed to have got it. The biggest argument came over the way wars were fought. Eventually, everyone agreed the largest conflicts must include alliances of church and sorcery, because bombs couldn't possibly avoid killing members of both. Once the Accord had been accepted, the Taverners tried to get to grips with the sheer scope of the power a sorcerer held. Absolute power belonged to kings in history books, not to a scrawny schoolboy who lived in a council house and hid from the school bully.

Everything belonging to the demesne belonged to Abel, personally, because that's how magical law worked. Despite that, Abel promised he would keep on giving away free magic, asking for advice, and would try to avoid murdering or imprisoning people. The Taverners agreed they'd provide the magical labour, mainly filling hexes on buildings or things like mowers and computers, to keep the sorcery business making a profit. Eric and Shawn, both in their early twenties, would each get a wage, a car, and a flat above one of Pendragon's places of business. Those two would run the business side, dealing with customers and organising the Taverners to carry out the magical contracts.

Up to now, everything had been a warm-up. The Taverners had actually gathered to agree on the aims of the magical Tavern, a set of rules, and penalties for breaking them.

*   *   *

"Before we get to the actual rules, some of you want to know why we need any beyond the Accord. The problem is we, the Tavern, are doing something new. Magical trainees are apprentices, tethered to a sorcerer so they can't disobey. Anything they do is the fault of the sorcerer, and he is judged by the Accord." Abel stopped at the storm of comments about apprentices living in luxury, and doing as they liked. He turned to Ginny, once just that sort of apprentice, and shrugged. "Ginny here can tell you how it felt like from her end. When I first explained how she'd serve her sentence, a tethered taxi driver, and magical guardian and mentor to a pair of young girls, she laughed at me. Ginny, please explain why."

Ginny waited until the cat-calls and boos died down. "I was offered Zephyr's tether rather than death or a church tether, which came as a big relief. I thought I'd be working as cheap labour, with occasional pain and a few punishments thrown in. It turns out my punishment might be better than my previous employment."

"In that case we should add some more punishment." The scowl from Rachel had no give in it. Her brother had been tethered and tortured by Pendragon, and Guinevere was the only survivor she could get at for payback.

"Guinevere is a slave, in effect. The tether is more of a collar than any of those we've seen in pictures, because it imprisons her mind. Zephyr can read Ginny's thoughts, and if she even thinks of rebellion can inflict mental pain, or force Ginny to hurt or kill herself." Abel looked around the room, settling on Rachel. "Exactly what would you do that's worse than that?" He waited, but Rachel kept her mouth shut. "Ginny, please explain what apprenticeship means for a would-be sorceress."

After a pause to sort out her thoughts, Ginny tried to explain. "As Pendragon's apprentice I was on call 24/7, using up my magic almost as fast as I absorbed it from the air. I topped up hexes protecting property or machinery, while Pendragon collected the payments. He gave me a salary, to spend on clothes and jewellery. The appearance of apprentices reflects the status of their masters or mistresses." Ginny stopped as several Taverners interrupted, pointing out that wasn't a bad deal.

"Better than not bad. Remember, I'm expecting a life as a burger flipper, and hoping Shawn will sell his scooter cheap now he's got a company car." Other voices agreed, with a couple bidding for the scooter.

"But when you leave work your time will be yours. Even if you don't get extras from Abel, you can decide how to use the magic you absorb from the air each day. It's not a lot, but it will be yours." Ginny paused, turning to look at all the unconvinced faces. "That's a lot better than apprentice life, because we were never off-duty. A tether means you have to watch what you think, every waking hour, because you can never be sure your master isn't spying. Before getting promotion, my only free choice was if I practiced manipulating air or fire. It was a difficult choice. Did I make my adequate air glyph stronger, or develop my weak fire glyph? I had barely any magic left after finishing my work, but I had to improve my skills so I would survive if Pendragon sent me into battle. I slept in a dorm, went where the tether sent me, did what the tether told me, and the only time I left the house and garden were for work."

"So why were you dressed like that?" Shannon shrugged towards Abel. "Sorry, but it doesn't add up."

The smartly dressed ex-apprentice looked down at herself. "You, the Tavern, killed one of Pendragon's senior apprentices in the leech nest. Pendragon chose me as Elrond's successor. My promotion meant a good salary, a car, my own room, and a collection of clothes and jewellery to make me look good. I bought more clothes, ones I preferred, for if the Master let me out for a night on the town. That only happened about once a month, but I literally had nothing else to spend money on for the next fifty-five years. Part of my promotion included Pendragon teaching me the glyph for water and how to shield. He didn't allow me any extra magic to practice them. In spite of the promotion, I still used up almost all my daily magic earning him money."

"How did you learn to cast them properly, with less magic than the daily ration from the air? It took me weeks and loads of magic, most of the extra I get in my lead bars, just to get to where I could hold a steady shield." Una looked down at her hands, one of them straying to her waist, where she now wore a belt full of magic instead of carrying a lead bar. Among the Taverners, those belts were a sort of promotion. Only Ferryl could make the belts, so only the most adept could have one. Muttering and little discussions broke out here and there, as others compared how long it had taken to master a glyph even with tree magic from Abel. Some tried to work out how long it might have taken, using just the natural daily dose from the air.

"Ginny will answer questions later. Just let her finish, please?"

"Yes, oh mighty sorcerer." Una grinned at Abel and sat down.

Once the laughter died down Ginny continued. "Pendragon also gave me the two witch charms, for numbing pain and speeding the healing of superficial injuries. He told me if I worked hard for the next ten years, he'd teach me the glyph for self-healing. Working hard meant giving up even more of my magic every day."

"We wondered why none of Pendragon's apprentices threw glyphs like Ferryl, nets and spikes. You all stuck to fire or air, with a few ice shards, though you'd all got shields." Rachel smirked, because the apprentice shields hadn't been any stronger than hers, or strong enough to stop Ferryl Shayde's attacks. "You didn't dent Zephyr's shield when she did her ogre impersonation."

At the mention of Zephyr, and her very realistic ogre, Ginny flinched and glanced at Abel's shoulder. "Galadriel and Denethor could throw ice, and a cloud that burned skin, but they were very senior. I used my spare magic to concentrate on my shield, to improve my chances of surviving. I'd seen the strength of your shields, at Redwolf's house, but it came as a shock to the others. Then half of you started throwing ice spears, combined air, reverse heat and shaped water glyphs!" Ginny sounded a little bitter about the next part. "Now I find out some of you have also learned combinations and glyphs for colour change, plant growth, veils, and how to place a Seeming on bandages to disguise wounds. Abel tells me you are all given extra magic, just to practice and accelerate your learning. As fast as you master a glyph to Ferryl's satisfaction, you get the next."

"Sort of. We have to show we are sensible enough to handle the stronger glyphs, because practice gets more dangerous." Una glanced around the room, then looked back at the group around Abel. "Abel, Kelis, Rob, Jenny and of course Ferryl and Zephyr are the strongest, but in theory we can catch up. We complain about the time it takes, but according to you I've got the same glyphs as a fifty-year-old apprentice." Some of the Taverners looked startled, while others nodded because they'd already worked that bit out.

"Possibly more than some seventy-year-olds. The rate of learning varies from sorcerer to sorceress, and apprentice to apprentice. Some of you are learning glyphs I never knew existed, like colour change, and I've no idea what really senior apprentices learn." Ginny now knew about some advanced glyphs, although they weren't common knowledge. The contrast had stunned the ex-apprentice, and now the Taverners. They'd seen senior apprentices, smartly dressed adults from late thirties up to their sixties, all driving flash cars. Now everyone wanted to discuss this business of apprentices having to manage on hardly any magic.

"So all of us, even the likes of me, gets more magic than a proper sorcerer's apprentice?" Tobias, who had only recently learned to cast his first shaky air glyph, looked around at the rest. "I wasn't keen on using up some of the extra magic in my lead bar, wasting it on filling hexes for contracts. If I complain at any time in the future, just slap me upside the head and remind me, I still get more than a senior apprentice." From the comments, several more had begrudged giving up some of their practice magic.

"How fast are we learning, Abel? Ginny is surprised by the ice, and shields, but what about the rest of us? How long does an apprentice usually take to learn air and fire? It can't really be twenty years like Ginny said, can it?" Diane, Jenny's younger sister, looked around the room. "Am I learning faster because of my sister?"

"Maybe, but only a little and only because you work hard." Jenny, the sister in question, looked slowly around the room then back to Ginny. "How long before you learned fire, Ginny?"

"I didn't even learn air to start with, not for the first two years. As soon as I could push magic out of my hand, I filled hexes to protect customers' premises. By practicing with every scrap of spare magic I could save, I finally mastered air. After ten years, Pendragon gave me the fire glyph." Ginny pointed at Diane. "This young lady is already ahead of where I was after five years, maybe seven or eight because she has already learned the colouring glyph. I really have no idea how many glyphs some of you know, and can only guess how strong you might be. You blew away Celeborn's shield in one attack, and someone told me you did the same to Denny, Denethor."

"My cue I believe. A little while back Creepio assessed us, the Taverners, for a report, and told me, Kelis, Rob, Jenny, Zephyr and Ferryl the result." Abel explained that Vicar Creepio Mysterio, the peripatetic archbishop who never gave a name except vicar, had been impressed. He'd thought that half the Taverners could already defeat the typical lesser apprentices. If Abel kept giving away free magic, within two years at least half would be the equal of the average senior apprentice. According to Creepio, the Magic Council only allowed the Taverners to progress so fast because none of them were tethered apprentices. That meant each one was technically a weak, independent, would-be sorcerer or sorceress.

*   *   *

The Taverners took a break for drinks and to discuss the first revelations, with a few approaching Abel with specific questions. Most of them were waiting to finally set out the aims and rules of their magical club. Another eleven Taverners were spread around the country, teenagers who had been involved as beta players and discovered magic, and they'd given their opinions by phone. Those were being kept up to date as the meeting progressed.

Once the meeting resumed, Rachel spoke up before anyone else got a chance. "It's simple really. We adopt Abel's mission." She looked defiant when some, including Abel, objected to the word mission. "Call it what you like, but Abel is willing to put in his cash, and the magic of his trees, to supply magical protection to people living in neglected areas. Now we've found out he isn't actually rich. He sold his family silver, in effect, to get us started." She scowled when a couple of people pointed out the money actually went to fix the house and game, but Shannon jumped up.

"The money did more than that, and so does all that extra magic Abel gave us. For starters we are all getting rid of the magic creatures around where we live, protecting our families and friends. That also stops the creatures preying on the other residents in our villages and estates, places that aren't wealthy enough for the church or the likes of Pendragon to protect." As Shannon finished, before anyone else could speak, Rachel stood and raised her hands to get attention.

She turned to Abel, head up and chin jutting in defiance. "That's what I think the Tavern should be doing, and what Abel thinks, and he's got other supporters." Rachel smiled as cheering spread through the room. Most of it came from a group of younger Taverners who treated her as a role model, a leader who despite her lack of years had already become a strong magic user.

"But will that be allowed? Won't the other sorcerers object? If enough of them are annoyed they'll gang up on us and squish, we're dead or on tethers." Justin, Rachel's seventeen-year-old brother, rubbed his shoulder. "Pendragon tethered me, briefly, before Zephyr broke me loose, and it's no fun at all."

"But Abel wants us to deal with the gaps, the parts that aren't under church influence or in a sorceress's demesne." Una, dressed as the mercenary game character Robin D'Ritche, with long boots and an enactment sword, nodded towards Rachel and Shannon. "We can't just charge in like Rachel wants, but once the game is on sale we'll get more recruits. Any teenagers who can almost sense magic, can almost see the creatures, will be tipped over the edge when they practice the meditation. Any who already see creatures, but think they're hallucinations, will see our illustrations and realise the truth. They'll all email the address for the mythical sorceress Ferryl Shayde, even if it looks like a joke, and we can send someone to help them."

Another voice rang out, even if she didn't stand up. "Someone to teach them the rules, how to avoid falling foul of the Accord and sorcerers. They'll learn how to protect themselves and their families from creatures, and we'll show them how to get a little extra magic from bushes and saplings." Petra, who had been the first accidental recruit, wore her furry catsuit, complete with her cat-sorceress leather shorts and top. Repairing her costume after the fight had obviously been a top priority. "Once they are competent with wind, that first recruit can join any more newly aware players in the area. Until it runs out, Abel's loot will hire them a room to meet and practice, if necessary. If Abel is skint they'll just have to meet in a field away from prying eyes."

"So why are we discussing it?" Tobias hadn't really got up to speed on the wider picture, despite his girlfriend, Kelis, possibly being the most adept of Ferryl Shayde's trainees. He'd probably been too immersed in mastering that first, essential glyph.

Abel grabbed his chance. "Because we have to agree on what sort of an organisation we are going to build. I'd prefer one that keeps doing what we've started. Any new recruits, if they're still at school, should place hexes to eject magical creatures. As there are more Taverners, and they become more adept, the magical and non-magical players can deal with bullying and abuse, thieving, drugs and persecution of minorities. Each new magical recruit will no doubt clear the immediate area around their houses, but then local groups should combine to drive the creatures from places like junior schools or children's parks." He shrugged, with a smile towards Petra to acknowledge the bit about his money running out. "Hopefully, once each area has a couple of Taverners who can cast wind, they'll be more or less self-sufficient."

"What if someone learns magic, then doesn't agree with our aims and rules?" From her look and voice, Rachel wouldn't be very diplomatic if it happened.

"Then they don't join the magical part of the Tavern, and don't get the training and extra magic. If they do join, and break our rules, there have to be consequences." Una looked around, letting everyone see her big smile. "So if anyone gets tempted, remember. If you want all that lovely extra magic, you stick by the Tavern rules." She turned back towards Abel and bowed. "Once we've got rules."

"Hang on. First off, exactly what did you mean by protecting people? We'll never persuade everyone to wear a Tavern hex." That finally got the discussion off the ground, explaining how to protect an area rather than individuals. Some wanted to go further, targeting specific areas to warn off or beat up muggers and similar criminals. Eventually most Taverners conceded that wasn't practical, not without attracting attention. The simplest way would be to let the police deal with that sort of crime.

"Unless it affects our immediate families." Sarah wasn't the most belligerent Taverner by far, and now she looked a little embarrassed. "If some yob starts giving mum or dad grief, I want to be able to deal with it."

"If you want to deal with someone like that, come and ask and we'll take half a dozen adepts." Abel held up a hand to stop Rachel, who'd already come to her feet to object, and finished answering Sarah. "That way they won't stand a chance, and we can make sure none of it makes the TV news."

Though he hadn't stopped Rachel entirely. "But if it's urgent, sort it out and we'll cover it up. Abel won't want someone hurt while you're waiting for him to answer his phone."

"True, but don't use that as an excuse. Cover-ups will be very expensive, and I really have sold most of the goodies." Abel didn't have a chance to say more before comments came in from all directions.

"I can live with that. I'm more interested in these punishments, because it can't all be either a tether or death."

"I can't see any of us doing something that bad. I'm more worried about the refuges. If there's no more money, how can we open Taverns, magic clubs or refuges? How many people out there found magic when they were over twenty-five and flipped? They'll need help as well."

"They're already crackers. We can't cure them so how are we supposed to help?"

"This place, the refuge, is for older people, those who had breakdowns when they saw creatures."

"No, it's supposed to help battered wives, or is that because of Kelis's mum? Or is it both?"

Despite the last one making Kelis blush a little, the comments finally started a real discussion. Nobody had a clear structure in mind, or not until everyone had suggested their own pet charity project or use for magic. Between some good-natured ridicule and sheer practicality, the ideas were gradually whittled down until there seemed to be a consensus. Not a precise plan, but a general feeling for what the Taverners should do with their new-found talent.

Taverners had to be a force for good, although magic gave them plenty of leeway to have some fun. Even the term Taverner caused some discussion. The magical world had a strict hierarchy based on power and skill, but all Taverners would be considered equal regardless of their magical skill, race, colour or creed. After some discussion, that included magical creatures, such as the goblins or dryads who had accepted the protection of the Tavern or wore the Tavern ward. Learning that one of the usually timid goblins had committed suicide, exploding itself to injure Pendragon, finally settled that argument.

Penalties turned out to be a contentious subject among those who had been attacked without warning, then faced with the options of stunting, killing, binding or tethering prisoners. Magical law had no alternatives, usually inflicting a long, lingering death on any traitors. Ordinary law couldn't help, because even a magical beginner could break out of any ordinary jail. At the time some Taverners had wanted to kill at least one of the survivors, the traitor, or tether her and make her suffer. Abel had chickened out, and let the church take almost all the surviving attackers. The men and girl would live out their lives gardening, or otherwise working for a monastery or nunnery, tethered slaves but not tortured.

None of the rules would work without some sort of sanctions. Working out punishments wasn't easy because the magical community used stunting, removing the ability to work magic, as the minimum penalty for minor offences. The Taverners found that a horrific idea, the magical equivalent to cutting off limbs or a lobotomy. Under the new rules any minor transgressors would be shunned, deprived of contact with Taverners and magic but only for a period. They'd be drained twice daily to remove any magic they'd absorbed. Shunning would hurt despite the culprit being able to talk to anyone non-magical. Magic users found it difficult to relax with anyone else, because of the secrecy.

"It's worse than that." Carl, a fourteen-year-old currently being shunned for three months for using magic to bully, cringed from the glares. He'd been allowed to this meeting as a special concession. "I've only been practicing glyphs for two months, and only been banned from using magic for a fortnight, but I can feel it. It's a sort of itchy, scratchy feeling I can't locate, and is really irritating." He straightened a little, answering with more confidence as others began to question him. The Taverners were more interested in the problem than his crime.

Claris, who had become magically aware when her leech-inflicted internal injuries were healed, seemed really interested. "Something like that might explain my mood swings. I used magic while Ferryl healed me, even if I can't remember the glyphs or quite what I did, but then stopped. Once I'd been cured, I didn't want anything more to do with it." Silence spread across the room as everyone listened, because Claris had been exposed to magic a lot longer than Carl. "Now I'm wondering if that explains my mood swings. I've always had a temper."

"Temper or maybe just plain nasty." Una shrugged when Claris's boyfriend glared at her. "Be fair, you wouldn't have gone out with her a year ago." He subsided but hugged Claris, who really had been the school bully's henchwoman at one time.

She looked guilty but carried on, though her voice dropped to just above a whisper. "But temper or nasty, I wouldn't have beaten a fourteen-year-old insensible with a baseball bat. I know she threatened me, but

Natalie couldn't cast really dangerous glyphs, and then I emptied a gun at Pendragon. I kept shooting, even after a few bullets got past his shield and I could see him bleed." The Taverners leant forward to hear as her voice dropped further. "I still don't know if I'd have shot Effy, an unarmed woman."

"Who could have set you on fire with a glyph." The rugby player hugged her tighter.

"Fair point, but Effy wasn't actually forming a glyph. There again, Claris didn't shoot her. So what's the answer?" Jenny, definitely the practical one, brought everyone back to the real problem. "Not for Claris, because she can learn the wind glyph, and chuck some magic about now and then. I meant how do we ban a Taverner from using magic, but let them use enough to stop the withdrawal symptoms. Unless that is a part of the punishment?"

A storm of comments disagreed with the last part. Nobody wanted an adept to get twitchy, then crack and lash out. Eventually the Taverners agreed that limited glyph throwing would be allowed, under strict supervision so the culprit didn't have fun or use the magic to practice their glyphs. Though even with the discomfort adding to the penalty, shunning wouldn't be enough for some crimes.

Learning just how much magic and training a Taverner received, compared to any apprentice, made the next penalty a real deterrent. Persistent offenders would now face banishment, which would include a permanent mark to warn all magic-users the culprit wasn't trustworthy. Taverners could choose to leave at any time, without the mark, but they would forfeit all access to extra magic or training. They would be restricted to the meagre amount absorbed from the air each day, or scraps gleaned from bushes and saplings.

The next level, tethering, magical enslavement in effect, would be reserved for captured magic users. After some discussion about maybe preferring death to mind slavery, captured magic users could choose tethering or death. The most discussion centred around the final punishment, death without option, only sanctioned for cold-blooded, premeditated murder or betrayal leading to death. Even then it would be a clean death, not the usual sorcerer torture. "Though I'm not sure who would carry out the sentence. It would be cold-blooded murder, in effect."

Nobody volunteered, or even met Una's eyes.

"We'll worry about that if it happens." Abel knew either Ferryl Shayde or Zephyr would snuff out a life in a heartbeat if he asked. Neither were human and both had a very tight set of loyalties, with preserving Abel and his close friends right at the top. Ferryl in particular had become fiercely protective after the fight. She'd been trying to learn emotions, and almost losing the first friend she'd ever had shook her badly.

*   *   *

When the meeting finally broke up again, Frederick, the fifty-four-year-old owner of the house, passed around menus from the local take-aways and phoned for fast food. While they ate, the Taverners mulled over the results so far. Abel sat with the other Taverneers, Kelis, Rob, Ferryl and Jenny, trying to work out how it had gone so far. Not too bad, they concluded. That might have been a mistake, because his phone struck up with "People are Strange."

"Hello, I thought we were off your Christmas list."

Creepio displayed his usual lack of humour. "You are, but I keep my promises. Amanda and Cecilia are on the way to meet their saviours." The 'vicar' might not have a normal sense of humour, but Abel detected a hint of vicious glee. "Since you are all gathered together, I thought this might be the best time."

"We've got a dozen walking wounded in here and the place is a mess after the battle, as you well know!" Abel calmed down, because visitors might lighten the mood a little. When the Tavern's bound leech had killed the seeds inside the two girls, Creepio had commented that they'd probably become nuns or join the Church Militant. Being rescued by the church, and then healed in a convent hospital, usually had that effect. Since the Tavern rescued these two he'd reluctantly agreed the pair should see the alternative, a non-church magical community. "When will they be here?"

"Half an hour, so you've got time to dust and polish." As the vicar rang off, Abel looked around the room. One door hung off its hinges, the paint and wallpaper were gouged and scorched, and the floorboards had been scored and charred in places. At least half the furniture would be rejected by a charity shop, and polishing wouldn't help the rest very much.

Abel warned everyone, which meant confessing he'd kept a blood leech alive. Even though it had saved three victims from seeds, and Ferryl had now bound it into a hare, that wasn't popular. Claris in particular thought that part, saving the leech, had been a bad dream, and now she wanted it dead. The argument still raged when Abel's phone rang with "I am the Law," the Judge Dredd song by Anthrax. At least Terese Green, his magical solicitor, would be on his side.

He never had the chance to ask, because she'd brought Abel another problem. "We have accessed the trackers on your captured vehicles, and took a look before passing control to your office. One of Pendragon's cars has been parked a long way outside your Sheffield demesne. I'm assuming none of your people took it there?"

"We are all here, every Taverner who can drive." Abel paused, wondering about the legalities of him now owning Pendragon's cars. "Can I report it stolen?"

"You could, because it is owned by the business, but I advise against sending police after a magic user. The protection on the car means it can only have been taken by one of Pendragon's apprentices, presumably after he felt his tether break. Now you have been confirmed as the Master, he won't be able to get into the car again until you have opened it. I suggest collecting the vehicle before he hires a magical locksmith to break the glyphs." Abel clearly heard Terese shuffling some papers. "A minor sorcerer lives at that address, so Gawain or Paragon, whichever it is, might have run there for sanctuary."

"I'm a bit torn really. I'd like the car if only to sell it, but I'd rather not start trouble with another sorcerer." Abel thought a BMW would fetch a good price, maybe enough to repair the damage to Frederick's house.

Terese sighed. She knew how Abel felt about getting into fights, and had actually advised him to keep a low profile for a while. "You cannot afford to ignore the theft. Right now you are a newcomer, being judged by the sorcerer community, and that would look like weakness. As your solicitor I advise a visit to collect the vehicle, with enough backup to dissuade any rash attempts to keep it. Start off politely, ask if a thief has turned up with a BMW. Either Valdar will deny all knowledge, which makes this a deliberate challenge, or he'll hand it over." A little humour touched her voice. "If he argues, ask your Taverners to show off their fire glyphs. If you take enough help, Valdar won't start trouble."

"Valdar? I don't recognise that name from any book or film. Where's it from?" Sorcerers usually gave their apprentices names from fiction or history. Abel hoped the source might give him a hint of what the sorcerer or sorceress might be like.

"Valdar was a legendary Danish king. All the apprentices serving the sorceress Sif were called after Norse kings, so he may be one of them. Sif encouraged them to be arrogant and belligerent, but after she fell the survivors seemed to understand their real place in the pecking order." Terese hesitated for a moment. "It might look better if you didn't take your solicitor. Otherwise some might think you rely on Woods and Green, and are not capable of controlling your own demesne."

Abel had been going to do just that, because Terese seemed to steamroller most opposition just by waving bits of paper. "Give me the address, please, and details of the car. We'll sort it out." He wrote it down, but didn't tell everyone for few minutes. "Zephyr, connect me to Ferryl please." Spooky-phone shot out so Abel could ask Ferryl to join him. He explained, expecting her to object to anything that might be risky.

Instead, the sorceress agreed with the solicitor. "Terese makes sense. There may be danger, but allowing others to think you are weak would be worse. If Zephyr unlocks the glyphs on the Mercedes minibus, we can fill it with Taverners." She nudged him gently. "The Master will travel in his BMW SUV so he can take his personal bodyguards." Abel didn't even try to argue. Although they were his friends rather than bodyguards, Kelis, Rob and Jenny would just gang up on him.

*　*　*

When Amanda and Cecilia, the rescued girls, were delivered by a priest, Abel didn't expect them to stay long. Both looked horrified at the goblins in the garden, flinching away from them. Their faces fell further when they saw the inside of the house, at both the battle damage and the creatures such as pictsies scuttling about. Some of the Taverners were quick to explain they'd recently beaten off an attack, and after being offered a drink and decent chairs both relaxed a little.

None of the magical creatures came near them, or anyone else, but some were clearly trying to tidy the place up. Cecilia's curiosity finally won through, unexpected because she'd been confirmed. Abel had expected her to be firmly wedded to the church view that all magical creatures should die. "There are no minions of evil in the convent grounds. Why do you allow them in here? Why are they working for you?"

Abel opened his mouth to explain they weren't minions of evil, but he never got the chance. A dozen others pounced first, defending their magical housekeepers. The Taverners explained about good and bad creatures, and how some of them were useful in houses. Brownies cleaned and dusted to collect scraps of magic that had leaked from humans, and pictsies hunted bugs and flies, while goblins ate scraps and small magical creatures. As they learned about ways to allow the useful sort inside, and banish the rest, both girls began to get really interested.

Shannon might have been the most help, when she admitted she'd been confirmed and still attended church, but wanted to stay in the Tavern. Shannon's cross and Tavern hex hung together, around her neck, and she finally convinced Cecilia to touch a Tavern hex with her cross. When absolutely nothing happened, it finally broke down the barriers. After hearing how Shannon learned about magic, met creatures, and talked to some, both girls followed her outside to meet a goblin and a dryad.

Since everything seemed to be going so well, Abel nipped off to sort out the Volvo Estate and the Mercedes minibus, both captured after the battle. Both were magically locked, because they'd belonged to sorcerers who had loaned apprentices to Pendragon. The Volvo had already been conceded after a standoff with the sorceress, though Abel still had to get past the lock. Zephyr or Ferryl tried first, rather than employ one the magical locksmiths Terese had mentioned. Neither entity was human, so their true-selves could see how magic flowed and could sometimes unravel a glyph. Despite that, after twenty minutes of trying, Ferryl admitted they'd been too confident. The glyphs on the Mercedes minibus had yielded at last, but those on the Volvo were much tougher. Abel gave up, phoning his solicitor to hire a professional locksmith.

By that time he had another problem, because while Ferryl and Zephyr worked he'd had another phone call. Verenestra, an apparently friendly sorceress in Sheffield, warned him the original owner of the Volvo Estate still wanted it back. Boudicca had been shouting to anyone who'd listen about being cheated, and that a schoolkid wasn't stealing her car.

Zephyr flew back to Frederick's house, where the Taverners were still entertaining their two guests, to find a driver for the minibus. While she'd gone, Abel listened to a frustrated Ferryl as she continued her inspection of the Volvo. "The glyphs on this are very good, much better than a weak sorceress like Boudicca could have cast. I want to be here when the locksmith breaks them, just in case I can get some hints for another time."

Despite wanting to laugh at Ferryl's obsession with learning every glyph she came across, Abel passed on the warning. "According to Veren the car might not be here by then, because Boudicca is making noises about getting it back. She might sneak over here in the night and drive off in it. According to Terese, the locksmith won't be here until tomorrow, and might not make it until Thursday, so we can't move it." Abel glanced back towards Frederick's house and chuckled. "If I tell Una that, she'll sleep next to it with her sword. She's still hoping it counts as loot." The teenager had claimed the Volvo Estate, acting out her game persona as the mercenary Robin D'Ritche.

Ferryl smiled at that, but something else worried her. "You should stop shortening sorceress's names. Verenestra doesn't seem to mind, but others will consider it a deadly insult."

"But they aren't real names, just whatever dopey name their master or mistress called them when they put the tether on." Abel didn't think he'd be very attached to what was essentially a slave name.

"The renaming is part of a process to break all links with their past. If an apprentice survives to become a sorceress, she will outlive everyone she knew. By then her name is her only true identity, recognised by the magical community as a statement of her power, wealth and experience." Ferryl held out her hand towards the estate car. "Speaking of experience, I might not be able to break these glyphs but I can cast a ward Boudicca won't get through. Not unless she hires someone, and a contractor won't break my glyph without seeing the name on it. They'll check who the Master of Castle House is, find out this is your demesne, and be very, very cautious." Ferryl's hand kept moving, a succession of small glyphs spinning out to create a web around the vehicle. She 'signed' the ward by spelling out 'Master of Castle House' in hexes invisible to the non-magical. "There, only a warded Taverner will get through that."

"Just in case Boudicca brings someone less than reputable, I'll ask the batlins to keep an eye on the car at night. One of the Taverners can keep watch in the day." Abel turned as he heard someone coming across the rubble covering the empty plot. "Ginny?"

The ex-apprentice looked a little abashed. "I thought I ought to make myself useful, a start towards my redemption. My tether can keep track of the girls from here, and they're in no danger in that house."

"Not a problem. After all you'll be living here in Stourton and they'll be in Brinsford and Kielby, eight and nine miles away. You aren't a close-in bodyguard." Abel wondered if the protection imperative might be a bit too strong, but daren't ask.

"No, but I remember when I first found magic, and the stupid ideas I had. Barely sixteen, already messing about with booze, boys and pot, I thought I knew it all. The combination might have been why I started seeing creatures. When I pointed at a couple and described them, my friends probably thought I'd moved onto something stronger. Somehow, a magic user must have heard about me. Galadriel, one of Pendragon's apprentices, turned up and asked me if I wanted power and money. She zapped a few creatures, took me to buy some flash clothes, and explained my future as a beautiful, powerful sorceress. Before I'd time to think it through I'd accepted a tether. I got the power and cash, but never had the chance to use it. Gally got a bonus for recruiting me." Ginny stopped, and now she looked really embarrassed. "Sorry about running off at the mouth. Maybe it's because I can drop the snooty superior sorcerer's apprentice act. The thing is, I know just how easy it is for a youngster to mess up, so I'm watching for the signs."

"She believes what she said, unless she can hide her thoughts in case I am listening. I do not think so."

"Thank you Zephyr." Abel gestured towards the Mercedes minibus. "With luck you can stop Mel or Diane before it gets that bad. We'd like this taken back to the house, please. Someone else will drive from there, because we are going to repossess one of the BMWs from someone called

Valdar. I don't want Melanie and Diane going in case it's dangerous," Abel explained properly.

"Valdar? He visited Pendragon twice, to combine forces for seeing off a challenge. He's not considered a strong sorcerer, but he paid for the help by backing Pendragon's monopoly in Stourton. Gawain stayed to look after the Sheffield office when we all came to Brinsford, so he probably took your car." The ex-apprentice hesitated because that had been when she'd attacked the Taverners.

"I thought all the real apprentices, the ones with cars, came on the attack." And died, Abel didn't add.

"Gawain and Paragon are only hex-fillers, they can't even cast air properly yet. They'd have access to cars so they could drive themselves to jobs if the seniors were busy. Gawain probably knew about Valdar, so he might go there for protection. I don't know if an apprentice can still use the cars if they take Valdar's tether. Speaking of which, you should hex this vehicle so that only Taverners can get inside." Ginny opened the minibus, climbed in and started it up. "Maybe I should come? Valdar knows me, so I can confirm your takeover." With a wry smile she tapped her shoulder. "Having me on a tether should be all the proof you need. If trouble starts I have these gold armbands full of extra magic, so I can help shield you."

Ferryl took Abel's hand, talking silently through the skin contact. "Zephyr can watch Ginny through the tether, and the imperatives mean she can't betray you. She is right about being proof you won. Without Terese, the solicitor, Valdar might dispute your right to the car. We'll all get home a little bit later, but Melanie and Diane won't mind staying here as long as we want them to. They are having a ball, meeting all the Taverners and the two rescued girls, and pestering Rachel about the new rules."

"Good idea Ginny, though we'd better get off. We have to get Rob's and Jenny's sisters back home for teatime."

*   *   *

When Abel came back into the house, Amanda and Cecilia were in the centre of an excited cluster of Taverners. The group were those who had barely learned to activate a wind glyph, so they were only fluttering

44

leaves or agitating handfuls of gravel. Despite that, the two newcomers were fascinated. Both were magically aware so they could see glyphs and creatures, but the church wouldn't even start teaching them to use magic. According to Cecilia, anyone learning glyphs had to sign up as a fighter or ancillary with the Church Militant. The idea she could sit on her own and practice with a leaf, at her own pace and without needing constant supervision, came as a revelation.

"Some of the church helpers, like that policeman who came after the fight, aren't taught glyphs. These two accepted that idea, until now." Kelis's smile didn't seem too worried about it. "Amanda isn't keen on learning magic, in case that gets her into strife, but she likes the idea of a ward and a few hexes to keep creatures away. Cecilia is really fired up."

"Creepio will be pleased. The next time we see her she'll be one of his God's SAS, smiting the godless." Though Abel hoped Creepio never put the Tavern in that category.

"No she won't, or she might not. Putting her with Shannon might have been a mistake. You remember when Creepio offered Shannon a place in the Church Militant?" Abel nodded for Kelis to continue. "She's just been explaining fighting for good within the Tavern, a sort of apprentice Saint Georgeous. I think Cecilia fancies white armour and a unicorn." Kelis burst out laughing at Abel's face. "Stop worrying, she knows that's just a game character but the idea really appeals to her. Creepio probably has Cecilia pencilled in for church use, with her being a believer and already confirmed, so he'll think we did this deliberately."

"Flobberclomps. Flipping, flopping curses. We can only hope she calms down once Creepio gets her back in the convent hospital. She'll be there for a while, until all the leech damage heals, so she'll probably change her mind again." Abel braced his shoulders. "But that's the least of our problems, right now we've got to go and get our car back. On the bright side, we can use the minibus now, so we'll take plenty of help."

"I will put a hex on it so only warded Taverners can ride inside, as Ginny suggested." Zephyr flitted off on her errand.

*   *   *

Once he asked, Abel had no shortage of volunteers to go and brace a sorcerer. From his point of view the fight with Pendragon should have been enough to put anyone off, but the Taverners didn't see it like that. Once Ginny gave her assessment of Valdar's level of competence, definitely less than Pendragon's, the main problem became cutting down the numbers to fit the vehicles.

Cecilia and Amanda wanted to know where everyone would be going. In a vain attempt to counter their enthusiasm, and the rosy view of magic the Taverners were giving the girls, Abel explained. He should have known better. Cecilia promptly insisted she ought to come and see a real sorcerer, one of the type she'd been warned about. The phone call to Creepio, to explain why the two girls wouldn't be leaving on time, didn't go well. After Cecilia pointed out she should take the chance see the real enemy, she handed the phone back to Abel. When Creepio finally rang off, Abel understood the message. If either girl ended up hurt, Valdar's headquarters would be a hole in the ground, and Frederick's house wasn't necessarily safe.

Cecilia's and Amanda's inclusion, because nervous or not Amanda wasn't going to be left out, meant adding an extra vehicle and guards. Abel found that he had six bodyguards, though luckily one lived in his arm. Another, Una, doubled up as driver for the big seven-seater BMW SUV or they'd have been a bit crowded. Jenny claimed the rear-gunner's seat, as she called it, the two fold-up seats in the rear. Una lost a bit of her enthusiasm when she had to take her sword off, but Kelis claimed the front shotgun seat and held it for her. Abel ended up sat in the back between Rob and Ferryl, feeling just a bit miffed about the guards. He could throw most glyphs as well as anyone except Ferryl. Zephyr's assertion she'd prepared a shield, ready to cast it over the whole vehicle if necessary, left him speechless.

The minibus held Ginny and eight more friends/guards, all adepts, with Shannon, Eric and Rachel following in a second BMW with Cecilia and Amanda. Those who didn't qualify for gold belts carried extra lead bars full of magic. From Abel's point of view, his friends' precautions looked ominously like preparations for an invasion or assault, rather than a friendly visit.

Repossession Plus

The trip wasn't boring because Shawn handed Abel a phone, then used its twin to call the Sheffield office to say Abel would be in town and explain why. The twenty-year-old couldn't officially quit his job until after Easter, but he'd already moved into the flat above the Sheffield office. The secretary had produced the business phones for him and Abel, spares because careless magic and electrics didn't mix. With that in mind, Abel put his own private phone in the pocket on the back of the driver's seat and the rest did the same.

Now, with the manager and the owner both headed their way, the secretary forwarded several queries. Five minor sorcerers had asked if Abel wanted to do business, had business for them, or they wanted to rent or buy some of his trees or one of his houses. Abel sent back a message via Shawn, promising to consider them all, and asking if the office had a phone number for Valdar. He'd been thinking, and turning up without warning might not be the best way if Abel wanted to ask nicely.

Despite hoping to leave all the magic business alone until after the exams, the messages showed that might not be possible. Shawn brought up other problems, like Pendragon's two houses that were magically locked down until Abel visited them with his dragon ring. Several Taverners had been to have a look, curious after Ginny described her own room, but couldn't get into the garden.

The next phone call from Shawn, riding in the minibus, threw Abel completely. "Valdar has been informed that you will be visiting, to repossess a stolen car. He's been given the registration and told about the tracker."

"Who told him that?"

"Your secretary, Bertram, from your office." Abel could hear the laughter in Shawn's voice. "According to Ginny, and Bertram, sorcerers don't call sorcerers. Their people call each other. More to the point, your secretary thought turning up unannounced might cause trouble. This way Valdar can save face by having the stolen car parked on the road, ready to go. Ginny suggests you drive up first, without the rest of us. We should lurk round the corner."

He'd been going to call Valdar so Abel didn't mind, but Ginny should have been the proof that Pendragon lost the fight. Though when he mentioned it there'd been some rethinking. "Call her forward if you need the proof. It might be best if Ginny isn't there upfront, just in case whoever stole the car has joined Valdar and panics. She might be here to recapture them. They are only beginners, not dangerous, but even running away might kick off a fight."

"All right. Just be ready."

"Ginny is calling on the tether. She will be two streets away, in gear with her foot poised over the accelerator." Zephyr sounded excited, ready to go. "Would you like an ogre this time?"

"I'd like a sneaky-quiet Zephyr, as a surprise if I need her, please." Abel really hoped that was all he'd need.

*   *   *

The small, quiet, leafy close seemed peaceful, as did the rambling old house showing through the trees at the end of the short road. "That house is warded, and so are the houses each side of the road." Zephyr had connected to everyone in the car, so six pairs of eyes inspected the houses.

"No BMW parked in the road, keys in and ready to go." Kelis sounded tense, ready for the worst.

Though Rob seemed less worried. "But no line of sorcerers and apprentices tossing glyphs at us."

"If the houses are warded, does that mean he has enough apprentices to fill both of them? How many apprentices has he got?" Una slowed the car a little, trying to work out how many might be hiding in there.

"Those houses aren't as big as the one Ginny described, so maybe the same number but split up." Ferryl looked at each house in turn. "Maybe less, because I can't see anyone coming out and there's only one vehicle on the driveway on the right. There can't be any at the other house because the driveway has been torn up."

"I have asked Ginny. Valdar had eight apprentices, four senior but the other four were hex fillers. Two could use fire, and might have been ready to learn a shield, but the other two were still stuck on air." Sudden excitement brightened Zephyr's 'voice.' "Magic users are leaving the big house, heading this way. I can detect three shields, two big enough to cover several people."

Jenny called from the rear. "Nobody behind us, but a shimmer just sprang up across the end of the road. Someone has put up a veil so they want privacy."

By the time Una pulled up, six men and four women had walked to the end of the driveway directly ahead and stopped. One man had his own shield, but Zephyr confirmed the rest of the group were under two large globes. Rob's hand stopped Abel as he undid his seat belt. "The rest of us discussed this before we left. The other mob are shielded so they might be looking for a fight. Ferryl, Kelis and me get out first, with shields. Una stays ready to drive away while Jenny can cover our escape. If Ferryl steps away from the door it's safe, follow her, then both Jenny and Una will get out as well."

"Did you know?"

Zephyr didn't sound surprised. "No, but Rob is making sense. After that talk everyone here realised that the Tavern relies on your money, and your blood link to Celtchar, so you must be protected. If you have to shield, warn me first, please. I will call Ginny on the tether, or fly free so I can do so outside the shield."

Meanwhile Ferryl had greeted Valdar. "Greeting visitors with raised shields is impolite at the least, or possibly threatening. Though with your people grouped like that it makes them two big targets."

Valdar looked startled, briefly. "Pendragon warned me you could detect shields, but I expected you to use a glyph. Since I am meeting the sorcerer who defeated him, and he seems to think I have stolen his property, the shields are a precaution." The sorcerer turned to Rob. "That would be you."

"Nope, I'm a bodyguard. We've had a bad few days so either you drop the shields or the other three will get out." Rob seemed quite cheerful. "We'll all be shielded as well."

"Boudicca seems to think you are dangerous, but with ten to your six, and your age, I'm willing to take a chance." A moment later Zephyr confirmed the shields had gone down. "Now do I get to meet the mystery man?"

"To avoid any misunderstandings, I will introduce myself first. Ferryl Shayde, sorceress, bodyguard to Abel, Master of Castle House and Pendragon Enterprises. I am not tethered, nor bound, so I will react to any threat without waiting for instructions." From her tone of voice, Abel could imagine Ferryl's big smile. "When you are counting, remember I killed five senior apprentices in the last fight." She moved away from the door, so Abel got out and took the proffered hand.

"You love doing that, don't you?"

"I told you, I've never been me before so I enjoy showing off." Ferryl's hand squeezed a little and she nodded towards Valdar. "If you look at how nervous those apprentices are, you'll see how well it works."

Valdar looked Abel up and down. "That part is right, you look like a schoolboy. I'm told it isn't a Seeming, which explains a sorceress as bodyguard."

Abel simply didn't want to go through the usual sorcerer taunting and bragging. He found the whole thing a waste of time. He only had one simple request, and all the posing in the world wouldn't change that. "I've come to collect my car, the BMW. Unless you've found a less than honest locksmith, it's useless to you anyway."

"Ah, that's a bit awkward. I bought that car in good faith, before you claimed Pendragon Enterprises, so it isn't yours." Valdar's face broke into a confident smile. "Why aren't you in Pendragon's Bentley? If he's still running about in that tank, you might not want to annoy anyone else. You'll need friends in a hurry if he turns up."

"We retrieved the gold from the Bentley, before sending what was left to the scrapyard." Zephyr fed the next words into Abel's head, directly from Ginny's tether. Shawn must be in touch with the office. "Gawain left the Sheffield office in the car after I registered a seven-eighths claim, which the staff would have confirmed if you'd asked. Buyer beware, so I hope you can get your money back." The flinch from one of the apprentices might mean they'd found Gawain.

"Sometime I'd like to know how you broke down the shield on that Bentley, fast enough to get through the armour as well." The sorcerer seemed genuinely curious but not for long. "Fair enough, collect your car. Though it's in the garage there." With a big fake smile Valdar pointed at the shattered driveway. "Driving it out might cause some damage, but that's not really my problem." He patted his pockets. "Oh dear, no you can't. The apprentice with the keys for the car and garage is on an errand. He should be back in a couple of days."

"By which time the locksmith will have visited, the tracker will be disabled and the garage will be empty. Then Valdar will claim the car was stolen back by Gawain after he had to pay back the money." Ferryl glanced up the driveway, then back to Valdar. "Though I'm not sure why he is so keen to keep one vehicle."

Abel thought he knew. "Boudicca is going crackers about losing one Volvo, so maybe he's only got one or two more. Though it shouldn't be a problem. Can you fix the driveway, Rob?"

"Probably, though it might still be a bit bumpy."

"The garage has a magical lock as well as a physical one. Both are stronger than necessary. If you break either, Valdar will pretend to be offended and want compensation." Ferryl inspected the garage door, presumably adjusting her eyes because she shouldn't have been able to see the details from fifty metres away. "The door itself hasn't been given extra protection. Ask him to drop the boundary around the house. If he does, at least he's willing to give us a chance at the car. If he refuses, call up the others." Her mental voice took on a little bit of anticipation. "Or give me the word and I'll kill a few apprentices. That should make him more willing to help?"

Her voice gave no hint if Ferryl was joking, so Abel ignored the last bit and went for negotiation. Valdar still wore his big fake smile, slightly mocking, when he agreed to drop the protection on the house and garden. It widened when he pointed out that he didn't want everyone wandering about his property, so only one person could collect the car. That had to be Abel, because the car wouldn't let anyone else in until the glyphs recognised the new master. By then Ferryl wanted to call in the reinforcements and simply demand full access, but Abel didn't want to fight over a car. So far the sorcerer had played games, but not threatened anyone. If that changed, Abel felt sure his shield would hold long enough for Ferryl to get to him, while the rest held off the opposition.

Abel couldn't look around for traps or lurkers as he walked up the broken tarmac, or he would have tripped and fallen, but Zephyr assured him there were neither. As he came near Zephyr explained there were still magical wards, very strong ones, though only around the lock itself. Unfortunately, the magic would stop her even attempting to trip the tumblers. Her voice continued in his head as Abel inspected the wooden doors, until something snagged his attention. "You can undo woodscrews?"

"Yes, but as I just explained, not these because the hasp covers them. Several of the Taverners started it as a game when they were repairing Frederick's house, because they didn't have enough screwdrivers. Not many can manage to compress wind enough to hold the cross cut into the screw end. Rotating is easy, the same as forming a whirlwind." Zephyr sounded frustrated, but she didn't come across many garages.

"But you can send a little bit of you inside the door, through the cracks between the timbers, and see the inside. The hinges should be screwed into the wood at each side. If you undo them, the doors will fall off." Abel thought it through, and remembered what Ferryl said about damage. "I'd better catch the doors and move them gently. If Valdar gets shirty, we'll screw them back on afterwards. Will the magic in the lock interfere?"

Abel felt the nearest thing to a mental giggle he'd ever experienced, very strange. "Not if you don't touch the metal, physically or with magic. If you stand closer to the door I can sneak a look without anyone seeing me." Abel moved up close, putting his hands on the wood well clear of the lock as if sensing something. A slim shimmer tickled across his chest and eased out through the front of his shirt before disappearing between two planks. A little while later Zephyr's suppressed excitement told Abel the answer before she confirmed it. "I had to clean some rust from the screws, but I have tested them. I will need plenty of magic, enough for ten bits of me to hold tight and twirl."

"All at once?" Only Ferryl could handle ten glyphs so Abel worried that Zephyr might be trying too hard, pushing herself too far to please him.

"Yes, but ten glyphs all doing the same thing. I will undo ten screws first, some on each hinge, then the other ten. I had to unpick eight of Pendragon's tethers at the same time. This will be easier. Magic please."

Abel took one hand off the door and hooked it into a gold belt, drawing magic until Zephyr stopped draining it. "All turning now. Some were very stiff. Be ready to catch the door." Abel formed air glyphs in each hand and raised them, letting the wind hook into the cracks between the timbers to get a firm grip. It wasn't easy.

Abel felt weight come onto the glyphs and strengthened them, just as Zephyr confirmed she'd got half of the screws out. The rest were now loose, barely holding hinges in place. More magic flowed down the link, then the door shifted just a little. "All done now. Putting the screws on the floor so I can hide again." As he felt Zephyr flow back into his tattoo, Abel's wind glyphs lifted the two timber doors, and he took a half-step back. The pair of doors followed him another two half-steps, then Abel rested the weight on the ground.

A quick glance each way only gave him one option, apart from tossing the doors into the shrubbery. Abel strengthened the glyphs, lifting the doors before shuffling slowly sideways. The corner turned out to be the tricky part, swivelling the lot without catching on trees, bushes or the fence. He finally got the unwieldy burden lined up, and set off sideways again. By the time he finally leant the doors against the side wall of the garage, Abel's hands were stiff from keeping the exact position, and taking the strain of the glyphs. With definite relief he released the magic, and relaxed.

As he stepped back, laughter startled Abel. He turned to find that Valdar and two of his apprentices stood at the end of the drive, looking frustrated and definitely angry. The laughter came from Kelis, behind them. Ferryl wasn't watching, she'd got her eye on Valdar's other apprentices. "As you can see, Abel doesn't need a sorceress to cast his glyphs."

With an obvious effort, Valdar forced a smile back on his face. "Now I want to see him float the car down the drive."

"Rob, can you steamrolla some rocks please?" Jenny and Kelis laughed again, this time at the play on Rob's game persona, Rock'n Rolla the earth wizard. Valdar didn't see the joke, especially when Rob began to cast glyphs. Nothing fancy, he turned two strips of broken tarmac leading from the garage to the road into dust, then solidified them again. As promised they weren't smooth, but the suspension on a BMW wouldn't be stressed. Abel went to the car, looked inside and tried the door, but it had been locked.

"Any ideas, Zephyr?"

"None, but Ginny has. I've been telling her what Valdar said, and when he told you the keys were missing, Shawn called your office. If you can delay a little longer your secretary will deliver the spare set. He will give them to Ginny, because the office staff aren't employed to fight and have no shields." Zephyr's tendril probed around the edges of the car doors. "I can get through the cracks to pop the door lock, if you want to sit down?"

"Let's not show him we can do that." Abel raised his voice. "I'll just inspect the car for damage. By then the spare keys will be here."

"But too late. I had to be sure you really were the Master of Pendragon Enterprises, and you've just proved it by touching that car. Better yet, I've got you separated from your bodyguards." Valdar started up the driveway with two apprentices, while the rest spread out to cover his back. "Consider this a takeover bid, and repayment for my two dead apprentices. When you die your sorceress will be unemployed, so the new Master of Pendragon Enterprises will hire her."

A familiar voice sounded from across the road, behind Abel's friends. "She might not be available. I told you this wasn't finished, sorceress. Let's have that duel now. I fancy the odds today." Boudicca! The sorceress who had sent an apprentice to help Pendragon attack the Tavern! The sorceress who wanted her Volvo back! She came out of the driveway on the opposite side of the road, followed by four apprentices.

Zephyr almost vibrated, wanting to come out, but Abel still hoped to keep her in reserve. The puff of wind could be badly hurt by sorcerer-strong glyphs. "Ginny is on the way in the minibus, but metal posts have come up out of the approach roads. She has cast a veil while the others burn them off. Shall I help now?"

"Just tell me what else you can see, please." Abel still didn't want Zephyr in a firefight.

"Boudicca and her four apprentices have shields, as do Valdar and the two with him. The other apprentices are sacrifices, almost unprotected though two are forming a shield and another two are trying."

Abel raised his shield, then his voice. "Una, you can beat all the rest of Valdar's apprentices on your own. They haven't got real shields." He did the math and didn't like the answer. A sorceress, Boudicca, and her four senior apprentices against Rob, Kelis, Jenny and Ferryl. Even if Una broke through her opponents, she couldn't tackle Valdar, and Ferryl would be busy fighting Boudicca. That wasn't good news because it left him on his own, against three. Despite his gold belts full of magic, Abel knew a proper sorcerer like Pendragon or Valdar carried magic in diamonds in his bones. The other two, a man and a woman, must be senior apprentices so they wouldn't be pushovers either.

As the first glyph hit his shield and flared, blocking his view, Abel heard shouting and then screaming in the road. His air glyphs plucked a trolley jack from the garage floor and hurled it at an apprentice, then a toolbox at the other. A spare wheel gave him options. Abel used wind to throw it at Valdar, but added fire so it burst into flames. The missile rebounded, but the woman apprentice had to stop to blow it aside before continuing. Encouraged, Abel threw everything flammable he could lift, so the three attackers had to stop and blow them aside. Return fire hit his shield causing sparks, cracks and patches of blazing light that obstructed his view.

Despite that, Abel kept throwing glyphs, even using growth glyphs on the bushes next to the driveway. Sharp branches lunging out, or roots thrusting through the broken tarmac, burned out on the shields, except for one that got through and jabbed an apprentice's leg. The three shields stopped most of Abel's glyphs, though the male apprentice now had a limp, and bleeding score marks on his face from a box of screws or nails. The woman's clothes were smouldering, so the heat from Abel's fire glyphs must be bleeding through. Zephyr kept throwing fire mixed with ice, clouds of tiny shards and sparks spread across all three attackers, trying to keep their shields glowing to disrupt their vision.

The trio kept coming, Abel's magic kept draining away, and another serious danger threatened. The hail of glyphs hitting his shield had set the garage on fire! Now Abel had to use precious magic to keep the smoke out of his shield, and cool the air so he didn't burst into flame. His concentration on the attack glyphs faltered, weakening them. "I will deal with heat and air. You can throw stronger attack glyphs than me."

Abel relaxed a little, tightening his next fireball while using angled ice to deflect an incoming ball of something that looked nasty. At least the fire glyphs from the apprentices had burned off some purplish, sticky stuff from Valdar, which stopped it draining magic from his shield. Unfortunately, as fire glyphs smashed into the walls and ceiling, Abel realised that Valdar had switched to deliberately setting the garage on fire.

Except the car! A deflected glyph glanced from the bonnet, bubbling the paint but not burning through so it must have some sort of protection. "Open the car door, Zephyr." Abel concentrated, pulling his shield into the skin on his back to let Zephyr out of the shield. He felt sudden heat, sharp pain, then blessed coolness. He'd forgotten the fire behind him!

"Quickly, get in. I put out the flames on your back." Abel opened the door and, hidden for a moment, dropped his shield and dived inside. He immediately slammed the shield back up to cover the whole car, just in time to turn aside a storm of fireballs. Just for a moment Abel nearly lost the shield, when the seat connected with his burned back. He sat forward a little and concentrated, ignoring the pain to pour everything into defence, because he couldn't cast glyphs from in here. Through the glare and flames Abel saw the three attackers closing in, while the inside of the car door began to smoke very slightly.

*   *   *

Ferryl Shayde whirled, saw Boudicca, froze as she realised what Valdar intended, then spun back round towards the sorcerer. Red rage swirled across her vision. "Una, deal with Boudicca!" Ferryl knew she'd made a mistake in the last fight, left Abel to fight a sorcerer, but not this time. She'd made her decision in the long dark hours afterwards; she would never desert him again. With a scream of rage Ferryl strengthened her shield and charged the seven men and women in her way, glyphs reaching out to burn and tear.

Una hesitated, until the man at one end of the line facing Ferryl flew backwards off his feet. He rolled away across the pavement, shrieking as a burning red net enveloped him. Another scream rang out as the woman at the other end of the line threw up her arm to stop a glittering spike, and it drove right through until the point jutted out the other side. As Una turned towards Boudicca, Ferryl's shield clashed with a feeble attempt by a very frightened-looking apprentice. Ferryl pushed harder until cracks ran through the man's shield, glowing brighter as the protection began to flicker.

Turning to face Boudicca, Una strengthened her own shield, though if the sorceress had any sense she'd just go straight after Ferryl. That meant finding a way to keep Boudicca pre-occupied, to give Ferryl a chance to break through. A big smile broke over Una's face and she raised her sword. "Remember me? Want your car back? Come and get it, bitch!" Moments later Una wondered if that might have been a mistake, as a hail of glyphs smashed into her shield. Bright fiery lines and sparks crawled across the normally invisible globe, but despite the onslaught, it held and Una steadied. As Boudicca headed across the road, closing in, Una's smile came back. Robin D'Ritche had just the thing for up close and personal.

Jenny turned when she recognised Boudicca's voice, and realised the sorceress might have spoken too soon. The Taverners weren't outnumbered yet, because three apprentices were still on the driveway. Jenny didn't hesitate, throwing growth glyphs with both hands, urging the hedge on either side to grow. The tough privet stems and roots twined together and thickened in a sustained surge, two metres high, right across the driveway, trying to bury the apprentices. Wood and leaves couldn't penetrate the shields, but Jenny didn't expect them to. The two women and a man stood back to back, frantically burning away the shoots closing around their shields, distracted for vital seconds.

Kelis and Rob both threw their first glyphs at Boudicca, though her shield stopped them. When Kelis heard Una's shout and saw the sorceress's reaction, then the hedge exploded into growth, she saw her chance. "Distract that apprentice, Rob!" Kelis concentrated, shutting out the rest of the fight, knowing she only had one shot at this. How well it worked depended on what Rob came up with. The tarmac footpath lifted right underneath the remaining apprentice, glowing and then catching fire as Rob pushed it against the shield magic. The sudden heat, right under his feet, took the man's eyes off Kelis and she thrust both palms out. "Stickybangs!" Fifteen small black shapes flew out, their little legs fastening onto the apprentice's shield.

His head came up, puzzled, and then horrified as the shield around each black beetle shape began to glow, and small cracks appeared. Rob sounded puzzled, then he remembered. "What the crikey gosh are those? You did that to Pendragon!"

"Be ready when they pop." Kelis kept her voice down, building an ice spear while Rob grinned, remembering what happened when those things hit Pendragon's shield. He built a fire glyph, concentrating it for long seconds until.... In a series of sharp explosions the black blobs exploded, and a network of glowing cracks brightened and spread across the apprentice's shield. Worse, the sudden explosions right in front of his face must have spoiled his concentration. Even as Rob and Kelis launched their glyphs, the shield flickered.

Moments later the apprentice dived for the floor as his shield collapsed, but glyphs were magical homing missiles. He managed to get an arm up to stop the ice spear, but as Rob's fire wrapped around his arm he rolled away along the road, frantically beating at the flames. For a few moments he forgot to raise his shield again, but luckily for him Boudicca's other apprentices joined the fight. They'd finally realised the bushes were only a diversion, and burned their way straight through to join their mistress. Now Rob, Kelis and Jenny were in a full-scale battle, though the injured apprentice couldn't take advantage. Even when he finally remembered to shield, he had to concentrate on stopping the blood pouring from the hole in his badly burned arm.

* * *

Despite their initial success, Abel's friends hadn't managed to strike a vital blow. The battle in the road settled into an exchange of glyphs with four casters on each side, Unfortunately, that wouldn't last. As Boudicca closed in on Una, the trainee concentrated on her shield, but occasionally cast the strongest fire glyph she could manage. Una wanted Boudicca to keep a strong shield, to use up some of her magic. The would-be mercenary knew her glyphs wouldn't break through a real sorceress's shield, so she saved most of her magic for when the shields clashed. Rob and Kelis were wearing down their opponents, and Jenny definitely had the measure of hers, but now Boudicca's injured apprentice started throwing glyphs. That might not be a disaster, not yet, but Boudicca kept getting closer. If she put Una out of the fight, the other three would be in real trouble.

* * *

As her opponent's shield failed and he fell away wreathed in flames, Ferryl ripped and tore at the remaining five apprentices. She concentrated on powerful attacks, accepting some damage so she could finish this fight as fast as possible. In a mad melee of flame and terror her shield burned two more opponents while glyphs smashed and tore the others. Ferryl staggered for a moment as the resistance vanished, the last apprentice turning to run, but the spikes already buried inside her burst apart. Even though it took precious moments, Ferryl paused to heal herself before running up the driveway to tackle a full sorcerer. Ahead of her, flames gushed from the garage, the garage where Abel had been! As she ran, a glistening shape grew between Ferryl's hands, and smoking droplets fell to burn holes in the shattered tarmac.

The woman apprentice with smouldering clothes stopped in her tracks, spinning round as she felt something sucking magic from her shield. A glittering web crawled across her vision, leaving black smears that smoked, and then began to eat through. She poured magic into her defences, then more, but the cracks spread until a silver spike struck and pierced right through! It jammed partway, but then a second and third struck. The fourth drove in through the centre of the others before exploding in a blizzard of tiny shards. Blinded, with her hands and face shredded, the woman's shield collapsed and the web and corrosive droplets took her down.

By then Ferryl had her hands full, because both Valdar and his other apprentice had turned and were casting glyphs. Her vision purpled out, but she recast the slippery spell and the gunk from Valdar's attack slid off her shield, far enough for her to see. Ferryl didn't clear it all, ignoring the drain on her magic so she could keep up a relentless onslaught. She hammered both with glyphs, desperate to keep them from targeting Abel, though she might be too late. Behind her opponents, smoke and flames gushed from the garage, too hot for a human to survive. Wind gusted briefly and Ferryl saw the car, the metal grill on the front glowing in the heat. More important, she saw movement inside it!

Just for a few moments Ferryl Shayde stood still, gathering strength and concentrating, ignoring the glyphs hammering away at her shield. She had always claimed to be the mistress of wind, well now she would prove it! With a grunt of effort Ferryl released the glyph, but not at her opponents. The reverse wind glyph flew through the gap between them, and at first it did no more than suck smoke from the garage. A blast of flame followed, some reaching Valdar and his apprentice. The flame didn't threaten their shields but it distracted them. The apprentice even stopped throwing glyphs, while he glanced back in alarm. Ferryl dropped to her knees as the strain hit her, pouring more magic and will into the glyph because it wasn't working!

Flames gushed further out of the garage, wrapping right around both Valdar and his apprentice, until with a groaning and shrieking of burning rubber and metal on concrete the BMW lurched forward. Again, despite the wrench on her legs and arms, Ferryl hurled power and will into the glyph. With a drawn-out, torturous screech the smoking vehicle lurched clear of the garage. The flames and smoke eased as Ferryl finally released the glyph, but Valdar didn't take advantage. He'd dived into the bushes to avoid the vehicle.

The apprentice had been stood to one side, so now as the smoke cleared he had a clear view of Ferryl. She'd slumped onto her hands and knees, her shield flickering, so he raised his hands to finish her. Flames roared around him again, stronger than ever, bathing the apprentice's shield in fire and blanking out any chance of seeing his target.

Ferryl shook her head, clearing it, looked up and recognised the continuous stream of flames. Abel's flamethrower! With a vicious grin she cast her favourite web, so familiar it took hardly any concentration. The apprentice had turned away as the fire burned away at his shield, frantically trying to see where it came from so he could fight back. It faded a little, enough so he could see a young man streaming smoke. No, steam, he realised, because even with his hands throwing fire the youth seemed to be casting glyphs to drag moisture out of the air to cool himself. The sudden powerful drain on his already weakened shield puzzled Valdar's apprentice, because the stream of fire from ahead had slackened. Realisation dawned, just in time to throw himself sideways as his shield failed, so the web of fire tightened around his legs rather than his body.

As the man rolled away, screaming and trying to drag enough water from the air to quench the net, another voice brought Ferryl's head round. "Too late." Valdar staggered out of the bushes and began to build a glyph, looking straight at Abel but speaking to Ferryl. "He's nearly done." Ferryl's quick glyph fizzled against Valdar's shield without even distracting him. She tried to get up, to get to Abel and shield him, but pulling the car had been too much for her muscles. Desperately Ferryl tried to form something dangerous enough to stop the sorcerer, if only long enough for Abel to stop coughing and realise what was happening. A shimmer in the air threw glyph after glyph, but Valdar stayed fixed on killing one person, the Master of Pendragon Enterprises.

*   *   *

Out in the road Una kept throwing glyphs, the best she could create left-handed, waiting until Boudicca came near enough. She'd learned a strange thing in the fight with Pendragon's apprentices, but had never got round to discussing it. That time Una hadn't known what she was doing, she hadn't prepared, but this time it should work better. Una really hoped so, because otherwise Boudicca's shield would drain hers, and Una didn't want to burn. She glanced to the side, but Kelis, Rob and Jenny were still embroiled in their own battle. From the looks of it they'd win, eventually, but only if Robin D'Ritche could handle her end of it. Boudicca stopped and Una's heart sank, because if the bitch didn't get close, those glyphs would eventually break through. The would-be mercenary gritted her teeth. If the mountain wouldn't come to her?

With a sudden yell Una leapt forward and crashed her shield into Boudicca's. As sparks flew she saw the look of triumph on the sorceress's face, because a sorceress would soon drain an apprentice's shield, but then Una played her joker. In the last fight, her sword, still holding the remnants of the magic put into it during the fursomnium hunt, had penetrated a shield. A weakening shield, and the sword only went in a third of its length, but while she'd been throwing glyphs with one hand Una had been feeding her weapon magic from the other.

Boudicca had relaxed, safe because nobody could throw glyphs while clashing shields, so the sword thrust came as a complete surprise. Una gave it everything she had. The sword hit Boudicca's shield, the blade flashed a deep red, a shock went up Una's arm and she thought she'd failed. Then the resistance vanished, and the glowing weapon slid straight through and into Boudicca's arm!

Only an arm, not her chest, because the sorceress's reactions were good enough to protect her body. Una's re-enactment weapon wasn't as sharp as a real sword, so it burned into the sorceress's flesh rather than stabbing, but Boudicca yelled something incomprehensible and tried to break contact. Una lunged forward to keep the shields locked. She could feel her magic draining, so she could only keep contact for one more thrust. Her sword pierced the shield again, but the sorceress blocked with her other arm! Una shrieked in frustration, but when Boudicca staggered back again she had to let the sorceress go. Dragging together the last dregs of magic, Una tried to build a decent glyph, because Boudicca's shield had failed at last. It flickered and stuttered as the older woman tried to stop the blood pouring from her charred arms.

Too late. Boudicca's shield snapped up as she steadied. Despite the bleeding and obvious pain, the sorceress raised one hand and a glyph grew in her palm. Una abandoned her glyph and frantically fed the rest of her magic into her shield. The small, tight fire glyph smacking into Boudicca's shield came as a complete surprise to both of them. Even though the shield stopped it, Boudicca's already charred arm smoked slightly. She jerked it away in pain, and lost her glyph.

Una's legs gave way and she sat down hard, holding her shield and staring as a succession of tight, intensely hot glyphs hit the sorceress's rapidly weakening protection. Some part of Una felt jealous because she'd never been able to get a glyph that tight, certainly not tight enough to crack a sorceress's shield. She'd barely thought that when a storm of ice and fire crashed in, and tossed Boudicca's burned and torn body down the road. Una turned to look up the street, just in time to see the glyph-storm retarget. Boudicca's three apprentices ran, fast enough for one of them to make it out of sight before her shield failed completely.

As her opponent went down Kelis took one glance up the road, registered the minibus surrounded by Taverners, and whirled all the way round. "Abel!"

*   *   *

Abel didn't hear her. He'd thrown fire as long as possible, until he grew dizzy, then collapsed to his hands and knees. He stayed there, coughing and spluttering, his eyes streaming, trying to drag enough oxygen into lungs that stung with every breath. Ferryl gave a despairing cry as Valdar took another step, casting a swirling purple cloud spangled with yellow glitter at the defenceless youth. Not quite defenceless! A shimmer flew down, too fast for Valdar to divert the glyph, and caught it on her shield. Not a strong shield, Ferryl knew. Zephyr didn't have enough magic to hold off a sorcerer-strength glyph for long.

But Zephyr didn't try to hold it off, she flew into contact! In the blink of an eye, before Valdar could banish it, his own glyph hit his shield. The flash as the magic short-circuited blinded everyone for a moment, but when her eyes cleared Ferryl groaned. Valdar still stood, while a shimmer wobbled away through the air, trailing smoke. Ferryl dropped her hands to the ground and began to crawl forward, hoping to get near enough to clash shields. She'd never make it, so Ferryl poured more magic into her shield, pushing it out as far as possible.

Just far enough, as Ferryl's shield flared against the sorcerer's. Magic drained away, too much magic, but Valdar's shield fluttered! Ferryl groaned, because if she'd got close enough she might have drained him, but pushed out like this her shield lost three times as much magic as Valdar's. He looked startled, then sneered and stepped back, too far for Ferryl to follow. "Abel!" Even as Ferryl recognised Kelis's voice, and slumped in relief, a series of ice spears hit Valdar's shield one after the other, each one leaving a star of cracks. He looked past Ferryl, and for the first time she saw fear on Valdar's face as he turned to run.

He didn't even make the first step before going down on one knee. Valdar looked down, trying to work out why, staring at the melted tarmac that had oozed through his stuttering shield and now bubbled and smoked over his foot. His shield popped, he jerked, and four thin branches thrust out through his chest. Even as the sorcerer raised a hand, trying to push them back or summon a glyph, a block of ice crashed down on his head. Ferryl put her head down and concentrated on crawling, heading for Abel.

Back in the road, as the triumphant Taverners swept forward to check the fallen, the apprentice with the burned arm pushed himself back into the hedge. Once the nine fresh, strong glyph-wielders passed him he clambered to his feet. Cautiously, keeping an eye on the fiasco behind him, he crept towards the end of the road. "Under the new rules, we are supposed to give you a chance to surrender." He jerked his head round to find two apprehensive young women standing in front of a BMW sedan, peeking between three very determined glyph-wielders. He raised his good hand, to surrender but it might have been mistaken as an attempt to cast a glyph. "Good." The youngest teenager, Rachel, released her glyphs a fraction before the other two. Still in agony, too startled and confused to concentrate on a decent shield, the apprentice didn't live long enough to hear. "I prefer it this way."

* * *

By the time Abel had managed to stop coughing, and look up, he found himself face to face with Ferryl. She wrapped her arms round him, despite them both still being on their knees. "Not again. Not on your own, never again." That wasn't exactly coherent, but Abel understood, and he didn't fancy sticking himself out front again anyway. Voices surrounded him and hands were on him, checking or just patting him. Even without seeing who it was, Abel felt the remnants of their link when Kelis gave him a quick hug. Cool, damp air surrounded him before Abel heard hissing. The Taverners were sucking moisture from the air to extinguish the fires.

"What happened Ferryl? Why can't you walk?" Jenny sounded really worried but Ferryl managed a shaky laugh.

"This is why I keep telling you to build up muscles. Magic lifts many times what your muscles can, but dragging a car turned out to be too much."

"Maybe Abel should have taken the handbrake off?" That had to be Rob, of course. The first scattered laughter broke out, maybe more relief than humour.

Zephyr flowed back into her tattoo. "Handshake please. Hurt, need magic. Do you have magic please?" If she'd had eyes, Abel thought he would have felt tears. "I lost lots of me. I don't know what I forgot."

"Nothing you can't get back, Zephyr. You can bop fae until you are an ogre again." As he reconnected and fed magic down the link, Abel realised exactly what she'd said. "You lose memories?"

"Ferryl warned me I would, because I have only me to remember. That's why I try to grow, to remember more. I have no bones, no wits." Though a quick discussion with Ferryl calmed Zephyr down. Even if she'd forgotten a glyph, Zephyr would have kept her experience, her control of magic, so it would be easy to relearn. Ferry promised to sit in

Castle House gardens and go through every glyph Zephyr knew, to be absolutely certain the sprite still remembered them.

* * *

By then Abel and Ferryl were on their feet, more or less supporting each other as they staggered down the driveway. A crowd surrounded them, happy at winning though they had questions. Kelis, Rob and Jenny were puzzled by how easily Valdar's shield had gone down at the end, while the others hadn't expected Boudicca to fail so fast. The good humour died when the victorious Taverners took a good look at the losers. The bodies were all burned to some extent, and most were torn by ice shards and broken by Windhammers.

When a few of those with stronger stomachs inspected the bodies, they found why their opponents' shields had failed. Both sorcerer and sorceress wore gold bracelets and belts, magic storage, under their clothes. Neither were experienced enough to embed diamonds or heal themselves. Ferryl could do both, so if she hadn't used so much magic defeating the others and dragging the car, or physically exhausted herself, Ferryl would have won without help. More startling to everyone there, if she'd had another gold belt or even a lead bar Una would have taken Boudicca!

The crowd stopped in the middle of the road, looking at the bodies, damage, and the smoke still drifting up here and there. Several Taverners looked ill, especially the ones who had inspected the bodies. "This seems worse than the last time." Shawn waved his arm to take in the scene. "We didn't see most of the bodies, because the God Squad took them away. I hope we don't have many fights like this. It might be self-defence, but I'm not comfortable with killing lots of people."

"Nor me, or any of us, but it's different when someone is trying to kill you. I concentrated on living until after, and didn't even think about the damage I did to anyone else." Petra grimaced, keeping her eyes away from the nearest body. "Not until now. Now I'm pleased I'm not cleaning up. Creepio will not be amused."

"He won't care because nobody saw us." Rachel pointed back towards the end of the close. "The Seeming across the end of the street dropped, so I put three lead bars on top of the BMW and raised a big basic veil.

Anyone driving past will see the cars and houses, but no bodies, nor any of us."

"A Seeming across the whole road? Where is the glyph? Did it survive?" Despite her exhaustion, Ferryl perked up. Abel smiled to himself, a new glyph worked better than medicine on some people. Unfortunately Rachel hadn't seen a glyph, just the view of the road changing from a peaceful street to carnage as it failed.

"Who lives in the other houses?" Eric looked nervously at the two either side. "They must have seen us, unless they're among the bodies? Even then, all these people must have jobs and friends. If they disappear there'll be an investigation."

"All three houses were protected so they belonged to Valdar, and his apprentices are dead so there are no witnesses. Though I don't know how much Creepio will charge for the church to mazzle their friends." Jenny looked the houses over again, suddenly thoughtful. "Has Abel just inherited these houses, sorcerer style?" Several Taverners looked pointedly at the dead sorceress. "And Boudicca's house and whatever?"

"None of the apprentices have friends, because the first thing a sorceress does is force the apprentice to leave home and their old life behind. Solicitors like Woods and Green remove the apprentice from public records, or arrange a funeral, so they are invisible to the government. Magical friends will keep quiet, because of the Accord." Ginny looked sad as she continued, very quietly. "I had to go home, just long enough to have a blazing row with my parents and storm out. The tether meant I had no option."

Ferryl looked up and down the short road with three houses. "No records, no neighbours, so as far as the rest of the world knows nothing happened. We will want to find any customers, to take over the work, but that's all. No need for Creepio, and Abel has three new houses once Terese fixes the legalities."

"Boudicca and Valdar will be official because they ran businesses, so they'll have to disappear. I'll bet Terese can fix that, when she transfers the property. One of Boudicca's apprentices got away, so she might claim Boudicca's house." Kelis looked in the direction the injured woman had gone, a wicked smile spreading over her face. "Abel, why don't you call

Verenestra? She's not exactly a fan of Boudicca's."

Though Abel didn't actually call, because Shawn pointed out sorcerers didn't do that. More to the point, Abel's office phone was a charred lump. Once he had the sorceress on his phone Shawn passed it to Abel. "Have you decided? Will you remove the traces of my tether?" Verenestra sounded cautiously hopeful.

Which answered one question, Veren hadn't known about this mess. "Probably. No, definitely, if you'll do me a favour. One of Boudicca's apprentices will be running for home. Do you know where she'll be going, and more to the point can you get there first and stop her?"

"Boudicca only has one house, the same as me, so I'll have to try for an intercept. Our apprentices live with us." Verenestra hesitated, sounding really cautious. "That could start an open fight with Boudicca. Will you back me?"

"If you can persuade Boudicca's gryphon to accept you, you can wait inside her house. She's laid in the street outside Valdar's place with three of her apprentices." Abel turned, looking up the road towards Valdar's house. "In a minute I'm going to try and get into Valdar's house and find his gryphon. Do I need a solicitor?"

He didn't expect the laughter. "I told you I hadn't seen a gryphon. The likes of me, Boudicca and probably Valdar don't have them. Our goods and properties are tied to our personal ward, so if we die it's all up for grabs." She stopped dead. After a long silence Verenestra continued, but with a definitely calculating tone in her voice. "How much of Boudicca's belongings are you claiming?"

"None, if I can claim Valdar's, or maybe her car to replace the BMW. I'm hoping someone in the house can explain the attack because it doesn't make sense. Not for one car." Abel looked at the big house again. "Zephyr, is that house still protected?"

"Yes, there is a magical boundary but not as strong as the one round Castle House. The protection around the two smaller houses has gone."

"Thanks." Abel spoke into the phone again. "Veren, how do I get rid of a barrier if the sorcerer is dead?"

"It will be tied to a glyph set into something holding magic, probably a block of lead. The usual way to break one is to collect a horde of magical creatures, hoplins and the like, and drive them against the barrier. The boundary will kill the first ones, but eventually it will be drained far enough for you to walk in." Semi-hysterical laughter echoed down the phone. "Or you can line up those scary apprentices of yours, and just smack it with glyphs until it breaks down."

"What if it's powered by trees?" Abel didn't fancy trying to drain one tree, let alone the eight he could see in the house gardens.

"You have got to be joking! I've only got six trees in my garden, and there's no way I'm wasting them on powering a boundary." She giggled, Verenestra sounded either high or drunk. "I forgot, you've got trees everywhere, forests full of the durned things. Oh, how the other half live."

"You can join the other half if you nip off and grab Boudicca's trees. We'll sort out your tether trace when people stop trying to kill us." Abel wasn't joking at all. He had to talk to Woods and Green and find out how often this sort of thing happened. He said goodbye to Veren, and raised his voice. "The trees around the two small houses shouldn't have any protection, not now. Check first, then everyone fill up." He took off three of his gold belts, surprised to find one still felt about half full.

"I'll take those." Going by the sparkle in her eyes, Jenny had recovered from the fight, or maybe it was the thought of tree magic. "By the time I've filled those, my belts and my diamond, I'll be a happy little puddle of giggle. Just pour me into a car to take me home."

The Taverners spread out to find trees, but Kelis stayed. At Abel's look she touched her second blouse button. "I'm good for now, so I'll wait here in case someone else is lurking. This diamond holds a lot of magic, more than bracelets and belts." Her eyes narrowed in definite anticipation. "The next minor sorceress to give us crap is mine."

"Abel? Cecilia and Amanda want to look in the big house. They're quite excited about seeing a real, murderous, treacherous, backstabbing sorcerer and sorceress get their just deserts." Rachel rolled her eyes, but kept her voice down. "They're probably expecting trophy heads on the walls and a torture chamber, or possibly a larder full of body parts." Behind Rachel both the girls looked excited, though they kept giving the bodies cautious glances. Neither seemed horrified, but they'd both hosted blood leech seeds. Gore probably didn't rate as horrific, not compared to drinking blood from live victims. The rest of the Taverners weren't as hardened; they were giving the bodies a wide berth. Rachel pointed up the road. "She might let us in."

The pretty, well-dressed young woman standing at the end of the driveway looked apprehensive. Half a dozen Taverners approached her, and Una spoke to the woman briefly before laughing at something. When she came back Una seemed torn between shock and humour. "That's Valdar's girlfriend, or his ex now. She has no ward but there's something in the barrier stops her coming out of the garden. If she could, I reckon she'd be borrowing my sword to make sure Valdar isn't coming back."

"She will have had a link, the same as we thought you had with Kelis. I knew it wasn't that type as soon as we broke it, because the usual reaction is for whoever was linked to take a strong dislike to the sorcerer." Ferryl seemed amused by the next bit. "That's why I kept pushing you to kiss others, to get away from the feeling when you kissed Kelis. You were never properly linked, but you were having trouble moving on."

Abel let it ride, because even if Kelis seemed over it he still felt a magical something when she hugged him. "Will you organise everyone please, Una? Ask them to throw wind glyphs at the boundary until it collapses, then we'll give Cecilia and Amanda a guided tour."

"Bagsy the big house for University digs." Shannon stopped, putting a hand to her mouth. "Oops. I blame Una and her loot claiming thing, she's taught me bad habits. Though if it's going begging? Just to borrow, not a gimmee? Mum and Dad want me to try for Oxford but I'd already decided on Sheffield. I want to stay near the Tavern and the extra magic. Now I looked at that place and realised I'd need digs." Shannon had a smile now even though she still looked a little embarrassed. "It's only thirty miles away from home, but I want some freedom from parental supervision. For all the hours of study of course." Still smiling, she headed towards the Taverners gathering near Valdar's ex.

As Shannon headed off, Una stopped and turned back. "That lass seemed puzzled why there'd been a fight, since we'd brought Valdar's minibus back. Valdar must be the one who loaned Pendragon the other two apprentices." She set off again, calling out to those who'd finished topping up with magic.

"He said something about payment for two apprentices, and he only had two who could shield properly. Now we know what this was all about. Both Valdar and Boudicca wanted revenge, for the apprentices and cars they lost by helping Pendragon." Abel sighed, looking around at the carnage while trying to blur his eyes a bit, to obscure details. "While the others sort out the boundary, I'd better check with my solicitor. The one who said she wouldn't be necessary." He braced himself for another lecture on not doing things the sorcerer way.

*   *   *

Oddly enough, Terese seemed to think he'd handled it right, except for exposing himself. According to her, Abel should have used a glyph to break the garage lock without even setting foot on the driveway. If Valdar objected he should have ripped the garage door right off. Now any paperwork Abel found should be passed to Woods and Green, to be added to Pendragon Enterprises under the protection of the gryphon. Kelis had been right about Valdar and Boudicca. The solicitor would fix the records to show both of them had allegedly left town. Both of them would 'sell' their property and businesses to Abel before leaving. Abel still had his lecture, but on the subject of takeovers. He wasn't inheriting Valdar's houses by either blood or power. Abel had simply taken them, by blood and power, perfectly legal if Valdar didn't object. Terese suggested cremating the bodies with fire glyphs, and using the ashes to feed the trees.

Even if the Taverners did that, there'd be fewer ashes than expected. One of Ferryl's victims had escaped. From the blood trail he might not survive, but by the time anyone counted up he'd long gone. The missing man might be Gawain or Paragon, because although Ginny did her best to identify the bodies, she didn't find either of the ex-apprentices.

Rob wasn't bothered about one live apprentice, because he'd come up with a real problem. "Flobberclomps. We'll need Creepio after all, because none of us will want to move the bodies. Unless you fancy a graveyard in the back garden?" He grimaced and pointed to the bodies still laid in the road. "I'll dig the hole if the rest use air glyphs to move that lot, then we can use air and vapour to scrub the road."

"Terese told me to burn them and feed the trees, but I don't fancy that either. We'll sort it out once we've had a look at the house." Abel didn't want to look at the bodies, and definitely didn't fancy a garden full. The Church had plenty of graveyards, so buying space shouldn't be expensive.

Twenty minutes later the house boundary went down. While the Taverners refilled with tree magic, Zephyr followed the lingering traces to a block of lead incised with glyphs. Ferryl inspected them before offering to design something better, so Abel melted the marks away. Three other Taverners asked about using the place as digs while they attended University, suggesting Abel rented the other two houses out. Abel let them talk in the background as he had his first good look at sorcerer accommodations.

Sumptuous, definitely, but to Abel's eyes the sort for show, not comfort. Valdar had a selection of expensive ornaments and paintings, but according to Zephyr all but a few of the smaller ones were created magically. There were no animated anything, which came as a relief. The bedroom and en-suite were modern and probably expensive, but not unbridled luxury, as was the clothing in the wardrobe. A blushing Karen, the young woman, admitted the bedroom through the connecting door was hers, as were the women's clothes.

Zephyr used spooky-phone to warn the Taverners against asking embarrassing questions, though Abel had to ask one. "Do you want to stay here? You can burn in a ward so the creatures let you alone, and learn magic if you stick by our rules."

"But what would I do? To earn my keep." Karen avoided everyone's eyes. "I quit sixth form college when I came here, so I haven't really got any qualifications."

"You can carry on do…. Er, carry on living here and learn magic?" Justin turned away to hide his own blush.

"Good idea, we'll need a housekeeper in the University holidays. The Tavern is supposed to find a place for people in trouble." Rob examined the door to Karen's bedroom. "Stick a lock on this or choose another room. You could learn enough to help Shawn with filling hexes, to cover your rent, then go back to school. We should have extra work from whatever Valdar did."

"Valdar employed three non-magical computer experts. They repaired computers as a cover for his magical business, protecting office

71

equipment in small businesses against Gremlins. He also sub-contracted for sorcerers like Pendragon, if they didn't have enough apprentices for some reason." Karen looked startled as the Taverners moved in round her, but they were just interested in sorcerer economics. Terese Green had tried to explain, but the version that solicitors like Woods and Green dealt with weren't exactly grass roots.

"That's your first job. Write down everything you know about Valdar's business, and any other sorcerer you know of and their business." Abel heaved a big, extravagant sigh of relief. "Do you know his solicitor? I'll get Terese to contact them."

"He didn't have one. I don't think many of the sorcerers do." Karen looked around the room, struggling with something. "Can I can live in one of the other houses? Please?" She glanced at Ferryl. "Will I be tethered, like an apprentice?"

"Karen believes she is part of the conquest, a possession like the house or any surviving apprentices." Ferryl eyed her for a moment. "She would make a good liaison with the sorcerers Valdar did business with."

"But warded, not tethered." The answering snigger in Abel's head probably meant Ferryl expected his reaction.

*   *   *

Despite the hundreds of questions he had, Abel couldn't stay long. After conferring with Shawn, he offered Karen a home in any of the three houses. She could pay for food and board by keeping the houses clean and tidy, while Abel worked out what to do with them. That should give her time to decide what she wanted to do next. He had to prise Karen loose of Amanda and Cecilia for that, because they wanted to quiz her about sorcerer life. From some of her cursing, Karen must be reinforcing the evil sorcerer part. After settling the basics, Abel left Karen and Shawn to sort out details.

Before going, he had to make up his mind about the bodies. Remembering how the Taverners avoided even looking at them settled it, he'd pay for disposal. When Abel asked Shawn for his phone to call Creepio, the local manager shook his head. "Save your breath. Ferryl moved the bodies onto the broken tarmac, and Ginny cremated them. There's a patch of odd-looking tarmac that's been melted and set, but the ashes are someplace in a garden. Zephyr has been acting like a little storm cloud to wash the road and footpath down." Shawn heaved a sigh of relief. "I'm really glad those three have the stomach for it."

Abel knew Ferryl and Zephyr didn't have stomachs, and weren't human, but wondered if Zephyr had ordered Ginny to help. However it happened, he couldn't object because they'd solved the problem. That left one problem, or two problem girls. It took a while because they wanted to inspect all three houses, but Abel finally persuaded Amanda and Cecilia they should go back to Stourton. Creepio would go crackers if he arrived to pick them up and the pair were still in Sheffield.

The little convoy formed up again, a bit larger this time. Shannon had claimed Valdar's Range Rover for the return trip, so Shawn could drive his company car, and Eric found a Volvo convertible for the trip home. Abel hoped the magic businesses made money, if only to pay all the car insurance.

He spent most of the return trip on the phone, though a business one not his private phone, thank goodness. Bertram the secretary had brought two replacements, because phones were fragile when glyphs were flying, so now Kelis had one. Just as well, Abel's or Kelis's mums would have had a lot of very searching questions if they'd seen these calls on personal phones. At least the personal phones survived because they'd left them in the car.

Within minutes Kelis started giving a clerk at Woods and Green a series of names and numbers, contacts and contracts, from the papers found in Valdar's filing cabinet. She finished with details of the cars and houses, including what was apparently Boudicca's personal Volvo convertible. Terese suggested writing to all the customers past and present, using Pendragon Enterprises headed stationery. Even while Abel wondered how Shawn or Eric would like dealing with that, Kelis laughed down the phone and passed it over. "For the Master." The smirk made that a joke.

Terese seemed cautious once he answered. "You wanted a way to let your mother have more income, preferably as a gift. One of our staff has a solution, but it might not be what you had in mind." She hesitated, almost long enough for Abel to ask what. "Will you be basing your operations in Stourton or Sheffield?"

"Stourton. That's if I can shift it away from the dragon, the gryphon." Abel had trouble with calling a dragon's head anything but a dragon, especially after it spoke in his head.

"The business can be based anywhere you choose, without moving the gryphon. From the glyphs worked into the door and room, very old, strong glyphs, you may not be able to move it. A major assault by several sorcerers might not reach the gryphon itself, and it will defend itself if they do." Terese paused again, definitely hesitant which worried Abel. "You mentioned your mother works part-time in an office at the moment. You could employ her at the Stourton office?"

Abel opened his mouth to say that wouldn't work, because mum would be exposed to magic, which might send her crackers, but then remembered the staff he'd seen there. Neither of them knew about magic, or what the business did except security work. His mind whirled, looking for problems, but the only one was him. He wouldn't be able to visit his own office on business. Rather than a worry, that made him laugh. "Sorry Terese. It sounds like a wonderful idea. Why were you so worried?"

"It's quite basic work, almost menial. Not what the mother of the Master of Castle House should be doing." The solicitor sounded absolutely serious, setting Abel off laughing again.

"Mum works odd hours for basic wages whenever she can grab them, and has done since dad died. She won't take a fulltime job, because she wants to be able to turn down work if I happen to be ill." Abel's mind raced. He'd heard enough on the news to know how to get round that. "If he gives her a zero hours contact, so she can turn down a day's work when she wants to, then Eric can offer her as many hours as she wants."

"You'll have to warn the staff."

"Eric, that's all. The other two know I'm the new owner of Pendragon Enterprises, but not my name." By now Zephyr had connected spooky-phone to bring the rest up to date, so everyone else had started smiling. "Once I can inherit everything legally, mum can have the option of retiring in luxury or carrying on."

"That will be a shock for her. We have already started trying to work out how to soften the impact, on her and the world in general. The simplest way is if your game is a success, then none of your parents will query you having more money." Once again Terese hesitated. "We, Woods and Green, might be able to help with that, the game." Abel heard her voice grow more confident, more like her usual self, as she followed up her idea. "Since we are on the cover and the box lid, and play a small part in the game, pointing that out to magic-users here and there would be seen as advertising ourselves. There are sorceresses all over the world who bemoan the lack of respect the general populace have for sorcery. We could mention that we are involved because this game advertises the Accord, so belief in magic may grow a little. I will consult with Woods."

Once Kelis took the phone back, the master and his bodyguards chewed that over. None of them could see the sorcerers having a big effect because they were by nature secretive, but a little extra business might make it worthwhile. By then Abel had to brace himself for the reaction when the priest picked up Amanda and Cecilia. To his great relief the man seemed unperturbed, pointing out the archbishop had warned him to expect the unexpected. The goblins and dryads being out in plain view had been a surprise, but since nobody in the Tavern had a pet dragon the experience hadn't been too bad. Kelis thought Creepio had picked the bloke for his sense of humour. After the priest left, everyone present admitted they worried much more about Creepio's reaction.

*   *   *

When the four friends called home and asked about staying in town an extra night, Abel's mum for one didn't sound surprised. Despite it being Easter Monday, none of the families went to church, so the only change would be when the teenagers finished their chocolate eggs. Talking about chocolate brought up another small side effect of magic. Ferryl had told them that anyone using magic, casting glyphs, healed a little better than normal, but now one of the Taverners wondered if that meant she could eat chocolate without breaking out in spots. The innocuous question, half-joking, sparked a big discussion.

After comparing notes it became clear that using magic helped with acne, greasy hair, and a few other minor inflictions. The worst acne sufferer had taken to wearing a copy of the healing glyph Ginny had brought, a witch charm, hoping it would finish the job. When several Taverners pointed out that Ginny looked younger than thirty-six, she told them Elrond had been forty-eight although he looked late-thirties.

The discussion moved on to battle injuries, and how the magic ointments would help everyone who'd been injured. After a few questions about physical exhaustion, and if the charm would help, Abel ended up watching a very strange procession going round Frederick's garden. "You had me doing that, running with logs, and I hated it. It's a sort of joke, almost, after the Rocky films. Now they're all volunteering." A long crocodile of teenagers jogged around Frederick's garden, each lap going right round the end of the orchard and back. Each person held a brick or log in one hand and cast small glyphs with the other.

Behind Abel, curled up in an armchair, the inspiration for the jogging had no intention of joining in. Ferryl wouldn't even be walking far for a day or two if she could avoid it. "I told you exercise would toughen you up, so that you could lift more with magic, and it has. I saw the size of some of the lumps of metal you threw at Valdar."

"I can lift or throw more than I used to, though I doubt I could have moved that car." Abel chuckled, pointing out of the window. "A few of them already look like I used to feel. I don't suppose it will harm anyone, even if they never have to try what you did. I'm surprised you could manage it, because you aren't exactly beefcake, all rippling muscles."

"My magic is more efficient. You should pay attention to how Ginny forms glyphs, sheer power isn't everything." Despite her efficient glyphs, Ginny was one of those running around outside. She'd spent some time inspecting the burned car, and the grooves where the wheel rims had scored the concrete of the garage floor. Ferryl stretched, cautiously. "I keep these muscles toned, magically, but even so I damaged this body today."

"We can't do that magically, so I'd better take up the jogging again." Kelis scowled at the mere thought. "I've let it slide a little, but now I suppose I'd better start again. Plodding through the mud, oh joy. Hey, could I get the same result in a nice clean warm dry gym?" The same thought must have occurred to the runners outside, despite being neither wet nor muddy. As they straggled in, several asked similar questions or quizzed Abel about how often he'd had to train, and if there was another way. The enthusiasm wouldn't last, or so Abel assumed, but right now every single Taverner wanted to get as fit as possible. Later in the evening, a small deputation asked Abel if he could buy a couple of bits of gym equipment for the cellar. That way the weather wouldn't matter.

Over the following day, Abel spent time talking to a succession of small groups of Taverners, and the takeover of Pendragon's and Valdar's demesnes settled in. Both businesses were assessed, as best the teenagers could, and with extra magic from Abel's trees the Taverners could easily fill the hexes and wards. The problem would be re-scheduling the work for schoolchildren, probably using the minibus to service as many contracts as possible at weekends. Shawn and Eric seemed confident that they, with Shawn's staff, could keep everything going until the holidays.

After the summer holidays they'd have more Taverners who had left school, plus seven living in Abel's housing while they attended Sheffield University. Abel's tenants would pay their rent in hex-filling, helping out the business. Four of the students had changed their options from other Universities when they'd heard Shannon's description of the digs, and realised how isolated they'd feel anywhere else.

Abel even came to terms with burning the bodies, though at least he hadn't had to do that personally. Ginny explained that apprentices usually volunteered for the job. The sorcerer would give them extra magic to dispose of bodies, so they got extra practice with fire glyphs. At least the clean-up had been cheap, no need for Creepio, but Abel didn't want to know which garden had been fertilised.

A local company would be laying a new tarmac drive, while the fire in the garage hadn't eaten deep enough to affect the structure. Once the completely untouched doors went back on, and the soot had been glyphed off the walls, the outside looked near enough. Shawn promised to get anyone staying in the other houses to help with the inside. They'd get it all clean and dry eventually, then either give it a lick of paint themselves or get a decorator.

After a long discussion with Eric, about hopefully employing a new secretary, he promised to remember to only refer to Abel as "the boss." The big smirk meant Eric would also be having some fun at Abel's expense. There might be plenty of secretarial work, because the present secretary didn't seem happy with the takeover.

After promising to find plenty of sorting and refiling of paperwork, to cover as many hours as necessary, Eric pointed out he wouldn't be hiding names or specific mention of magic. All the paperwork, including contracts for non-magical work, referred to Pendragon Enterprises and maintaining installations. Ferryl, Ginny and Terese the solicitor confirmed that sorcerers used titles if they had one. Abel had two, Master of Pendragon Enterprises and if that didn't do the job, Master of Castle House.

As Ginny drove him home, Abel still had one main worry. His mum knew Eric as a game player at the Taverner parties, so would she accept a job offer from him?

With This Ring

Once back in Brinsford, Abel stayed behind at Kelis's house while Rob headed home. Ferryl wanted another of those talks in her room, though this time she seemed content for him to sit quietly and hold her. Even so Abel had to solemnly promise, several times, to never leave her behind while he walked into danger, not again, not even a few metres behind. To be honest Abel didn't fancy getting trapped like that again, not if he could avoid it. He didn't stop too long, in case mum had seen Rob going past.

Though when he arrived home, Abel's mum seemed more interested in his new haircut than what he'd been doing at Frederick's. Abel denied working his way down to a crewcut, though it really was short now all the charred ends had been cut off. He wore a thin glove on one hand, to hold a Seeming of undamaged skin, and a completely new set of second-hand clothing. The staff in the charity shops had started to recognise Abel and his friends, when they came for more clothes.

With twenty-four hours to work on the damage, the ointment from the magical doctors had managed to more or less get rid of the red from Abel's scorched skin. The extra day in Stourton had been a blessing, though all of them were still hiding more serious wounds from the first fight. Abel had a piece of cloth, coated with magical gunk on one side, covering the new burns across the back of his shoulders. Even with the magic in the ointment, he still couldn't lean back against anything. Hopefully, any smaller extra bumps and scratches that showed would be put down to the car accident three days ago. According to Jenny it was all an incentive scheme, aimed at getting them to learn to heal. Since Ferryl hadn't got a mark on her, the rest knew what she meant.

Abel ate his tea, while he explained all the fictional work they'd managed to get done in Frederick's house. He hoped she never checked, because the lounge still looked like a bomb site. His mum kept joking she didn't want much to eat, she'd rather finish her chocolate egg. Abel hadn't bought her an Easter egg for years, but this year he'd even managed to get one with hard centred chocolates inside, which completely threw her. Since she seemed to be really relaxed and happy, Abel decided to leave the new job until tomorrow. The pair of them enjoyed a quiet evening laughing at old films, and spoiling themselves with chocolate.

When he finally went upstairs, Zephyr surprised Abel by wanting to hunt, even though she'd done so on the way back from Kelis's house. When Abel asked why she needed the extra, Zephyr hadn't been catching her usual prey. There weren't many fae in Brinsford these days, only those inadvertently brought through the barrier inside vehicles. According to the sprite, Abel and Ferryl attracted tiny sparks of magic so she'd been after them, but she needed bigger prey to regrow herself after being damaged.

Before setting off to hunt across the farmland, Zephyr wanted her own long discussion. The puff of wind had been frightened by how much of herself she'd lost in the fight, how much she'd forgotten. She worried about not recovering lost glyphs, leaving her too weak to protect Abel. Abel suggested making up a notebook containing all of Zephyr's glyphs, in case she ever ended up very badly damaged and forgot them.

*   *   *

Waking up stiff and sore seemed almost normal for Abel after the last few days, except for waking up lying on his front. Not too stiff and sore except his back, because a combination of his own magic, the magical medicines, and Ginny's witch charm made a big difference to minor injuries. He dithered a bit before going down for breakfast, because he still wasn't sure of the best way to approach the job thing, but in the end stuck to almost-truth. "You keep saying we're skint, mum. Would you be interested in extra work? Office work, in Stourton?"

"A bit more wouldn't hurt, especially now I've got a decent car so I can be sure of turning up. I nearly lost the job I'd got when the last one kept breaking down. They couldn't rely on me." She looked Abel up and down. "I could work a few more hours, now you seem to be growing up and getting all independent, though I still like to be here when you get home."

"Do you remember Eric, Warren's big brother?" Abel waited for a nod. "He's got a job as a branch manager. The business has expanded, and the local branch needs more clerical staff. I'm not sure exactly what the work is, or the hours, but he asked the Taverners if they'd got a relative who might be interested." Very casually, Abel took out his phone. "I've got his number if you want to call him?"

"I'll leave it until tomorrow. Spoiling his holiday by phoning as soon as he gets back into the office wouldn't make much of an impression." As his mum copied the number, Abel stifled his sigh of relief. He hadn't been sure she'd fancy working for some young bloke who played board games with her son. The relaxation continued because Abel stayed at home all morning, pottering around helping his mum in the garden. Abel helped more than she'd ever know, casting surreptitious glyphs to give most of the plants a little boost. At least he wouldn't need to persuade his mum to let him plant a tree, because Rob had already managed that. Dryad Sycamore's seedling would be moving into Rob's garden, once a sapling had been planted and the young dryad ripened.

Two messages from Ginny, passed on by tether to Zephyr, reported that she'd been using the tether to supervise Melanie's and Diane's glyph practice. That came as a relief, improving Abel's already mellow mood. Ginny's tether also passed reports from Stourton, a bonus Abel hadn't thought of. Boudicca's death had banished the protection glyph on the Volvo estate, so Una had driven it round to Frederick's house. She'd asked about insurance for 'her' loot, Valdar's motor, and the Volvo convertible. In Sheffield, Shawn found a Volvo saloon in the other apprentice house's double garage, with a Peugeot estate. Abel sent a reply through Zephyr and Ginny's tether. Eric and Shawn could look into car ownership and insurance, once everyone went back to work.

Over the next couple of days Abel, Kelis, Rob and Ferryl stayed in Brinsford. They all needed some peace and quiet, and time to heal, and there were plenty of Taverners willing to investigate and organise the new property and business. Better yet, adding the cars to Pendragon's possessions and insurance cover turned out to be simple. They were 'bought' by the business. That meant six of the Taverners and Ginny now had a vehicle, so they could drive groups of youngsters to wherever they were needed to get the contracts serviced. While sorting out the paperwork, Bertram confirmed that Pendragon's Bentley and business really did have insurance covering magical injury and damage to others. Shawn spent some time listing the damage to vehicles and people, in both attacks, then adding the details from the magical doctor. The gold in the armbands recovered from four of the dead apprentices should repair

Frederick's house, without touching the extra from the Bentley.

Ginny ended up driving the BMW SUV, because it would hold Abel and his friends, and it turned out all Pendragon's cars had built-in resistance to glyphs. She used the car to visit both Melanie and Diane, meeting them away from their houses to help them with controlling their air glyphs. In common with most Taverners, they tended to use more magic to compensate for lack of skill, but Ginny wanted 'her' students to learn how to economise. The extra magic in her armbands allowed Ginny to cast a huge veil, so the trainees could stand in the middle of fields and throw their glyphs further.

Shawn and Eric, the two older Taverners now managing Abel's business, didn't rest much at all. Both spent their time racing around Stourton and Sheffield, and various businesses nearby, to explain the change of management. Since the name stayed the same, none of Pendragon's customers seemed too worried as long as they received the same service. Either the fancy letterheads reassured Valdar's customers, or they'd already heard or been told by others, because the only reaction came from a few who tried to get a price reduction. Valdar's three computer technicians met Shawn in the Sheffield office. Bertram laid on tea and nibbles, Shawn explained how Pendragon Enterprises were moving into the market and wanted to keep their expertise, and all three signed up.

Shawn, with several other adept Taverners, had inspected Valdar's houses and the street, finding a glyph in a block of lead set into the road. They weren't sure if it would reinstate the Seeming that disguised any magical activity, or set up some sort of defence. So far nobody had found the magical trigger for the posts set into the approach roads, but they'd been destroyed anyway, so creating a replacement defence moved up Ferryl's to-do list. Not the very top of the list, because Ferryl had copied every glyph she'd seen on the cars and houses and wanted to test them.

Ferryl also had a much more mundane chore, her holiday homework. Learning came down to inscribing the information on her bones, but understanding and then completing her schoolwork took time and effort. Even Abel finally conceded that he had to inscribe more schoolwork onto his bones, because with all the distractions he'd never learn the usual way. The other three teenagers had already come to that conclusion, especially

Jenny who had her A levels coming up. As she pointed out, cramming for exams was always a pain, but now it hurt her bones as well.

Jenny's dad, Jake Forester, called a Bonny's Taverners shareholders meeting to tell Abel's, Kelis's and Rob's mothers about all the exposure the school dance had given them. Not only on the local TV and radio, and local newspapers, but there'd been a short snippet on national news. There'd only been one shot, of all the children in fancy dress arriving at the dance, with a few words contrasting the Tavern's charitable aims with a national upsurge in school violence. Now Jake wanted to cash in.

Eventually it came down to education versus business opportunity. Jake wanted Jenny to spearhead the launch, to start her career in business with invaluable practical experience, but she couldn't do that before leaving school this summer. Worse, right now Jenny had to concentrate exclusively on her A levels if she wanted good grades. Once again the launch went on hold, but only on hold. The game itself had been completed, the boxes were stacked up ready for distribution, and Bonny's Taverners had enough cash in the bank to make a reasonable ripple in the national gaming media.

On the charity side, a local business called Pendragon Enterprises donated a Mercedes minibus, which gave Stourton Refuge two once the original came back from being repaired. Jake really liked Frederick's idea of using it to transport Taverners to tidy up local areas overrun by graffiti and rubbish. That idea had come from one of the Tavern players, a non-magical, who suggested starting with Stourton's public park.

Abel's mum sprang her own surprise. She had an interview for a job at the same firm, Pendragon Enterprises, some sort of private security business. Eric, the local manager but also a Bonny's Tavern player, explained how the firm knew about the Tavern, and might explain why they were so generous.

Jenny, Rob, Kelis, Ferryl and Abel pretended to be surprised, then volunteered to go along and help with the clean-up. That also gave them a chance to get over to Sheffield and release Pendragon's houses, and hopefully some trees. The last day of the Easter break, with their homework completed and their minor injuries healed, the five Taverneers dressed in their oldest clothes and borrowed brushes, trowels, shovels and a wheelbarrow.

*　*　*

Abel had worried about how their parents would react to a complete stranger, Ginny, collecting him and his friends. He ended up stifling his laughter at the perplexed reaction from Kelis's mum. Ginny, looking considerably younger than her thirty-six years, had dressed down for the day in designer casual jeans, long leather boots and a Barbour wax jacket. The apprentice really had spent all her money on looking good. She certainly didn't match the usual Taverner look, casual schoolkid, nor did her big SUV.

Mrs. Ventnor had expected one of the usual Taverner drivers, a teenager in either a parent's car or the newly donated minibus. Instead, Ginny cheerfully insisted on loading the wheelbarrow and tools aboard her SUV, claiming that the vehicle was supposed to be designed for this sort of work. On the way to collect Jenny, Kelis warned Ginny to expect a polite but firm invitation to stop for a cuppa and a chat, when she delivered everyone home.

The next stop wasn't as bad, because Jenny's dad wasn't there. "Blimey, that's a bit snug." Jenny squeezed past a rake, and patted the wheelbarrow sat next to her rear-facing popup seat. "Armour plating? Why didn't you use the minibus?"

"Because we'll be going to Sheffield later, and the Tavern minibus has no protection." Ginny might not have a strong magical imperative to protect Abel, but she seemed very keen. "If Pendragon's Bentley had survived, I would have insisted we used that."

"Crikey, mum would burst a blood vessel." Kelis twisted in her seat, looking back. "Would the wheelbarrow have fitted in the boot?"

"Easily. We once put three bodies in there, trespassers." Ginny shrugged without turning, keeping her eyes on the road. "Much more discreet than in the back of an SUV with all those windows." The conversation turned to how many bodies Ginny had stashed away for Pendragon, and the answer turned out to be none. The cremations after the Valdar fight weren't for convenience, they really were the usual way to get rid of any bodies. As a sort of bonus, the flames thoroughly destroyed any hint of diamonds in the bone, or any other sorcerer or apprentice anomalies. Abel hadn't liked the idea at the time, but now he found his only alternative was to start up his own personal graveyard.

*   *   *

Abel forgot all about graves when the car pulled up at the entrance to the park, the Leferrier Memorial Park because a local lady had donated the land in memory of her husband. A tall, heavily weathered pillar in the centre of the boating lake supported what might have been an eagle at some time, but nobody seemed sure. Right now the late Lady Leferrier would have been impressed by the number of vehicles and young people clustered in the car park. A couple of council workmen were talking to some of the adults, casting helpless glances at the crowd of wheelbarrows and eager volunteers building up around them. From a quick glance nearly all the captured vehicles were here, so the Tavern had turned out in force.

Shannon and Una pushed through the crowd, Una raising a hand and her voice to greet him. "Abel, come and talk to these men. They reckon we need all sorts of insurance and Health and Safety before we can work in the park. They're talking about getting the police to stop us." A tiny smile touched Una's face, softening her indignation as she lowered her voice. "You could mazzle them, the confusion thing, or put them to sleep?"

"Not on TV." Ginny nodded towards two men and a well-dressed woman setting up a camera and sound gear. "Unless you can mazzle cameras, whatever a mazzle is?"

"Mazzlement confuses people, from puzzled up to forgetting the last hour or two. We could black the camera lenses?" Kelis's quick glance and smirk at Abel suddenly changed to surprise, as she saw something that diverted her. "Why is Mr. Gordon here?"

"The headmaster?" Abel turned and sure enough, saw a familiar figure in the crowd. "Now we really do have to be well behaved. Did all the Tavern come, the non-magical ones as well?"

"Not quite, but this crowd includes non-Taverners. Some kids just heard about it and decided to join us." Shannon waved to a small group. "Those are from my school, St. Agnes Catholic Grammar. I doubt they've ever played Bonny's Tavern, though the group over there have." Her face dropped at the raised voices around the Council workmen.

One rose above the rest. "My boy spends his life in his room killing things on a bloody computer. Now the first time he wants to get some fresh air, and do something bloody useful, you turn up and tell me he can't." Behind the man a teenager with a rake and hoe seemed torn between dragging his dad away and hiding.

Abel caught hold of Ferryl's hand and Zephyr connected them. "Maybe a bit of mazzlement, Ferryl, to quieten things down?"

"Confusing him a little might make things worse. He could lash out." From the looks on some of the growing numbers of annoyed parents, violence looked like a real possibility. Ferryl spoke aloud, hoping to head off the belligerent looks on both Shannon and Una. "If a fight starts, it will look bad for the Tavern."

"Then we'd better sort it." Kelis raised her voice. "Taverners, to me!" She started walking steadily towards the waving arms and shouting. It wasn't far but Abel, Rob, and Jenny soon caught up as did Una and Shannon. Others took up the cry and a score of teenagers were soon closing in from all sides. A couple of the parents looked startled as Kelis kept going, turning sideways to slip through the group towards the workmen. Annoyed looks turned to confusion as more young people joined the crowd, easing their way forward.

The council employee found himself facing a tall slim schoolgirl instead of irate parents. "Who are you?" Kelis smiled at the workman, but didn't answer him until she'd turned to the parents.

"I'm Kelis, a Bonny's Tavern player. We want to clean up the park, but we don't want to break laws and we don't want to cause trouble." Abel wondered why she'd raised her voice so much, then noticed the camera pointed straight towards them. "Bonny's Tavern does not believe in violence, or lawbreaking." A scattered cheer broke out as the nearest Taverners heard, though some were smirking at the no-violence part.

"That works better than mazzlement." Ferryl might sound amused but the adults had looked around, seen all the children watching them, and were rapidly reassessing.

"I just want Pete to do something useful for once." This time the man sounded more petulant than threatening. "That's not a crime."

"Daa-ad." Ripples of laughter spread as an embarrassed Pete tried to will himself to disappear.

"We can supervise the kids. Won't that cover Health and Safety?" Several voices backed the anonymous parent.

A woman's voice joined in. "It should. I've been running around staving off death and disaster since mine could crawl." A good few agreed with her as well.

"There's no public liability insurance, not for non-council employees. The law is clear. I'm sorry but if I let them start work I'll get sacked." The workman didn't want to argue about parents being competent guardians, not to a crowd of parents.

The cameraman had moved closer, and now the woman reporter pushed a microphone towards the workman. "As I understand it, these children want to carry out a public service. This Bonny's Tavern," she paused to let the cheer die down, "think the park is a disgrace. Since Stourton Council has failed to clean it up, they'll do it themselves."

"We haven't got the men, not now, not after the cut-backs." The second, quieter workman looked embarrassed.

"Shut up, you'll get us in trouble." The spokes-workman turned back to the camera, and the crowd. While he tried to justify the state of the park, Zephyr warned Abel another car had drawn up, one covered in magic.

When Abel turned he saw Redwolf and his senior apprentice, Mannan, coming towards the crowd, so he moved away to meet them. He smiled a little as both Ferryl and Ginny moved slightly in front of him. The sorcerer sketched a brief bow towards Abel, then Ferryl, before turning to Ginny. "Guinevere. Congratulations on surviving, again."

"I'm a fast learner, and everyone calls me Ginny these days. These Taverners are more informal, and, as you already know, they aren't vindictive. Us Taverners, because I've been recruited." With a wry smile she raised a hand to tap her shoulder. "I'm the only tethered apprentice, but that turns out to be an improvement over the usual version."

At the inquisitive look Ferryl took Abel's hand. "Not his apprentice, nor mine. These days I usually introduce myself as Abel's bodyguard, to save misunderstandings. In that capacity, I'm wondering why you are visiting another sorcerer's park?"

"There's no harm in it, and no danger as long as I leave his trees alone." Redwood looked over at the camera and crowd. "I came to look at the clean-up, though I didn't expect this."

"The council won't let us do anything in there. Health and Safety and insurance." Abel knew he sounded disgusted, but with so many parents supervising and magical help only a glyph away, there really shouldn't be a problem.

"Pendragon had insurance. All sorcerers have to cover their parks, just in case a hex misbehaves and fries a dozen passing innocents. It isn't to compensate the families, just to pay for the cover-up so it doesn't get in the news." The sorcerer tutted. "You didn't know? I hope you get Elmwood Park insured before putting in the hexes."

"Pendragon had…?" Abel pulled out his business phone, handed over as soon as he'd got into the car, hesitated then went for the solicitor. Pendragon might not have told his office staff. Within a minute he had the answer, without even talking to Terese. According to the woman on the phone, sorcerers always worded their public liability insurance to cover anyone and anywhere they chose. A second call, to Pendragon Enterprises, dealt with the rest. Abel turned back towards the increasingly embarrassed and frustrated council workman.

The reporter had the poor man on the ropes. She must have known that legally he couldn't let the teenagers carry out the work, so she used the opportunity to berate Stourton Council over the state of the place. Abel waited until she paused, then dived in. "If we had public liability insurance, would you let us sort out the park? With the parents to supervise of course."

All eyes turned back to the workman and the microphone waggled under his nose. Abel could almost see the poor bloke figuring it out. If he said no, the legal answer, he'd just accused all these parents of being incompetent. He chickened out. "Well technically I couldn't, because of Health and Safety, but with all these responsible adults supervising? I can't see how it could hurt, and the park would look better. Unfortunately, that would cost a fortune, and I'm sure it would take days to set up."

Before the reporter could accuse the man of wriggling, or pick up on the state of the park again, Abel dropped the hammer. "The paperwork will be here in a few minutes." He'd never be sure what the workman said, because the cheering started and spread out to people who probably had no idea why they were yelling. As he raised his voice enough for the workman to hear, the reporter pushed her microphone forward to catch it. "I've just been told a local company will cover everyone here."

By the time the taxi drew up, and the receptionist passed Eric a copy of the certificate, half the crowd were already inside the park. Abel wasn't, he'd found himself the target for the reporter and camera. He stuck to just being the bearer of good news, and being one of the game designers, though the woman wanted too many personal details for his peace of mind. Abel fobbed off questions about the mystery firm, his love life, and parents, until Eric held up the insurance. The reporter re-targeted, because now she had a representative of the mystery firm to interrogate. Better yet, the headmaster went to look at the paperwork so she included him.

With a sigh of relief Abel headed into the park. "That turned out more amusing than I expected. I must get out more often." Redwolf had tagged along. "Especially now you are taking an interest in the place. Some sorcerers take pride in keeping their parks neat and tidy, but too many of them leave it to the local councils. I have a nice little place in Birmingham, but letting the public in leads to problems. I dealt with several groups taking drugs and generally being a nuisance, but I had to burn the bodies. A few ashes under the bushes aren't much of a warning, so more kept coming. It wasn't safe to walk through the place after dark." His short laugh held a lot of malice. "Not for others anyway. An attempt to mug me was amusing, but the last straw. I haunted the next group and set my apprentices to terrifying any more undesirables. Word soon spread. Now I occasionally get ghost hunters but no troublemakers."

"You seem more friendly than the last time we met." Abel didn't trust the bloke, and couldn't understand why he'd turned up.

"I'm a fast learner, as Guinevere puts it. Pendragon taunted me, swore I'd been bluffed but here we are. Your delightful young sorceress is intact, and you are strolling in Pendragon's park with his apprentice on a tether." A glyph flicked out and a dandelion growing from a crack in the path withered. "Kills the root better than any weed killer, and eco-friendly as well."

"So this is what, a peace meeting?"

"This is me showing the local ruling sorcerer respect, and that I bear no grudges. So far five sorcerers and a leech nest have been disrespectful, starting with the sorceress who raided your village. I enjoy being the only survivor, and can take a hint that big." Redwolf gestured towards five big beech trees. "You don't exactly need them, considering how many trees you have around Castle House, but they will be handy if you are in town." He paused, looking down at Abel's hand, holding Ferryl's. "That seems to be a habit of yours. Mannan tells me you shook his hand."

"It's polite." "Zephyr, is he shielded?"

"No."

Abel stuck out his hand. "I'm pleased to meet you on better terms."

Redwolf looked at the hand for long moments, then took it. "Novel. As apprentices we learn to stop doing this. Senior apprentices find it funny to hold out their hand, but keep their shield up. That hurts like hell, and takes a long time to heal, and in the interim the sucker has to cast glyphs through a blister." He turned to Ferryl, and held out his hand. "Mz Shayde?"

"I agree, this is much better than our last meeting." Ferryl held out her hand and Redwolf lifted it to touch the back with his lips.

He turned to Ginny and repeated the hand kiss. "Now I'm going to enjoy the air, and all these young people who aren't vandalising anything at all." Mannan followed him, after bowing a little to Abel and Ferryl, then nodding and smiling to acknowledge Ginny.

*   *   *

Once Redwolf left for his walk, Abel, Ferryl and Zephyr, soon joined by Kelis, Rob and Jenny, got down to the real work. According to Ferryl, the warning around this park felt similar to the one she'd put around Elmwood Park: Beware, this is claimed. The glyphs inserted under the bark of the trees, however, were much nastier than expected. From what Zephyr and Ferryl could see, there wasn't a limiter. Anyone triggering the defence would be hit by all the magic in an adult tree. Probably fatal, even for a strong sorcerer, and definitely a reason to insure against accidents. Abel had visions of a Council workman trying to prune a branch and being blasted into ashes, but Ferryl thought not, as long as the workman wasn't magically aware.

Having Ginny along came in handy, because Pendragon sometimes passed his apprentices extra magic when he wanted extra work out of them. The sorcerer didn't cut a glyph before touching his trees, so Abel put out his hand, very cautiously. Zephyr watched the magic flows and assured him it wasn't objecting. With his hand flat on the bark, Abel imagined the draining glyph and fresh tree magic surged into his hand. "Hold my hand." Ginny eyed the tree cautiously, then Abel. "Did Pendragon cast a glyph to pass magic across to you?"

"No. He touched my shoulder and the magic came down the tether. Sort of like a smack across the back of the head, only inside the skull." Ginny still didn't look keen, but Abel wouldn't have been either.

"I'll pull magic from the tree, and push it down my other hand. Cast the draining glyph on your hand and pull it from me." From the shocked look that couldn't be right, but Abel and his friends had passed magic like that before. "What's the problem?"

"You are." Ferryl started laughing. "Sorcerers don't let others draw magic directly from them, because it could be hard to stop. Doing that is a sign of trust." She turned a little, looking at Ginny, and all the humour drained from her voice. "Taking advantage would be a mistake. After all, her tether is held by a very unforgiving entity."

"Abel does it that way so he can hold hands with girls." Kelis's smile faltered. "Though not for everyone."

"Though when he does, it's nearly as good as getting it straight from the tree. I got my magic that way a couple of times, before I perfected my glyphs." Jenny giggled, in anticipation. "Be careful, it really is a rush."

Despite the reassurance, Ginny still seemed cautious. Moments later a huge smile lit up her face. "Oh boy, I can see why you like it. We never got to take magic straight from a tree." She sniggered briefly. "Sorry, it's just that the apprentices might have combined and hired someone to kill Pendragon if we'd known how this feels. Then we could have shared out his trees."

"You didn't fill up at Frederick's?" Abel couldn't understand. "Or Valdar's?"

"I'm tethered, so I didn't think it was allowed. The Taverners at Frederick's gave me enough lead bars to replace all my magic, once I'd been safely tethered. At Valdar's I would have asked several to bring me lead bars, to refill my arm bands, but the first one said not to bother. She kept refilling her lead bars until I'd got enough." Ginny's big smile hadn't wavered. "Now I know why she seemed so happy. It's better than any drugs or booze I ever tried, and I've tried a good few."

Even as Abel opened his mouth, Ferryl's 'voice' filled his head. "Don't give her direct access to trees. Or only give her limited access until she has proved she can be trusted. Zephyr can tell when she has used up any extra magic and needs to top up, and the tether will mean she can't cheat. No access to Dead Wood or Castle House gardens."

That meant Abel quickly amending what he'd been about to say. "Once Ferryl and Zephyr figure out how to do it, you'll get access to one tree. You can use it to fill up those gold armbands, but you will also fill up lead bars for those who are just learning. That way you'll always have plenty of magic to protect Diane and Melanie, or anyone else who gets into trouble." From the look on Ferryl's face, she still thought that was too much.

Though when Ferryl spoke, Ginny wasn't mentioned. "That might not be easy. Whoever originally placed this protection wouldn't have thought of modifying the glyphs. The gryphon gives the sorcerer automatic access, and he wouldn't allow others to actually touch his trees." After an hour of Zephyr helping her to inspect trees, from a safe distance, Ferryl had only confirmed that even the saplings were protected. She suggested they went to Sheffield, as planned, so that Abel could use the ring to get into Pendragon's houses. On the way Ferryl and Zephyr discussed what they'd seen, and hoped the trees in streets weren't as heavily protected.

*　　*　　*

The trip didn't take long in the BMW, but Abel spent all of it on the phone. He'd called to let Shawn know he was on the way, and the office had a short list of people wanting to talk to him. He broke into the silent discussion about glyphs. "Excuse me Zephyr, Ferryl. Ferryl, have you heard of a sorcerer called Capone? He wants to talk to me about a boundary."

Ferryl shook her head, but Ginny replied. "With that name he must have been made an apprentice sometime in the last seventy or eighty years. He won't have been free of his tether for very long, and can't be important because Pendragon never mentioned him."

"Veren! Ask Veren about him. She's only a newbie and maybe they have a club or something." Rob waited until the rest stopped laughing. "All right, from what she told us, and the evidence so far, it would be a fight club. Even so, she still might know him."

"Veren wants to see me if possible, so I'll ask her then. That way we can see her reaction." After a couple of calls back and forth, Veren would come to meet Abel outside Valdar's house. Capone said he'd wait for a call. Abel relaxed because he would be wandering around among some trees first.

The first wanderings around trees, in the streets near the office, didn't take long. Shawn came to meet them, with a rough sketch map showing the best guess at Pendragon's Sheffield demesne. "From what the staff say, it's all a bit fluid. The actual ownership of trees or buildings are set, and the locations where someone is paying for magic, but not the actual streets. If dryads have snaffled the trees and nobody is paying for magic, the rest is allegedly worthless." Three arcs cut into the map, from different directions. "Those are the boundaries of the protection given by three churches, all perfect circles on the larger map in the office. That one is actually a mosque. Bertram reckons there are sometimes skirmishes where church and mosque protection overlaps, but there's some sort of treaty because of the one God part."

While talking the group had gathered around a tree in a perfectly normal residential street, so Abel walked up and cautiously put his hand on the bark. "No problem, I can draw magic. Ferryl?"

She approached very cautiously but stopped short. "I can see the magic gathering, so no thanks. Ask Zephyr to try, on her tether." A few moments later Zephyr floated right up to the tree, and kept going until she touched it.

"I can draw magic, but when I am attached to Abel I can draw through him anyway." Zephyr detached her tether and tried again. "No, I can see very nasty magic waiting to get me."

"Bertram has a solution." When Abel turned, Shawn brandished his phone. "I've been explaining our problem. The nearest he's heard of is if a sorcerer dies but the protection on their property still works. Magical locksmiths break the glyphs protecting vehicles and buildings for a living, so they must come across a wide range of protection methods and glyph combinations. The best one he knows of has a really good reputation, legally, so maybe he can break into a tree?" That brought some smiles, but Ferryl thought it might be their best bet. With luck, if she hid nearby, she might get some hints on how it was done.

"Will the locksmith object to Zephyr?"

Ferryl produced a magnificent smirk. "The locksmith won't send the customer, a sorcerer, away from his own property. I expect some sort of screen, but if you stand here and I hide the other side of the street one of us should get a hint." Frustration replaced the smirk and Ferryl took Abel's hand. "I should be able to do this! I need my wits!"

"Think of how much fun you're having, learning all over again. Now calm down or Ginny will find out you've lost your memory." That silenced Ferryl; she really didn't trust Ginny. "While we are waiting, let's go and open up Pendragon's houses."

*   *   *

Everyone liked that idea. Shawn had been round to visit them, as had Ginny when she drove to Sheffield to help fill hexes for a contract, but both houses and gardens were locked down. That had to be the gryphon, because Ginny couldn't even get at her own clothes. She hadn't wanted to bother Abel, and Zephyr didn't think it was important, so nobody told him. "Eric, the manager in Stourton, bought me some cheap clothes from a charity shop, out of petty cash." Ginny looked down at her designer gear. "All the senior apprentices kept a spare set of clothes in Stourton, for emergencies."

On the way Abel asked again about Pendragon's house, but Ginny swore only Gally, Galadriel, had gone inside. The apprentices had seen a housekeeper, over the fence, because although the houses were on different streets the apprentices' garden backed onto Pendragon's. As expected, when they arrived Abel walked straight through the gate without any trouble, which restored Ginny's access. Unlike Valdar's apprentice houses, this barrier stayed up until Zephyr traced the controlling glyph in a block of lead. Abel spoiled the glyph a little, enough to stop it working but leave it clear enough for Ferryl to read.

When Rob pointed out any toerag could wander in, Ferryl offered to design a new barrier. She'd need time, because Taverners weren't tethered so she couldn't easily identify them. She'd used the tavern hex for identification on the cars, because most of the original Taverners had drawn the hex on their skin. That wouldn't work for everyone, because some of the later ones stopped wearing or carrying the hex once they had a ward. Shawn laughed and showed them a box full in his car boot. Various people had been making Tavern shield hexes ready for the launch of the game, so anyone who wanted to visit the house could take one.

Ginny's remarks about a barracks were soon explained. All ten apprentices used to live in this one big house. She used to sleep in a bunk in the same room as the other junior female apprentices, until promotion entitled her to a personal bedroom. Another room held bunks for junior male apprentices. The four bedrooms for senior apprentices were more palatial, all having en-suites, and one of those held all Ginny's treasures. Abel took a slow look around. Despite what had been said, some of the clothes didn't look too old for the likes of Una or Claris. "The best idea is for you to pack up all your personal stuff, because you'll be living in Stourton where you can easily reach Mel and Diane. Make sure you get it all, or you might find it decorating one of the Taverners after we've shared everything out. If we haven't got room in the car, ask Shawn to store the rest in the office for now."

Instead of starting on her packing, Ginny glanced at Zephyr's tattoo. "Some of this is already loot. Technically mine, but I didn't buy it and I'm not sure who did. A good bit of the jewellery belonged to previous apprentices, but when they died Pendragon kept it. The idea was for me to look rich, so he looked wealthier. I didn't pay for any of the pictures and ornaments, and some of the clothing isn't any style I would buy." She still looked unsure, and Abel realised why.

"Pack up anything you bought, though you won't get all the jewellery back straight away. You'll have to work for that." Abel would have given her it all now, because he wouldn't steal it anyway, but Ferryl and Kelis had been adamant.

"I won't be buying any more, because Pendragon kept my money so I've lost it. He kept everyone's money, and if someone died he kept their stuff. The other three rooms for seniors are the same as this, a mix of inherited and bought. The latest, Denethor, has nearly as much as the others because he 'inherited' from his predecessor, Aragorn." Ginny hesitated, then carried on with a definite question in her voice. "Aragorn had a leech, but didn't die when Elrond did. Some of the Taverners told me he died after the Magic Council insisted on seeing him?"

"Pendragon killed him, so he couldn't answer awkward questions. I'll leave you in peace while you finish up." Zephyr might be in her head, but Abel didn't want to be in Ginny's room while she sorted through her clothes.

*　　*　　*

While Zephyr peeked now and then, so Ginny didn't get greedy, Kelis, Rob and Jenny cornered Abel. "This looting thing needs sorting out, even Ginny is on about it now. Are you really giving Una that Volvo?"

"Probably. Ginny will have the BMW SUV to act as my taxi, and cart Taverners about, and Eric and Shawn have a BMW each as part of their pay. There aren't many Taverners who can drive, and Una can use the car to cart people about." Abel looked around his friends and they definitely disagreed. "I don't know who claimed the other cars."

"Exactly, you idiot. Shannon drove Valdar's Range Rover back to Stourton and still has the keys, but at least three others are eyeing it up because it's top of the range. Actually she's offered to trade it for Boudicca's Volvo convertible, another tasty motor. There's even some Taverners casting hopeful eyes over the Peugeot estate used by Valdar's apprentices, though Shawn keeps the keys unless he needs someone ferrying about. Some are even on about capturing more cars, because they'll be passing their tests this summer." Kelis shook her head, baffled by Abel's bewildered expression. "The only reason nobody is trying to commandeer the minibus is because you gave it to the Refuge. They all belong to you, but now some people think cars really are loot, and are wondering about all the other tasty stuff left behind by dead apprentices. More to the point a few think it's first come first served, which will cause real trouble."

"That is how it usually works, as far as I know. The sorcerer owns everything, and the apprentices get privileges and the choice of things like cars based on rank. Oh." Now Ferryl looked baffled. "Taverners don't have ranks, do they? I never really thought about how this sort of thing is decided, because it didn't affect me personally."

"How do I decide who to give cars to? I could sell them and buy a fleet of bikes?" Abel sat on the bed, since he'd been cornered in a bedroom. "Flobberclomps at least. It seemed funny when Una claimed the Volvo, and sort of stuck it to Boudicca so I went along with it. I haven't even looked at the cars since then, not properly because I can't drive. You could have one, Jenny, for when you pass your test?"

"Good idea. Ooh look dad, Abel just gave me a Range Rover. No, it's nothing to do with being his ex, he just had a spare one." Jenny rolled her eyes. "That Range Rover is worth more than dad's Merc, and you really would just chuck me the keys, wouldn't you?" Abel shrugged, then nodded. "You can't even give me the Peugeot estate, you clot. They all belong to you so they'd only be loans." She paused, and thought harder. "Actually you really could give them away, but which Taverners deserve a gift worth tens of thousands of pounds? How would they explain them to parents?"

"How would anyone insure them, because even my little car will cost me well over a grand when I pass my test? Some will get cheaper insurance if it's done through their parents, but then they've got to explain to dad and mum about the nice man giving out cars." A smile tugged at Kelis's mouth. "What will your mum say, if you park the Range Rover outside your house and chuck her the keys?"

Even Ferryl laughed at the look on Abel's face at that thought, though eventually he brightened. "A Seeming? We could disguise them as some cheap second-hand car?" His face fell again. "But the real make would go on the insurance."

"I might be able to cast a detailed Seeming over a car, and anchor it to a lead bar, but it will use quite a lot of magic." Ferryl seemed quite interested in trying that, but then looked resigned. "Even that wouldn't be enough. A Seeming doesn't work when people touch, so someone will trip over the bonnet because the car looks smaller. If you get in and out, the Seeming will waver, which really will cause trouble. Worse, once you shut the door it'll look as if the seats are still empty."

"That doesn't solve the real problem, because the people who drove them would still know they were Volvos and BMWs. Abel could loan the cars instead, sort of, because we need them on the road to transport Taverners for contracts." Rob paced up and down, completely serious for once. "The most adept who have a driving licence could be given custody of a car, providing they agree that the first priority is working for the Tavern. Taxi drivers, but if the motor isn't needed they can go shopping in it or whatever? If the car is needed and they can't come, then another Taverner drives it."

"Will Una be upset? Curses, what about Eric and Shawn? I gave them a BMW as part of their wages. Will that cause trouble?" Abel threw his arms up in exasperation. "Why don't I just sell the lot?"

"Because as Rob just said, we need the transport? Though you could get more cars, just cheaper ones." Kelis preened a little. "I've already got a car, from mum, once I learn to drive. Then I can come into Stourton, and use one of the others if it's for Tavern business."

"Selling might not be a good idea, or rather you can only sell to sorcerers. Every one of those cars has some sort of magical protection, which might bite a non-magic user at some time. At the very least they might realise it's almost fireproof, or the insides are genuinely stain-proof without any wiping." Ferryl nodded at the startled looks. "Honestly, try spilling coffee in the Volvo convertible. I've been checking all the glyphs I found." She smiled down at Abel, though it had a wicked edge. "Worse, all of Pendragon's vehicles are linked to his gryphon. Good luck with breaking that link, though it can probably be done. For all I know Terese has linked the rest to Castle House."

"You could keep one at Brinsford, until it's all sorted out?" Jenny didn't bother with innocent, she downright smirked. "One of the Taverners could use it to come and get you, the same as we did with Kelis's mum's BMW? According to Ginny a sorcerer has to have a posh car, it's expected. The best one is the Range Rover."

Kelis dived in while Abel still stared, dumbstruck. "Not kept in Brinsford, and not the Range Rover. There's only one motor that will take all five of us and a chauffeur, the BMW SUV, so Ginny drives that.

She can also use it to cart Taverners around, or pick up any of us five whenever we need a lift. Better yet, it means that if Diane or Melanie are in trouble she can get to them." She nodded gently, satisfied with that. "Then we only have to explain this posh woman picking us up, and Ginny can claim she's just supporting the charity."

At least the interruption gave Abel a chance to get his wits back. "I was going to suggest a veil to hide a car, but then someone would try to park in the empty space and crunch, invisible fender bender." Though now he felt happier, sort of, or at least about one car. "Now what about Una, and from what you say Shannon, and maybe Eric and Shawn and whoever else fancies a car?" He looked around the room. "And loot in general, because going by what you said all this lot is mine as well. Jewellery doesn't suit me, the suits won't fit, and those dresses just aren't my style."

"When he won a battle, Pendragon would allow the senior apprentices to take something valuable. He kept the rest." Ginny had finished packing and come to find them. "I heard some of what you said about the cars. I hadn't realised how you had to hide things, because sorcerers don't. They brag, so you really should have the best car possible."

"Tell everyone in the fights they get a souvenir, loot, but limit it. The cars are yours, and if they want to drive one you set the rules. Shawn and Eric said yes please to the jobs without asking for details, so their cars can be used by others if they are busy in the office. After all, they've got a free flat and a decent salary. Shawn is downstairs so we can give him the happy news right now." Kelis smiled happily and headed for the door. "They'll ask more questions next time instead of going ooh, yes, gimmee."

Abel stood up to follow. "Now I've just got to put up with all the pouting and sulking."

"And begging." Jenny's smile had a lot of anticipation. "But you only tell everyone once. Putting up with that sort of aggravation is why the managers get the big bucks."

"Not only that, but even if someone cries on them Shawn or Eric aren't allowed to hand over the keys to the Range Rover. A certain sucker might fall for that, or possibly a pretty face swearing it went with her shoes and handbag." Kelis swept out while Abel was still trying to sort out an answer to that.

Shawn, waiting downstairs, didn't seem too worried about the car being used for work. "It's a company car, so it belongs to the firm, and the main reason I get it is to do my job. My uncle's firm won't let him use his for any private journeys, so I'm better off than him. Twice, because I've got that flat, which is a definite improvement on my old digs." He hesitated, definitely worried. "Bertram, the secretary, told me the freezer and fridge were kept stocked for apprentices. Do you want me to pay for what I've eaten up to date? I can get some cheap burgers in once I get some wages."

"Just don't get greedy, no caviar on your steak. We'll reassess if the business doesn't make enough." A quick glance at his friends showed Abel that none of them thought he'd overdone it. "After all Kelis might drop by, and she'd be miffy if she didn't have any posh fish eggs to put on her toast."

"No hogging all the unicorn pate." Rob and Kelis started inventing more and more improbable sorcerer delicacies.

*   *   *

The hilarity died when the group walked round to the front of Pendragon's house and were met by a very apprehensive young woman. She stood just inside the gate, not quite touching it. "Hello, I'm Abel. Are you Pendragon's housekeeper or, um…." Abel tailed off, because he didn't want to ask if she had another of those 'special' links.

"I'm Tess, and the housekeeper. Can you tell me what's going on, please? Mr. Pendragon hasn't been back for days. I'm getting worried, because I'm out of milk and there hasn't been a grocery delivery. I'm not allowed to use the phone."

"Why don't you nip down to the shops?"

The housekeeper looked embarrassed. "I can't," she whispered. "I've tried but I can't get out of the garden. I don't know why. Even if I could, I wasn't allowed any money and I don't get paid."

"Why do…." Kelis tailed off, because being unable to leave the grounds explained why Tess hadn't quit. She glanced at the rest, took a breath and went for it. "Pendragon is dead."

"Nothing too easy, I hope. Was it lingering and painful or is it too much to ask for?" Tess wasn't either embarrassed or shy now. "Did you kill the nasty sod?"

"Sort of, between us. You seem, er, sort of happy? Was he, did he, you know, hurt you?" Now Shawn tried to be diplomatic, but didn't know how to ask.

"I met him in a dance, when he bought me a drink. Next thing I know I've volunteered to be his housekeeper and moved in. Oh, and had a blazing row with mum and dad for reasons I can't even remember. A couple of weeks later, while I was still trying to figure out why I wasn't being paid and couldn't leave the garden, he showed me a local newspaper." Tears had started trickling down the young woman's face. "My parents died in a car accident, hit and run. Within a couple of weeks I could see weird things in the street, and wasn't keen to go out there anyway. It took a while, but the arse wasn't bashful so I found out the things were magical. Then about him being a bloody wizard, and what a nasty shit he is, was." A big sob broke loose and the tears ran faster. "Three years, and he's finally dead, but I'm still stuck in here!"

"Maybe not. My friends can probably fix the garden part." Abel caught hold of Ferryl's hand. "Well? Why didn't her link die? Can you break it?"

"It isn't a normal link or tether, or they'd have failed. I can't see any sort of magical compulsion. I'll give her a friendly shoulder to cry on, and if Zephyr helps me we'll find it."

Abel walked through the gate without any trouble. "Give me a minute to let these in, and then you can explain properly. There's two sorceresses here and neither are like Pendragon, I promise." He fixed the glyph so the rest could follow, and gave Tess a Tavern hex. "Wear this, even in the shower, or you'll be really unhappy."

Ferryl promptly installed her temporary 'keep out' barrier, while Tess ended up sobbing on Rob's shoulder. He'd stopped as he came through the gate to sympathise, which was all the housekeeper needed. Rob tried to lead her out of the gate, but she simply couldn't do it. When Rob picked her up, she began struggling as he got to the gate, even though she swore she wanted to leave.

It took a while, but by a process of elimination Ferryl settled on Pendragon using his Command voice, probably repeating it now and then to drive it home. There wasn't a cure as such, just a way of cancelling it out. Ferryl took Tess into the back garden, but the rest could still hear her shouting as she used her own Command voice to overpower Pendragon's instruction. Tess looked pale when she came back round the house, but she walked through the gate without any hesitation.

"Brilliant. Now could you show us round the place?" Abel pointed to the hex. "Just remember, if you take that off you won't be able to come in."

"I don't want to, ever. Oh, er, botheration! All my clothes are in there." Tess looked down at herself. "He didn't exactly push the boat out, but they're all I've got and I've no money." She looked up, shock and fear warring on her face. "Where can I go? Don't make me go back in there, please?"

"Would you mind being a housekeeper someplace else, like the apprentice house?" Abel wondered why Tess looked decidedly wary, then realised he'd just offered her the same job she'd just escaped. He thought fast, because no money meant Pendragon hadn't paid her, so she was broke and homeless. "How about some other houses we've just taken over, to help the lass there?" He tried for bland smile, not easy when Kelis rolled her eyes and mouthed 'sucker.' "Just so you have a room and wages until you work out what you want to do?"

"Karen might want to move here." Shawn looked a little embarrassed. "I didn't say because you've got a lot to deal with, and there wasn't any real alternative. She doesn't mind the work, keeping the houses clean and tidy, but she isn't truly happy even in the apprentice houses. Valdar's house is next door, and Karen sees it every time she goes outside."

After some discussion Tess agreed she really didn't have anywhere else to go. She'd look at Valdar's houses, and maybe move in as a housekeeper while she worked out what to do next. Kelis's repeated "sucker" might be right, but this time it didn't have any real bite.

One quick look around Pendragon's home, a large detached house with extensive gardens and over twenty mature trees, decided one thing. The Taverners wouldn't get this loot, because flogging the contents would make a significant contribution towards supporting the Tavern and the Refuge. The décor and furniture were a definite improvement over Valdar's, with an emphasis on small statuettes and paintings. Some of the figurines were gold or had gold or jewelled inlays, genuine not magical. Unfortunately the gold in the bathroom fittings was magical, as were most of the fittings such as doorknobs, so Ferryl and Zephyr would have to check everything. For now the Taverners took photos to check prices on the internet, and Shawn would get the paintings assessed. Ginny collected Tess's gear and put it in Shawn's car. He would leave her at the office until the locksmith finished with the trees.

*   *   *

By the time a large panel van arrived at the chosen tree, Ferryl had found a suitable hiding place. She'd been right about the locksmith being cautious. Abel never got to meet or even see the expert because the driver, wearing a smart set of overalls with "Piklokk Security Consultants" on the back and front, inspected the indicated tree. "Please touch the tree, sir. No offence intended, but you might not be the legitimate owner." Abel put his hand flat on the bark, drawing a little magic to prove the point. "My employer has detected a magical creature in your arm, possibly a bound spirit. Please keep it inside the tattoo. We will be erecting a screen to protect trade secrets, but such a creature might still see too much." He circled the tree, warily, with a palm raised towards it, a pose Abel recognised from when both Creepio and Pendragon had tested the Castle House barrier. "If we break this protection, a dryad might move in."

"I don't want the tree left unprotected. I can access the magic, as you can see, but I want my allies to have access as well." Abel pointed down the street. "There's a lot more trees, at least a couple of hundred, and more elsewhere. Can you give me some sort of glyph to cast, so I can give someone access to all of them? Otherwise I'll end up paying you to fix one here and one there."

"One moment sir." The apprentice disappeared into the back of the vehicle for about five minutes. When he came out he seemed mildly amused. "My employer is intrigued. Our usual jobs entail breaking glyphs, but the locksmith can see three ways to meet your requirements. Two really, because paying us to adapt each tree to each ally would be too expensive." He showed Abel a small metal badge with a glyph inscribed. "We can supply you with a personalised version of this, tuned to the permissive aspect of your signet ring. Anyone holding the badge will be able to draw magic from your trees or access your properties."

103

"What if it's stolen and copied?"

"That is the downside, though we would make sure copying it would be difficult." His tone of voice suggested almost impossible. "The alternative is more expensive, but more secure. We can devise a glyph you can place on anyone who trusts you enough, giving them permanent access to anything protected in the same way as this tree. That can't be broken except by changing the glyphs on every tree or killing the person."

Abel opened his mouth to point out the glyph could still be seen and copied, then remembered Ferryl drawing invisible marks on his friends to allow them inside Castle House gardens. "How expensive?"

"Seventeen thousand pounds, sir. The price reflects the extra work involved in circumventing the glyphs, fooling them rather than breaking them. That is unusual, and these are very strong glyphs." He hesitated for a moment, before continuing. "My employer wondered if you knew who set them, because they are a very old style."

Abel knew the glyphs were strong, or Zephyr and Ferryl would have broken them, but neither had mentioned age. "Someone told me Pendragon's gryphon and the room were designed for a much larger demesne, and very well protected. The gryphon is a dragon's head, still alive somehow."

"Pendragon is an old name, once powerful, so this may be a fragment of the original demesne, one split between apprentices and possibly more than once. A dragon's head sounds like an original gryphon, so the access glyphs could be centuries old. In return I should warn you about prying in the gryphon room. An old room like that one might hold unpleasant surprises, though it might also hold treasure." The driver held out the badge. "Have you decided, sir?"

Talk of treasures reminded Abel he had no idea how the managers had paid for anything, or if they had. "Just a moment, please." He phoned Shawn, who had just dropped Tess off at the office. "Did you find a cheque book or something? I've no idea what we can afford."

"There's just under two hundred thousand quid in the account, and there's a box hidden somewhere in the room with the gryphon that might contain cash or valuables. The secretary, Bertram, has seen Pendragon taking valuables in there but told us not to go and look. The room is protected from anyone but you, now you've met the gryphon. At the moment Bertram is using his company credit card to pay bills, but he's asked the bank to issue one for you." Shawn sounded a little uneasy. "The day to day would be easier if you put a few quid into a different account, and let me have a debit card for it. Just for petrol and topping up the coffee machine, that sort of thing."

"I'll sort it, and we'd better set up how you and Eric get your wages. Ask Bertram if he knows how. I know I'm technically the boss but you're the real one, running the place to make a few quid for the Tavern." Abel rang off, cutting off the protests. He couldn't handle having to be a boss and a schoolboy as well, so Shawn and Eric would have to do the job. On the way back to the driver, Kelis, Rob and Jenny intercepted him.

"You can't give anyone access to all those trees."

Even as he opened his mouth to ask Kelis why, Rob butted in. "You haven't even met some of the Taverners, not properly, so how can you trust them? If one of them runs off they can nip into the park or one of these streets and top up any time, and you can't stop them."

"Banishment wouldn't work. They'd just keep stealing magic from trees, and might get a really good deal from a sorceress. Then they could fill lead bars for her other apprentices." Jenny stopped as Abel put up his hands in surrender.

"I get it. I'm an idiot, and hadn't thought it through, but you've made the point. Let me talk to the driver." The driver didn't exactly laugh when Abel asked about individual access, just pointed out that a separate glyph for each person would be very expensive.

While Abel tried to think of another way round his problem the driver inspected him, not brazenly but obviously trying to decide on something. "My apologies sir, no offence intended, but I am told you really are as young as you seem. Would you mind giving some idea of how adept you are? Just enough to let me know if you can manage one particular possibility?"

"Even if I can't manage what is needed, I can tell you if Ferryl will be able to."

Abel nodded, and the driver relaxed. "Can you alter a glyph just a little, to make it unique without destroying the meaning? If you can, sir, we might be able to help." Abel agreed he could, after the smug little voice in his head pointed out she had already broken a tether. He wouldn't need Ferryl to alter a glyph. "I will speak to my employer."

The consultation took some time, but Shawn re-joined them and amused everyone by telling them about Tess. Bertram and Marianne, the office staff, had made her a cuppa and were entertaining her with stories about Abel and the Tavern. According to Shawn, Bertram was a sort of magical snob, so finding out that Abel really was the Master of Castle House had elevated Pendragon's holdings into the magical peerage. By the time Tess met Abel again she'd be suitably impressed, and terrified of what she'd probably thought was a minor apprentice showing off. Since Abel had dressed for gardening, Tess would have thought the smartly dressed Ginny was in charge.

Another short conversation when the driver came back, another price hike, and the locksmith swung into action. The driver wasn't kidding about a screen. The van backed up near the tree, a canvas contraption slid out, and Abel never even found out if the expert was human. According to Zephyr, the canvas had magic woven into it to scramble her view of the flows. Abel would have left and come back later, but he had to put his ring hand through a flap and onto the bark for about ten minutes. He drew a little magic when asked, to help the locksmith analyse the ring's reaction with the tree. The locksmith asked for a repeat several times as the work progressed, just for a minute or two, to check the results to date.

Eventually the screen drew back but the driver and locksmith stayed in their van. When the driver finally came out he called Abel away from the rest, careful to turn so nobody could see what he did or overhear. He handed over two small, carefully drawn, intricate glyphs, each with a tiny gap clearly labelled to prevent accidental activation. They didn't look like twenty-eight thousand pounds worth.

Abel's reaction must have shown, because the driver explained they would work on any object that could be unlocked by Pendragon's ring. "Work like that takes very specialist skills, and the fee also covers our confidentiality guarantee. Once you have tested the glyphs, the locksmith will voluntarily accept removal of all memories since arriving here. That will include any knowledge of the glyphs worked into your ring."

"Which is which?"

The driver pointed at the drawings. "The glyph labelled one is the original as requested, and simply drawing it on someone's skin will give them blanket access. Number two is the variable neutralising glyph, a version of the original protection that you can place on a tree, under the bark. If you draw the identical glyph on a person's skin, that will bypass the protection but only on the object bearing the glyph. It is designed to incorporate any distinguishing alteration providing the extra becomes an integral part. Drawing any random line or curve won't work, but you said you could manage the work?"

Abel nodded, after a moment for Zephyr to exercise her smug. "Is there a limit on how many variations I can make, or put on one tree?"

"None. You can place a hundred variations on one tree, each one allowing one person access. Remove one version of the glyph, and one person is denied access. The blanket glyph is designed to bypass any version of that glyph as well, as will your ring of course. The second glyph only cost eleven thousand because we had already broken down the original protection, to create the first glyph. Both are very unusual, especially a blanket access?" Despite him keeping a more or less straight face, Abel could almost feel the waves of curiosity coming off the driver. With a little smile he phoned Ferryl, because he didn't trust himself to draw a magic glyph on anyone's skin.

A sharp ringing from inside the van must have been when the locksmith recognised the approaching woman as non-human. The driver certainly looked very wary after he'd been inside to answer the summons, keeping well clear of Ferryl. As far as Abel knew, being able to tell the difference without a glyph, or touching, made the locksmith a non-human as well. Abel handed Ferryl the glyphs, with a quiet explanation. "So will you draw that on a volunteer, the same way you gave Jenny access to Castle House gardens? Pick someone who will access all the trees. No need to nag, the other Taverneers have persuaded me only a very few people will get that one."

"Good, on both counts. Me drawing the glyphs might be safer than you doing it and binding them all." Her smile took away any sting, as Ferryl's hand took Abel's. "You will have to draw mine first, carefully because that glyph is very complicated. It is important everyone sees you give me the access first, personally, to demonstrate you are the sorcerer.

Don't worry, I'll make sure you don't link or bind me." Before Abel could answer she turned to the driver. "Since I'm his bodyguard and a sorceress in my own right, he uses me to test any unknown magic." Ferryl extended her bared arm, turning so nobody else could see what Abel did. "Don't stop or take your finger away until you complete the glyph. Just your finger so there's no visible mark. Leak a little magic, but don't push it. Without a physical mark, such as ink, you won't get any side effects."

Abel really didn't fancy it, but Ferryl had more chance of surviving a mistake than anyone else. About a minute later he heaved a sigh of relief. "Now what?"

"Now I take a little magic from that tree, and the next one along the street. If I survive we test the other glyph on someone. If they survive you pay up, and I'll mazzle the locksmith." Ferryl didn't seem worried as she walked up and placed her palm firmly on the bark, but Abel saw her shoulders relax just a little when nothing zapped her.

As she headed towards the next tree, Abel turned to the others. "Now to test the other glyph. Shawn?" The manager looked startled. "As my manager you get access to a few trees here and there. That lets you fill up lead bars so the others can fill contracts. It also means that if you are attacked, no matter where you are in the demesne, there'll be extra magic nearby."

Everyone turned to Ginny when she laughed, while the driver definitely looked startled and then intrigued. "If you are attacked, slap your hand on a tree, cast a really solid shield, and raise your free hand to aim a glyph. Anyone less than an old, strong apprentice, someone stronger than Boudicca or even Valdar, will start running. A tree-driven glyph will punch clean through an average shield." Abel noticed the driver nodding gently, so he thought the same.

When she returned from testing the second tree, Ferryl drew Shawn's glyph on his arm, then beneath the bark on two trees, and he tested it. When the big smile proved it worked, even before Shawn confirmed it, the driver moved in. "Since both glyphs work, the fee is due sir." Shawn handed Abel a cheque, already signed by Bertram, and he filled it in. That really did need sorting out. "Thank you sir. If you cast the confusion glyph at the patch of skin, please? Just enough to wipe out two hours, from when we arrived. No more or the penalties will be substantial."

When Abel turned, the side door of the van had opened, showing another canvas screen with a square cut out to show light brown skin.

Zephyr had been keeping very quiet, as requested, but that caught her attention. "That skin is a Seeming!" Abel hesitated, because he didn't want to cause an upset. With definite relief he remembered Ferryl would be casting the glyph.

"My bodyguard is better at confusion than I am." Ferryl took one look and went into a huddle with the driver, then approached the van close enough for a quiet, private conversation.

Once she came back to Ferryl turned and cast her glyph, before taking Abel's hand. "That is a very sneaky entity. The usual strength would not cause complete confusion, so the locksmith probably has the magical key to every customer it has helped. Except you of course." From the tone of her mental voice, Abel didn't have to look to know Ferryl wore a little smirk. "We have agreed there's no need to tell anyone else about that little lapse, and no need for anyone else to know who your bodyguard really is." Abel noted she hadn't even told him what the locksmith was, but he didn't push.

Once the van drove off, Ferryl drew the blanket access glyph on Kelis, Rob, and Jenny. After hesitating when Abel told her, she drew a variation of the second one on Ginny and on the same two trees as Shawn's. Abel ignored the looks from his friends as he explained. "Ginny, you have access to the same trees because you'll need the extra source to help with contracts in Sheffield. You can also help Shawn fill lead bars if you are visiting. I'll give you access to a couple of trees in Stourton as well. You'll need those because Melanie and Diane will be learning as fast as possible, and they'll insist their siblings supply extra magic. You have to stay ahead of your students, and can also supply them with a little extra now and then as a reward." The ex-apprentice had a huge smile after she collected her first belt of pure tree magic, straight from the bark. As soon as she could get a quiet word, Kelis suggested a long talk about who else had access.

*   *   *

Ferryl had been thinking about access, but to houses and gardens rather than trees. For now she'd created a lesser barrier around each garden, deterrence, but not enough to kill anyone. Anyone wearing a Tavern shield could get in, but she wanted to refine them later and tie the new version into tree magic. Abel started to worry about all these special glyphs, but Ferryl assured him she'd etched the variations in her bones. She would draw each one, labelled with a name, for Abel to hide in the room with his gryphon.

Now he'd got the chance to ask, Shawn wanted to give a couple of older Taverners, those who had left school, a permanent job as house-sitters and glyph-fillers. That would mean paying them wages, because Shawn needed them available in the week, not just at weekends. Valdar's houses had been locked up during the week, though Taverners were using them this weekend while filling hexes for contracts. Ferryl promised to protect the gardens when Abel met Veren, but first Abel wanted to eat.

He meant a burger, but when Shawn called the office Bertram offered to book them a table. When the cars pulled up Abel for one had second thoughts. "Did Pendragon bring you here, Ginny?"

"Not likely. I might have eaten at some very nice places when I got the chance, but he didn't socialise. This looks like the sort of place that only admits members." Ginny looked back at the four schoolchildren dressed for gardening. "Even if it isn't, I doubt you'll get in dressed like that."

Shawn, in the car behind them, must have thought the same because he called Abel. "I just phoned Bertram, and this is the right place. He reckons that the Master of Pendragon Enterprises has a booking, regardless of how he's dressed, and the Master of Castle House shouldn't need to book anyway." The tiny giggle spoiled Shawn's serious manager act. "I think he's high on snobbery."

"I'll tell them who is here, then if they say no it's only to an apprentice." Zephyr didn't need her tether for everyone to follow what Ginny said next. The uniformed bloke on the door went from snootily indifferent to superior but agreeable, then on to politely welcoming with a touch of impressed as Ginny rolled out the titles. Abel really hoped Shawn had taken a video clip for the secretary, he'd love it. The doorman soon had his face back under complete control; not a muscle flickered as the gang of kids piled out of the car and trooped inside. By then Ginny had spoken to the smartly dressed woman inside, and the whole party were shown to a booth.

The whole thing should have been a bit of a circus, a big posh place with a bunch of kids stuffing their faces, but the booths were magically screened. The staff were non-magical or had a pass glyph to enter, but nobody else gave a second look. By the time Kelis wiped the cream from her sticky toffee pudding off her face, they'd sobered up, and even discussed the morning. Leaving without paying seemed weird, but Bernard had told Shawn the bill would be sent monthly to the office. By then the group were more interested in what Celtchar's house and park would look like.

Walnut's Grove

The group had barely left the restaurant, when Bertram called from the office with a message from Capone. The sorcerer had called, suggesting that as the Master of Pendragon Enterprises seemed to be heading for Valdar's old house, they could meet on the way. Someone must be watching. Zephyr, and Ferryl, wanted to find the spy and administer a sharp shock, but Abel didn't see the point. "Whoever it is has already reported in. I'm more worried about the actual meeting. It could be a trap." Abel had started to feel a little paranoid about meeting magical strangers.

"We are filled up to the brim after testing access to trees, and I put in extra diamonds after Pendragon and again after Valdar." Ferryl took Abel's hand. "Better now, when we have Ginny and Shawn along, than an ambush sometime unexpected?"

"If it's an ambush, it can't be too blatant because according to my phone map, that car park is out in the open. If someone starts casting veils and glyphs we can run for Valdar's house? If we can reach all those trees, it'll be game over." Kelis touched her blouse front. "If I drain my diamond to make a shield, it should hold long enough to get there. On the other hand, if this Capone isn't that good I can just flatten him."

"If this Capone wants to start trouble, we should go there first and protect all the trees. That might be what he wants. Maybe he's already been nicking magic?" A short phone call later Rob shook his head. "Shawn doesn't think so."

"How about we don't argue and we don't fight? He asked for the Master of Pendragon Enterprises, so does he even know about Castle House? That might slow him up a bit." Jenny sounded a bit fed up. She'd been looking forward to testing Celtchar's trees and having a look round a senior sorcerer's house. "Though since he's poked his nose in, he can make himself useful by telling us about the other local sorcerers, and boundaries." Abel gave in, because the meeting place really was on the way.

As the two BMWs pulled into the car park, they found Capone waiting. Five men and four women climbed out of four cars parked along the far end. Abel's phone rang, Shawn calling from the other BMW. "Going by their cars, that Nissan 4x4 means that Capone is Valdar level at best." He smiled at Abel's startled glance towards him. "I always liked cars, but now I've found out they are a public guide to a sorcerer's status. Bertram has it all worked out."

When Abel shared the news, Rob and Ferryl got out while Zephyr spooky-phoned Shawn to do the same. Abel rolled his eyes and stayed put, as instructed. One of the waiting men hailed them, introducing Capone, an overweight man who looked to be in his late fifties. That probably meant sixties for a magic user, while the grey hair and waistline meant he wasn't advanced enough to self-heal. All those opposite watched spooky-phone, so they were all magic users. "Only four have shielded. Two are only adequate and one is showing real weaknesses, flaws in the magical flows. I will hit that one first if trouble starts, to let everyone know which apprentice to target first."

"No fighting, I hope." Abel listened to the exchange of names. Ferryl toned hers down to just bodyguard, though she included Castle House as well as Pendragon Enterprises.

To the Taverners' surprise, Capone cut straight to a dispute about a strip of land. According to him, there'd been an ongoing negotiation with Pendragon, about the demesne borders. Capone had reached an agreement in principle with Pendragon, and now he wanted the line on the map agreed with the new master. An apprentice brought Rob a map, so Kelis got out to collect it.

Kelis inspected the map before leaning into the car to show Abel, and tap the long shaded strip outlined in red. "This shaded strip is supposedly Capone's, as agreed with Pendragon. This side is Valdar's demesne, and this side is Pendragon's. I've no idea if it's accurate, but according to this, Capone's demesne almost cuts Valdar off from Pendragon." She turned the map back round so she could read the notations. "That could be true and wouldn't have mattered, but now you own both sides so it's a bit awkward."

Ginny turned round, took the map to inspect it, and handed it back. "I never heard of anyone worrying about travelling to Valdar and back, so either Capone is very weak or this bit isn't his."

"Sorted." Kelis produced a pen and neatly drew a line connecting Valdar's and Pendragon's demesnes, cutting off the long bit. "I'll point out this is all one demesne now, so the negotiations are over." Before Abel could come up with an objection, she'd gone to hand it back. Kelis didn't even stop to argue, just handed it over and got back into the car. From his reaction, Capone wasn't happy.

"Zephyr, tell Ferryl we don't want a fight." That seemed possible, because Capone seemed to be getting a bit heated.

"Two cars coming. Magic users." Two Volvo saloons screeched into the car park and parked well off to one side. The doors flew open and everyone piled out. "It is Verenestra." The sorceress lined up with four apprentices, one heavily bandaged.

She might have been off to the side, but Veren shouted loud enough for everyone to hear. "Have you got a death wish, Capone?" She looked at Ferryl and back to the sorcerer, baffled. "Did you listen to the introductions?"

"Yes, and if this is all they've got it isn't a death wish. I've been pushing and the sorcerer daren't even get out of his car." He pointed at Rob. "He seems to be more interested in boundaries, so they don't even know who owns what. If you join me we can maybe get all of Valdar's houses. They're stood empty, because they haven't got enough apprentices to guard them."

Veren threw up her hands in exasperation. "Not a chance. I bust a gut getting here to stop a fight, not join the casualties. This is the Master of Castle House you fool!"

"She said something about that, but I've never heard of it so it isn't important. If you won't team up that's your loss Verenestra, but you ought to ally with someone, and soon." Capone's sneer put a nasty edge in his voice. "There's a few rumours, about you having a lot of trees and not enough apprentices to keep them."

Abel reached for his door handle when Verenestra flinched. She turned towards his car as the doors opened, then started to smile when Ginny, Kelis and Jenny dived out to face Capone before Abel could. Capone looked startled, then straightened, and his apprentices definitely got ready for trouble. Abel ignored him, waving to Veren. "Hi. We just wanted to find out where the borders run, but Capone tried to nick a bit of territory and trade it for some of Valdar's. Ferryl, introduce me again please. Properly this time." That kept Abel amused, because the smartly suited man had obvious trouble marrying the kid in jeans with the titles. Master of Castle House still didn't have any real effect, which Abel found a bit disappointing.

Capone picked one part out of the torrent. "Sorceress bodyguard? Why is that different to senior apprentice?"

Verenestra dived in straight away. "She means a proper sorceress, and a real bodyguard, so back off Capone, I really mean it. This one doesn't play all the dominance games, or he plays for keeps. You've always been fair with me, so I broke the speed limits to get here before you screwed up. I've heard that bodyguard introduce herself like that before, and the last sorcerer to argue is ashes. Since then I've asked around, and she killed up to a dozen apprentices in three days. At least six were as good as me, or maybe you. Killed them in job lots, not one at a time, while these other four held Pendragon to a draw. Then the rest arrived and killed Pendragon." The sorceress relaxed a bit when Capone started looking wary rather than belligerent.

"I heard about Valdar dying, but no details. How come you know so much?"

Capone probably didn't expect the laugh from Verenestra. "I was waiting at Valdar's house, Abel's house now, to say thanks for Boudicca's house and one of her senior apprentices. The last one." The bandaged woman bowed, very low, presumably instructed through her tether. "They took out Boudicca and three senior apprentices, at the same time as Valdar and all his, just because she stuck her nose in where it wasn't wanted." The broad sweep of Veren's hand took in all the Taverners. "Forget what they look like. Castle House is an old title, one of the biggies, Magic Council big. Abel has inherited the lot." Capone still seemed baffled until Verenestra added, "He's got a great big park full of trees, here in Sheffield." The sorcerer looked shocked, then wary and definitely worried.

Abel relaxed. Capone had calmed down and seemed to be more interested in information than a fight, while Veren seemed to be having fun telling him. Eventually both of them turned back towards the

Taverners, so Abel took his chance. "Sorry about the confusion. We were trying to avoid all the titles, because they are a bit much every time I meet someone. My bodyguard just wanted to ask you about the local boundaries, because there isn't a proper map. Then you claimed that strip and tried to rip me off, which annoyed Kelis. I'd appreciate it if someone talks to Kelis, and helps her mark a map up properly?" As Kelis headed towards the big open space in the middle of the car park, pulling out her pen, Abel turned to Veren. "Are you really in trouble?"

"Maybe?" The sorceress hesitated before giving a big sigh. She looked around the car park at the three groups, and Kelis with Capone's apprentice in the middle. "That's why I wanted to meet at Valdar's place. It would have been private, because it's a bit embarrassing if you say no."

"So come closer and whisper."

Veren jerked, then smiled before leaving her apprentices and walking closer. She kept her voice low. "I forgot you don't insist on a big clear space all around." She glanced at Ferryl, now coming around the front of the car to join Abel. "I haven't forgotten why you don't need space, Ferryl Shayde. The reason this could be embarrassing is that Capone will know I am desperate, and might round up some friends and come calling. We aren't enemies, but when there's trees up for grabs?" The sorceress stopped talking and tried to stand up straight, but she still looked more wary than confident. "I am willing to offer all my knowledge, and help at any time you ask, if you will accept me as a vassal."

"What is a vassal, Ferryl?"

Veren carried on talking, and answered Abel anyway. "It probably has some medieval name, but as far as I can work out vassal means a subordinate ally. Someone not tethered but under your protection, and control. From what I learned it is offered as an option if a minor sorceress can't be defeated without serious losses, but the stronger sorceress wants to control an area or asset." She shrugged, meeting Abel's eyes with a wry smile. "You can run right over me so I can't negotiate like that, from strength, and my demesne isn't much of a prize anyway. You might not even want it, but I've got to try something. I'm between the troll and the ogre. I really don't fancy becoming a tethered apprentice again, but I need some sort of protection."

"But you seemed to be set up, you and Boudicca. You've got trees and apprentices, and I thought sorceresses didn't risk themselves fighting? According to an archbishop, they daren't risk all their wealth and knowledge on what might be a miscalculation." Though Abel reflected that several seemed to have done so recently.

The touch of bitterness in Verenestra's voice might mean some sorceresses weren't keen on the fighting idea. "It might look that way from up on the mountain, but it's dirtier down in the mud. The likes of us have no real wealth, or power, and have never been given much training because most of us never served our full apprenticeship. My master dying seemed a wonderful opportunity. There I was, free of the tether, with a house, a nice car and a few apprentices, and feeling pretty good. Then you killed Boudicca and Valdar in one go, before casually giving me a house and half a dozen trees. You even tossed in a senior apprentice and a car. Reality bit me really hard."

Verenestra paused, glancing at Ferryl with a little shrug. "I really am what your bodyguard called Boudicca, an ex-apprentice who had a careless master. Freedom didn't suddenly reveal lots of glyphs and make me a real sorceress, and four mediocre apprentices isn't much of an army. Three and a bit until she heals. Your apprentices really hurt the last one, which is why she surrendered when I ambushed her. That's a wake-up call on its own, and so was her telling me that lass with a sword held Boudicca to a draw, got through her shield. That kid in her fancy costume, not even your senior apprentice, could probably take me in a straight fight."

Veren looked at the rest of Abel's party, slowly, nodding gently to herself. "I'll bet any of these could, or they wouldn't be facing Capone. I've spent a few days sat in my lovely new house, weighing up my chances and looking for a solution. I've even considered giving up the old apprentice house, hopefully by selling it, but my neighbours would take it as a sign of weakness. Then I thought of an alternative, which is why I wanted to meet you." Her sad smile admitted the next bit hadn't worked out. "Without witnesses."

"The not having knowledge or power sort of explains why Valdar and Boudicca stuck their necks out. I suppose they thought that because I'm only a schoolboy, I'd be in the same position." Abel kept talking, half-thinking aloud as he reassessed the sorceress community, and the place of freed apprentices. "So until an apprentice has survived long enough on her own, it's more or less open season? How many of them go for this vassal idea, until they can get themselves sorted out?"

The question seemed to depress Verenestra; she sort of slumped into herself a little. "I've never heard of an actual vassal, just what they are, but thought it might be worth a shot? You already admitted you don't know much about boundaries, or other sorcerers in this part of Sheffield. This way you get everything I know, and I stay sort of free. That's if information is enough to make me useful?"

Even as Abel wondered if this might be some sort of a con, he felt Ferryl take his hand. "There were equivalents, both magical and among the knights and lords. Feudal servants, who held a small area in return for service. How badly do we need her information?"

At least Zephyr meant that Abel could answer silently. "You were the one who suggested keeping Veren near, giving her a morsel to get information. We don't have to trust her with anything, or even support her, because she already has trees and apprentices. Unless she'll drag us into a war?"

"No. Capone didn't recognise Castle House but stronger sorceresses will, or Veren will tell them. Anyone at her level will run a mile if she is truly allied." Ferryl paused, obviously inspecting Veren's apprentices. "With the extra magic in her new trees, her apprentices will hold against a low-level attack. If she allows them extra magic to practice, they will get stronger and she can take on a couple of glyph-fillers. As a vassal, Veren would be under your control as well as protection. I would put a decent barrier around her houses, tied into a tree, something that will stop Capone cold. You will be able to pass if you wish, but we will not tell her that."

That seemed to be enough for Abel, because he really didn't like the dog eat dog idea. He'd given Veren a house, and it made her a target! "I accept, but don't start any wars."

"As far as I can work out, I'd need your permission to do that. Vassal means a sort of apprentice without the tether, and is supposed to be shaming, but I'm not stupid. I've been looking at maps, and asked around, and being protected by your sort of power will make up for a lot of snide remarks." Verenestra blew out a long breath. "Shall we get it over with now, so I can sleep at night?"

"What about the privacy bit, Veren, sorry, Verenestra?" She'd lost Abel again.

"Since you've accepted, the more who know the better. Capone will tell everyone he knows, once I explain Castle House properly, and as fast as possible so they don't make a mistake. Except a few enemies, he'll probably encourage them to attack me or you." Veren seemed really relieved, babbling a little. "You may as well all call me Veren now. It'll look like you've renamed me, and it will stop your apprentices mangling my full name. The name Verenestra hasn't got much of a history anyway, so no great loss." With an obvious effort she stopped and firmed up. "I don't suppose you know how it goes, the exact wording?"

"The wording will have varied because, as usual, intent is what matters. I will understand if she alters the meaning, tries to give herself a way out." Abel passed that on, and Veren went down onto one knee. Everyone else in the car park stopped whatever they were doing and watched, baffled or surprised. Veren's formal statement more or less said here, you can have anything I've got if you need it. Ferryl prompted Abel to promise protection, for as long as Veren remained faithful.

"I'm supposed to kiss a ring or a sword or something. It's the really important bit and seals the deal." Abel held out his hand when Ferryl silently prompted him, trying not to giggle at what Creepio would think of it. Veren kissed the Pendragon ring, then jerked back in surprise. "What was that?" She looked up, really frightened. "I said not tethered!"

"No tether, I swear." Though Abel had felt something, a connection, a feeling of inspection, then approval. "What was that, Ferryl? I felt something when Veren touched the ring."

Ferryl might have answered Abel, but she watched Veren. "That was the reason clients keep their word. Your gryphon just accepted the contract, a magical oath sworn freely. You are both bound by the terms, unless one of you formally dissolves the agreement. That has to be done face to face."

"What happens if we break it, the oath?" A nervous smile flitted over Veren's face. "Not that I will. I don't fancy having a dragon's head looking for payback, not one that can open its eyes and bare its teeth!"

"Your oath was sincere, or the gryphon would have known and rejected it. I've no idea what happens if you change your mind without a formal meeting, but I wouldn't want to be the one to find out." While Veren stood up and pondered that, Ferryl turned to look at the rest of the car park and burst out laughing. She raised her voice, or magically enhanced it. "Abel hasn't tethered her. Veren has become a vassal of Pendragon, so probably Castle House." She pointed at Capone, who still didn't seem to be impressed. "You might want to go over there and explain the second part, Veren. If Capone turns that sneer into an insult that offends me, we'll have to change the maps again."

"I'll tell him exactly that." The way Veren strode off, to explain why the sneer might be a bad idea, didn't look very shamed at all. However she put it, Capone didn't think he should sneer again, and the pair ended up having what looked like an animated but friendly conversation. Meanwhile Kelis drew what information she could get onto her map, and everyone loaded up again. By the time Ginny pulled out of the car park, Veren's group had loaded up and were following.

Discussing the vassal idea at length, and what Veren knew about the demesnes bordering Abel's, kept the rest interested while Tess moved into Valdar's house, and Ferryl started on the protection. Karen promptly volunteered to move to Pendragon's house and housekeep there, anything to get away from her memories. The various sorts of magical compulsion really did leave a strong reaction once lifted.

Veren arranged to meet Shawn at the office in a couple of days, to help with the demesne maps, and left to go home. Shawn left soon after, to get Karen settled in and arrange milk and groceries. While Ferryl reinstated the Seeming across the end of the road, the Taverneers, and Ginny, had a little time to kill. Rob started teasing Kelis about all the houses up for grabs, and for the first time Kelis actually wavered. "Not give, but if I go to University?" She started blushing! "Just one room, and I'll pay rent, but it would be nice to have decent digs so mum could visit now and then?"

It might have been a bit mean, but Abel couldn't resist. "That seems reasonable, because then I can do the same for my other ex-girlfriends. I'll give you Pendragon's house, then you can take in student lodgers and your mum can run the place. Jenny could take Valdar's place and do the same. Does Claris qualify for a house, or just a flat?"

"Don't you dare!" Kelis almost thumped him, until Abel collapsed laughing. Rob and Jenny were soon laughing as well, though a baffled Ginny probably wondered why Kelis said no. When Kelis finally calmed down, she accepted that Abel simply wouldn't accept rent for her room, though she'd only keep it until she'd finished at University. Jenny accepted the same deal, mainly so she'd have some free time where her dad couldn't get over-protective. By then Ferryl announced that she'd finished the temporary barrier, so did anyone want to go and play in the park?

*　*　*

The next visits, inspecting Celtchar's properties, should be the highlight of the trip, except now Kelis thought of a problem. A subdued, whispered argument blew up, because Kelis and Rob weren't keen on Ginny knowing too much. Eventually they conceded that the five of them needed a discreet chauffeur. Ferryl and Zephyr didn't trust Ginny, but were adamant her imperatives meant the apprentice couldn't betray Abel.

Celtchar's Sheffield house came first, and this one belonged in an entirely different league to Valdar's or Pendragon's. The detached, modestly carved, three-story stone façade had that air of genteel nobility that just screamed old money. It had probably belonged to some minor noble, unless Celtchar had the place built to order. The six of them walked past several times, but didn't detect any active defences. There were some dormant hexes, and when Abel tried the front gate Ferryl and Zephyr spotted several of them waking up. Ferryl pushed in front as the rest came inside the garden, and walked up the footpath. Since there hadn't been a problem, Abel tried to work out what to say when they reached the door, but Jenny sniffed and pulled a face. "Yeuk, what stinks?"

"Drains? A dead dog?" Kelis looked around at the neatly mown lawns. "Where is it and why didn't we smell it from the street?"

"Because the house is doing it. Keep going, but slowly." A few steps later Ferryl slowed. "The warning is getting stronger."

"It feels like a definite 'go away,' without words, but the stink speaks volumes. That house really doesn't want us." Rob turned to Abel. "What about you, Master?"

"I'm not the master here. I wondered how Woods and Green could rent out my house, but I couldn't get access, and now we know. My house doesn't want me anywhere near, though I can't smell anything odd." Abel could feel an irritation inside his head, now strong enough to promise real pain if he kept going.

"The smell is to deter magically aware visitors, the go away is for persistent magic users, and the house recognises Abel but knows he hasn't been accepted by Celtchar's gryphon. Pushing further could be painful for all of us." Ferryl turned back towards the gate and the rest quickly followed, except Ginny who had waited outside. "I suggest leaving the hexes as they are, unless you are determined to break in?" Ferryl frowned, assessing the magic involved. "That might be a bad idea, and damage your property."

"Nope, that's enough. I probably won't need this place even when I get access. Not unless Kelis wants an upgrade?" Abel turned away with relief because the house really had started to push, mentally. "At least we can all go into the park, because that's public access."

Kelis held out her phone, with a map on the screen. "After seeing this place, I thought I'd better look up Millponds Nature Reserve on the internet. It's a bit more than just a park. According to the Council website, there's just over five hundred acres of woodlands, and streams with a bluebell valley and daffodil hill. Hiking or horse riding only, no vehicles or bikes. There's real millponds with kingfishers, fish including pike, otters, and the remains of an old forge and waterwheel." Kelis turned her phone so the rest of the passengers could see the screen. "We should have looked it up before coming. The whole lot was donated to the city in the eighteen hundreds, by a local who'd made his fortune in steel."

"Or donated by the sorcerer who owned it, so nobody wondered why hikers kept disappearing." Nobody laughed because Ferryl wasn't joking.

Kelis kept them all amused during the short drive, by feeding them snippets from the website. Despite that, the extensive picnic grounds among the scattered trees at the edge of the real woodland, and the huge car park, came as a big surprise. "Blimey, now we know where to go for the next summer Tavern meeting. There's even tables, and the Council will clean up the rubbish." Jenny carefully inspected the immediate area before pointing. "Apart from that one, all the trees in the picnic area look too young to have been here back in the eighteen hundreds. Does that mean they aren't protected?"

"Maybe all Celtchar's woods are the same. If so dryads will have moved in by now. After all, nobody has been putting glyphs on any trees for over a hundred years." Abel looked past the picnic ground, at the big, old trees pushing up above the woodland. "Even if the dryads have moved into these, the big ones back there should supply plenty of magic for everyone."

"I'll check for dryads." Jenny's little skip forward turned into a startled yelp and a scramble backwards. "Who did that?" A long strip of blackened ground, between the group and the nearest trees, still smoked where the grass had burst into flame. The shimmer of a veil hid the damage from non-magical sight, as more glyphs landed. Mist dampened the area and grass began to sprout again. All eyes turned to the spreading branches and massive trunk of the tree stood all on its own, clear of the main woodland.

"That was protection. Protection using a tree, and capable of both a reaction and then covering up the evidence. A dryad." Ferryl took a long look at the strip of blackened earth, now almost covered with green shoots, and turned to Abel. "I can't come with you. If there is any sort of warning, come straight back and we will contact Woods and Green."

Abel took a long look at the blackened strip, and the wide expanse of untouched grass, and nodded. "Too true. If the tree bark looks even slightly annoyed when I get nearer, I'll come back." He braced his shoulders and walked straight for the old tree, raising his voice. "Greetings, dryad and tree. I am the Master of Castle House and wish to talk to you." When nothing happened he considered repeating it, but dryads could hear mouse whispers. Abel quickly killed any curiosity about other entities that might live in trees, and maybe dislike sorcerers, because he didn't need his nerves shredded any further. He almost stopped before walking under the branches, but that zap would have nailed him in the car park so a falling branch wasn't much of a threat.

"Greetings, oath-breaker. Or sorcerer. The same word." Two big, dark brown eyes opened in the trunk.

"Greetings dryad. I have never broken my oath to any dryad. What

123

would happen if some impolite sorcerer insisted on taking magic from those trees?"

"I would channel the magic from the older trees deeper inside the woods, to destroy him or her." The large, deep brown eyes turned from Abel to look at his friends. "Or it, in one case. The younger trees are not individually protected, but no trespasser could carry enough magic to survive my attack. Only the master has access to the magic in this wood."

"The non-human is a friend, dryad, called Ferryl Shayde. I'm sorry, I would call you after your tree as I usually do, but I don't recognise what it is." Abel looked up at the branches overhead. "Thank you for looking after my magic for so long."

"This tree is a Walnut, very popular once a year, but only among those who like the nuts and have no magic. There are no thanks due for guarding your magic, because I am a dryad and that is what I promised. You are a sorcerer, which is why I have not received payment." Branches rustled above Abel, but didn't sound threatening. "Perhaps I would have left once the sorcerer broke his word, but it was too late. I could not because he had removed all the nearby trees big enough to hold me, and marked the edge of the woodland to bar me entry." Branches moved and leaves fluttered, definitely agitated but still not a threat. "Since I must stay I have kept the bargain, because life and a good tree are better than an annoyed sorcerer and a charred stump."

Abel tried his best to make his face and voice show his sincerity, even though he didn't know if dryads recognised expressions or tones. "If I had made the bargain, you would have been paid. I cannot undo what Celtchar did, but I will honour the agreement from now on."

The branches rustled again, and for the first time Abel heard curiosity, and a lessening of the bitterness. "I have heard whispers of sorcerers who keep their word?"

"True ones, Dryad Walnut." Kelis might call him a sucker, but Abel didn't like what had been done to the dryad so he made a snap decision. "If you tell me the terms, I will honour your contract, pay you up to date even if Celtchar is long dead. After that I would like some help, and might want answers to questions now and then, but we will pay for those with honey." Abel turned to take in all the trees and bushes around the picnic tables. "What were you promised?" Now he'd opened his big mouth, Abel hoped it wasn't heaps of gold sovereigns.

"A home for my young, one every fifty years, in a tree already strong enough to protect it. My kin would have helped to protect the other trees of course." Leaves fluttered again, but gently in a pattern that usually meant Chestnut found something amusing. "Though with the magic from so many large, old trees available for me, help is not necessary."

"Pick four trees, Dryad Walnut, fully mature ones, and get on with ripening. One extra tree if you can allow my companions to take magic whenever they wish." Jenny would giggle at that, because there were enough big trees here to keep her spaced for several lifetimes.

"The older trees have glyphs, so I cannot allow anyone to take magic from them, but the younger ones here and further into the woodland rely on me for protection. If the Master of Castle House placed his hand on my bark and commanded me, I would accept that as an alteration to our contract. Especially now the master has paid up." Abel moved up close and put his hand on the tree. "No, on my bark." The dryad materialised out of the tree. Even this close Abel couldn't tell if it slid out, appeared outside, or sort of smoked out. The brief fuzziness hid any detail.

Behind Abel, Ferryl raised her voice in alarm. "Caution, Abel. A dryad draws magic directly from a tree, and from humans if they are charmed into making contact. We would not be able to overcome a dryad backed by so many mature trees." Her tone hardened as her eyes fastened on the dryad. "Though I'm sure fire, and the right mechanical equipment, would deal with the problem eventually."

"No dryad has ever cheated me." Abel held out his hand.

"I thank you, though trust is not needed. Any attempt to harm the Master of Castle House would leave him with plenty of walnut charcoal, and a vacancy for a dryad." No branches creaked, so that wasn't an attempt at humour.

Abel knew dryads didn't trust people, especially sorcerers, but they'd always been truthful so he laid his palm on the gnarled, twiggy entity. He'd expected the same sensation as the bark of the tree, because a dryad matched the patterns, but not how soft and pliable the 'skin' felt. Resisting an impulse to stroke the dryad, Abel dragged his mind back to business.

"Any special wording?"

"None needed, just intent. Those allowed access will touch a tree and let a little magic leak out. After that I will always recognise their true-self."

"Silly me, I should have known about the intent part." That seemed to be a constant in magic, intent mattered more than words. "This first person will only be allowed to draw magic from two of the trees. If she ever tries to take magic from the others, kill her." Abel turned back to the rest. "Ginny, choose two trees. Place your palm on each one and leak a little magic so they recognise you, and will allow you to draw magic in the future. Make sure you memorise which trees, because the others will kill you." Ginny advanced cautiously and put her palm on a tree, then another, straightening with a relieved smile before re-joining the others. "Everyone else, choose your tree and do the same, leak magic." Abel turned back to Dryad Walnut. "All of these, including the entity now known as Ferryl Shayde, can draw as much magic as they wish as often as they want to."

"Entity or human, as long as you have given permission I will allow it."

The rest of the group took turns to choose two trees each, and Abel realised they thought the same restrictions applied to everyone. With that in mind, he asked about giving more people access. As expected, Abel had to give each one permission, personally, though discussing that and the true-self part gave Abel an idea. "I carry another entity, one that is still growing. If she touches a tree, untethered, can you give Zephyr access as well? Just in case she needs magic and can't get to me."

"As long as it has enough of a mind for me to read its true-self."

Abel wasn't having that. "She is Zephyr so it will be her true-self. Ferryl Shayde is also her and she. Mouse and wind whispers might have mentioned that?"

"Rumours about you are very unclear and confused, because some do not believe them. Zephyr should touch a tree, however she accomplishes that, firmly enough to leak magic deliberately. After a moment she should draw magic so I know how it will be done. She will be recognised in future, regardless of her appearance." This time the rustles were definite

126

humour.

"If you are not here, why would I be here looking for magic?"

"One day you will grow too big for the tattoo, or might wish to fly free and travel the world. Ferryl keeps saying that in wind form you are vulnerable, so you need a safe place to hide or recover. As long as you can get to this wood, you can recover from any damage. There will be plenty of fae and bugs for you to hunt, and lots of strong trees for magic if someone tries to hunt you." Abel chuckled, remembering something else. "We can bury a copy of your book, the one with all your glyphs, in the woodland. I'm sure Dryad Walnut will find a very safe place if we bring honey."

"I will never be too big for the tattoo, but one day I might travel. Thank you Abel. If I ever leave, and you need a Ffod or a watcher in the night, ask a dryad to whisper to the wind." Zephyr slipped free before Abel could answer, and floated over to a tree.

"Dryad Walnut, many people are trying to find out who or what Zephyr is. Please do not let any whispers about what you see drift on the wind, or crawl through the grass. That includes whispers about her being able to draw magic from all these trees." As he spoke Zephyr plastered her wind-self to a tree trunk for long moments.

"No whispers or rumours, Master of Castle House. Zephyr has a very strong, clear sense of self, more than enough to give her access. If she survives and grows, you will have a strong, clever ally. Should you be betrayed, finding out how strong and dangerous your invisible friend can become might be a good lesson for a traitor." Leaves danced in definite dryad laughter as Zephyr left the tree, then flew back into contact.

The dryad and the leaves fell silent as Zephyr drifted back to Abel and into her tattoo. "That felt strange. I drew magic, just me, just for a moment. It tickles and fills me up very quickly. Handshake please." Abel wanted to talk about messages on the wind, but a voice behind him interrupted.

"Can I mark my two trees with a pen or a cut, so I don't make a mistake?" Jenny asked, but when Abel turned everyone but Ginny had come to talk, though none had ventured under the branches. Ginny watched warily from near the car, so Zephyr asked why, using the tether.

Sorceresses and dryads were rivals for tree magic, so all apprentices were warned not to end up all alone near dryads, or get too near a big one.

"Spooky-phone but not to Ginny, please Zephyr. Explain they all get to use any tree that has no glyphs, except Ginny but I don't want her to realise." When she passed that on, Zephyr didn't mention being able to draw magic for herself, leaving Abel to wonder if Dryad Walnut had already whispered to her.

"We'll all mark two anyway, so Ginny doesn't realise. Thank you very much, kind sorcerer and dryad. Can a person die of a magic overdose? Or giggles?" Jenny turned to look at the woodland, more like a forest in places. "We still can't touch the older trees, those with glyphs, so how will we know which are safe?"

The dryad must have decided it could talk to this group at least. "Approach my tree, or any of the large, old ones deeper in the park. You will feel uncomfortable if it has glyphs, becoming pain if you persist. Don't push back hard enough to actually touch the tree. You will die before you feel the bark." The dryad closed its eyes, leaving an ordinary looking walnut tree. "Try." Three of them tried, reporting an ache in their teeth when they stood under the outer branches. The ache strengthened as they came closer, though none took more than two steps. Ferryl simply pointed out she could feel the glyphs, and understood them well enough not to be stupid.

"How many hundreds of trees are there in this wood?" For once Kelis seemed overwhelmed. "There must be hundreds of new ones, the ones we can use. Even so, I'll bet that's nothing compared to the magic Abel can get from all those really big ones."

"Not many hundreds, or not until the master speaks to the other four dryads who guard sections of this woodland. The glyphs will not allow us to contact each other, in case we conspire, but the wind whispers so I can tell you where they live." This time even the branches creaked, dryad humour since nobody ended up brained by one. "I will enjoy the whispers when they tell me of their visits."

Half an hour later Abel had twenty fewer trees, mature ones for seedlings, and his friends had access to enough tree magic to last several lifetimes. In a private moment Abel and Zephyr agreed that her first access was more than she'd ever need. More than that, she didn't fancy exposing her true-self to the other dryads. They were scratchier than Walnut, less forthcoming, though all of them accepted homes for their young and new instructions. None of the others came out of their tree, accepting Abel's hand on their tree's bark as sufficient confirmation. Privately Ferryl thought Dryad Walnut might have been testing Abel in some way. When she suggested that the dryad might be more sociable after years of people picnicking nearby, the Taverners dissolved in hysterical laughter. Once the hilarity died down, Ferryl admitted sociable and dryad didn't really go together.

On the way home, all seven of them, including Zephyr, tried again and again to make sense of the amount of woodland in Millponds Nature Reserve, and couldn't. Abel couldn't use the magic in all those trees, no sorcerer could even if their bones were pure diamond and they wore a suit of gold armour, so why didn't any of them share? Ginny had no idea, the sheer number of trees stunned her. Pendragon had boasted of his trees, but the lot would disappear into Abel's park without a trace.

Ferryl probably came up with the answer. "It must be a combination. Claiming that many trees is greed, and also stops anyone else taking the magic. Fear might play a part because all that magic is a sort of insurance. Standing in that woodland and connected to all those trees, a sorcerer would be almost invulnerable." A nasty little smile came and went. "But only almost, if they face someone willing to die as well." She clammed up and nobody pushed her too hard, because that had been a very nasty smile.

*   *   *

The following day Abel had a short but stormy meeting with as many adept Taverners as he could round up. As soon as he mentioned sorting out the captured cars, people started shouting at him!

"I thought it was sorted. Do I have to give mine back?"

"How come this lot got all the cars? There'll be none left when I pass my test."

"Not everyone. I can drive but I didn't get one."

"Do we have to be at a fight?"

"I was here to fight Pendragon, and I didn't get anything."

"Never mind the cars, I'll settle for some loot from Valdar's house."

Abel sat there stunned. The Tavern was coming apart in front of him as arguments broke out about who should get what.

"Listen, please." Ginny stood and held up her hands, repeating herself until most of the talking stopped. "Abel has asked me to explain what usually happens if sorcerers win a fight. The senior apprentices don't choose, they are given a little something and the sorcerer gets the rest, all of it. The junior apprentices are just thankful they survived. Apprentice cars don't belong to the apprentice, nor do over half their clothes and jewellery, they are loans."

"But Abel isn't a real sorcerer."

"Well he is, but he's head of the Tavern, and we are all equal."

"What about the cars, can we still get one?"

When Kelis stood up everyone quietened down straight away. They all knew her and respected her, or her temper. "First off every magic user in the country knows that Abel is real sorcerer, except apparently a couple of people in here who didn't get the message." She glared at each culprit in turn. "The titles are a big hint? Secondly, just suppose the idiot here put all the car keys in a hat and you drew one, then what? How will you explain a new car to your parents, or pay for insurance, MOT, servicing, repairs or road tax?"

"But the business pays that, doesn't it?"

"For your private car? Not likely. My insurance will be fifteen hundred quid, then there's the MOT and tax, and petrol is six quid a gallon." Kelis explained how much her own insurance would cost, then the loan option for drivers, and answered questions. Most of the Taverners were thinking now, nodding or agreeing that there had to be some sort of system. Not all of them, neither Kelis nor Ginny had really persuaded the hotheads. A small number, mostly newer arrivals, had set their heart on a four-wheeled prize, though some would settle for pillaging the captured houses.

"Stop acting like spoilt kids!" Abel actually heaved a sigh of relief when Una spoke. He really had wondered what she'd say when she stood up. Now she stuck her hand on her sword hilt and glared at anyone still arguing. "I never really expected Abel to give me that Volvo. Flipping heck, I only claimed it as a joke in the first place, to stick it to Boudicca. Then I looked up a few things, and insuring that thing would cost me nearly three grand a year." She turned to Abel with a big grin. "Though if you pay the cursed bills and let me run about in it, I'll play taxi driver whenever you want." Una fished in her pocket and threw Abel the keys.

He'd barely pocketed them when Shannon stood up. Those who'd started to argue again shut up as she threw the keys for the Range Rover over to Kelis. "If anyone had a chance to score a car as a gift, it would be Kelis, Jenny or Ferryl, and I don't see any of them with new wheels. Jenny has already passed her test, and I'm sure it wouldn't take the others very long." She laughed when a couple of Taverners pointed out there were more than three cars. "Don't look at me, I crashed the last motor anyone let me drive." The wink at Abel as she sat down made his mind up. Maybe not right now, but sometime soon Shannon would get the keys to the Volvo convertible. She really had crashed the minibus, but to save his life. Una had challenged a sorceress to guard Ferryl's back, and fought Boudicca to a standstill. She would get the Volvo estate, but neither motor would be a gift.

"I've already agreed my deal. The BMW is a company car, so it was never mine. That's how it works in business. If I'm busy and someone needs a lift to fill glyphs, I'll toss the keys to the nearest driver." As Shawn sat down Petra shot to her feet.

"In that case I'm sitting between Shawn and Eric, sort of convenient?" Eric waved his keys, then snatched them away as a laughing Petra made a grab for them. Several others promptly offered to sit near a manager, or on Shawn's knee in one case. Despite the laughter, some were still muttering about getting proper loot, like in the game.

The lingering discussions about cars stopped smartly when Abel stood up. "The magical Tavern isn't Bonny's Tavern, the game. We do not charge off on quests for treasure caves, we try to make sure kids and grandmas aren't bitten by fae. Even so, on this occasion there is some loot. Ginny explained the usual solution, but I think Robin D'Ritche has rubbed off on me, just a bit. In the Tavern, everyone who risks their lives gets some loot, but not enough for some idiot to start a fight for."

A couple of people who'd started to speak were quickly shushed, and dead silence fell. "Everyone who fought Pendragon can choose a prize from his apprentice barracks. There's some really nice stuff in there, especially in the senior apprentice rooms. You all get one item, jewellery, a pair of shoes or a suit, that sort of thing." A ripple of laughter greeted that. "Don't laugh." Abel shot a quick glance towards Ginny. "I am assured that some of those shoes are almost worth dying for."

"What about her?" Rachel pointed at Ginny, then looked a little guilty. "I mean Ginny."

"Ginny isn't the enemy now, so we don't steal her personal property. Whatever Pendragon gave her when she was promoted is still in Sheffield, and will go into the pot." Abel turned towards a definitely apprehensive Ginny. "Ginny has to drive a car to cart me about, to get to Diane, Melanie or anyone else in trouble, and to be the Tavern taxi driver. Remember, her tether can call Ginny in from anyplace if she's needed, so her car isn't a gimmee."

"She fought for Pendragon!"

Abel deliberately misunderstood. "True, so no loot from the first fight." He gave a huge grin, and some of the others caught the joke and laughed. "But Ginny gets to pick something from Valdar's place."

As voices were raised to object, Una came to her feet again. "If she doesn't, I'll give her my share. I was about down and out when Ginny's glyphs arrived." No hand on her sword, but Una had a definite challenge in her voice. "Though it'll cost her. I want lessons in how to keep a glyph as tight as that."

"I've already asked." Petra turned so the rest could see her smile. "She says manage without spare magic for five or six years, but I'm trying to find a better way." The argument about Ginny getting loot fizzled out as others tried to come up with faster ways to learn tighter glyphs. As he carried on to tell everyone who fought Valdar they'd get something from those houses, Abel noticed a definite trend. Una, Petra, Shannon, and sometimes Shawn, Justin or Eric, the original beta testers, neatly diverted any objections before they picked up much support. A few others were very quick to pick up the diversions and run with them.

Kelis winked when Abel glanced her way, after she'd made a joke about not being able to claim a house. When some griped about missing out on both fights, Shawn asked if Cecilia and Amelia qualified for loot. Ferryl finally took pity on Abel and took his hand. "The details weren't worked out, but some people agreed to stop anyone getting too greedy. We didn't expect the car keys, not like that, but both had already agreed that the loan and taxi idea made sense. Just so you know, we didn't promise either Una or Shannon a car." Zephyr explained what Abel had decided to do about those two, and why, and Ferryl agreed but only in a week or two.

Once Abel explained that the rest of the loot would be sold to help the Tavern and the Refuge, a few diehards asked why it couldn't all be shared out. Abel never got to answer. Several voices pointed out Abel had already donated his own personal goodies from Castle House, so by rights he should keep the loot as repayment. That ended Abel's meeting because Rob claimed he had to get home, but the rest were still talking as he left. Jenny assured him there were enough of the right people, mostly the original betas, personal friends, to stop any attempts to alter what had been decided. Once everyone had a chance to think, they'd realise it all made sense.

*　*　*

School, or more particularly swotting for exams, stopped Abel worrying about business or woodlands in the next few weeks. Eric and Shawn buckled down, trying to learn what they needed to run the business. Both wanted to keep the job, thoroughly enjoying their improved conditions, wages, cars, and the unlimited magic from the nearby trees. Although they called Abel now and then, they'd usually reduced the problem to a few clear options and preferences, so that wasn't too bad. Now they both had bank cards, Abel could more or less ignore Pendragon Enterprises.

Taking away the boards to reveal the shop window made a world of difference to the Stourton office. Within a week Abel's mum had accepted her first day's work, describing the place and the people to her amused son. Although she didn't realise yet, there would be plenty more work. The current secretary had put in her notice, probably unhappy about the first meeting when she'd been magically influenced, put to sleep and then mazzled. She couldn't quite remember what happened, but felt uneasy. Abel left it all to the managers, telling them to only call him if they had a big problem.

A few letters arrived, one of them a map of the area around Pendragon's and Valdar's demesnes. Veren had spent long hours with Shawn, drawing in the boundaries she knew, then travelled around the whole perimeter to settle any discrepancies. A note from Shawn reckoned she'd been talking to the neighbours, and probably scared most of them glyphless. According to the map, none of the neighbours were much bigger than Valdar had been, because there wasn't much business in the mainly residential area. Despite the big parks here and there, none of the locals had access or even knew who owned them. Sheffield City Centre seemed to be a free-for-all, where lots of different sorcerers had contracts but none claimed it as a demesne. Another letter listed all the non-magical businesses Pendragon and Valdar had serviced, providing security equipment or computer repairs.

Two half-day visits to Sheffield, and a trip to the Leferrier Memorial Park in Stourton, gave a score of Tavern adepts access to selected trees. In return all of them agreed to fill lead bars for the other trainees. Ferryl finished her work on the houses in Sheffield, fixing strong barriers around Veren's houses while Zephyr removed all traces of the sorceress's tether. Veren seemed keen, liaising with Shawn and occasionally loaning him drivers so the younger Taverners could fill glyphs.

Once Ferryl drew them for him, Abel took his copies of all the glyphs for barriers, and tree access, to Sheffield. The dragon head opened its eyes and greeted Abel when he entered the gryphon room, but didn't speak again. Finding a safe spot didn't take long. Abel found a wooden chest, tucked away behind the pedestal supporting the dragon's head. The chest already held three bags of sovereigns and a stack of tiny gold ingots, Pendragon's stash, so Abel added his sheaf of paper. A hook on the pedestal held a sword and dagger, in scabbards fastened to a broad leather belt. Abel felt he shouldn't ignore the dragon, but wasn't sure if he should, or what he should call it. In the end Abel just couldn't stand it any longer. "Do I call you dragon or gryphon? It's just that you aren't a gryphon, so, well…."

For a moment nothing happened, then the dragon's voice echoed in its head. "Gryphon is my burden, but I am still what remains of a dragon. In the old days I would have left my knowledge and skills for the next holder of this position, and passed into memory. There are no other dragons, so I persist."

"Can't you do that anyway, pass on? It can't be much fun stuck in here." Abel thought he'd want to let go, but Zephyr thought she knew why the dragon stayed.

"Nobody to leave everything to. It doesn't want all that knowledge wasted."

"I can look after the whatever for you? Then you can decide to put all your memories and skills in there if you've had enough." Though now Abel wondered if he could make a new gryphon, or had he just shot himself in the foot again.

"Tradition dictates an acorn as the magical receptacle for the iuloch, the Giving. A symbol of the potential within, just as an acorn holds the potential to become an oak tree. Though I have continued long past the death of my race, so mine would have been a very large acorn. I thank you for the offer, but no. A Dragon Kin-oath sworn freely to a Dragonfriend cannot be broken." The sheer finality in the dragon's 'voice' didn't leave any wiggle room.

"Okay, and thanks." That seemed a bit inadequate for a dragon's life. Thinking of what the dragon actually did prompted a question. "How do I add things to the demesne, so you know about it? Trees for instance?" That would be handy, because then Valdar's could be protected without Ferryl spending hours designing complicated glyphs for partial accesses.

"Press the head on your ring onto the object, then picture this. Be precise. You will feel me connect." An emerald green shape drifted to the wall, then the lines firmed up to form a glowing dragon's head. Presumably an adult, because this one had horns and a much more pronounced snout with bigger teeth. It looked thoroughly pissed off at something.

Even while Abel grappled with remembering that shape precisely enough, a voice in his head let him off the hook. "Got it. I will draw it in my book so I do not forget." Maybe the dragon overheard because they were both in Abel's head, or maybe Abel had a time limit. The head faded from the wall.

"Many thanks. Anything else I need to know? Is there a secret treasury?" That wasn't flippant; the Tavern seemed to be a money pit. The cash in the bank wouldn't last long if Abel had to open Taverns all over the country.

"Searching this room could be fatal for anyone but a Dragonfriend. There are no more, and never will be because only a free dragon can gift the title. That is all I can tell you." Not an answer about the treasury, but a definite warning about searching. Abel thanked the dragon again and got out. He talked it over with the Taverneers on a trip to mark all Valdar's trees, but there wasn't a way round it. They all felt sorry for the head, trapped by an oath that could never be lifted because there were no more Dragonfriends, in a job it couldn't leave because there were no more dragons. Jenny offered to grow a giant acorn for the job, just in case. She really did like her plant glyphs.

*   *   *

Abel made sure to give Shannon and Una access to several trees, with nobody else there to see him add a little extra. He told them both why they got car keys, and which cars, and left the explaining to them. Una told everyone she got the Volvo because otherwise Robin D'Ritche would have stolen it, while Shannon explained that she'd prayed really hard for the convertible. Eric and Shawn arranged for all the Taverners who qualified, including Una and Shannon, to pick something from the goodies removed from Pendragon's and Valdar's houses. The carefully assessed selection contained clothing, jewellery, ornaments and even a few paintings that seemed to be about the same value. According to Eric, at least one Taverner chose a pair of shoes. Abel heaved a sigh of relief, and got back to revision.

Though even at school he couldn't totally ignore the Tavern, because of the Leferrier Memorial Park clean-up. The local TV had covered it properly, with before and after pictures and interviews with Eric, the headmaster, parents, some children and a very reluctant Council spokesman. Abel for one hoped nobody noticed that a few shrubs and plants had definitely grown, or flowered, between one picture and the next. If Pendragon Enterprises had been looking for real, non-magical security business they'd have been pleased at the publicity. Eric did them proud when he was interviewed, explaining the boarded up windows had been temporary, because the firm had only just expanded into Stourton.

Ginny settled into a routine, monitoring or mentoring Melanie and

Diane, or helping out filling hexes or lead bars when the pair were at school. She found a niche in the Tavern, because once reports of her concentrated glyphs spread, many of the newcomers asked for lessons. As a result, the less adept began to produce tighter, neater glyphs. Stung, the adepts tried much harder, and as a consequence became more economic with magic. Most Taverners allegedly continued their physical exercise, some of them using the two running machines and weights in the cellar at Stourton Refuge.

With the usual cramming for exams in full swing, the older Taverners had to spend most of their weekends on schoolwork. Kelis, always deadly serious about study, even told Tobias she didn't have time for a boyfriend as well as swotting. He didn't seem too bothered. Already deep in his own swotting for A levels, Tobias admitted he found Kelis's magical abilities downright off-putting for a beginner. Several others pointed out there'd be all summer for boyfriends and girlfriends, while other couples simply combined their studying.

The managers tried to fill the magical contracts by using younger Taverners, transported by drivers who had left school, though occasionally older adepts were needed. Four older Taverners, and a couple who had left school at sixteen, now lived in Sheffield to cover any weekday work. Many of the younger trainees were keen to get to the Tavern in Stourton at weekends, because Rachel had carried on the clean-up. Once they'd all contributed, filled hexes to help the business and earn extra magic, car-loads would target a new hot spot. Rachel stuck to public areas, like grassy areas used as dumping grounds or places like the town square, though none attracted quite the same attention as the park.

*　*　*

As May rolled by without any big ripples Abel began to relax a little. He should have known better. The first intrusion on his revising started as a phone call. Not a particularly welcome one, because after the last meeting Abel had hoped he wouldn't see Creepio for a while. Worse, the archbishop didn't seem happy. "I thought we understood each other. You promised not to poach potential magic users from the church."

Abel, still trying to drag his brain out of the economics of the Norman feudal system, had no idea what Creepio meant. "Who? When? Did we?"

137

Not coherent, but Creepio got the message. "Cecilia. A confirmed member of our church. Now she wants to become the Last Paladin."

"Who? I mean the Paladin bit. Do you mean Saint Georgeous? We explained she couldn't have a unicorn, not really." Abel's brain began to mesh. "We didn't try to recruit her. We thought she'd be horrified, once she got back to the convent and had time to think."

"You showed her a churchgoer, Shannon, storming into battle to defeat the wicked and rescue a maiden! Compared to that, we promised her several years of careful, dedicated learning until she could handle glyphs, then a position guarding the faithful." The vicar slowed up a little. "She spent an afternoon watching children younger than her juggling fire, then a fifteen-year-old blasted a full apprentice into oblivion in front of her eyes."

"Rachel? Shannon and Eric helped, and the bloke had already been hammered. We left Amanda and Cecilia at the rear to keep them out of danger, but Rachel spotted that one escaping." Abel wanted to bang his head on something, because he'd thought Shannon and Rachel would be less threatening for the two visitors. Instead they'd been inspiring?

"Rachel? Ha! She's filled that girl's head with nonsense about a mission, to defend the weak. Cecilia watched you stomp into a sorcerer's stronghold and flatten him, while I had to tell her we can't touch sorcerers unless they attack us or break the Accord." Creepio had definitely started running out of steam, but he still didn't sound happy. "When they came back, both girls were thoughtful. Amanda seems to be edging towards living a quiet life, away from serious magic and possibly back home with her parents. She's torn between the Tavern and church as the best people to help her with that." After a long pause, Creepio seemed to finally calm down. "Cecilia seemed really interested in magic, and how we trained the Church Militant."

"So why am I getting earache? Wasn't that why you sent her to see that mess at Frederick's?"

The odd noise on the phone didn't deny it. "Unfortunately that mess made you the valiant underdogs, doing the jobs the clean, rich churchmen don't. Though she didn't say that at first, not until we'd carefully explained how we'd never risk our people or their homes like that. Sweet

Cecilia asked lots of innocent little questions, some about the characters in your game, and the nuns saw no harm in talking about them." Creepio's complaining tone changed, becoming totally serious. "The Last Paladin is real. There are reliable records of his or her appearance, as a glowing figure in armour, riding a magnificent white charger. The real Last Paladin wields a sword of light that will cut to the heart of any evil, and is covered in white armour infused with the power of prayer. What Cecilia has seized on is that the Last Paladin only appears to those with a just cause. It doesn't matter if you are church or heathen as long as your fight is just, and hopeless." He finally managed a chuckle, definitely black humour. "If you see him or her approaching, even as an ally, make your peace with your gods."

"You can't blame us for any of that." Abel tried really hard to keep his smirk out of his voice. "So Saint Georgeous is real?"

"No, but near enough for a starstruck seventeen-year-old. She has rewritten her own rescue." The vicar paused, definitely calmer now. "No, not rewritten, just looked at it from a different perspective. Your Tavern stormed the leech nest, killed most of them and made off with a rescued victim. The church mopped up afterwards. We found Cecilia and Amanda in the cellar and freed them, but we couldn't remove the leech seeds. We killed their companion when we tried. You pulled the seeds out of the victims, something the entire church couldn't manage." A heartfelt sigh sounded down the phone. "She asked a lot of different people, just a question here and there, and pieced her own version together. Brace yourself, because she'll want to start a crusade."

"What!" Abel paused. "Zephyr, you heard all that. Let Kelis, Rob and Ferryl know, then contact Ginny on the tether. She can tell Frederick, and use the tether to tell Diane and through her, Jenny." He went back on the phone. "When will she be here? I thought she'd been badly injured?"

"Not for a week or two, but any time after that. Cecilia wasn't as badly hurt as Amanda, which I accept was my fault. I'd rather Cecilia didn't live in that mess?" Another long sigh sounded. "She'll think it's noble."

Abel told Zephyr to call off the panic. Cecilia wasn't on the way, not yet. "The bedrooms are perfectly respectable, and we've had the workmen in to fix most of the rest." This time Abel let his humour into his voice. "If your bishop had let us lease the church, that might be ready and she'd feel right at home. We've had some substantial donations so we can afford it now."

"I must make another confession. You should take the cloth if I'm going to do this very often. On top of my worries about how power would affect you, I have been a little upset about you taking the girls into that fight." Somehow Abel didn't think that could be the confession. "The bishop asked me to contact you, but it slipped down my in-tray. I'm still not comfortable with heathen sorcerers using church property."

"He's agreed to the lease?"

"No, to meet you. Then he'll decide. Try not to blow up more of his city in the interim." Although the vicar finally sounded amused, it wasn't good news for Abel. "That's Sheffield. He'll meet you in the Cathedral Church of St. Peter and St. Paul."

"Will you be there?" Because with Creepio in this mood it would be the kiss of death on the whole idea.

"No. Our branches of mother church have differing ideas on the exact nature of our worship. The Church Militant defends all those who worship the One God, but we don't exactly socialise." For the first time in this phone call Abel heard the vicar's familiar, slightly mocking tone. "As an Englishman you may feel more comfortable with his version."

"Not really, I tend to lump you all together. Have you told me about this meeting in time to attend, or will I have to apologise and try again?"

"You have his number. He might have expected you to call earlier, but I wanted to be sure your moral stance had survived your victory over Pendragon and promotion. I'm sure Valdar and Boudicca think so." The parting shot sounded a little waspish. "Perhaps you should take your church contingent with you, to make a good impression." Abel stared at the phone for a while, trying to get it all straight, but however he looked at it he'd been stuffed. Thirty minutes later, after answering calls from Stourton, Jenny, Rob, and a combined Kelis and Ferryl, Abel tried to drag his mind back to his history revision.

*　　*　　*

One worry never materialised, because Rachel and Shannon volunteered to look after Cecilia, and stop her getting carried away. They could only meet up at weekends and evenings, but Shannon could run them about in 'her' new motor. Cecilia would spend her days in Stourton Refuge with Frederick, but only until the summer holidays. By then Frederick would be ready for the inspections. Once he accepted the first real charity cases, the place would stop being a social club for would-be sorcerers. He'd even arranged to hire staff, until those Taverners who wanted a career in caring could qualify. Eric had started looking for an alternative location for Taverner practice, though they could keep using Frederick's cellar for a while without any residents noticing.

Eric's call about new training premises seemed innocent enough, until the "so our security staff can train there as well."

"They're all Taverners, so how can they practice as well as the Taverners." Garbled, but Abel's brain felt that way.

"You said to manage the business, to make a profit for the Tavern. Didn't your mum say anything?" Eric suddenly sounded cautious, so Abel made an effort to sound less stressed.

"Sorry, I'm revising so I'm a bit wound up. Mum tells me bits of social stuff, but never discusses actual work. Maybe it's a privacy thing, or she doesn't expect me to be interested." By now Abel had his brain aimed in the right direction. "Security work, or people. Non-magic staff?"

"Yes. It was all that publicity after the Easter dance, then the reports about the park clean-up. Several people called asking us to supply door staff, for a dance or a wedding, and a couple of people wanted us to patrol their premises at night. I told them I'd get back to them and called Shawn. He's already got some ordinary business, supplying security equipment or maintaining it." By now Eric had started warming to his theme. "We reckoned it could work. Some of the Taverners won't get many qualifications at school, so they'll be after any job with a wage. Shawn is a case in point, and I'm not much better. We aren't really qualified to do this job but the staff do the real work. Security is steady work but can be dangerous, unless they can throw a glyph."

Which made sense to Abel, because a glyph-wielder didn't need as much muscle. "I'm all for it, but why do we need non-magical ones?"

"Because they know what to do, proper unarmed non-magical training, procedure, laws, that sort of stuff. We'll team them with a

Taverner beginner, then if things get rough the beginner can add a bit of magical help. Meanwhile it's on the job training, and we make some extra money. I thought that if our people spot a customer who sees things, hints of creatures, we could offer hexing as well?" Eric didn't sound as sure about that, but Abel liked the idea. The more who paid for hexes, the more poorer areas the Tavern could afford to protect. "Remember we asked for gym equipment?"

"I remember. You brought in a couple of running machines, so you can all drag a car about like Ferryl."

Eric chuckled, because that really was the reason. "Two wasn't really enough. I've found a unit for rent, on a run-down industrial estate so it's cheap. Security won't be a problem for us, so we can put in training equipment for Taverners and the security staff to tone up. Shawn snapped up some kit from a business that went bust, and thinks it might be worth opening a proper gym eventually. It all ties into the security aspect, even the magical side." Eric waited, but not for long. As Abel tried to work it through in his head, the amateur manager just had to ask. "Well, what do you think?"

"Rent the unit, and I'll bring Ferryl and Zephyr round there this weekend to put in security hexes. Have a word with the batlins to see if they'll fly around the place at night, as a sort of backup." He thought hard, but Abel had told the two managers to manage, so… "Go for it, but keep the costs down to start with. Please walk, don't run. I'll talk it through with you both, properly, at the weekend. Meanwhile Physics homework beckons."

"For me as well, to help me learn the dirt-sieving and rock-making glyph. And Biology, for the healing. Shawn is talking about an Open University course in Business Studies, while I'm doing more school work than I did at school. Though only when I can fit it in." A relieved Eric rang off, while Abel abandoned homework to call his friends. They'd mull it over until the weekend, then meet to talk properly. Abel remembered those security men of Pendragon's. Even without the guns, a couple like them might come in handy in a situation where nobody could use magic. With a smile he thought of one possible candidate, providing Claris could keep her temper until she actually needed to hit someone.

*   *   *

142

Before the weekend Ginny added one more worry, because this time there wasn't any doubt what Melanie saw. From her bedroom window, the red cap on the metre-tall, thin toadstool-like creature, just outside the back fence, couldn't be missed. Since Ginny could peek down the tether, she'd done so after Melanie had called her. The tether showed thoughts, not a view, but Melanie totally believed she'd seen the thing. After a very quick meeting in Castle House, called by a furious Rob, Ferryl suggested traps. Not like those she'd once installed in Abel's fruit bushes, something stronger because this creature must be able to pass the boundary posts.

Rob seemed happier when Dryad Sycamore confirmed it had a seedling ripening, though the process would take weeks. Abel made a phone call to alter the original tree order. The red maple sapling Rob had allegedly bought, for his garden at home, would now be much larger and stronger. The firm would suddenly have a problem getting the right size, and would offer the more expensive mature one as compensation. Abel didn't even know which of his woods it would be coming from, but Terese sounded confident. With a mature tree nearby to supply magic, Ferryl could catch even a strong mystery watcher.

Meanwhile, the batlins would watch Rob's back fence at night, as much as they could while they were out hunting. Rob really was tempted by the idea of a goblin in his garden, on permanent watch. Unfortunately, even he couldn't come up with a reason he would buy a large, grotesque, expensive-looking garden ornament. More to the point, none of them really trusted the goblins to keep it looking exactly the same all the time.

Despite everything else, Kelis seemed most preoccupied by the SOLD sign outside her old house, complaining that she hadn't finished with the dryads yet. She'd nipped round to the gardens and removed the iron spikes that held the security cameras, so at least the dryads talked to her. Now Kelis had a deadline, trying to persuade them to supply magic to a part of the village boundary before the new owners moved in, and stopped her trespassing. She'd offered a young tree in her own garden as a home for a seedling, but the six dryads wanted one each or none of them would help. Kelis couldn't plant six almost mature trees in her mum's garden, even if the landlord allowed it. Abel ignored the sharp glance at him when she mentioned landlords. Kelis still wondered if he'd bribed the letting agents to add a convenient extra bedroom, just so that Ferryl could move in as well.

Kelis's complaints to the other Taverners encouraged some of them to talk to dryads in other locations, about protecting areas around their own homes. Abel might be asking Terese for more trees to house seedlings. Even a trickle of magic from a willing tree would power the hexes to clear creatures from a whole street, whereas replenishing the magic in hexes on fences and lamp posts turned into a continual, boring necessity. As the protected areas spread, filling enough lead bars to supply magic for all the hexes would become a logistical nightmare. The problem came down to finding places to plant the trees, places the Taverners could collect magic without being noticed and also, hopefully, where a guardian dryad would feel safe. Abel felt sure the Taverners would find a way, sooner or later.

Abel called the bishop, or his office, and explained that he really wanted to lease the church but couldn't come until his exams were over. The delay put a bit of a crimp in Abel's half-formed plan to install Kelis's mum as the secretary, housekeeper or some other position in the old church. She didn't have much of an education, and her husband had kept her secluded and subdued, so Mrs. Ventner had neither a driving license nor job skills beyond her brief modelling career. A job as house mother in the church, with a qualified assistant, would give Kelis's mum some income.

Abel hoped the bishop believed him about exam pressures, because according to Ferryl, and Ginny, sorcery and advanced education didn't usually go together. The two of them explained that magic activated any time after puberty. As a result, those who discovered magic naturally usually did so during the years they should be swotting for exams. If a sorcerer offered them an apprenticeship, the youngsters spent their days filling hexes instead of attending school. If not, the visions of creatures wrecked any chance of studying anyway. Even if the teenager managed to stay at school, few stopped on for sixth form or college.

Most of Abel's problems were being put off until after the exams finished, but then he'd have to cram everything in before the start of the school holidays. Jenny would be launching Bonny's Tavern as soon as school broke up, so Abel wouldn't have time for much else. He expected a few emails almost immediately after the launch, in reaction to the artwork. People who had become aware of magic, but hadn't really learned what it was, would recognise the creatures, realise they hadn't been hallucinating, and make contact. Others, who were close to becoming aware, would be tipped over the edge when they started playing and meditated, or tried to float a leaf.

At least opening the next door inside Castle House wasn't a problem, because nobody had any idea where the key might be. The first exams hit, and after that Abel didn't have time to think of anything but school until he'd finished the last one.

Cherubs and Souls

In retrospect, Abel should have realised that leaving the likes of Rachel unsupervised might cause problems. Not that the younger Taverners actually broke the Accord. Ginny had heard gossip from other sorcerer's apprentices, about some sorcerers skirting very close to breaking the Accord or actually breaking it. Pendragon even boasted that the leeches in the two apprentices were deliberate, part of his plan to take control of Abel and gain access to Castle House. He also hinted of larger plans, but Ginny never heard any details.

Abel and his friends had read the Accord, then been embroiled in exams. Now they were over, Abel found a list of problems needing his attention. There'd be no peace during the two weeks before school officially ended for the summer, because he had to get them all settled. This time Jenny wouldn't delay the release of Bonny's Tavern. The publicity about the charitable side had grown, locally, and she wanted to take full advantage. Mr. Forester egged her on. He'd been chafing at the bit ever since Easter, and tweaking his daughter's preparations while she took her exams. At least he'd been persuaded to keep the first launch concentrated in a few locations in the UK, to help Jenny cope, though the internet meant word might spread.

Now Abel found out that while the older students were busy with exams, Rachel had pushed on with her own agenda. Together with her willing accomplices, mostly younger Tavern players, her magical clean-up crews made a real impact on the public areas of Stourton. Especially magically, because Rachel could now put a glyph or hex below the surface of solid objects so the areas stayed clear of creatures. The public might not notice the lack of magical pests, but they definitely saw the removal of rubbish, and how the areas stayed clean.

As expected there'd been a reduction in littering, once the likes of hoplins and thornies weren't raiding rubbish bins. One reporter even noted a reduction in insect bites, an unexpected by-product of fae being kept away by glyphs, and the lack of rubbish attracting other pests. Encouraged by their success, the magical Taverners had taken to occasionally walking through the cleared areas, extending their rubbish-clearing game beyond school. Using discreet, carefully controlled wind glyphs to tidy up litter, while practicing wind and water glyphs to clean off new graffiti, doubled up as magic practice.

Now several Taverners told Abel about rumours of fly tippers, and even some casual litter louts, being subjected to very strange experiences. The rumours were only among Taverners, none had shown up in the news or even at school. Even so, mystery voices in ears, burst tyres, tripping over nothing, and gangs of kids pointing and shouting at people dropping litter went far beyond what Abel had agreed. Barely minutes into his first visit to Frederick's after the exams, Abel found his way blocked by Rachel and Cecilia. "We want to move on to the next stage." Abel looked at his four friends, but they seemed as baffled as he was as Rachel continued. "We should clean up the not-so-public areas near infants' schools and playgrounds, and anywhere the yobs hang about causing trouble or leaving needles. We could wander around at night and cut down on muggings as well?"

"As far as I can remember, the meeting decided to leave police work to the police. From what I hear you've already gone beyond that." Abel noticed a dozen Taverners lurking nearby, pretending indifference. "Who is we?" He spotted Diane and Melanie. "Zephyr, use the tether and ask Ginny if either of her pupils has mentioned crime-fighting."

"Ginny hasn't heard any hints. Mel and Diane have helped in the public clean-ups on Saturday afternoons, because their parents allowed them into town for that."

At Abel's glance towards Ginny, Rachel smirked. "We didn't use much magic. A gang of kids waving cameras reminds most people where their litter should go. We didn't tell Mel and Diane about encouraging gremlins to concentrate on fly-tippers, because we know who else holds Ginny's tether. We include most of the magically-aware Taverners who haven't been taking GCSEs. That includes seven from St. Agnes Catholic Grammar School, some from the college, and a few Taverners who have left school."

Despite being reluctant to turn the fan club, or activists, loose where they might be seen, Abel found himself losing the argument. He'd even suggested cleaning up places that kids played, so protecting infants'

147

schools and any playgrounds from creatures and discarded needles was a natural extension. Rachel made her points quietly and clearly, and she was right, nobody else would clean the town up. Though Abel soon realised that Rachel wasn't being patient, she was just very determined because she just kept going. Eventually, he agreed to a limited campaign, to prove it could be done discreetly, but only because Shannon and several other adepts had offered to join the clean-up. "Make sure everyone can cast a glyph, without being obvious, just in case."

Una added the final touch. "If we meet something truly dangerous, a magical something, Robin D'Ritche can charge in to rescue them." She tapped her leg significantly.

"She has something hidden under a Seeming." Abel didn't have to guess what it was, not after the game character reference, though he asked for a quiet word later.

"If we're taking real adepts along, then the volunteers like me can go as well. I've been practicing glyphs, making a leaf flutter, but I can't really cast anything useful, not yet. That doesn't stop me using a brush and shovel." Cecilia spoke politely, but sounded very determined, so Abel gave way on that as well, but Cecilia wasn't finished. "The church will not deal with filth, disease, robbery and murder, and neither will sorcerers so it is down to us. I have read the Accord, and you have the right to deal with any crime in your demesne." The would-be Paladin paused, looking puzzled. "How big is your demesne? Does Castle House demesne include part of Sheffield, more than the park and that one house?"

"We've got a map. Didn't Shawn pass it round?" Ferryl's hand told Abel she had no idea. "Ginny, is there a map in the Stourton office, one with the combined demesne on it?"

"Veren and Ginny helped Shawn and Eric to draw the one you saw, with Pendragon's and Valdar's demesnes, and we included the villages with Taverners. We don't know what Celtchar claimed in Sheffield, or what part of the local area is technically part of Castle House demesne."

Abel spoke up before Ginny did more than shake her head. "Sorry Ginny, Zephyr has just reminded me we don't know enough. Is there a master map someplace, one for all the sorcerers to use?"

"As far as I could work out, bearing in mind he didn't really explain much, Pendragon claimed any area he could control. Stourton for a start, even though he bribed others to let him claim it." Ginny's little smile held definite malice. "Though he never mentioned the bribery part, just his monopoly. The office might have a map, though Eric never mentioned it?"

"I'll call by…." Abel stopped, because he couldn't call in at his own office. Mum would be there, and if the receptionist recognised him as the new owner the gremlin would be out of the magical sack. Abel decided against calling Terese, he had to learn to manage without running to Woods and Green for every answer. "Will someone call Eric about the map they made, and ask him to look through the papers in the office for a sort of super-map of all sorcerers? I'll ask Shawn to do the same. We can put it up on the wall." He paused as another thought struck him. "Frederick's first refugee moves in next week, a battered wife, so even if there is a map we'll have to find another headquarters in Stourton. Or I will, because everyone else can use my offices."

As the laughter died down Una's voice butted in. "Most of us already switched to the new place, the rented unit. Ask Eric to build you your own office in the gym." Abel laughed then followed as she started to move away.

He assumed she wanted to have that private talk, but before that? "An office?"

Una answered while the Taverneers followed her towards the door. "Why not? It could go above the showers. I've already asked for a room to practice sword-fighting, the real deal. Laurence has promised to give me lessons."

Abel never had a chance to ask about showers and sword-fighting. "Laurence? I thought he was off to Germany again, or was it Scotland?" Rob's smile grew as two pink spots appeared on Una's cheeks and she glanced cautiously at Kelis. "Is Robin D'Ritche capturing nobles for ransom?"

That stopped any chance of Una being embarrassed. "No, but it's a good idea. I need some better clothes now I'm driving a flash motor, even if I daren't let my parents find out. I have to wear a big hat so nobody recognises me around town, so it's a good job I looted a car that's big enough to wear one." The big grin showed she still loved the idea of looting. "I'll get my fencing lessons in Germany, because I've been invited to visit Laurence's relatives for a fortnight." Una turned to Kelis with a calculating look. "Hasn't Emst asked you yet?"

"Yes, but, well, with the launch of the game I won't have time. Jenny needs all the help she can get, especially from the designers." Kelis looked a little embarrassed. "Emst has got a thing about playing Bonny's Tavern with a real sorceress, though the real part is a joke because he doesn't know about magic. He kept emailing because I wouldn't talk on skype, not until the exams are over."

After the teasing about reasons why Emst really wanted to see a certain sorceress, Jenny looked very thoughtful. "Having one of the game designers in Germany could be useful. I've included a proper mini-launch there, because Emst and his cousins translated everything free of charge. Since you've learned to speak German, Kelis, you could meet reporters and answer any questions. I doubt anyone will activate their magic in the first week or two, but you could look at how to set up a Tavern in Germany if they do."

"How about in a proper hunting lodge, in a forest? According to Laurence he rescheduled from Scotland because Emst fluttered his leaf, several times, and wants to know if a certain somebody really is a sorceress. From the lack of surprise, I reckon there might have been a bit of surreptitious coaching going on." Una turned back to Kelis, her hand going to her mouth. "Tarnation, don't tell either of them I blabbed. It's supposed to be a surprise."

"It is a surprise!" Kelis dithered a little, then firmed up. "I'll ask mum. Laurence's parents will vouch for the German relatives. Flobbities! What about Rachel's project and meeting the bishop?" With a big smile Kelis relaxed again, turning to Abel. "I forgot. Someone has employees, a sorceress bodyguard, and all that filthy money so he can deal with it."

Abel couldn't really argue about anything but the cleanliness of his money, most of which he still couldn't get at until he reached eighteen, so he turned back to a patient Una. A quick glance showed nobody had followed them outside. "So how come you're carrying your sword all the time?"

Una confessed that she hadn't told anyone, but she'd taken to carrying the sword in case of magical trouble. She wasn't keen on fighting people, but the sword gave her an option after clashing shields. "That's something I want to ask you, Ferryl and Zephyr about. Something weird happened when I ended up fighting Boudicca." Once she explained what the sword had done to Boudicca's shield, everyone turned to Ferryl.

Ferryl had seen magical weapons that could allegedly penetrate shields, but they were all studded with gems in the hilts and had glyphs on the blades. "The Tavern hex glows red because Una filled the blade with magic, which will harm magical creatures. The blade glowed when it cut through creatures, so that might be a reaction to any magic." Ferryl sounded really puzzled. "Boudicca wasn't an experienced sorceress, but even so a defensive magical hex shouldn't have penetrated her shield. There's something odd about the Tavern shield, maybe because of how it came about. The way it acts tickles something in my memory, but I don't have the right information to work out what." She meant the right wit, shard of inscribed bone, not something to discuss in public. Ginny came over, looking curious, so Jenny told her they'd been discussing how the Tavern hex came about. Explaining how Kelis had drawn it based around part of Abel's personal ward, to expel slimies from her bedroom, neatly diverted the apprentice from weapons.

While Ginny brought the car, Una quietly agreed to keep the effect quiet from most of the Taverners until Ferryl figured it out. She'd email and ask Laurence to keep quiet about what his rapier might do, possibly the same as her sword because she'd re-burned his hex in return for sword-fighting lessons. At least the other swords used on the fursomnium weren't a problem, because Abel had removed the hexes after the fight. Talking about swords, but not how the hex worked, kept them all occupied on the short trip to the industrial park and their new gym.

*   *   *

The gym inside the utilitarian, slightly worn-looking building came as a shock to Abel, because it looked like one. He'd expected the running machines from the Refuge, with maybe a couple of rowing machines and a few weights, not lines of gleaming apparatus. Una had appointed herself as the guide. "According to Eric, Shawn picked up all the equipment dirt cheap from a gym that went bankrupt. He's working on buying more matting someplace, the same way because little businesses are always failing. We've only used a third of the floor space here, but that's more than the gym that shut down." She swept a hand up and around the concrete floors and metal walls. "The place needs a coat of paint at least, but we haven't got that far yet." The fifteen teenagers working up a sweat didn't seem to mind the decor. Three men and a woman didn't even look up, engrossed in keeping their definitely toned bodies in shape.

Abel wanted to ask why strangers were in here, people too old to be discovering magic, but Una kept going. She put her hand on a grill in a door in the block wall, before opening it to reveal an alcove big enough for three or four people. A second door, to the side, let Abel out again without anyone in the gym seeing what lay beyond. He stopped for a moment, staggering a couple of steps when Kelis pushed him, and looked around. "Crikey." The wall, which Abel could now see had been built much thicker than necessary, separated the gym from a completely different sort of exercise area.

At the other end of the huge area, a rough-cast concrete wall absorbed any stray wind or fire as intent teenagers took turns casting glyphs at painted targets. The more adept Taverners were coaching the beginners, while others practised controlling water, meditated on cushions or jogged along the opposite wall levitating leaves, pebbles or half-bricks. Even as Abel watched, a beginner, coached by Petra, practiced wind glyphs to scour away scorch marks.

Petra saw Abel, told her pupil to take a break, and strode over with a big, welcoming smile. "Well Abel, what do you reckon to it?"

Abel took his time answering, looking slowly around to take it all in. The chairs, small tables, several mats and makeshift targets were mismatched and well-worn, strictly utilitarian and not all that impressive. All the activity, carefully organised with warning signs and marked out practice areas, came as a complete shock. "When did all this happen?"

"It sort of grew, a bit at a time. Frederick's house passed the last inspections, so it will soon be a refuge and we needed someplace else. Eric said you'd okayed renting the unit, and the gym equipment doesn't use even half the floor space, so we had a brainstorm." Now Petra looked a little apprehensive. "Some of the Taverners put up the first part of the wall, which is why it's rough, then Eric paid for brickies to come in one weekend. The thickness more or less stops any noise coming through into the gym. You kept saying you hadn't time for Tavern business until the exams were over, but anyone who wasn't cramming, or wanted a break from revision for an hour now and then, pitched in here."

Abel turned to the door, but Una answered before he could ask. "It's locked against non-magicals, and the alcove and side door stop anyone seeing straight in when it's open. You'll need decent control of wind glyphs to open the outside door, so nobody can wander in by mistake." Abel nodded, that explained Una putting a hand to the grill in the door.

Encouraged, Petra's enthusiasm came back as she explained the system that the adepts, the more proficient magic users, had set up. "There's a rota, but adepts earn extra time to practice against the wall by teaching beginners. Either that or they take extra lead blocks to the park and fill them with magic. In here we can really cut loose without anyone non-magical noticing."

"Did you ask about a village tree yet?"

"No." Petra looked a little abashed. "I wanted to work up to it, but there's no point now. Abel, what's the chances of getting a tree transplanted to some of the villages, a biggish one without a dryad? Like we are trying to do in town? We can use it to protect the village properly, start a boundary like the one round Brinsford. As a bonus, if any of us are grounded or can't get to town for some other reason, we don't lose out on practice." She stopped, hesitated, then ploughed on. "I know you charged Laurence for his trees, but most of us can't afford those prices. We'll dig the hole? With magic? Good exercise and a bit of practice combined? We can take lead bars home to fill them in our own time?"

One part of that snagged Abel's attention. "Whoa, back up. When did I sell Laurence a tree?"

"You sold him a lorry-load, six of them. He didn't realise until the same delivery man brought them as took the dryad seedlings away. When Laurence asked, the driver told him Woods and Green organised the sale." Petra looked puzzled, as did Una and several others who had drifted over to join the group.

Abel racked his brains, until Zephyr prompted him. "Someone from Woods and Green asked if you'd sell the trees used for transporting dryad young. You never asked who bought them."

"Zephyr has a better memory than I have. The phone call didn't mention Laurence, just asked if I'd sell the trees instead of putting them back where they came from." Abel shrugged. "Since replanting would have cost me, but selling the trees paid some of the costs of resettling dryads, I said yes. To be honest, I have no idea what trees cost."

That led to a couple more questions, including why Abel had been rehoming dryad seedlings. Laurence might have guessed, but he hadn't told anyone. Now everyone knew about Castle House, Abel confessed that's what he'd paid to get the magic for fixing Laurence's house. "Laurence said he'd pay for getting magic if he had to, so he won't mind. He's too busy crowing about the extra magic from his trees, and the baby dryad guarding them." Petra tried to sound casual, but couldn't. "So what's the chances of a village tree here and there? The ones in my village are all claimed by the church, but in other places it's dryads."

Although he hadn't thought about it, Abel should have. He'd been able to fill up with magic from the trees in Castle House gardens, so topping up hexes on posts wasn't a big drain. Elsewhere the Taverners had to use up their lead bars, which would cut down on their practice. "I'll sort out where there's a spare tree, and the best size." Abel would ask Terese, since she'd organised Rob's tree as well. "Working out the practicalities, and digging the hole, will be good practice for if we have to do it anyplace else, once the game goes live. I can give you the tree, but digging up and carting it about costs money. Any help will be appreciated."

*　　*　　*

Petra gave Abel a hug before going back to her student, but Una wanted to get his verdict on the room. "Can we keep going with this place, Abel, improve it? We'd like to extend the concrete wall, thicken it and make it an open-sided cube so no magic escapes." She looked at Abel's tattoo, then Ferryl. "Then we can ask one of your sorceresses to put a shield around it, just in case someone gets too enthusiastic. We can use the top of the cube as a floor to store things, or put a coffee machine?"

"I'd rather not, just in case something leaks upward. We could build a second floor along the side, to free up the floor space down here. That way trainees will have somewhere to sit and relax, and compare magic, where we won't get in the way of the runners for starters." Warren, one of the original betas, pointed upwards. "The roof must be fifteen metres high in the middle, and except for the concrete practice wall, any space above three metres is wasted. We need a disabled toilet as well, now we've got disabled Taverners, and a ramp or lift if we build an upstairs." As Warren pointed here and there, several Taverners nodded enthusiastically.

Justin, Rachel's older brother, noticed Abel's startled look at the mention of disabled Taverners. "Two of our latest recruits turned up at Frederick's house in their wheelchairs, rather than email a mythical sorceress when a leaf fluttered. They'd put the Bonny's Tavern game and the publicity about the Refuge together, and come up with a magic club. Now they want to know if magic can help them walk again." Justin looked hopefully at Abel's tattoo. "We told them about healing injuries, eventually, but we weren't sure if magic could fix old damage or birth defects."

"I rebuilt this body, so providing they are capable of advanced glyphs, the two in wheelchairs will eventually walk again. That level of expertise might take more than a normal life span, so perhaps you should just promise healing might make some difference." Abel passed the last part on, and was promptly dragged off to see where Warren wanted the additional toilet. That wasn't as simple as expected, because those sort of facilities had to serve both training areas.

Once he'd seen the changing rooms and showers, just bare pipes and breeze blocks and no proper lockers, Abel sat down to look at what else the Taverners had in mind. Eric arrived part-way through, after someone told him about Abel's visit. He brought a list of things he wanted Abel to authorise, even if he'd already gone ahead with some like the gym. Despite trying to let Eric and Shawn run everything, Abel couldn't get away with it. Both managers, especially Shawn, relied heavily on the experience of the staff in Sheffield and were influenced by their attitude.

When Abel repeated that everyone seemed to be doing fine without needing his permission for every little thing, Eric shook his head. "We all know it's down to you, and we're never sure if you'll okay what we've done. Ask the staff at Sheffield, the ones who know about the magical part. Bertram the secretary and Marianne the receptionist saw you claim the gryphon, and have no doubt about who their boss really is." He tried to take the sting out of the next bit, but the smile didn't change the harsh facts. "They'll remind anyone who needs it exactly how much power the master holds. To be honest, most of us got the message at that meeting about loot, even if you didn't rub our faces in it. Under magical law you personally own everything, including the bank balance." Eric's hand swept around to include the building and contents. "If you say so, this closes down in five minutes flat."

He might change that in time, but for now Abel gave up on a lost cause. "What about cash? Do I need to sell anything else?" He hoped not, because he'd already sold most of the valuable antiques from Castle House. He didn't expect Eric's laugh.

"Ask Shawn if you need cash. The bank balance is healthy, but if you need to sell any ornaments he's got plenty. A few Taverners helped him strip the best out of the houses in Sheffield, Pendragon's and Valdar's, and stashed everything so you can sell a bit at a time. He offered the rest to anyone entitled to loot, then after they'd chosen put the remainder into the war chest or whatever. According to Shawn and a couple of those who are living in the houses, some of the rest of the pictures and ornaments are too good to be left in student digs. The collection isn't even close to the standard of what you sold from Castle House, but there's more of it." Eric slowed up, sounding more cautious now. "That's if you go for that. We don't know if you want to rent the houses out or sell them, though we are assuming you'll keep one for when you go to University?"

"Maybe." Abel made one snap decision. "I'll keep one for any Taverners who want to live in Sheffield permanently, probably Pendragon's apprentice house. We have contracts from both Valdar and Pendragon, so the tenants can pay rent by filling hexes with magic. I'll keep another one at least for the likes of Shannon to live in while they are at the Uni. I'll have to look at them all properly first." Abel had only seen the houses once, briefly while Ferryl fixed the magical barriers around them. "I got a rough idea of what was in the houses, but it was rushed so I'm not sure if all the goodies are real or magical fakes."

"Who knows?" Eric glanced at Abel's tattoo and then Ferryl as he realised who could tell. "Does it make a difference?"

"Only if we sell to sorceresses. Even then, they can't always tell without testing." Ferryl smirked, because the gold blocks in Eric's belt were actually magically transformed lead. The created gold stored magic as efficiently as real gold, unless the glyph in the centre failed when the whole thing turned to worthless gravel. "Pendragon's valuables should be better quality than Valdar's, so I'm sure Abel will sell off Valdar's for starters."

None of them expected Eric's laugh. "The secretary in Sheffield, Bertram, reckons the Master of Castle House will consider anything Pendragon had is cheap tat. Abel will apparently sell all Valdar's stuff, or possibly just make a big bonfire of it." He sobered, glancing around at the Taverners who had gathered to listen. "There's some really good stuff still in Pendragon's house, like gold bath fittings and door knobs. We can sell the jewellery from the apprentices, but what about all the good suits and dresses?"

"Forget the bath taps, because Zephyr reckons they aren't real gold, but we could have an upmarket market stall with the rest?" Despite the jeers, Rob stuck to his guns. "The clothes are better than those in the charity shops, and we could get rid of the last remnants of the dead apprentices." Eric for one promptly asked if he could buy a suit at market stall prices.

Una teased Abel about not being able to drive so he didn't get a car, only a chauffeur-driven taxi, but Shannon shot a glance at Ginny. "You should upgrade anyway. I'm surprised your chauffeuress hasn't already suggested that Range Rover of Valdar's, because it really is top of the range." As Shannon began to list the umpteen extras, Abel smiled quietly, remembering how she'd gone on about the leather seats in the car Creepio once loaned them. He wasn't surprised she liked Boudicca's convertible. "Eric and Shawn only let the really level-headed Taverners drive it, because a bump could be really expensive. A couple of us worked it out, and we reckon it cost about a hundred and eighty grand brand new."

"But it isn't big enough." Ginny shrugged and glanced at Abel. "I'll admit I'm not against driving around in a better motor, but if Abel wants all the Taverneers along he has to take the BMW SUV. Sorceresses always have much better cars than apprentices, it's a status thing, but I'm guessing Abel doesn't care."

"The Range Rover stays as a pool car, unless anyone can figure out how to give it to my mum?" After laughing at Abel, Una pointed out he'd probably choose a tranny van that could take Kelis, Rob, Jenny and

Ferryl over any car that wouldn't. The discussion turned to poser motors in general, and where they'd come from.

*   *   *

"I told you the car shows the status, but sometimes a surviving apprentice inherits a good car when their sorcerer dies." Eric looked over the list. "No wonder the apprentices all want to get off the tether, there's a hell of a gap between the boss's motor and even the senior apprentice. Valdar's apprentices shared a Peugeot estate car and the Mercedes minibus we captured in Stourton, while he drove the Range Rover. Shawn also found four really nice motorbikes in a shed round the back of one house, 125 cc so anyone with a CBT can use them."

Several of the Taverners visiting Sheffield to fill hexes had asked about the bikes, so Shawn had added them to the company fleet. "It's another of those things we need you to decide, Abel. They're dead handy for nipping around town to fill hexes, and anyone who passes their CBT can ride one?" Eric shrugged uncomfortably, not sure if they'd done the right thing. "Shawn uses one to go into the city centre, to get through the traffic, but the others are locked up most of the time. I could do with one of them here."

"You were going to buy a bike with the fifteen hundred quid from the jewellery we sold, so you could zoom off to inspect your trees." Kelis's smile had a lot of mischief in it. "Though now you've got a driver and choice of motors?"

"Good idea. Then I can get into town without Ginny or one of the other drivers turning up to get me. Mum is already wondering how come so many people with nice motors want to pick us up." Abel grinned back at Kelis. "Better still, it's a freebie." His face fell. "No it isn't. Flobberclomps! I'll have to buy it from the firm, and pay insurance, or mum really will have some awkward questions." After a moment while everyone processed that, Abel had to put up with the laughter and teasing about being the only Taverner paying for his vehicle. Worse still, Ferryl announced that she didn't mind riding a company motorbike.

Faced with an opportunity like that, Rob dithered, but decided against buying one. He'd have the same problem as Abel if he brought a 'free' bike home. Since he wanted to hang onto his cash for now, he'd stick to the free taxi. Kelis wasn't interested. She already had her little car once she could drive it, and Jenny had her scooter.

Abel spent a couple of hours at the industrial unit, and really enjoyed himself discussing the business, and plans, and who could now cast which glyph. During the exams he'd missed meeting the other Taverners, swapping gossip and comparing notes on magic, but now Abel found one big difference. The loot meeting, followed by his self-inflicted absence to concentrate on exams, had given the Taverners time to really understand the Master of Castle House and Pendragon Enterprises titles. While they all still joked with Abel, when it came to the actual business all the Taverners treated him like a real employer. They were respectful, but definitely not deferential because they still went to the same school.

On the way out Abel met the three men and a woman he'd noticed on the way in, all in their late twenties. Eric introduced him as the boss, which made Abel twitch a bit but he couldn't use his name in case they talked about him in the office. These were the first of the new security staff, so they would be meeting the new secretary, Abel's mum, now and then. All four had experience, and were willing to take on trainees. Another two would be joining them, giving Eric a dozen with the Taverner trainees. The continuing local publicity for the Tavern included occasional pictures of the minibus, now sporting a sign stating it had been donated by Pendragon Enterprises. As a result Eric had contracts to patrol two industrial estates and two gated housing estates, and a scattering of bookings for functions and dances.

While heading home, Abel and his friends made plans for a full day visit to Sheffield, though Rob kept being distracted by his new toy. Eric had bought some security equipment, including telescopic steel batons, so Rob finally had a replacement for his ruined rounders bat. He even had a little holster for it, and would be hiding it under a Seeming just as Una did with her sword. Ferryl eventually had a look at the baton, and became very interested. The steel tubing would hold a lot of magic if Rob inscribed the Tavern hex on each section. The sorceress suggested everyone in the car carried one under a Seeming, hexed and loaded with magic, because the modern world frowned on carrying swords and daggers.

*   *   *

A week later Abel might have felt more comfortable carrying a sword, or possibly a machine gun. Now the exams were over he had time for his appointment with the bishop, hopefully to finalise leasing the church in Brinsford. Abel's nerves weren't helped by Ferryl and Kelis fussing about getting his four magic belts topped up. Kelis even offered to lend him her diamond, Rob offered his baton, Jenny her pink version, and Una asked if her sword would help. Eventually everyone accepted that if Abel ended up fighting clergy in a cathedral, no amount of magic or weaponry would help. The formal letter, extending the personal protection of the bishop for the duration of his visit, should mean Abel wouldn't need either.

Abel thought Ferryl would try to come inside as a bodyguard, but a quarter of a mile from the cathedral she asked Ginny to stop the car. "I can't get any nearer to the cathedral." Abel, Kelis, Rob and Jenny understood; Ferryl might be possessing a human body but she was a magical creature. Ferryl shot a warning glance at the back of Ginny's head, they couldn't let the apprentice know. "I have several hexes embedded in my bones to protect me from church magic, and the cathedral is rejecting them. I'll stay here, where I can see the front entrance."

"We've got it covered." Kelis patted her hidden baton. "If Abel needs us, we'll get him out." The rest agreed. Abel checked with Zephyr, but the tattoo seemed to be shielding her. Ginny pulled up a hundred yards away from the cathedral, because Abel didn't want to take everyone close enough to make any watching churchman nervous. After another round of nervous hugs and good wishes, he straightened his tie for the twentieth time and set off towards the huge spired building.

The new suit felt strange, the tie choked him, holding the new slimline leather briefcase would stop that hand forming a glyph, and Abel couldn't shake the feeling that a lot of very unfriendly eyes were watching. Someone must have had a photograph of him, because long before Abel reached the doorway a priest came out and headed his way. The priest's eyes were definitely unfriendly, and wary, when he planted himself in Abel's path, though he spoke politely. "You are the Master of Castle House and Pendragon Enterprises?"

"No, I'm Abel but everyone else seems to think that's not enough." He hadn't meant to say that, but then Abel hadn't expected the titles.

Now the grey eyes looked calculating. "Full titles are always used for initial introductions. After that the usual form of address for a bishop, and a sorcerer, is My Lord."

"I looked it up, and according to the internet the modern way is to call them bishop. I couldn't find an entry for sorcerers, but I really don't mind Abel." Abel didn't fancy calling the bloke My Lord, and really didn't want to answer to it. He wanted as close to a friendly talk as he could get, and My Lord seemed very formal.

"Bishop is acceptable from anyone who is not a sorcerer, and is preferred. Sorcerer-Bishop meetings are more formal." For the first time the priest's expression softened a little, impressed in spite of himself. "This is the first such meeting during my lifetime."

"Not really. I've met an archbishop several times." Abel tried to remember Creepio's real name, but didn't think he'd ever heard it. "A peripatetic archbishop from the Church Militant who prefers to be called vicar."

The priest knew Creepio but didn't like him, judging by the curled lip. "I meant a formal meeting at a cathedral. That particular archbishop tends to dispense with formality, though he doesn't usually meet sorcerers more than once or twice." Now the priest looked inquisitive, though it barely showed because he still didn't like the idea of Abel near his cathedral.

"I amuse him." Abel looked past the man. "Have all your colleagues had a good look? I'm out here in the open, I'm not carrying the equivalent of a magical nuke, and to be honest I'm not that good a sorcerer so you shouldn't worry."

"You carry a great deal of magic, and those titles mean you are a significant power. I'm told you also carry a tethered spirit, a very strong one? Such creatures are usually repelled by the cross in a church. The effect is much stronger near a cathedral." Now the priest looked definitely inquisitive, and had gone back to wary.

Abel hadn't considered that because Zephyr hadn't complained. "Is the church magic hurting, Zephyr? If so you should leave now because it'll be worse inside."

"I am safe in here. It is like when we went inside Castle House, right at the start. If I start to come out the air burns a little. I would like to stop with you, because if you need a Ffod bop I can stand pain for a little while." Abel almost smiled at the reference to Ffod, the Flying Fist of

Doom.

"Stay in there unless the fighting actually starts, because coming out might cause strife." Abel glanced at his arm, deliberately. "Zephyr is tethered, and inside the tattoo. She is unique, so maybe her tolerance is due to how she came to be?" Which Abel wasn't talking about, even though the priest left a long silence.

Eventually the priest turned towards the cathedral. "Providing the spirit remains inside the tattoo, that is acceptable. Please follow me, and stop immediately if challenged." As his escort turned, Abel saw a tiny ear bud, so the church used radios rather than spooky-phones or holy tethers. He followed, wondering what the man meant by challenged. As he came nearer, Abel tensed a little, but even so he wasn't prepared for the guards. Just inside the doorway were two deep niches, one each side, containing larger-than-life statues of a man in a robe holding a bible and a medieval knight. He'd barely started wondering if they were saints when the knight lifted its sword! Abel froze.

"The other one is full of magic as well. There wasn't any until you stepped inside the door, which is why I didn't see them. What should I do?"

"Nothing. I'm invited, so that must be an automatic reaction to you or my magic." Abel tried to keep his voice level, even if his heart still raced from the shock. "How come those two haven't been warned about me?"

"Some of us have wondered about you, and your protection. Your Tavern hex co-exists with the cross, even carried by the same person, and can be tattooed onto a confirmed Christian without negating their mark." The priest touched his forehead, but Abel understood anyway. "Those who are responsible for protecting churches wondered if our guardians would recognise you as a threat. Even now the answer is unclear. The saints have woken, what you would call a warning light, but they are not actually moving to block or expel you."

"I'm not moving either, not until you drain the magic back out or turn them off." If either of the stone figures started towards him, Abel would do his best impression of a startled rabbit, out through the doors and down the path.

"The bishop guaranteed your safety, so they will not attack you. They should have blocked your path, and we expected them to advance and force you to leave if you didn't retreat." Despite the assurance, Abel stayed put. He'd seen how fast magical attacks could be launched and oops, sorry, wouldn't fix his charred body. "I will ask, because I would prefer to keep them active. Just as a safeguard, because of what I read about the Master of Castle House."

"Not me. Celtchar is dead." Abel forced a chuckle. "I'm seventeen, and I haven't learned to self-heal so I won't be causing trouble."

The priest didn't seem to be listening to Abel, and didn't like whatever the earbug told him. Abel knew the answer before the priest spoke. "Magic is lessening. It is not draining away, just retreating deep inside, back to the shade or glyph inside the stone." The knight lowered its sword. "Both seem to be plain stone again, but not quite. Now I have seen them activate I can detect a trace, enough for them to sense each person who comes through the door. Next time we will not be surprised."

"Next time? Not likely."

"The bishop has given permission, another first. I have never seen the saints completely inert. Since you are the first sorcerer to visit him here, the bishop has asked me to show you our cathedral." Abel found himself on a completely unexpected conducted tour of the whole place, with a running commentary. While he walked a steady trickle of priests and what looked like ordinary people arrived to watch, from a distance. Some of them had quite animated discussions before leaving again, while others just seemed curious. Several looked either offended or worried, presumably by a sorcerer being allowed on their holy ground. The priest never mentioned the spectators, but he watched both Abel and his arm when they came closer to some areas like the altar. Abel wondered if the bishop wanted a test. Abel asked, privately, and those places had stronger church magic but Zephyr wasn't uncomfortable.

Under the priest's explanations of the layout, decor and carvings, Abel could hear a different version from his tattoo. The bishop might have skipped the tour if he'd realised Abel's passenger could see the sentinels, the carved guardians and the holy hexes in the roof and on the pillars. Even as the priest chose a path that went through some, and avoided others, Zephyr described the magical tripwires. Despite appearing to be defenceless, the whole cathedral would be a magical killing ground for the unholy. There might not have been many priests, but their creatures and fixed defences were formidable.

Abel would have loved to ask about the swords and bayonets forming a screen in St. George's Chapel. Not their history, because the priest explained that the chapel was dedicated to the York and Lancashire Regiment, and the weapons were donated when the regiment was disbanded. This chapel had been inspired by the number of local men, the Sheffield Pals, killed on the first day of the Battle of the Somme during the Great War, the First World War. The history part interested the history student side of Abel, but the blades captured his magical interest. The invisibly etched crosses, and the church magic Zephyr could see suffusing each blade, would definitely injure any magical creature, but Abel wondered if it would also pierce magical shields. According to Ferryl even a non-magic user would be able to wield Una's sword, once it had been charged with magic. If these worked the same way, any sorcerer attacking this place might find that even the congregation could be dangerous.

Eventually the priest took Abel through a small arch to a wooden door, insignificant against the sheer scale and splendour of the rest of the building. He didn't knock, just opened it before stepping back out of the way. "The Right Reverend, the Bishop of Sheffield. My Lord, this is the Master of Castle House and Pendragon Enterprises. Or Abel." The last bit sounded downright sarcastic, but Abel ignored it and walked in.

*   *   *

"Abel?" The white-haired man in a pale purple frock with a sash smiled, and held out his hand. It looked a totally natural gesture, but Abel caught the hint of calculation in the bishop's eyes.

"Zephyr? Is he shielded?"

"No, but the room has guardians."

That was all Abel needed, he took the hand and shook. "Yes, but I've been told to call you My Lord." The bishop must know what had been said, through the priest's radio link even if nothing else had been reported. Zephyr had spotted entities, magical creatures, moving about the cathedral and they probably reported to this man. "I was going to call you Bishop."

"Bishop will do, because you have just confirmed at least part of the reports. Coming into this room without a shield shows an unexpected level of trust. Please sit down." The bishop indicated a comfortable chair in front of a plain desk.

Zephyr must have known what Abel was thinking. "There is no magic in the chair. It is not like Redwolf's."

Abel sat and tried to relax. "I expected a lot more robes and a big hat, a mitre?"

"The archbishop assured me you wouldn't turn up in sorcerer's robes, and this is more comfortable. How much do you know about bishops?" Once again a little something in the man's eyes warned Abel, though he wasn't sure what the man wanted to know.

The answer wasn't difficult. "Not much more than what I found on the internet, which didn't mention magic. I know you are the equivalent of a sorcerer, but not what sort of strength. Going by the magic and defences in your cathedral, I would guess at a senior, powerful sorcerer?" The next part came without thought. "How old are you?"

That startled the bishop before he smiled, a genuine one without any edge. "That isn't a question one should ask a magic user. Since you have been honest and volunteered your age, I will tell you. I am approaching sixty. This is a relatively junior appointment, but no serving bishop is older than seventy. The biblical three-score years and ten." He chuckled, obviously reading the next question on Abel's face. "A bishop who lived several hundred years would be difficult to explain. We retire, allegedly die, and serve the church in less public roles. Even then there are restrictions on how long we can do so. Unlike sorcerers, we do not believe that man should have eternal life on Earth."

"Eternal life might get boring. I'd settle for a peaceful life, but that's not going to happen." Even as he said it, Abel realised he'd no idea how long sorcerers lived. Ferryl and Woods had survived over a thousand years, maybe a lot more, but neither was human. "How long do sorcerers usually live, human sorcerers?"

"An interesting distinction, because the church only recognises humans as sorcerers. All magical creatures are considered the agents of evil, though some must be tolerated and others can be useful servants. The oldest sorcerer I know of has lived just over seven hundred years.

They are capable of living much longer, but are either killed by rivals or make a fatal mistake experimenting with glyphs. Rumours insist some are older, but confirmation is difficult because they change identities and appearance." Now a wary curiosity showed through his pleasant smile. "How old are the non-human sorcerers? From your wording I am assuming you have met some?"

"I'm not sure." Abel wasn't mentioning names, though now he thought about it he genuinely didn't know their ages. "Defining the term sorcerer could be a problem in some cases. Dryads cast powerful glyphs and can be very old, while leeches move from host to host though they don't seem to be adept with magic." Now that he actually thought about it, he realised dryads didn't seem to use many glyphs. "What makes a person or entity a sorcerer? Is it their skill, or the amount of magic they control, or the number of glyphs they know?"

"So you know a very old being who probably qualifies in all three, and you are protecting its identity. Even so, I will answer your question. To be counted as a sorcerer, a human must know enough glyphs, wield enough magic, and be adept with enough glyphs and shields to remain free of a tether. Many are killed when they annoy a stronger sorcerer, or to keep the competition down. Dryads are skilful and command a great deal of magic, but because they can only cast through their tree, their glyphs are limited. They would not be considered sorcerers. Even so, most sorcerers and priests should steer clear of challenging an old dryad with access to mature trees. Why don't you join the church?"

There'd been no warning, so Abel answered the question without real thought. "Because you are as bad as sorcerers. You don't care about those who can't pay."

"Not because you don't believe in God, or believe in a different god?" From the way he'd hunched forward a little, eyes locked on Abel, the bishop had got to the real questions at last.

"I believe your God exists, but as I understand it any sorcerer with enough power and will can become a god. I've been told other gods still exist, but none of them have done much to help the average Jane Doe." As he spoke, Abel recovered, getting back on balance, but the bishop's mouth fell open in shock.

"You know how to become a god! That is forbidden knowledge!"

"Magic is building. We must leave. Ffod bop ready."

"We'll never make it." Abel put both hands flat on his head, a sign of surrender that stopped him casting glyphs. "I heard it could be done. I don't know how!" The bishop relaxed, only a little, but according to Zephyr the magic build-up paused. "An entity told me, when I asked if it was a god. Your knowledge isn't forbidden among the magical creatures." Zephyr murmured that the threats were easing a little, so Abel pushed on. "I only asked when it told me someone's dog had its own god. It meant the dog's owner. Apparently a huge amount of magic and believers are needed to make a real god and a heaven." The bishop seemed to have relaxed, but the magic hadn't dropped all the way, not yet. "Believe me, I have absolutely no ambitions beyond surviving to get the Tavern running, and maybe meeting Celtchar's gryphon. Though after meeting a gryphon that's a dragon's head, I'm not sure about the last one."

The bishop's lips twitched in an almost-smile. "The knowledge was supposedly purged from both the sorcerer and general church communities, anyone below very senior sorcerers and bishops. There were too many new gods and the wars between them, and between their followers, were creating chaos. This was long before the Accord. Because sorcerers tend towards secrecy and sudden death, the knowledge has almost died out. There have been no new gods since, and many of the old ones have faded away." He blew out a breath, relaxing, and smiling just a little as Abel cautiously lowered his hands. "Perhaps we were foolish to believe no magical creature knew that Gods were made. It would be best not to spread your knowledge, because some sorcerers are arrogant enough to be tempted. Though if magical creatures know, then some sorcerers must have learned despite what the church believe, and might already be experimenting. I will pass the news to the Church Militant."

"Why?" Abel didn't want Creepio coming after anyone he'd mentioned god-making to. He couldn't even remember who else knew, if anyone, though Ferryl might have told someone. "I can't un-hear it, but I'm not likely to shout about it. I don't fancy new gods either. I'm not keen on the ones we've got, or a visit from God's SAS." He froze, remembering where he was, but the bishop didn't seem too offended.

"I won't be sending the Church Militant after you, but I will warn them to watch for signs of someone gathering worshippers. As you said, any potential god needs a good number of them. Unfortunately, nobody knows the number." The bishop had either decided Abel wasn't a threat, or that he didn't want trouble in the cathedral. "Perhaps we can get back to the reason you believe in charity, dislike sorcerers, but won't join the church. Apart from not being keen on gods." The bite in the last bit meant Abel had offended the bishop after all.

"You take the money from believers to use in God Wars, to extend your influence, instead of looking after the villages and council estates in your back yard. From down in the dirt, there's not much difference between churches and sorcerers. Why isn't that priest out there leading the faithful to clean up Sheffield, or opening a church in a village overrun with creatures?"

"A good question, and one that is sometimes asked within the church. God Wars, as you put them, are often defensive. We must protect the souls of the faithful from the followers of other beliefs." For the first time he glanced at the papers on his desk, though he didn't seem to read any. "The church supports charitable acts all over the world, helping famine victims or taking medicine into jungle villages or plague areas. We have refuges for the homeless and the abused, and distribute food to those who need it."

"But look at this place." Abel waved his hands about to take in the whole cathedral. "Gold, jewels, fancy carvings and stained glass while some people sleep in cardboard boxes. More to the point, a cross or a hex would cost nothing, and keep the creatures from them even in a cardboard box."

"Not all of the gold is real, nor are the gems. Most of the genuine valuables are used by the Church Militant, to hold magic because they won't crumble if they take battle damage." The bishop settled back a little with a rueful smile. "The idea was for me to interrogate you, yet now I must admit to some truth in what you say. Our priests could place hexes where the homeless sleep, but we don't have many who are magically adept. Those we have either join the Church Militant or are sent as missionaries, to try and convert non-believers. Our intention is to save their souls, which can provoke a reaction. In some places that can become God Wars, as you call them, which are not strictly defensive. As far as wealth is concerned there is a substantial amount of gold in this building, to store magic. Enough gold to make a significant difference to the lives of my parishioners, but not enough to cure poverty or stop drug abuse and petty crime."

"You aren't saving souls, because their god will already have a heaven waiting for them. You are harvesting them, diverting them towards your God, and ignoring opportunities on your own doorstep. The wealth of your cathedral might not solve all the problems but it would help, make a start? Though even your charitable acts are to convert the hopeless and helpless, even if it's a gentle sort of persuasion. It's all a part of God Wars." Abel relaxed, deliberately sitting back when he realised he'd copied the bishop's pose. "Nothing I say will alter that, though I'm relieved you already recognise the problem and some church members are at least discussing it. Meanwhile I will be trying to help out a few people here and there. The people who live in the gaps, where there isn't any protection from magical harassment."

"The witches were supposed to fill the gaps." The bishop sat back as well, with a hand raised to stop the reply. "And places of worship keep closing because they aren't economic, leaving more gaps. Your reaction is what I wanted to see, the initial reaction before you thought about it. There is no hatred of the church; you are not our enemy. The next part is exactly what I had been told. You dislike our methods but feel the same about sorcerers. Now persuade me you won't use our building in Brinsford to recruit members for your Tavern."

"This meeting was supposed to be about the building. I brought plans, because Cre... the archbishop said you'd be worried about alterations to the structure. He knows we aren't actively recruiting." Abel tensed up again, because he'd no idea how to prove that.

"Why doesn't the church recruit?"

Zephyr had a point, because the likes of Shannon should have been a definite target. It had taken ages for the church to notice Mark, and he'd been pestering his priest about seeing creatures. "Why aren't you doing that, recruiting magic users? I'm told there are people out there who find magic on their own, and end up in therapy for the hallucinations. The sorcerers pick them over for apprentices, so why don't you set your missionaries on the same job? You could find the teenagers who worry about hallucinations and tell them about God, then send them out to put hexes on all those cardboard boxes." Abel leant forward, keen to make the point. He didn't really like the church, but now Zephyr had got him thinking. Becoming a priest had to be better than a mental breakdown.

That certainly stopped the bishop for a moment, though when he answered someone had obviously asked the question before. "Church dogma is clear. If someone is pure enough to accept the gift of God's power without being corrupted, God will lead them to the light. Mankind has free will, which includes the right to misuse God's greatest gift." Now the bishop tapped a finger on his papers, definitely unhappy. "Though you are taking some of those already chosen for God, confirmed teenagers, and putting your Tavern mark on them."

"Which doesn't affect their cross, or faith. Any of our Taverners can leave and join the church if they wish. One has, and he took his Tavern hex with him. We've got Taverners who wear a cross, or a Star of David, or possibly something else." Abel realised he'd raised his voice and deliberately relaxed again. "I don't even know what religion most of them are, if any."

"You are referring to Mark? A very confused young man, though he has since found peace and certainty. He still has the Tavern hex, though he is not allowed to wear it." The bishop thought for a few moments. "Aren't you worried that some of those wearing crosses might be spies for the church?"

"So what?" Abel opened his mouth to say more, then didn't bother.

Now the bishop leafed through his papers for a minute or two, actually reading them. "Perhaps one will find out if you really carry the shade of an untethered sorceress, or only a bound spirit? Though your question about what makes a sorcerer might mean the creature can be both, in your eyes. Since you don't see a difference between them and human sorcerers, do you believe magical creatures have souls?"

"I'm not sure I have one. If I do, then so do dryads and goblins, and probably a lot of others." Abel realised he had exactly the right person here to find out. "Why are you so sure we have souls? Can you see them?"

"No, but very experienced senior clergy, the magical ones, can detect them. When any life ends a tiny part continues for a while, a spark we call the soul. If the person is a believer the soul is called to the afterlife, their heaven. If not, it wanders until its magic fades."

That seemed a pretty definitive answer, though not a complete one. "When any life ends? So magical beings have souls?"

"No, though because they are formed from magic any fragments can persist for a while. Sometimes their fragment disappears quickly, according to some because it is drawn back to the adversary, while others find enough magic to eventually form another magical creature. Many just fade, or are eaten by magical hunters. Creature fragments may be the basis for the Hindu belief in multiple reincarnations." The wry smile admitted the Bishop had been caught, the church didn't have a definitive answer. "If you find a dryad preaching to magical creatures, let me know."

Abel remembered what Ferryl said after she purred to a cat in Brinsford. "He will worship, in the way of cats." He didn't know what the cat would worship, only that Ferryl wasn't a goddess so he kept his big mouth shut.

Zephyr broke into his thoughts. "I see them, the little sparks. I told you I hunt them. Should I stop? Are they souls? They seem to drift about without any real direction."

"Later. Stop hunting them for now, until we know." Seeing the curious look from the bishop, Abel knew something showed on his face. "My passenger sees the fragments, but didn't know what they were. Maybe we'll follow a few, to find you that preacher?"

"I really hope it isn't a dryad." That had been pure reaction, a strong one. The bishop recovered, then sighed in resignation. "Perhaps you should know. Dryads are magical creatures, so the church believe they are evil and should be destroyed. Haven't you wondered why there are still so many, and why we leave them in peace?" The bishop didn't wait for an answer. "If the church set out to destroy dryads we might unite them. Then we would be defeated, crushed. Most of the wild forests in the world, an incalculable amount of stored magic, are held by dryads. Luckily the creatures are insular, and generally peaceful if left alone. Dragons were their only real threat, and we destroyed the last one centuries ago." He chuckled, but still didn't seem entirely at ease. "Perhaps we should discuss those church plans, rather than unlikely disasters."

While he took out the plans Abel thought about what the bishop had said, both about the power of dryads as a race and the fragments that might be souls. Not for long, he soon had to concentrate on the job in hand. The bishop really did want to know how the alterations would be fitted in. The church would be de-sanctified and leased out, but the bishop wanted the building intact if an upsurge in faith made it a viable place of worship again. Abel felt really pleased he wasn't the sort to desecrate, because he found that de-sanctification meant disconnecting the Yew trees' magical connections. There were no wards stopping even goblins from entering the building, but damaging the altar or the graves would have brought extreme pain.

When Abel explained about the windows, and wanting to rebuild them, he ended up in a detailed discussion over what the stained glass would show. There were records for the designs on most of them, but two of the windows were plain so Abel wanted to put in his own pictures. Eventually the bishop conceded that Abel could replace clear glass with the Tavern sign on one window, and a scene with peaceful magical creatures and humans in the other. English heritage would insist the other windows were rebuilt exactly like the originals, which reassured the bishop. As he put it, that way both faiths were represented for any refugees. Abel showed where a clear path would be left to allow any relatives to visit graves, and promised the rest would be tidied and the church wall repaired.

Once they'd agreed, the bishop talked for a little while about the local area, magic versus faith, and Bonny's Tavern. They discussed both the actual game and what the magical members hoped to achieve. Abel told the truth, because one of the church-going Taverners would probably tell a priest anyway. The bishop touched on Sheffield, on the unofficial truce among sorcerers, and hoped that Abel didn't disrupt it any further. He suggested Abel meet the senior sorcerers, just to introduce himself and explain his plans so none of them caused trouble. Getting rid of Valdar, Boudicca and even Pendragon didn't seem to bother the bishop, as long as their replacement didn't make magical waves. According to him the whole area needed tidying up, but he refused to suggest ways to do so.

Eventually Abel had to ask. "Most sorcerers, and churchmen, are very tight-lipped. You are talking very openly, about the church and magic, so

I wondered if that's because you are a bishop."

"Firstly, this meeting is unique in my lifetime. Sorcerers never meet bishops, not formally, because a bishop represents more power than any one sorcerer can wield. Magic users don't like to feel inferior. I tried to find a record of the last meeting in this cathedral, and there has never been one because the sorcerer would be at the mercy of the bishop."

All his relaxation disappeared as Abel glanced around, waiting for the trap to spring. "So why did you ask me to meet you here? Did you expect the bound shades to kill me?"

Despite the pause Abel kept quiet, because he could see the churchman working on the answer. "Firstly, those statues aren't controlled by bound shades. They are inhabited by the souls of true saints, who have volunteered to forego their reward in Heaven to guard the faithful. Eventually, when another truly selfless holy soul volunteers, they will go to God."

"Crikey. How long? Sorry, never mind."

"Too long. There are few modern souls that are that selfless." A sad little smile flitted over the bishop's face. "As to the invite, I was told you weren't arrogant so I tested you. My test failed, completely, because you accepted. You had no hesitation in putting yourself at my mercy, and even brought a tethered spirit onto holy ground. That makes this meeting even more important than expected." Another long pause followed as the bishop inspected Abel, his eyes going back time after time to the arm with the tattoo. "You are an anomaly, a very young sorcerer who holds a very old and powerful title. You also control the gryphon that once belonged to another very old, very powerful magical family, and something of their power may remain. The last holder had nowhere near the strength to investigate or control the Pendragon gryphon. Please be very careful before trying to wake it any further. Though even before you took over Pendragon's demesne, you were of great interest to the church."

"I know. Half want to kill me, but the rest hope I'll do something useful before dying horribly." That wasn't quite what Creepio said, but Abel had no illusions. Most of the church would hold a party if any sorcerer died, and him in particular if Castle House stayed safely locked up.

"Not quite." The bishop chuckled and shook his head gently. "Though you have summed up some points of view very neatly. One faction, which includes me, would rather have you alive for a long, long time. Do you know what is kept in the centre of Castle House?"

"No. I've been told it is very powerful and hates the church, and the archbishop told me it is evil." Since the bishop seemed to be helpful, Abel told him the conclusion he'd come to. "Celtchar supposedly controlled it, which means I'll have to because I'm betting it guards the gryphon."

"Celtchar definitely controlled whatever it is, though the magical community maintain none of them know exactly what. My concern is that when the heir gets to the gryphon, the entity or artefact might end up in control, giving free reign to its malevolence and awesome power. The alternative is the sorcerer gains control. Even then he might be influenced, tempted to use that power to make a bid for dominance of the sorcerous community. The entity would have little or no regard for the consequences." The bishop relaxed, his shoulders dropping a little as he let out a long sigh. "This meeting has confirmed my original beliefs. You will be a relatively benign sorcerer, so I prefer having you wield that power. I really will pray that your belief in good, and your tolerance, survive the encounter, and you control it completely. We will not help you, and even if we wanted to the Accord will not allow it. The best I can offer is prayer, and my promise that I will not interfere. Even so, if you even look like failing, the Church Militant will act against any perceived threat."

"Thank you. I wish I could be as confident that the Church Militant won't decide I'm a threat and descend on Brinsford. They, or a certain archbishop, seem to be a law unto themselves." Rather than defending Creepio, the bishop confirmed that if the opportunity offered, the Church Militant might try to seize the object so it could be locked away.

Having mentioned the archbishop, the bishop moved on to the Bonny's Tavern game characters, and then to one in particular. The bishop, and some other clergy, found the creation of the game character Creepio Mysterio amusing, because the description only fitted one man. Abel took the opportunity to ask about the Last Paladin, and there really was one. The bishop confirmed that, unusually for the church, many clergy believed the armour hid a woman.

Eventually, the bishop sat looking at Abel's arm for a long time, deep in thought. "Part of my asking is raw curiosity, but part is pragmatism. You told my priest that you carry an entity deliberately created, a unique creature, which has now penetrated to the heart of a cathedral. I would like to see your passenger, please, to make my own assessment. Enquiries have suggested a name, but using an entity's name can upset it. It can be seen as a threat, an attempt to command it."

"Zephyr? What will he see? There's no need if you are worried."

"I will not extend myself, just stay small and tight so I will be a shimmer. Ask the bishop if the two guards can move round behind him, and banish their magical attacks. Both are poised, so they might be fast enough to hit me."

Abel passed that on. The glance up above and behind Abel showed where the guards were, but the bishop wasn't keen on moving them. Eventually his curiosity about Zephyr won out. Two tubby figures fluttered down past Abel to hover just behind the bishop, tiny wings blurring as they replaced tiny arrows in quivers. The pair were just too much for Abel's sense of humour. "What do those arrows do, make me love you? Cherubs seem a strange choice as guards, unless they are under a Seeming." Two chubby, cheeky faces smiled at him, showing rows of tiny, sharp, pointed teeth, while Zephyr assured Abel they weren't Seemings.

"These two are not disguised, nor are they cherubs. Real cherubs are allegedly irritated by the popular misconception. These are amorini, the cupid-type version of Putto, a chubby boy. The artform wasn't religious, but belief in Cupid and the power of faith created the real thing. Since they were amoral, the church recruited them. Despite their appearance amorini are fast, very hard to kill, and those arrows carry something much less pleasant than love." The bishop glanced back at the pair. "That makes amorini excellent messengers, much more secure than radio or telephones and impossible to hack. If their arrows are enhanced, amorini become superb guards. Their magical presence is hard to detect so most people mistake them for carvings." He leant forward in his seat, intent on Abel's bicep even if the tattoo didn't show. "Now I really would like to see what manner of creature noticed them, and even that they were aiming at you. Send it out, please."

"A she, not an it, and using her name will not cause offence. Bishop, this is Zephyr. Zephyr, please come out far enough to let the bishop see you."

"But I will be ready to duck. I will not stay out long." Abel felt her flow out of his arm, but not all of her. A small, steady drain of magic puzzled him, but something definitely shocked the bishop.

"How? How can it tolerate the cross?" The bishop looked rattled and both the amorini made a half-move for an arrow. "I expected it to fail, or for you to ask me to provide protection from the cathedral cross. Just being inside the cathedral should destroy any creature of darkness, even if it is protected inside a tattoo. I had assumed your tattoo must be enhanced somehow, but this is impossible! The holy power in here would kill an ogre in seconds!"

"It hurts, but I can manage. Do not tell him."

"Zephyr is a she, and unique, and was not created for evil so perhaps the defences don't consider her an enemy?" With a little smile, Abel tweaked the bishop just a bit. "There's a new thought for you, a magical being that isn't evil by nature. A 'she' not an 'it'." Abel saw the calculation as the bishop grappled with that idea, and decided Zephyr had made her point. "Come back in now, Zephyr. Thank you for putting up with the pain, but I don't want it to actually damage you."

"The church magic has caused damage, but I used your magic to replace me and kept all my memories inside the tattoo." Abel could feel her relief as Zephyr flowed back in. "Now he will wonder, and might stop to think before attacking a magical creature just because it exists." The experience certainly gave the bishop something to think about. Within minutes he'd wrapped up the meeting, and the same priest escorted Abel off the premises. Two hours after entering, a somewhat bemused Abel walked out of the cathedral with an agreement. Brinsford Tavern Refuge was a go!

The BMW picked him up, collected an impatient Ferryl, and the cross-examination started. Halfway back to Brinsford, Abel pointed out the interrogation might be worse than the actual meeting. Not all of it, he could have cheered when Jenny suggested Kelis's mum as a manager for the new refuge, better than him bringing it up himself. Rob wanted to get started on the windows and renovating the stone inscriptions, but he'd have to wait until the bishop did his de-sanctifying thing.

Ferryl seemed most interested in the tiny fragments, the souls. Through her hand, privately, she confessed to occasionally hunting them while in her wind form. She'd never given any thought to what they were, except an extra source of magic, but now she would leave them alone. After a short, lively public discussion everyone agreed that since five of them were learning self-healing, finding out what might happen to their souls wasn't exactly an emergency. For now Zephyr would stop eating them, just in case she snacked on something which would have regrown. A message down Ginny's tether stopped all the casual talk. Melanie had seen a toadstool again!

*   *   *

Ginny didn't quite break the speed limits getting back to Brinsford, or not by much. A wasted effort because despite Melanie being certain, and Ginny confirming how sure she was, once again nobody else caught sight of the creature. Ferryl had laid several traps, but despite more sightings the creatures seemed to avoid most of them and never came when batlins were patrolling. Ferryl and Zephyr had finally combined to create a better trap, buried deep enough so the traces weren't detectable. Now it had sprung, but whatever it was had broken free. Worse, the small surveillance camera only caught a vague fogging, the same as pictures of a skurrit or hoplin. Some visible creatures like goblins could be photographed, but the pictures were always too fuzzy to prove they weren't faked.

This time Rob promised to catch whatever kept coming back. None of them were sure if it looked over other fences, and they could hardly ask the villagers, so this was the only spot for his pit. Ferryl admitted Rob impressed her. Sometime during his practice Rob really had hit on the knack of earth, how the parts held together. Now he compressed the surface soil, just enough to support itself, and then loosened the ground underneath. Once loosened, he removed fragments, leaving a delicate honeycomb of soil grains, then made the edges denser to stop worms and ants interfering. Because Rob only altered how much space the grains had between them the work left no magical signature, and no trace of digging. After four days of working on the trap, Rob declared the potential pit finished. Ferryl added a magical trigger, to seal the top if something fell in. If this didn't work they'd have to wait until the dryad seedling moved in.

Ghosts and Revelations

With everything else going on, Abel hadn't spoken to Dryad Chestnut for a while, too long apparently. "Greetings, negligent and stingy apprentice. Do you have so many dryads to talk to you cannot spare the time for this one?"

Abel turned with a smile, because he knew what really annoyed the dryad, a lack of honey. "Plenty of time for you, Dryad Chestnut, but I thought dryads preferred privacy. Or was it honey? No charge for the answer."

"After so many years of silence, I became used to your chatter. Sometimes you made more sense than mice and grass. Will you be binding the churchyard Elms?"

Abel laughed. Dryads had no patience when they wanted to know something. "The church will release them, but I doubt they will agree to being bound again. Why do you allow the church and sorcerers to treat dryads like that?" Abel stopped, cursing under his breath because he'd asked a straight question. "I have no honey for answers, but I can bring a whole pot tomorrow?"

"After such a long time I can barely remember the taste, so waiting a day will not be too bad. Sorcerers or the church give us a choice, obey or burn. Sometimes a dryad chooses to risk burning, and sometimes it wins so the sorcerer dies. That keeps them cautious. The church bring more priests and the dryad always burns, eventually. Some last long enough to keep the church polite." Branches creaked gently. "I have been silent too long. I am giving long answers without negotiating."

"But if the forests and trees all around the world combined, all the dryads, you could stop even the church. You could protect your own areas for seedlings." The dryad stayed silent until Abel thought he'd realised why. "All right, I'll make it a question. A whole pot of honey, a large one, for all the answers including this one. Why don't dryads combine to defend each other?" Instead of an answer the tree remained silent, until Abel wondered if this was the dryad saying no without risking upsetting a sorcerer. Though Dryad Chestnut never seemed to worry about that before. "Dryad Chestnut...."

"I am deciding if I should answer. You should veil, or others will wonder why you are here so long." Silence fell again. The last time Dryad Chestnut thought hard it had taken over an hour so Abel cast a veil, settling down to practice tiny wind glyphs. A cool breeze had sprung up so he sent counter-wind, and added a trace of heat. Not too much or the dryad would object, they were very sensitive about fire near their trees. Engrossed in his glyphs, trying to train his right hand to be as skilful as his left, Abel didn't notice someone else coming to join him.

"If you want to hide from me you'll need a better veil than that. Why are...?" Kelis stopped and rephrased her question. Dryad Chestnut had a habit of answering questions addressed to others, then claiming payment. "A passing trainee might wonder about another trainee sat by a tree, veiled."

"I'm waiting until Chestnut decides if I can have an answer or not. Not a negotiation, we've agreed the payment." Abel glanced up at the branches, but the only movement seemed to be from the wind. "I asked why dryads didn't gang up on sorcerers."

"You said the bishop told you about that, about them never combining. Maybe nobody told them all the dragons are dead?" Kelis's big smile turned to alarm as branches rattled and leaves fell. "Sorry Chestnut, bad joke." The branches fell silent. "This is annoying. I've got a question for you but if I ask, it'll cost me honey when I get an extra answer." She laughed when Abel started to get up. "Don't bother, it's good practice at careful phrasing for when mum asks awkward questions." At Abel's quizzical look she shrugged. "She'll have a list when I come back from Germany. I'm supposed to leave in a week, two days after the big launch, but there's a problem. We were going by air, me, Una and Justin, but Jenny wants us to take about a ton of promotional gear. It would be easier and cheaper if we drove over in the Volvo estate, and we'd have our own independent transport. The thing is, I'm not sure if the owner will be okay with that."

"Neat wording, even if you should know the answer. If you want it, any car including the Range Rover is yours once you've passed your test. The owner considers the Volvo estate, or any other car, yours as much as his, and will make sure Pendragon Enterprises agrees. He reckons that if Jenny wants you to cart her stuff about you should claim the petrol costs, but all he'll want is a souvenir. Not lederhosen." Abel froze as Kelis gave him a quick hug, but couldn't help enjoying the little flutter from his ward. "Hey, be careful, I'm still sticky with all that power and money. Worse, that was public because you've popped my veil."

Kelis promptly reset the veil. "In that case I'd better hide us so we don't upset your girlfriend. Where is she?"

"Blasting around the countryside on that motorbike, well over the speed limit and without a crash helmet. If she's stopped by the coppers she'll probably use mazzlement, or a seeming to show a completely fictitious driving license." Abel hesitated, but Kelis didn't seem to mind him and Ferryl these days. "I worry about Ferryl crashing, too hard to heal."

"That body isn't Ferryl, remember. She'll fly out if it dies and can even make another one look like that." Kelis must have seen the shock on Abel's face; he sometimes forgot his girlfriend was more than flesh and blood. "Quickly moving to an entirely different subject, the goblins will want a holiday home while the workmen are in the church. Your problem, while I'm off enjoying myself." Before Kelis could crow any more, branches rustled.

"I will give you a dryad answer, though humans may remember differently." The dryad still hesitated before continuing, leaves rustling gently without any wind. "Humans were more devious than expected, and better with glyphs than any entity before them. At first our races lived in peace, side by side, each using their powers in their own way. Humans multiplied and wanted to clear trees and plough the land. Their sorcerers turned dryad against dryad with lies, bribes of trees and honey, and trickery. Some used the threat of dragons or the offer of protection from dragons, and if defied sorcerers started huge forest fires. Hordes of non-magical humans cut down too many trees, leaving the dryads in the populated areas isolated. Even then, some sorcerers still pretended to befriend us, offer help so they could take our trees or enslave us. We eventually learned not to trust any human, but forgot how to trust each other, and now there is no guidance on the wind." A not-wind rattled the branches of the other five trees on the village green, then the biggest Yew tree in the churchyard joined in. "I cannot say more."

"I thank you, Dryad Chestnut." Abel started to get up. "I'll bring the honey tomorrow."

"I've got a question about something else. Hang on." Kelis searched in her pockets. "Half a bar of chocolate?" She threw a tiny piece near the tree and a shoot sampled it.

"Acceptable."

"When things die, are the little sparks of magic they leave behind really souls? I mean the bits from magical creatures as well as humans. The church say the human sparks are souls, but not the others." Kelis glanced at Abel, shrugging slightly. From the last answer dryads came before humans, so they might know. They definitely existed before organised religions and talk of souls.

"Some sparks can grow into another creature, but it will not have any memories. It may hold a sense of the old self, the character, though we cannot prove that without knowing which creature left which spark. Human gods attract and trap what they call souls, possibly to steal the remaining magic. They promise much, but who can tell?" Dryad Chestnut hesitated, unusual but then the other trees had never interfered before. "Dryads only come from seedlings, not surviving fragments, but since magical sparks lodge in tree bark they may persist in tree seeds or our seedlings. Goblins believe their remnants join the magic in the air, and are absorbed by others so they will live again in some form. The oldest, most powerful dragons had a way to contain some memories, and much of their power and skill, after the body died. It could be quickened in some way, giving a new-born dragon the experience and temperament of an elder dragon. Even so, the memories and self of the elder did not survive." Two large brown eyes examined the chocolate. "Deprivation has made me careless. A big answer for a small payment. Even Sycamore's seedling will laugh at me."

Abel thought of how often Dryad Chestnut had helped them, and how little a pot of honey cost. "I have a Horse Chestnut tree, young but mature, that needs a guardian. It will be planted in Kelis's garden to help power the village boundary, but where would I find a dryad seedling for it?"

"I have a short answer, barely worthy of payment?" The Horse Chestnut tree stood silent, not a leaf moving despite the wind.

"You gave a large answer for a small payment, so perhaps I should give a large payment for a small answer. Please let me know when a Horse Chestnut dryad has ripe young looking for a tree." Abel stood up and broke the veil. "Come on Kelis, it's chilly out here in the wind." Kelis looked startled, but then glanced at the tree and leapt to her feet.

Chestnut's voice sighed gently, sounding almost like a breeze and nearly too quiet to hear. "Sneaky humans. Though some are surprisingly generous. My thanks, sorcerer."

Abel raised a hand in farewell. "Trainee, remember, because I still have to ask a dryad for answers."

Kelis grinned, nudging Abel like she used to before the accidental link. She kept her voice down, glancing back at Chestnut. "Still a sucker, because you owe it honey for the first answer. Now what are you going to pay me, to accept this completely unexpected tree I'm getting?"

"Pay? It's a gift." Despite wrangling about that as they walked through the village, both of them were wrestling with the dryad's answers. Why would dryads want guidance, and why did the other trees stop Chestnut saying more? The answers about souls confirmed something survived, but didn't really prove what, though the dryad had an entirely different take on what a heaven might be. Abel and Kelis passed the answers on to the other Taverneers, but none of the six of them had a chance to think about the answers too much. Though perhaps they did, privately, because Abel found himself wondering about magical sparks now and then.

*   *   *

Abel paid his debt, a large pot of honey, but carefully avoided any mention of seedlings or souls in case the other trees were upset again. He'd have liked to ask Dryad Yew about souls, because it was much older, but would wait until the Bishop freed them from the church. Abel had plenty to do before then, because at least half the Goblins needed a place to stay while the workmen started on the church. Only half, some Goblins had to stay or the villagers would wonder where all the gargoyles on the church had gone to. The church only had four genuine ones, and they were just heads directing rainwater from the guttering.

The goblin meld didn't want to split permanently, so half moved into the shrubbery at the bottom of Kelis's old garden, still in Brinsford, and swapped members over at night. Abel left them a small stack of lead bars with a veil glyph on them, to be activated if prospective buyers came to look round. An old would do so, because summoning magic brought a risk of the goblin bursting into flame. That explained why goblins didn't cast glyphs.

Meanwhile Jenny took care of everyone's spare time, running around organising the big launch. She drove the Taverners half crazy, but at least all the projects stopped Rachel's crime-busting campaign. Once the launch finished, Abel wanted to sort out some real rules for that. He also wanted to get in touch with the senior sorcerers in Sheffield, whoever they were because Shawn asked but Bertram didn't know. As part of Jenny's preparations, Shawn arranged for a Bonny's Tavern leaflet campaign in parts of Sheffield, especially near the University. Although it was supposedly closed, the Open University and others used the facilities during the holidays. The Taverners were also trying to identify all the student accommodation, to target them and the secondary schools in Sheffield after the holidays.

Jenny's dad lined up interviews on local radio, and one with the local TV. Abel didn't fancy any of it, but there wasn't an option. Rob reckoned it should be a doddle because there'd be nobody throwing magic about, though he kept threatening to take a goblin along to help sell the game. Other Taverners would have their moment of local fame. The eleven smaller Taverns dotted around the country, places where relatives of the original beta players lived, would be hosting reporters or visiting local radio stations. The nearest and first detached Taverner, Kieran in the Hope Valley, would be giving interviews to boost the local tourist industry. Magic could be tied into local attractions promoting legends of witches, ancient cave dwellers, the various caverns and caves and old traditions like Well Dressings.

Only seven of the locations had magical Taverners, though Kieran and a couple of others were well past leaf fluttering. At least the experience getting Kieran through his discovery of magic had helped to get others past their initial fear and disgust of the creatures appearing around them. Now the captured cars meant the original betas could visit their relatives, to iron out any problems and get them set for launch day. Abel passed his CBT, helped by having the Highway Code etched in his shinbone, so he bought his motorbike.

Despite riding into Stourton, Abel still didn't use his bike for long trips, because Ginny drove him. So far Abel had managed to meet representatives from the three most advanced Taverns. Only two trips because two Taverns were near enough the same wood to share, a big help with time running short. Abel still hadn't seen any of the alleged accommodation, even though there should have been something habitable. At least extending the actual access turned out to be simple. The dryads had heard whispers and were keen to get paid up to date.

Two of the dryads had been enslaved as seedlings, bound into their tree. Abel consulted with Terese on the best way to free them, then offered both a contract and pay for the full period. As part of the contract Ferryl and Zephyr connected to each, implanting the safeguards to be certain neither would betray the Master of Castle House, Abel. Despite being keen to collect their pay, none of the guardians were as forthcoming as Dryad Walnut so Abel only put his hand on tree bark. Ginny had access to two trees in each wood, so she could help the local Tavern if necessary, while Kelis, Rob and Ferryl also touched two trees but were given access to all the younger ones. Jenny would catch up later.

After more comments about breaking agreements, Abel arranged for Woods and Green to arrange real contracts for any dryads in his woods. The dryads would normally have little choice other than stay and sign up, because the youngest had been in their tree a hundred and thirty years. Traveling to find a tree outside Abel's wood would have been slow, painful and dangerous, and the odds of finding a vacant, mature tree before running out of magic were astronomic. Terese didn't waste any time, reporting that the contracts included the dryads extending limited access to younger trees, ones without protection glyphs. The only proviso stayed the same, Abel had to personally authorise each access.

Despite all the rushing about, everything seemed to be more or less on track until two days before the launch. A reporter arranged to meet Jenny at home, not the first one to do so because her dad let Jenny take over his study as her office. After a couple of questions Jenny put this woman off, promising to talk to her the following day in Brinsford. As soon as the reporter left, Jenny called Abel. "Can you join me for an interview tomorrow, in Brinsford, and make sure Ferryl is there? We might need mazzlement, because going by the first questions this reporter is going for the supernatural angle." A look on the internet showed that the reporter specialised in strange sightings, hauntings and other unexplained phenomena. She'd debunked several mediums, but her articles seemed to accept ghosts as being real. None of the articles that Abel could find mentioned magic.

*   *   *

When she arrived in Brinsford the following day, and found all five designers waiting on the village green, the smartly-dressed middle-aged woman seemed torn between triumph and caution. She passed out business cards, but before she could ask questions Abel pointed behind her. "We'll be holding the interview in there, for privacy."

Her interest definitely sharpened. "The church? According to my information, your charity has leased it. Is holy ground significant?"

"No, just private. There are workmen all over the place, but there's a small room in there where they won't bother us." A room that now had six ordinary dining chairs but no sign of Ferryl ever living there.

Abel watched carefully, but Mz Fisher wasn't put off by the church glyphs so she must be an active church-goer. Some of the workmen had hesitated, unsure, before passing through the gate. As the group moved through the churchyard Abel kept watching, and thought he might know why she'd started reporting supernatural sightings. Once inside, Rob did the honours. "Only cold drinks I'm afraid. We haven't organised a proper office yet, because the whole thing might flop."

"Maybe not." The reporter didn't wait until everyone had a drink, she placed a small recorder on the table and dived straight in. "You have a novel set of magical creatures in your game, especially the smaller ones. Your giants and ogres look a little different to some other games and films, basic fantasy types. Why are piskies and brownies so different?"

"We don't think the Disney versions are realistic. Not just Disney, though their films probably set the basic look in the public mind." Kelis always answered that common question, because she drew them.

"But why those exact shapes? What gave you the idea?" Kelis gave the usual answer, imagination, but it wasn't good enough this time. "Why are there no ghosts?"

"There's undead, creatures brought back to serve necromancers, but we decided actual ghosts wouldn't fit the gameplay." Rob glanced at the rest, but they'd agreed on that.

"But you've used them, just called something else." Mz Fisher obviously thought she'd caught them out, but the laughter threw her. She rallied. "Don't try to pretend, I recognise some of them."

"Zephyr, make sure that recorder doesn't record any of this. Wipe anything it's recorded up to now. No flames or smoke." Zephyr had set a TV remote on fire by mistake. "Check to be sure she isn't carrying another but be very careful. She might see magic." Abel thought it likely, since the woman saw creatures well enough to recognise Kelis's less frightful versions.

"I will use a thin shimmer that sneaks in shadows, and shake the molecules in the recording disc just a little."

"It might be tape, and fragile. Take care."

Jenny had come to a conclusion, about an adult who saw creatures. "I mean no offence, but have you had some sort of illness? Hallucinations maybe?"

The reporter looked surprised, then annoyed. "That was cleared up years ago. I'm off all my medication now, because I realised the truth. I can see ghosts, and so can at least one of you." She rallied, confident she had the right idea. "Since none of you seem the slightest bit worried by the idea, all of you know about it, unless you can all see them. Is this game, and the Taverns, a cover for séances?"

"No. I'm sorry but none of us believe in séances, nor ghosts as you mean them." Jenny may as well have saved her breath.

"But you see them, because you've drawn them. The resemblance is obvious. Are you hoping to recruit mediums and open a network of Taverns?" She sat forward, excitement creeping into her voice. "Did you get the ghosts to answer?"

"We don't talk to ghosts." Abel cast a glance at the others, because he wasn't making any impact. "Why do you think what you see is ghosts?"

"Things nobody else can see, that waft through walls or through impossibly narrow cracks? What else could they be?" She produced an advance copy of the game literature, pointing to a piskie on the wall of an ogre's lair. "Things exactly like that? There was one on the wall near the church door as we came in, but it ran away. I saw other types, not unusual in an abandoned church. There are none in active churches, of course, because the priests will have helped them to pass over." She'd got the facts right, just not the reasons. The church cross kept any magical creatures a long way away.

"How many do you see now?" Abel knew the answer because despite never being threatened, the magical creatures in the church tried to keep away from magic users.

"None in this room. Did you banish them? Where do they go?" Mz Fischer narrowed her eyes. "Are you able to send them on, to the afterlife? I checked, and whatever your Tavern players do works. There are hardly any left in the big square near the council offices, or the other places that were cleaned up." She lowered her voice, leaning towards them. "What is heaven like? Do you know?"

"Nobody knows what a heaven is like, even the religions who believe in one." Abel thought fast, though Ferryl had an answer.

"Zephyr can follow her. I will visit her tonight, well away from here, and mazzle her until she cannot even remember how to use a fork. She has a history of mental illness, so if I destroy any notes about the Tavern creatures, that will be the end of it."

Mz Fischer might see Zephyr connect spooky-phone for Abel to answer, so he pressed on with answering the reporter. "You've come here telling us you see ghosts that look like the creatures in our game, but you haven't any proof. I can definitely tell you our drawings are not based on ghosts, and we don't send anything on to any afterlife. We don't even believe in one."

"No, they are too accurate, you've seen them." Her eyes moved from one to the other, a calculating look on her face. "You'll tell me, or I'll write a story claiming you want to suck kids into séances. True or not, you won't want that made public because other investigators will look into it. They'll write their stories about you being frauds, and your game will become a joke to most people."

"Sleep." Ferryl's wind glyphs caught the reporter as she fell, and lowered her gently to the floor. "That gives us time to talk. Is she right, Jenny?"

"About ruining the reputation of the game? Possibly, because she's got credibility from debunking scams, people trying to get money on the basis of contacting ghosts." Jenny's look at the prone figure wasn't even slightly friendly. "Mild mazzlement won't work, because she's got to have been working on this for a while. There'll be records. That means we're stumped, because despite how annoying she is she doesn't deserve to be left a drooling idiot." Abel's tattoo and Ferryl's hand suggested something more permanent. He assured Zephyr the reporter might be annoying, but she wasn't a genuine threat, and this time Zephyr passed the message to Ferryl.

"If she can see creatures, could she cast glyphs?" Rob had a half-smile now. "She might be handy, a secret Taverner who is a reporter? It's almost traditional for superheroines."

"Sort of Mz Spiderwoman or Superwoman with an alter ego?" Kelis considered it, briefly. "No, she could go the other way. A reporter screaming about magic could bring Creepio down on her, and us."

"So we show her magic, and tell her we'll get her if she doesn't keep her mouth shut. Prove we can do things that look like accidents, but could kill her." Ferryl warmed to her theme. "Lock her in her car, then start filling it with water. Or grab her feet with earth, and her arms with bushes, then cast a flame that would char her. I could stop up her nose and mouth and cover her eyes with black fog, leave it just long enough to terrify her, then release her? No evidence."

"No. Though we could warn her about Creepio, without names?" Which Abel knew she wouldn't believe. "How about a lesser fright? Take her someplace a bit more private and explain. Tell her that spreading the truth will kill her and cause panic. Explain upfront before floating her up a tree. As a demonstration, not a threat."

"It would work as a threat as well, even unspoken. Plant growth really persuaded me, because it's a normal thing acting abnormally." Jenny suddenly giggled, her hands out in front of her as if holding something the size of a big melon. "Give her a piece out of a giant apple, not enough to prove the fruit was outsize, and defy her to prove it isn't normal."

As they each chipped in, the suggestions about what to do settled into something along those lines. They'd give the reporter a list of impossible options, ask her to check for mirrors and wires, and then cast the glyphs.

"Wake her up Ferryl." As wind glyphs sat the reporter in her chair Rob put out a hand, then pulled it back. "We'd best support her with wind. If we're holding her she'll realise she collapsed." Seconds later Mz Fisher woke up, instantly alert.

Her eyes darted from one to the other before she picked up her recorder. "What happened then? Something did, everyone jerked as if you'd all moved a bit. There was a draught, just for a moment." She hit the buttons, frowned and tried again before looking up, alarmed. "What did you do to this? It still works but it didn't record."

"Maybe there's a ghost in the machine." Abel held up a calming hand as Mz Fisher looked around in alarm. "How about we take you somewhere private, where we can show you how we actually came up with the drawings?" Unfortunately, being knocked out, or the slight disorientation, had left the reporter very wary. She eventually agreed to visiting this mystery location, but Abel had to promise she could phone someone to say where she'd gone and who with. "You can't mention ghosts, just that you're going to an interview." Though when she agreed, the Taverners realised they hadn't decided on a place.

* * *

Though after a moment's thought, only one place would do. Kelis headed home to tell her mum she'd be delayed, but actually to get the pebble glyph, while the others walked Mz Fisher slowly through Brinsford to Castle House. With some sort of resignation, Abel paused outside the gate while the reporter made her phone call. If this went wrong, Brinsford would be getting a lot of unwanted attention.

Mz Fisher told the someone she'd be going into the grounds of the old house near Brinsford because she'd got an exclusive, but her phone would be turned off. When Jenny asked for the phone and recorder, the reporter admitted that wasn't unusual if she wanted the real story. The shallow cave, still containing five plastic milk crates for seats, didn't look very impressive. Mz Fisher said so, but Abel insisted this was the right place. "That's if you want proof."

189

"Absolutely, though there aren't any ghosts in here. Are they banished?" She looked hopefully from one to the other. "Can you banish them from anywhere you like, such as a kitchen?" That settled it, she could see creatures in her food. "What sort of area can you clear, because some crosses work better than others?"

"We can clear your kitchen, because your ghosts are actually magical creatures and can be driven away using hexes. The stronger crosses are blessed, filled with church magic." Abel stopped because he could already see the disbelief.

Scorn as well. "Typical of children. You've all read that woman's books haven't you? Suddenly everything strange is magic, but hidden from all us muggles."

Kelis burst out laughing. "So close, yet so wrong. You've just told us our magical creatures aren't like any in fiction, so they aren't from books or films. The bit about being hidden is right, which is why we're telling you. If you write your story, there are people who will shut you up."

"Don't be absurd, I've been threatened by experts. I have enough research in my files, ones you'll never find, to point the police straight here if I disappear." Mz Fisher looked from one to the other with contempt. "I expected better."

"It's not a threat, it's the rules. We had to get permission to put real creatures in our game, and we can't put them all in." Rob had started to get annoyed. "The people who come for you, or us if we mess up, won't bother with threats. Look at your foot." As she looked down the earth surged over one short practical boot and held it. "That isn't hurting you, but try and pull free."

"Rob, we agreed to explain first." Abel sighed, then smiled reassuringly at the growing fear in the reporter's eyes as she tried to free her foot. "He'll let you go because it's just proof, a demonstration. Rob?" The earth crumbled away.

Mz Fisher took a quick step backwards, inspecting the disturbed earth and shaking her foot to check it was really free. "How did you do that? I suppose you got me to stand in the right place first."

"Back to plan A, now Rob has tried a shortcut." For once Jenny's bright, innocent smile didn't work. Mz Fisher looked unimpressed. "You had a short nap in that room, while we decided what to do. We'll give you a range of options. You can stand where you like, look for mirrors and wires, and then we do whatever you choose. After that you'll believe us, or maybe go stark raving bonkers."

"Hah! The things I've seen, a few parlour tricks won't even give me bad dreams. What are these options? Mystery voices, waving sheets, an Ouija board, or shall I pick a card and you guess it?" Though despite the words, Rob's demonstration had rattled her.

Kelis took over, giving a range of options covering plant growth, colour changes, small fires, ice out of thin air and a hole in the earth or rock anyplace the reporter chose. "Or we can lift you up from anyplace you choose, and set you down someplace else, even the top of the cliff. Choose several options and we'll do them all."

The reporter took them totally seriously. "I must warn you, I am very good at finding out how people manage their special effects." First she used a small canister from her bag to spray smoke, to detect hidden light beams that might produce reflections or trip automatic effects. A magnet and a very long, thin retractable wand were used to check for wires or anything metallic. Her bag gave up gadget after gadget as the search of the clearing, and the bushes and trees along the edges, went on and on. Eventually Mz Fisher pointed to the circular stone slab covered in glyphs. "What is that?"

"A source of magic. Don't ask us to do anything to it, because it's dangerous." Abel walked over and put his hand on it. "Not to touch, but if we break it or even crack it enough it's a magical bomb."

"How do you know I won't come back and test it?"

"That will be your final proof." Abel meant she'd never get back into the garden, but he knew the reporter wouldn't realise that.

"I've decided. Those are perfectly ordinary trees, so if you can make them grow I choose that branch there." She pointed up at a Larch tree. "The second shoot out from the trunk. Grow it about thirty centimetres, without going near it, and let me go and inspect the result." Before anyone could do so she turned towards the cliff, taking a couple of steps to reach out and draw a circle with a felt tip pen. It didn't draw very well on the rock, but left enough marks on the pale limestone to show the shape. "I want a circular hole there, forty centimetres deep." Taking a couple of steps back she looked up the cliff. "Then I'll choose a place to stand, and you transport me right next to that holly bush." With a triumphant smile she turned to Kelis. "Well?"

"Not a problem. Jenny, Rob?" Both agreed it wasn't a problem. "The tree first." Mz Fisher kept her eyes on Kelis so she didn't see Jenny cast the glyph. Kelis pointed at the tree.

"Sorry, I'm a bit excited so I overdid it." Jenny giggled, but the reporter might not have heard. Her attention stayed riveted on the shoot as it grew out a little further than she'd asked, even producing a few leaves.

"Now the rock. Where do you want the heap of dust, because it doesn't disappear?" Rob's annoyance had gone, replaced by a silly grin. "Though I could hide it?"

"Just there." The reporter looked decidedly wary now, nothing like as confident. "I'll want to check it."

"Feel free. Hang on a sec, I have to concentrate." Rob took his time, casting air straight afterwards to funnel the dust down to the indicated spot. "The heap is a bit untidy because I'm not very good with that part." The teenagers watched as the puzzled woman, now definitely getting worried, cautiously put her hand in the neat round hole in an otherwise untouched rock face.

"Ready to fly? Pick your spot." Kelis wiggled her fingers. "I'm doing this part."

All the confidence had gone. The reporter dithered before choosing a spot, then hesitated before moving to a different place. "Is this safe?"

"No, it's really dangerous, but I'm good enough for this. You'll feel a draught around you, and the air will press in which will feel really strange. If you put your arms out I can use them instead of blowing your body up there. It's easier." Mz Fisher's arms shot out to each side. "Perfect, now keep them there." Moments later the reporter's feet left the ground, not a happy moment from her expression, and she wafted gently upwards to join the holly bush. "Stamp a couple of times, so you're sure you are there, then I'll bring you back down."

Mz Fisher hugged herself, then realised and stood up straight. "Is there another way down?"

"About sixty metres along there, to your left, there's a set of steps cut into the rock." Abel pointed, but couldn't resist tweaking her a little. "Aren't you worried we'll mess with the evidence while you're out of sight?"

"Coming down the steps is the bloody evidence!" Her hand went up to her mouth and she shook herself. "I'm sorry, but that felt really creepy. Something took hold of my arms, but I can see ghosts so nothing did. I'll be back down there in a few minutes to look at that branch, but then I think I'd better listen to your explanation."

As she made her way towards the steps, all five teenagers looked at each other. "Why didn't she go crackers?" Rob shrugged at Jenny's frown, unrepentant. "We just showed an adult magic."

"She's already had her breakdown, I reckon. You heard her on about the medication, and how she found a way to live with it, ghosts. My mum thought creatures were ghosts, among other things, and we know two other adults who see them." Abel had thought long and hard about those three. "I reckon if a person first sees creatures when they are young, but they aren't fully awakened to magic, it just knocks them off the rails a bit when they get older. Not a complete breakdown, because their mind has sort of got used to it."

"So if we got Stan and your mum to work glyphs, like Frederick does?" Ferryl didn't sound certain, a big warning to the others.

A warning Abel didn't need. "No! I'm not risking mum, and Stan doesn't see things clearly and tries not to." He looked towards where the reporter had gone. "But if there's no other way for her?"

"At least Rob can bury the body nice and neatly." Abel opened his mouth, shocked, but Kelis beat him to it. "Joke! A joke, for flipping flopping heck's sake." She glanced at the hole in the rock and a little smile tugged at her lips. "Though if that was a bit bigger?"

"Ashes, proper sorcerers turn bodies into ashes. We could put them round the flowers you and Jenny planted." Ferryl pointed in the direction of the patches of wildflowers that were replacing some of the undergrowth. At least joking about hiding the body, definitely a joke because only two of them considered killing Mz Fisher, kept them amused while the reporter made her way down off the cliff.

*   *   *

The reporter started with breaking off the lengthened Larch shoot, then snapping it into shorter lengths and splintering small pieces. Switching to the cliff, she sifted Rob's dust through her fingers before giving the hole in the cliff a thorough examination. Eventually she sat on one of the milk crates. "I give in. Either explain how you tricked me, or tell me what that was. It wasn't ghosts." Looking round the teenagers she produced a cautious smile. "You don't look like the sort of people to bury bodies in the woods, but I'll promise to keep whatever you tell me quiet. I can't prove how you did any of this anyway." Her waved hand took in the branch, dust and hole in the rock. Luckily she didn't see Abel flinch about the bodies part.

"It's easy, we told you. Magic." Jenny looked around the clearing, then at Abel. "Since she seems pretty stable, we may as well hit her with the lot. How about we go and sit someplace more comfortable?" She turned back to the reporter and pointed at Abel. "You will see things that will definitely persuade you, but they'll kill you unless you hold onto his hand very, very tight. I mean it."

Abel understood the suspicion on Mz Fisher's face, and didn't want her to let go just to test if his hand really was the protection. "I can scratch out the mark afterwards?" The rest nodded understanding, so Abel turned to Mz Fisher. "You hold my hand until I say so, regardless of what you see, but then I've got another hand I'd rather hold." Ferryl already had a firm grip.

"Are you sure? She will see secrets."

"Zephyr, a spooky-phone please." Abel waited a moment for her to connect. He'd been right, Mz Fisher saw it but kept quiet. "She already has, but she won't tell anyone, not without proof or she'll lose her credibility for her other work."

"Or she'll disappear." Ferryl must have felt Abel tense. "We won't have to do it, Creepio will, if only to question her about Castle House. I will insist on holding her other hand until she is accepted by the toad. I can put her to sleep if she panics." Abel wasn't sure he liked the calculation that came into Ferryl's voice. "This will be a good test. If Chris begins to activate her magic, we will know how much to tell her."

"Even if this goes well, we aren't risking mum!" After a silent tussle while walking to Castle House door, Ferryl agreed to leave well alone.

*   *   *

Abel should have remembered Mz Fisher's reporting background. The questions started even before he opened the door. "Isn't it locked? It should be if it's dangerous." Explaining didn't work, so out of pure curiosity Abel let her touch the door. The reporter nursed her tingling hand, and conceded nobody would open the door without permission. She hadn't even made contact. Kelis answered the next round of questions, about why nobody on the road could see them, or the door opening. An attempt to explain Fraggon failed entirely.

"Remember." Abel took her hand. "Don't let go. I'll ask Fraggon to move so you realise how dangerous some things are. He's a huge dragon-frog statue that can animate, just a guard so he usually stays put."

"He's a sweetie. Unless you're a…. never mind." Jenny mimed zipping her mouth. "Nerves."

Abel opened the door, but for a few moments Mz Fisher didn't react, just taking in the view. "That's a very large sculpture, and very detailed. I don't recognise the style, but the frills give it a hint of oriental. Obviously stone but according to you, if I walked in on my own it would attack me. So would what appears to be a very dead potted vine of some sort."

"Yes." Abel raised his voice a little. "Fraggon, we need to persuade this lady you are real, but without hurting her." He shut up, because Zephyr had flown in and connected to Fraggon by spooky-phone. A look at Mz Fisher showed that she'd screwed her eyes up, squinting, obviously trying to see what had just flown into the house. As Jenny explained Zephyr, Abel felt the hand in his tighten before trying to pull away. He held tight, looked into the room, and understood. "Far enough, thank you Fraggon."

Fraggon had partially uncoiled, which brought him two metres nearer the door where he'd bared his impressive array of dagger and sword-like teeth. "Good boy." Jenny went in and patted the guardian on the head. She looked back at Mz Fisher. "Dangerous, but I've been introduced. You haven't, so hang onto Abel." That got through. Abel started losing the feeling in his hand, and hoped nothing ended up crushed.

"Let's get this over with." Ferryl's grip on the reporter's other hand came in handy, to help support her on shaky legs as she went past Fraggon, saw the octopus in the ceiling open its eyes, and met the speaking, three-horned furry toad. At least Mz Fisher recognised the toad as a rare ghost, though she'd never heard of one speaking. Abel lifted her hand to push the back onto the wood, and a glyph appeared. Despite that, neither Abel nor Ferryl let go until they'd lowered the woman into an armchair in the library. Rob nipped off to make drinks, because he liked using the glyph-controlled hotplate, while the others did their best to calm Mz Fisher down. The aquarium helped, something apparently normal, as did all the books. Being able to see out through the supposedly boarded-up windows threw her again.

When Kelis showed her some of the books, the reporter became quite excited about their age and condition. Mz Fisher ended up walking up and down inspecting the shelves, finding original works by Victorians such as the Bronte sisters and Charles Dickens. She also discovered poetry by Browning, Tennyson and Byron, but reluctantly gave up the search when the rest insisted. Some of the interest might have been keeping herself thinking of mundane things, but when she finally sat down Mz Fisher still clutched an original Pride and Prejudice. "Have you any idea what these are worth? For study, not the money. Though they'd fetch a lot of money."

Jenny answered with a question. "If you were asked, where did you find that book?"

Mz Fisher looked down at it, then up. "In an old library, in an old house just outside Brinsford."

"A house guarded by a fraggon, which will kill unwanted visitors. Try explaining that when someone wants to see the library." Jenny smiled sweetly and nodded as she saw the reporter remember those teeth. "Once you've left, you won't be able to get back in. You won't even get into the garden."

"If you drive a car at the fence, as fast as you can, and shut your eyes, you'll still miss. The magical barrier will force you to swerve. If by some fluke you got inside, the garden would kill you without leaving a mark. You'd go insane first, screaming in pure terror at what's in your head." Rob's stone cold sober voice sounded odd to the others, more used to his jokes. "If you tell anyone, they'll come as far as the gate, but magic will tell them not to bother coming in. They'll persuade themselves you were lying."

"Are you in my head now, doing things?" Mz Fisher looked around herself. "No, that thing, Fraggon, is real." She patted the book. "This is real."

"We could make you forget if you'd prefer it? Everything, back to where you'd never heard of the Tavern." Abel opened his arms to take in the room and everyone inside. "Or we come to an arrangement."

It took a while, at least partly because Mz Fisher assumed he meant bribery or threats. Finally realising Abel meant blanking out her brain, her actual memory, frightened her badly until she understood nobody wanted to do that. Eventually she seemed to realise the Taverners weren't sure what to do, exactly, and started trying to work out her own deal. "I know my way around the occult world, but that's no real use to you." Mz Fisher's eyes drifted to the aquarium and she swallowed, hard. "Except you keep insisting occult is actually magic. I could tell them, people who see ghosts?" Before anyone could answer she shook her head vehemently. "Not a chance."

"You could assess those people, to see if any of them should know the truth? We don't mind people carrying out séances as long as they don't use them to harm people." Rob seemed to have shelved his usual joker personality, sounding almost wistful. "A séance helped my aunty when her daughter died. The bloke gave her a couple of happy messages about not being too upset, and said she'd be moving on to the afterlife. My aunty settled down after that, because she knew her lass was happy."

"If you explain about magic, tell me more, I'll help with anyone else who claims they've seen ghosts? I have credentials so I could get appointments." Mz Fisher nodded to herself, working through her own idea, then sat up straighter and suddenly more business-like. "I can assess if they ought to know the truth, then introduce them. Meeting others like me would also help me come to terms with what's happened. I'll be able to help people, maybe stop them having the breakdowns?" The rest pitched in, because that sounded feasible. Now she knew her own mental problems were normal, at least for older people exposed to magic, Mz Fisher really seemed to want to help them cope. So did the Taverners, but they'd had no idea how to manage it.

As the visitor left the garden, Zephyr neatly removed the pebble from her pocket. Mz Fisher drove off still unsure, but with a lot to think about and an original Pride and Prejudice on loan. Abel went back inside and scored through her glyph, which glowed once and disappeared. Despite hashing the whole visit over, nobody knew if the reporter would keep quiet. They hadn't time to worry too much, tomorrow they'd launch Bonny's Tavern!

*　　*　　*

Launch day! A mad whirlwind of new faces, many throwing questions faster than Abel could answer, and a succession of new locations that should have been memorable. Instead, looking back afterwards, Abel could never remember any of the first day clearly, just chaos blurred into one long, confused meeting. Despite Ginny turning up in the BMW, his mum insisted on being Abel's chauffeur, and becoming some sort of dresser, prompter and bodyguard. Abel might not have needed his mum checking his hair, or brushing his shoulders before each interview, but having her there helped him stay centred. Kelis, Rob and Jenny had their own proud parents along, with siblings because even Rob's older sister, Samantha, took a day off work. Four of the parents had a legal reason to be there. They were directors, although all of them stressed the appointments were only to meet the legal requirements.

Frederick came along to explain Stourton Tavern Refuge, a separate organisation though Bonny's Tavern had donated a vehicle and plenty of volunteer labour. From the comments, some of the newspapers and other reporters had already been to see the house.

Abel, Kelis, Rob, Ferryl and Jenny all had their moment of fame. By the time the TV cameras were ready, Abel wished he'd brought a goblin after all. Wearing a coat of makeup, because of the lights, just put the topper on it all. Jenny seemed to be in her element, Rob made daft jokes now and then, and Kelis came across as shy but knowledgeable. Ferryl stayed cool, calm and collected, even when answering questions about her allegedly dead parents. Abel knew he'd been flustered, and stumbled a bit over some answers, and wasn't sure how many times he'd blushed. One reporter went for the Abel-Ferryl romance angle, and had a field day when she found out both Kelis and Jenny were ex-girlfriends.

*   *   *

The Bonny's Tavern dance in the evening, in full costume, came as a relief. No TV or reporters were invited, and nobody gate-crashed because Pendragon Enterprises supplied the door-persons. The door-creature as well, because Zephyr lurked in the shadows to let the Taverner security trainees know if she saw something suspicious. She detected two magic users under Seemings, strangers who turned away when challenged. Ferryl thought they were probably apprentices sent by curious sorcerers. Redwolf's apprentice, Mannan, turned up with a legitimate invite, dressed as a sorcerer in robes and a pointy hat. He made a point of telling Abel his master had noted how fast the Taverners learned, and had now given Mannan limited access to a tree.

The organised chaos continued the following day. Abel, Rob and Ferryl visited four local shops to sign copies of the game, then headed for Sheffield to do the same at several much larger stores. Kelis had her own special interview, dressed as K'liss Windcatcher. Several photographers had taken shots of the costumes going into the dance, and one had seen Kelis, looking enough like her ex-model mum for the reporter to ask for a full photoshoot. Ferryl pretended to be annoyed at missing out, because she had to guard Abel. Maybe she really was, because Una, Petra and a score of the Taverners with the best costumes spent three hours strutting their stuff for the cameras. The photographers used Leferrier Memorial Park, which meant the 'models' had to be careful which trees they touched. Kelis staggered off home to finish packing, too relieved it was over to ask Jenny if she'd set the whole thing up.

Jenny didn't have time for interviews or photo-shoots, too busy checking to make sure every advert went in on time and the copies of the game hit the shelves on schedule. She also found herself trying to coach the members of the smaller Taverns, when local reporters turned up wanting interviews. Luckily none of the panicking teenagers realised that even Jenny had been caught out by the number of requests. By the time they'd attended local signings and promotions, and answered the same questions several times, most of the victims were enjoying themselves or were at least resigned to their fate.

*   *   *

The following morning Abel made a real sacrifice, getting up at six to see Kelis on her way to Germany. A willing sacrifice, well worth it for the long hug before she got into the Volvo. He wasn't sure if Kelis felt anything at all, but the lovely tingle from the remnants of the link would keep him thinking about her long after she'd gone. Abel felt a little guilty because he liked hugging and kissing Ferryl, his girlfriend, but it didn't feel the same. Wondering if Kelis or Ferryl realised, and if the fortnight's absence might help him get his head straight, kept Abel occupied as the Volvo disappeared down the road. Seeing Kelis as the car drove away might have given him even more food for thought. She sat with one hand tucked under the other arm, touching the unmarked skin where Abel had once drawn a flower, a little smile on her face.

At least getting up early gave Abel time to eat breakfast in peace. He'd be able to relax a bit today, between appointments, because mum would be at work. Remembering not to talk about magic, even in the car, had been awkward to say the least and it would have been harder today. The first email for Ferryl Shayde had arrived!

Unfortunately none of the Carlisle Tavern, initially recruited as beta players by one of Abel's friends, had discovered magic. That meant none of them could mentor a youth who had already seen creatures. The purchaser had taken one look at the graphics for his new game, and immediately recognised the small creatures that crawled through his food, and life. The description might have said they were relatively harmless, but if the little ones were real he wanted to know about the rest! Rob sent a reply telling him help was on the way, but not to talk about it to any other players.

Ginny only picked up three Taverneers, because Jenny couldn't help with either interviews or dealing with magic users. She had a full-time job monitoring the launch, with her dad looking over her shoulder. Worse, although it was only a small launch compared to a real games company, and mostly concentrated locally, she'd booked the other Taverneers solid for the rest of the week. A quick run through the drivers who were also adepts brought a big smile, and Abel made the call.

Petra had passed her driving test long before school ended, complaining that she'd just missed out on claiming a free motor. She'd been making a joke of it, offering to drive Taverners around the industrial estate so she could get enough experience to qualify as a Tavern taxi driver. "Petra? It's Abel. Can you get away for a few days?" Abel explained about needing someone to visit Carlisle, up on the Scottish borders, to mentor a new possible Taverner.

"Mum won't be happy, not at short notice. I'll go to the next one, hopefully somewhere nearer where I can be dropped off back home every night." Petra must have remembered something else she'd been pestering for. "Unless it means I get my village tree first?"

"The trees have been organised, delivery as soon as you've nailed down the location. Our problem with this newbie is we haven't got a spare driver, to take an adept to meet him. You are already an adept, so if you'll take the Range Rover?" Abel had put his phone on speaker so the rest heard the squeal.

"Really? I'll run away from home, or leave a ransom note. If this is Rob's twisted humour…?" Eventually Petra promised to drug her parents into agreeing, or leave them tied in a cupboard until she got back. Abel just kept laughing, and suggesting other drivers who might go along in case she got fed up with driving. Eventually Petra calmed down enough to agree she ought to leave her catsuit off until she arrived, or a traffic cop would pull her over. "Are you serious, Abel? I haven't got many hours of practice on the road, on my own. I could take one of the other cars, let a more experienced driver have the Range Rover? I'd rather not, but it might be safer."

"I asked Eric, and he said if you didn't get to drive a decent car soon you'd steal one." Though even as he said it, Abel raised his hand for a high five from Rob. He hadn't asked at all, but Eric had commented that Petra could drive any of the cars. She'd be too frightened of messing up to do anything stupid. A real recommendation, because Eric had become very protective over the vehicles, banning a couple of drivers who had been speeding. Some of the others were restricted to the minibuses or the Peugeot, because he felt they were too keen to show off, or maybe test the protection glyphs.

That phone call turned out to be the high point of the day, though this time there were fewer stores to visit because Jenny had spread her net. Claris, resplendent in her new Pendragon Security uniform, drove Rob to Derby via a short stop in Ashbourne. The blue 'giant' who accompanied them would help to take some attention off Rob, allegedly to stop him reverting to humour out of pure nerves. If that didn't work, Claris reminded him she had a perfectly legal club.

Abel and Ferryl, with Ginny driving, covered Birmingham and Manchester. Only a couple of stores in each, one a chain store and the other a dedicated gamers' outlet, but the reporters and queue of purchasers were long enough to keep them busy. The questions were different today because of the morning news. A Methodist minister had made a statement claiming that Bonny's Tavern represented the problems in modern Britain. The monsters were pollution, crime, disease and poverty, while the sorcerers, corrupt nobles and priests were big business, corrupt politicians and the established hierarchy of the churches. The players were apparently lawless, violent people and creatures who actually protected the common man, and were on the path to redemption.

The statement hadn't made national TV news, but spread through a snippet on national radio. Within the hour the story had been picked up and repeated by local media, then internet news and social media. By the time Abel reached the second shop, three reporters had turned up for a reaction. After explaining he wasn't anti-church, and it was just a game, Abel took a moment to check that Rob hadn't said something too outrageous. Ferryl didn't mind taking the heat for a while. Reporters didn't worry her because she reckoned she could mazzle someone pushing too hard, just enough for them to lose track. A text on his private phone asked Abel to ring his mum. "Mum? Is everything all right?"

"That's my line. Yes, even Rob is behaving, though I've had half a dozen calls asking if he's said anything to upset the church. Claris assures me he hasn't. The call is because I'd like you to meet me straight after work, if you get back in time. Jenny thought you should be finished by then." Abel opened his mouth to ask where, but soon had the answer. "Come to the office will you, please? There's someone wants to meet you." While Abel racked his brains for excuses, his mum made them all pointless. "He recognised you on TV. I've cleared it with Eric."

"Okay mum, no problem." After a few minutes talking about the religious questions, Abel rang off. Why hadn't Eric warned him? A glance at Abel's business phone showed him a waiting text. He hadn't felt the vibrate when it came in. According to Eric, he had no idea who'd recognised Abel, or from where, but couldn't really tell Abel's mum her son wasn't allowed to visit the office. His head whirling, Abel headed back into the fray.

At least by the time Abel and Ferryl headed back to Stourton, the religious controversy had been sorted. Several other religious representatives had been asked for a reaction, and poured some common sense on the whole thing. According to most quotes, nobody should read too much into a children's game. A few took the opportunity to comment on the charitable aspect, an innovation some of the established gaming franchises might consider copying.

*   *   *

When he knew where Abel was going, Rob chickened out of calling by the office. He phoned to say his mum didn't seem to be keeping any secrets, so maybe there wasn't a problem, then asked Claris to take him straight home. That kept Abel hoping he might get away with his dual identity, right up until he opened the front door and walked into reception. The receptionist, who had only ever seen Abel once, looked up, did a double-take and obviously recognised either Abel or Ferryl. A remaining faint hope died when Abel's mum came through from the rear, held the door open, and beckoned. "In here."

As he went through the doorway, Abel had to ask. "Who wants to meet me?"

"The boss."

Abel stopped dead. That didn't make sense because... While he floundered, a door down the passageway opened, and one of the security men came out. "Hi boss, finally come to see what we get up to?" The hired staff had all met Abel at the gym, most of them more than once. They'd found it funny that Eric only ever called him boss, and picked up on it. When one asked why he never came to the office, Rob told him the boss didn't want to find out what they really did instead of working. All harmless fun until now.

"Yes, it's time we all met the boss." At least his mum wasn't angry, she sounded close to laughing. "We might even find out his name."

"It's Abel. He's been on TV, but Eric never calls him that." The security woman following the man covered her mouth with a hand. "Oops, now I've done it."

"This is why he never visited. Eric warned him the staff would take liberties." Ferryl took hold of Abel's hand. "Now what?"

"Okay mum, you caught me. Is there actually anyone to meet, or just a big surprise poster, balloons and silly string?" The looks on both the other adults showed they'd had no idea Chris, the secretary, doubled up as the boss's mum. Abel shrugged at them and forced a smile. "Now you know the real reason I don't visit. It looks bad when the secretary tells her boss to eat his greens and polish his shoes." The pair of them headed out through the front, laughing.

"There's a very nervous someone waiting in that office, the one saying manager. You should give Eric a bonus because he still won't confirm a thing. I only found out because I heard one of the security men talking about the boss being on TV, and his real name being Abel Conroy." Mum's humour seemed to be dying back, and Abel knew what came next. A full explanation, one that covered however much she'd already found out and as little more as he could manage.

"Now you'll have to tell her everything." Abel couldn't even risk answering Ferryl through Zephyr, in case his mum saw her.

Though so far mum was still having fun. "Here we are. Eric, I've brought Abel to meet the boss, a bit difficult because you won't say who it is."

"It's all right Eric, mum knows. She's just winding us both up." Abel sat down, then got up again. "Do you want a drink, mum, or will you leave the inquisition until we get home?"

"I should get the drinks. It's my job." His mum picked up the phone and asked the receptionist to organise coffee and tea, please. For the boss. "I should ask for a raise."

"Pick a number. You don't actually have to work, mum. Not now." Abel sat again and braced himself. "What did you find out?"

"Oh no, it's not that easy. I already know some people think you are called Pendragon, and the business papers call the owner the Master of Pendragon Enterprises. There's another office in Sheffield and the firm deals in some sort of security, for people who pay a lot of money. Others pay horrendous prices to have their computers protected, horrendous enough for your manager to drive a very tasty BMW. I'd started to wonder if this place was a cover for something illegal." Her eyes narrowed, looking at Abel's hand. "Definitely Pendragon." Abel looked down at the signet ring on his pinky finger, the one with the dragon head. He usually hid it under a Seeming before going home, though before he could say anything mum moved on. "Speaking of BMWs, does that mean the smart-looking woman who keeps volunteering to pick you up actually works for you?"

"Ginny is a sort of chauffeuress and runs errands when Abel can't." Ferryl shrugged at Abel's look. "It's obvious now."

"Is she sat out there waiting for you now?" Abel confirmed that Ginny worked for him, the BMWs were company cars, he'd donated the Mercedes minibus, and some of the Taverners worked for him. After a long silence his mum pointed out he'd missed the industrial unit with the gym, and some sort of accommodation in Sheffield. The security staff had mentioned big houses when they'd stayed there while helping out the other security staff, the Sheffield ones. Then there'd been talk of computer repairing as well as protecting, another part of the business though they didn't charge as much.

Abel tried to play it all down, dismiss it as not much, but his mum had seen the list of company cars and that made the business lucrative. With a wry glance at Eric, Abel gave up. "Fancy a Range Rover, mum? Long wheelbase, top spec, all the extras? Straight swap for the Fiat? None of this lot will use it, because they reckon it should belong to the boss and he can't drive. You'll have to wait a couple of days because Petra is using it on Bonny's Tavern business." At least that stopped her in her tracks. "I'd rather explain all this where everyone can't hear my mum chewing me out, please?"

"All right, but I want you there as well, young lady." She fixed Ferryl with a glare. "None of this is the slightest surprise to you. How about Rob and Kelis, and Jenny? Should I call their parents?"

"Not until you hear me out. It would be a really bad idea." Though Abel thought the gremlin must be well out of the sack now, and the globhoblin in the chicken pen as well. In retrospect the secrecy had never been going to hold once he'd met the non-Tavern staff, and then been on TV. After a brief argument, Eric arranged for someone to drive mum's car home, because Abel insisted on her coming with him in the BMW. He didn't want her running into a tree on the way home because she was thinking about this lot. He wanted to curse Ginny when she called him boss, and opened the car door for his mum. It hadn't taken long for word to spread.

At least having Ginny there gave Abel a breather from mum-questions on the way home, though he had to answer several phone calls. The look at his business phone meant there'd be more explanations. A text from Jenny just asking "how serious" had to be her wondering if her dad would be asking questions. Rob's text just said, "Eric phoned." The one from Eric, asking if Mrs. Conroy would need security in the future, really threw Abel. Did his mum count as magically aware, a legitimate target under the Accord? Once home Abel's mum held off until her car arrived, because Ginny stayed to give the driver a lift back. The big grin as the driver handed over the keys meant all the Taverners would know by morning.

*　*　*

Once inside the house Abel opened his mouth but his mum got in first. "Before we go any further, is that all legitimate?"

"Totally, mum. Signed off by Woods and Green, the solicitors. It's a...."

"The same ones who organised the sale of that convenient vase I never saw? Is it anything to do with the creatures, or Castle House? I know you've been going in there but I can't. I kept meaning to bang on the door and surprise you five, but I kept changing my mind." The hand to her arm might not be a conscious move, but it showed Abel how often his mum stroked her mark, the Tavern shield he'd drawn and she'd had tattooed.

"Some of each. You can't get...."

"It can't be legitimate, because you are too young. Who is the real Master of Pendragon Enterprises?"

"Your son is. He'll explain if you give him a chance?" Ferryl spoke gently but it brought Abel's mum up short. "I promise, it will all make sense if you don't interrupt until he's done. He's been wanting to tell you right from the start, but knew there'd be these sorts of problems." She gave a short laugh. "You should have seen the amount of thought it took to find a way to buy you a better car." Ferryl nodded gently at the startled look. "He's been beating his brains out for ways to give you money. That's why Eric offered you the job, though he really did need a secretary. Now will you let Abel explain?"

"Zephyr, connect me to Ferryl, please." Abel nodded gently as his mum's eyes followed the spooky-phone. "If you can see that, mum, it's time you knew. If you feel funny, panic or anything, stop me."

"I remember, flying unicorns and stuff like that." She turned to look at the magical creatures on the sideboard. "So it's to do with them." Only a couple of brownies were still there, because despite them working up some tolerance to Abel, Ferryl had frightened the rest away. "Go on then, tell me everything. I'm as ready as I'll ever be."

Abel absolutely and definitely didn't tell his mum everything. What he did tell her became a slow reveal, with pauses to see if any of it had a really bad effect. The business turned out to be dead easy, because Abel had stopped creatures coming into the house, her car, and her work cubicle. The business did the same, sort of. When that information had no adverse effect on his mum, Abel answered more questions. He had to explain the prices people paid, and how come so many people knew. Finding out that only a few people could provide creature protection, which made it hideously expensive, raised a laugh. Her protection, personal, house and car, hadn't cost a bean.

As Abel gradually explained the signs, the marks, being magic, he stayed well clear of possession or rescuing beings from pits. Spooky-phone obviously came from his tattoo, which had to be explained. Since she'd be just another creature to his mum, Abel confessed about Zephyr. He held his breath while she flew out and hovered until his mum had inspected her, worried that would be enough to spark the insanity. Once revealed, Zephyr wanted to say hello but Abel told her no, for now. Abel sort of explained the Accord, an agreement to keep the creatures secret to avoid panic, but avoided words like sorcery and magic.

He needn't have worried about those particular words. Abel's mum already knew the small magical creatures in the Bonny's Tavern game were real, which helped more than expected. Sometime after finding that out, her mind must have more or less accepted the creatures had to be magic in real life as well. After a laugh when she wanted to know if he had a message owl and a broomstick, Abel confirmed he could cast what looked like spells. He explained that spells were glyphs, shapes like the protection on the doors. That brought a slow nod, as if it explained something. Finding out why the vicar had insisted on speaking to Abel and his friends rather than the directors, to see if they were good or bad magicians, brought another slow nod. The inheritance part caused more trouble, because it shouldn't be possible.

Abel found out quite a bit as well. His mum knew they all went into Castle House, because she'd seen muddy footprints on the path. She accepted something bad lived in there, so she couldn't go inside, but wanted Abel to keep out as well. When Abel asked her to keep it all quiet, she laughed. "Kelis will be having this talk when she gets home from Germany, because Jess can see creatures now." She laughed again at Abel's shocked look, though her humour had a slightly manic edge. "You think adults can't keep a secret?"

"No, I'm worried about, you know, the effect?"

"Jess knew I saw things, and I told her they were ghosts. The first time she saw something odd she came to see me. Did you know they're clearer if she strokes that tattoo, the Tavern sign?" Abel shook his head, flummoxed as his mum ploughed on. "We found out by trial and error, because sometimes she couldn't see them. Stroking lets me see them better as well, their glow is brighter. Jess can't see the glow, unless she's in the dark." Her eyes narrowed as she pounced, again. "Though I still can't see whatever that fuzzy thing is, the one that comes out of the trees and goes into the house. Or to the house door, because it never opens. That happens just after you and your friends have supposedly gone to that little hut that Rob bought."

"A veil, mum, so most people can't see us. Not a real veil, or cloak, a magic one. The bit in front of the door is called a Seeming, so it looks shut while we are going inside." Abel stood up, still not sure. "Would you like to see a veil?"

From the shocked look, maybe not, but after some thought his mum decided she wanted to see some of this magic actually work. Despite Ferryl still not being sure, Abel let go and stepped away from her. "Now you see me, now you don't." His mum wouldn't have heard the last part because veils muffled sound.

He stayed still as his mum squinted, then slowly stroked her Tavern mark and nodded. "Something, but not a person. Just a fuzzy globe. Can I touch it?"

Abel couldn't answer so Ferryl did. "Yes, but gently or you might poke him in the eye." A moment later Abel and Ferryl learned something new. A non-magic user could penetrate a veil without breaking it, and could see through it as soon as their hand penetrated.

Veil led to Ferryl's careless comment about a shield being harder to poke a hand through. After trying to explain why he needed one, without admitting to more than meeting the occasional larger creature, Abel asked Eric's question. "Since you can't shield, would you like a bodyguard, mum? That would stop any creatures getting near you? Chauffeur as well if you like." The question bounced back and forth, as Abel tried to minimise the danger to himself, but insist mum should be protected. After admitting that some magic could be dangerous, Abel had to agree to the next demand. His mum wanted to see what the dangerous magic looked like. She settled on a visit to the gym, in a few days when she'd got her breath back. The Taverners could show her, then Eric could explain her options.

"Though I'll be safe enough at work, if all your friends can protect themselves."

"Not all of them, but you don't need to go to work anyway, mum. I can buy this house, or you can have a house in Sheffield, or we'll flog one and buy something wherever you like. Then you can put your feet up." Abel still hadn't really touched on what Celtchar's legacy included. He might not have much cash yet, but he could give his mum a choice of houses.

"Not likely, I'll be keeping an eye on my son's business. I wouldn't know what to do with myself if I quit work now." The look wasn't taking no for an answer. "You can get someone to explain it all properly, so I can make sure nobody fiddles the books. That Bertram from Sheffield can do it. Eric is always phoning him with questions." Abel agreed, adding a phone call to Bertram to his list of things to do.

Several subjects were put on hold because of the game launch, or because Abel insisted on his mum having time to absorb what she'd already learned. After some frantic phone calls, the rest of the Taverners agreed to downplay the Master of Pendragon Enterprises bit, and never ever mention the Master of Castle House. Discussing his mum going inside the house itself went on hold, because Abel wanted Kelis back and recovered from her own parental showdown.

The other parents would be kept in the dark, for now, because Abel's mum didn't want any of them going through her experiences. She reckoned that living for years with the Pig, Mr. Ventnor, beating her, then getting her mark while on drugs after he kicked her insensible, had kept Jess sane. Or as she put it, "Jess lived with a real monster for years, so a few odd looking creatures that don't actually hurt her aren't really frightening." Though Jess had been worrying about seeing more of them, so a demonstration of magic might reassure her. Abel assured his mum, Kelis knew the dangerous sort of glyphs so her dad wouldn't get near his daughter or ex-wife again. The look in his mum's eyes reminded Abel of Kelis, some version of "he'd better not try."

Abel walked Ferryl home, and stayed for a while because this time he needed reassurance. So far so good, but it could still go horribly wrong. At least he'd stopped worrying about the game launch.

Bonny's Tavern Lives!

Abel gradually introduced his mum to the Taverners, real magic, and the refuge, but not goblins or dryads. Frederick, the fifty-five-year-old who ran the refuge, enjoyed the opportunity to compare notes on childhoods filled with hallucinations and psychiatrists. The highlight turned out to be the trip to the gym. "I've never been chauffeur-driven. I keep wondering how much it will cost and looking for the taxi meter." Abel didn't laugh, because he recognised nerves talking. He felt nervous as well, because watching people she knew chucking magic about, children, might flip his mum over the edge. Abel had already thrown a little fire glyph in the garden, and ruffled the bushes with a wind glyph, just to give her an idea.

"The gym, boss."

"You can stop that boss business, Ginny. You never used to say it."

"But I've got to show due deference while your parent is here. It's in the chauffeuress rules." Ginny jumped out and opened a door. "Though the rules aren't totally clear on this. I've opted for opening your mum's door, because I want her on my side."

"Zephyr, what's got into Ginny?"

"She is enjoying this, and wishes she had been able to show her own mother her magic."

Abel kept that in mind as Ginny escorted them to the door, and Eric opened up with a flourish. "Now I can see why you've taken a day off, Chris. Since you do most of the work I came to hide here, but now the boss has found me. I hope you'll put in a good word?"

"A lot depends on if I get a decent cuppa and a comfy seat. Is there a viewing gallery?" At least his mum seemed happier now she could joke with her boss, the non-son one. She stopped just inside the door, turning to speak quietly to Abel. "It really is a gym. How do they practice magic here, and how do I know who I can talk in front of?"

Abel raised his hand, to wave back at several Taverners and two employees who were working out. "Not in here mum, this is non-magical fitness, though Taverners have to be fit anyway. The door over there, with the grill, is magically locked."

"Let me try it." Abel stood back while his mum tried the door handle, then put his hand over the grill. A wind glyph lifted a sneck, and she opened up without any trouble. "Very clever." She turned and inspected the sneck from the inside. "You can control wind enough to lift that?"

"Yes, all the better users, adepts, can do that. The beginners need someone to open the door. We go out through this side door."

"To stop anyone peeking. Is it that obvious?" She opened the second door. "Oh." Abel stared as his mum actually giggled. "Yes, that would be a bit startling."

Four metres away three Taverners were jogging on the spot while keeping a half brick levitated using wind. "That is so that we can throw glyphs while running away, just in case." Rachel, dressed in a black blouse and jeans with a hooded red cloak, threw out her hand with a flourish. "K'ress Bloodclaw bids you welcome to Bonny's Tavern training centre. If madam would step this way, we have a demonstration of how trainees learn to master their first glyph." Abel opened his mouth, but both Zephyr and Ferryl told him let it go. His mum needed to know. She'd be learning a lot, because at least half the Taverners were here, all busy practicing.

"Hello Mrs. Conroy. My name is Tobias. You may have seen me hanging around with Kelis, after Valentine's. I'm training beginners, because that helps me to practice. A couple of months ago I would have been doing the same as they are. The idea is they must push magic through their palms to lift the leaf, or the gravel, without losing control." A row of four teenagers sat against the wall, staring at their hands. Each one stroked their arm, and with a sinking feeling Abel saw his mum unconsciously copy them. One leaf trembled, one jumped off, gravel scattered while absolutely nothing happened to the last little heap of gravel.

"Allow me." Ferryl's glyphs scattered across the floor and lifted the gravel, depositing it back in a stunned trainee's hand.

"That is what we are all aiming at. I'm a million miles away yet, so thank the sorceress for saving you some time with a brush and dustpan." To Abel's huge relief, Tobias winked at his mum as he turned away from the thoroughly impressed trainees. He turned back to point at them in turn, using his other hand to hold a gently rippling heap of gravel just off his palm. "You pair pushed too hard, you have to moderate it. Your leaf trembling means you are nearly there, you just need to catch that feeling and get behind it." Tobias squatted by the lad at the end. "Right, you can feel the magic?" The lad nodded, glancing at Abel and Ferryl. "Forget them, concentrate on that feeling. Learn to recognise it." Tobias glanced up to smile as Rachel led Abel's group towards those actually throwing glyphs.

Rachel turned as Abel's mum touched her arm, hesitantly. "So it isn't instant. Can anyone do it, magic?"

"We don't know. Some don't find magic unless they meditate, some see creatures, but it's best if they do so before they are twenty-five. Older than that and it can send them….er, sorry."

"Crackers. Been there, come back. Why is there a great big hollow cube made out of concrete? Is it really that dangerous?" She stopped to watch as a succession of Taverners threw glyphs, watched by two who were giving advice.

"No, because there's also a shield around it, but better safe than sorry." Rachel raised her voice. "Shannon, will you please show Mrs. Conroy a really hot fire glyph."

"Okay. Hello Mrs. Conroy. This is as hot as I can get. Abel's are hotter and Ginny's are neater." Moments later Abel saw his mum flinch as a patch of concrete blackened and cracked.

She looked at the smoking circle, then back at Abel and then Ginny. "Neater?" A short succession of small glyphs hit the concrete, leaving a straight line of smaller circles, all smoking. "Well at least I know Abel is safe with you. That's wind and fire, what else is there?"

"My turn?" Rachel cast several ice spikes, then turned to Ferryl. "A web please?" Ferryl cast a web that left a perfect impression of itself eaten into the concrete. "Rob? Can you do the earth thing with the concrete please?" With a big smile, Rob pulled the floor up into three spikes and then flattened them. "Anyone for colour?" A dozen nearby Taverners grinned, and a kaleidoscope of brightly coloured shapes and splashes spattered across the concrete. Everyone loved the colour glyph. Rachel pointed to four teenagers, she'd really started enjoying herself. "Clean-up?" Wind picked up the gravel, collected for wind glyph practice, and scoured the concrete wall clean except for the painted targets. She turned with her hands on her hips. "Those four are adepts, and teach the rest."

"We learn moving targets as well." Warren's and Shannon's hands cast glyphs, and half a dozen round balls lifted up and bobbed about. Several Taverners fired off tiny glyphs, trying to knock the balls back to hit the concrete without bursting any. "Julie, Carl, remember. Watch your glyph all the way home and it won't miss." The targeting improved.

"Definitely protected. Can you do all that?" Despite the smile, that had been a bit much, and Abel could see the worry in his mum's eyes.

"Yes mum, but we don't use the glyphs for fighting." That didn't work, she didn't believe him so Abel pushed on. "These exercises are a means to make our magic stronger, and we are all better at one particular sort. Rob is best with concrete or earth, I'm good with fire, Kelis is brilliant with wind and ice and Jenny will make your garden grow. Ferryl is good at them all, but prefers wind. Now would you like to sit down for that cuppa, and catch your breath?"

"Oh yes, definitely. Then you can explain the people running about, and those targets, and the heap of metal bricks. Is that a real sword?" She pointed and yes, another Robin D'Ritche swaggered across the floor while producing wind glyph hand claps of varying volume. A male version this time, but with long boots and the same sort of swagger as Una, and what might be a real sword. A very proud Rachel led them across the room and up a ramp, explaining it was for the disabled Taverners. One of those waited at the top, and demonstrated moving his wheelchair using just wind. Abel noticed three Taverners poised to dive in, so it must have been a new skill.

Over a cuppa Abel steered his mum's questions onto mundane subjects, such as the café. "Does the other bit have its own café?"

"Yes, but the toilets and showers are shared. There's a magic door to keep this side private." Shannon had joined them, and now she pointed down the ramp. "We even put in disabled facilities once we had wheelchair Taverners. Abel agreed to pay for a full set of lifts and everything." Totally unware of the sharp look, she went on to gleefully describe the improvements over the original breeze block and bare pipes. "We have to keep both lots of facilities the same, because the Taverners use the non-magic gym as well. We all want to tow a car."

"Hang on Shannon, mum is still learning." Abel could see a long debrief coming tonight. "I just expected her to see a couple of people throwing a glyph or two."

"No chance. We all knew you'd be bringing your mum, and we want her to be proud of what you've done, with, er, with the tree magic." Her quick embarrassed glance, as she almost spilled the Castle House part, slowed Shannon up a bit.

But Abel's mum had picked up on something else. "You said that on the way in, that your Taverners, Tavern players, needed to be fit. Is that for running, like those down there?" A short line were running along a marked track holding a log in one hand, while blowing half bricks into the air and catching them again using just air. Most of them had to use their hand at least occasionally.

"No, or just partly. Magic, the glyphs, can only increase what you can already do." With a little smile Abel used a wind glyph to collect a half brick. "I can lift this easily, using ordinary muscles. I can lift it easier with air. The stronger I am the more I can lift because the wind glyph lifts a multiple of what I can. All the Taverners use those machines to get stronger so they can lift or throw more, even if they never need to. Learning to control that strength teaches us to be more economic with our magic. Then we can fill more hexes for hideous fees, so I can afford fancy taps in the washrooms." As he'd hoped, the reference to fees cheered his mum up, and she spent a little while laughing about how she'd got free service. She relaxed even more as a succession of Taverners came to say hello, and how pleased they were to see her. Quite a few wanted to show her their own special trick, floating sparks or rippling fringes, with varying attempts at Petra's glyph clap. Someone had passed the word, because none of them mentioned titles or who paid for what.

Once the subject came back to training, Rachel explained that the archers practicing down below were supposed to be Bullseye the Bowman. They were already members of an archery club, with varying degrees of expertise. All of them were hoping to find a hex to enhance their arrow heads. Other Taverners were catching some of the arrows, or knocking them off course, or redirecting them, to practice hitting fast targets.

Once she'd finished her cuppa, Rachel led off for the rest of the tour. There were three enactment swords on the fencing room wall, and a few Taverners wore swords as part of their costume. So far, nobody could use them properly, but two Taverners had joined a fencing club. They hadn't got past epees yet, but were passing on their lessons. The rough metal bricks stacked along one wall were lead bars, one heap full of magic and one waiting for an adept Taverner to fill them. Filling ten bars gave them an extra turn on the adept exercises, mixing combinations of glyphs while keeping them precise. Other adepts watched and advised them. Rachel managed to avoid the office, where the maps showing the scope of the Tavern mission might lead to questions about the cost.

The amount of work needed to train for glyphs seemed to reassure Abel's mum, much to his relief. She confessed to being worried about a world overrun with spell-casters. Seeing how hard all the would-be magicians trained on the gym equipment also explained another puzzle, Abel filling out and needing new clothes. Despite his attempts to hide them she'd noticed Abel's second-hand replacement clothes, but thought he'd been ashamed because someone gave him them.

Despite his fears, Abel didn't get the third degree that night, because his mum seemed stunned and went straight to bed. The questions started the next morning, but only now and then. So far mum seemed to be pacing herself, not pushing but thinking it all over and then dealing with any anomalies.

*   *   *

Day by day Abel's mum learned an edited version of Abel's business, one that skipped around life and death and concentrated on protecting machinery and buildings. Having seen gremlins at her other job, slipping in and out of computers, she understood why firms paid to keep them out. Learning that some expensive cars and better makes of equipment were protected reassured her, the higher prices really did make them more reliable. The slow reveal continued with a few questions each night, after Abel came back from the latest publicity trip. Sometimes she just wanted clarification of a chance remark at the office.

At work magic could only be mentioned to Eric or known Taverners, in the back offices, because at least half the staff had no idea magic existed. Having had years of treatment, Mrs. Conroy made sure she wasn't responsible for sending anybody crackers. The Sheffield secretary came over to show her the proper accounts, and how to update them, but he turned aside any attempt to pry. Bertram stuck to his sorcerer's instructions, to the letter, while treating Abel's mum with careful courtesy.

Even while Abel dealt with his personal crisis, easing his mum through discovering magic, he had to deal with the rest of the world moving on. Bonny's Tavern had plenty of sales in the Stourton area, and a smaller bump in Sheffield and near the eleven established Taverns. Sales in the rest of the country, and Germany, started off as a scattering. The interviews and visits to shops died back, but the calls and emails claiming to have managed to flutter their leaf increased. After the first two hoaxes, the Taverners came up with a few questions about the actual effect that eliminated time-wasters.

When Petra came back, after extending her trip to see another two new magic users, she had an explanation for the speed of response. "All three already saw creatures. None of them actually fluttered their leaf, but they won't be long. Since they're already aware of magic, I explained about drawing the Tavern mark on their arm, and the glyph on their palms to get the hang of using it."

"We've got nineteen more that aren't hoaxes." Rob, along with other Taverners, scowled. The hoaxers had really annoyed some people. "Then there's the three adults who've seen the publicity and recognise the creatures. I'd hoped Mz Fisher would help with that but we've heard nothing."

"Maybe she's frightened? Or maybe she came to Castle House, just to check first, and the barrier told her not to bother." After beating it about, Ferryl might be right so Abel made the phone call. He thought Mz Fisher sounded pleased to hear from him, and she certainly agreed to come and visit. Insisting on Castle House might mean she'd tried and failed, and wanted to try again.

Now Petra had returned the Range Rover, Abel got a little light relief by tossing the keys to his mum. She took a short drive, but confessed she'd been terrified of pranging it. After two more short trips, to take staff to the gym, she borrowed it for a shopping trip to Sheffield. There wouldn't be a repeat. She complained it wasn't any fun because she couldn't take

Jess, Kelis's mum, with her. Despite his mum thawing a little, the car would definitely stay in Stourton for the Taverners to use. If it turned up parked outside Abel's house there'd be too many questions, from Rob's parents for starters, because she could easily buy her council house for what the car cost.

*   *   *

Meanwhile the Taverners concentrated on the big problem, the sudden rush of potential magical Taverners. Hopefully the numbers would die back, but if they continued at twenty a week the drivers couldn't cope. After trying to work out the logistics, Abel made his own call, on Woods and Green. As usual, Terese seemed to have a gap in her diary at just the right time.

Once he'd been shown through to Terese's office, Abel didn't beat around the bush. "The launch has thrown up a lot of teenagers who can see creatures, so I'll need some of the money from selling the ornaments, please." Abel glanced down at his quick scribblings. "How long will it take to get me five thousand in cash, for now?"

"As long as a messenger takes to collect it from the bank. No need for you to go." Terese spoke briefly into a phone, stipulating used twenties if possible. As Abel wondered how often she arranged anonymous cash, the solicitor turned back with an inquisitive look. "How many so far?"

"Twenty-three in a week, plus three older people who thought they were crazy or saw ghosts. We've already visited four teenagers and none had actually fluttered a leaf, just recognised the creatures. We've had several hoaxes, which isn't helping."

Terese read the annoyance on Abel's face. "Maybe you should take the hoaxers seriously? Show them magic and leave them trying to work out what happened?" She laughed at Abel's shock. "The Accord won't allow that, unfortunately. To be honest, I'd expected you to find a lot more who had been awakened without realising. Perhaps they just haven't seen the game yet."

"More? How many?"

"Who knows? Though now you ask, I've never thought of an actual number. A few teenagers cause trouble now and then, raving about visions, but they are hushed up." She paused, looking intrigued. "Now I think about it, there must have been more magic users in the past, even with a smaller population, because most lay priests could cast a real blessing. All the witches and warlocks came from somewhere, so there were plenty of youngsters who weren't snapped up by the church or sorceresses." Terese sat back, deep in thought, obviously following her own train of thought and trying to give Abel a real answer. "Count up the villages and towns over two hundred years old, and start with at least one witch or sorceress for each, or a priest if there's a church. There must have been that many actively magical humans at least, and towns had several of each. So maybe twice that, or four times? I hadn't really thought about numbers before, because there are always enough to supply apprentices."

"But according to Creepio, most villages without a church have no witch either. There could be hundreds of kids out there who should have been trained for those jobs and weren't. Thousands?" Abel looked down at his list. "Flobberclomps at least. Will other countries be the same?"

"Some cultures still believe in the unseen and the power of spells, so they still support sorceresses or witches and there'll be fewer who are never discovered and trained. The larger monsters and many of the characters you invented are based on European legends or authors, so the main impact of your game should be restricted to the UK, the Americas and Australia, possibly Europe. The language difference will slow the game's spread in the Americas south of the USA, even though the rest of the continent has been exposed to European religions and legends. The Far East, the Indian sub-continent, Africa and Asia have different cultural deities and demons, though films and TV are blurring the boundaries. So is the English language, and the movement of peoples, and the smaller pests like ganshbaal and hoplins have spread across the world. Sort of magical rats and cockroaches." The solicitor pointed at Abel's list. "You will definitely need a bigger piece of paper, and your trouble-shooters will need passports." A little smile flickered on her face. "Or magical assistance to pass borders."

"We can't handle all that!" Abel stared from the list to Terese, then back. "There aren't enough Taverners to train them."

"Your original plan will work, the one you came up with in this office. The first one to discover magic in any area will found a Tavern, then train subsequent Taverners." From the glance at her desk, Terese had taken notes at the time. "It seemed ambitious, but workable since you were willing to help with finance. You won't get everyone of course. How many recruits did you expect, world-wide?"

"Recruits? World-wide? I was thinking of England, maybe the UK, and wasn't thinking of actively looking for magic users. The launch only covered a few towns fairly near here, and eleven very small sub-launches, but the internet has already thrown up a scattering." Abel firmed up, because it was too late now. "We've already launched in Germany, but once again a fairly local affair. How will that go?" Abel stifled a laugh as he remembered. "We've already got two German recruits, but from playing the beta version of Bonny's Tavern. Kelis is over there dealing with them."

"You will find recruits, probably quite a few. Germany has plenty of wild forest and a tradition of supernatural tales, but is too civilised to have many true believers who will pay witches. There'll be potential Taverners in the villages, but sorcerers should pick up most of those in cities. Where will you launch next?"

"Nowhere once I've spoken to Jenny! Or not until we've dealt with this, and worked out some way of handling it." Though one person might help. "Did you look into Mz Fisher for me?"

"Yes, she really does believe in ghosts. Her journalism seems fact-based and impartial so I'd suggest using her if she'll agree. Ask her to call in here and we'll get a suitable contract drawn up." A wicked gleam came and went in her eyes. "I will explain the sorcerer response to breach of contract."

"My mum asked about helping out. She knows, or some of it, and will be visiting you at some time." Abel explained briefly. "I'd rather not get her actively involved, and definitely want to take her education very slowly. Especially the parts about Master of this and that and what they really mean. I explained that I inherited Pendragon Enterprises from some distant relative I'd never heard of, and you had the details."

"Solicitor/client confidentiality takes no account of mother/son relationships, so we can refuse to give her details. If she pushes we can use your age. We are the trustees and can keep everything confidential until you reach eighteen. In the interim, we will tell her exactly as much as you want us to, certainly not enough to cause her any problems. You may be right about why your mother, and Kelis's, remain sane and it might mean she is now safe." Terese looked at Abel, hesitating before speaking. "I can find help for any teenagers you can't deal with. Some sorceresses are better than others, and might take them as apprentices?"

"With tethers? I'd rather not."

"But better that, or even the church, than insanity. I'm sure you will do your best, but I will prepare a list of what are considered benevolent sorceresses. Just in case. At least meet some of them and explain your idea. They may come up with a way to help." The solicitor, made a note, looked up at a knock on the door and smiled. "Your cash is here. If you want larger amounts I'd prefer some notice."

"No problem." Abel worked through his mental to-do list. "Zephyr, what did I forget?"

"Trees."

"Zephyr reminded me to ask about trees. The ones for Brinsford and the villages."

"Two are on the way to Brinsford, large mature trees without dryads, a red maple and a horse chestnut. The contractor will arrive with the machinery to dig the holes. We have already selected nine trees for villages, mature but not as old so they'll be cheaper to move. Dryad Walnut sends greetings." She chuckled and tapped her papers. "Whole trees for trainees? There are sorcerers who will tear out their hair at the thought."

"Redwolf, the sorcerer who rents a house in Stourton, has allowed Mannan, his senior apprentice, access to a tree. He keeps saying he's a fast learner." Abel sighed, because he had enough to do but…. "Then I've got to race around all those trees to protect them before a dryad moves in."

"We have a glyph we use on your behalf, as your legal representatives, to claim new property. We could put the glyph on these trees? It has come in useful since Celtchar disappeared, especially for claiming trees that are outside a wood where there is no convenient dryad on guard. The protection will only answer to Celtchar's heir, but he can adapt, replace or remove the glyph. Having heard what you did with Pendragon's trees, and spoken to Dryad Walnut, Woods thought it best to create an additional glyph that will allow you to extend access to selected others. I will give you the glyph and explain how it works, but the trees will be safe until you get there. Or we can take two trees to each location and arrange for a dryad in one of them?" A wide smile answered Abel's look. "Properly contracted, not bound. That would be a good idea, if you wish to establish a grove or protect an area. Do the trainees own the ground?"

"Another job for me because I don't know. I only asked them to find locations. Hold the village trees until I get answers, please." After working over the benefits of two or more trees with a dryad guardian, Abel finally left, with a bundle of cash. He'd try to give some to mum though she still seemed reluctant, much like Kelis, Rob, Jenny and Ferryl. According to her, Pendragon Enterprises didn't make him really rich unless he sold off all the houses. She wanted Abel to be careful, because his windfall had to last a lifetime.

Abel's lifetime might be a lot longer than his mum expected, and he had already started plotting with Ferryl for if his mum could handle glyphs. Judging by how slowly Frederick learned she'd never become immortal, but lifetime might mean a bit longer and much healthier than the average.

In the meantime, after Terese's estimate of the numbers of teenagers who might be needing help, the Tavern had to get organised. They had to get to as many of them as possible, as fast as they could.

*　*　*

Having his mum in the know made some things much easier. "I need to go on a trip, mum, four or five days. Jenny has a long list of people who have emailed, teenagers who've found magic and want help. Now the launch is over I can do my bit. The smaller Taverns have picked up anyone near them, but there's a scattering of teenagers who only need one look at the graphics on the adverts to start yelling for help." Abel smiled happily at the next part. "I'm going by motorbike, because Ginny has her own list. They're all day trips so she can take Diane and Melanie, to give them some experience of other magic users. Knowing that pair, they'll want to cram in some extra training while they've got her to themselves."

"And she can keep an eye on them. When are you going?" The day after tomorrow brought mild teasing instead of twenty questions. "It's about time you managed on your own, without a baby-sitter. Just tell that girl of yours to be careful and make sure she wears her helmet. Call me to let me know how it goes."

Once more Abel tackled the same old problem. "I'd be happier if you had a bodyguard. Not obvious, just someone in sight of you or the house." Eric had tried, but she'd just changed the subject.

"Or I could invite that young man, the one who seems to like hiking in the area, to use your bedroom while you're gone." As usual, his mum nodded as she read the answer on Abel's face. "I have one already, don't I?"

Abel nodded, cautiously. "Sort of. The Taverners insist." At least that part was true. The Taverner volunteer allegedly hiking nearby had a tent round behind Dead Wood, and Ginny on speed-dial.

"Introduce the poor lad, and I'll consider him as a temporary lodger. When you get back we'll talk, because if I'm getting a nanny I'd like to set the terms." Her easy acceptance should have warned Abel there'd be more. "I'd be safe if I went with you to visit these other Taverns. Then I can help you with the new teenagers, or visit any older people who see things?"

She'd offered several times, but Abel declined. He didn't want to introduce his mum to the actual process of learning to use glyphs, not yet, not until he had time to watch over every moment. With luck Mz Fisher would deal with adults who saw creatures, long before mum pushed really hard. Instead his mum helped him plan a route, and decide what to take. This would be Abel's first long trip on the motorbike, and his first trip with only Ferryl as company. Rob had a chauffeur and his own list, and all the cars were needed for other visits or business, so Abel seized a chance to get clear of the bedlam.

Jenny's list didn't have many, all of them within an hour's driving, because her dad, Jake, still kept a watch on how she handled selling Bonny's Tavern. Luckily Jake had his own business to run, which he'd neglected for several days over the launch period.

*   *   *

Abel would be setting off early to miss the traffic, so he took his motorbike to put in the shed Rob had bought. Since it was in Castle

House gardens, the bikes wouldn't wake up half the village when they set off the following morning. Taking the bikes also gave him and Ferryl a perfect excuse to be in Castle House gardens to meet a visitor. Now she knew about magic, his mum tended to ask what he'd be doing there, and Abel didn't want her involved.

Despite the visitor knowing Castle House had been opened, Abel and Ferryl waited in the cave with Zephyr on lookout. She danced above them as if hunting, but there shouldn't have been any fae inside the protection. When he asked, Ferryl glanced up with a smile. "She's playing with the magical sparks, chasing but not eating any. They seem to slip through any barrier or shield, but never cause any trouble so those who can see them tend to ignore them. Now I know they could be souls, which might explain everything. One day, if our luck runs out, that could be you or I." She looked around the clearing. "Not a bad place to fade, flying free in peace without any fae hunting me. There might even be some concentrated magic left over from glyph practice, enough for me to regrow."

"But not as you, the you we know. According to Chestnut, and the bishop, I don't even have that option. Maybe if I've got enough thought left to dive into that slab? You said there's lots of magic in there." With his improved sight Abel could see faint glowing lines where his blood had cracked some glyphs, freeing Ferryl Shayde.

"Maybe enough to make you a god. It takes a lot, but the ones I saw didn't need as much as you'd think." When Abel jerked round, Ferryl was giving the slab a calculating look. "It's hard to tell, collected in a rock like that, but the slab has been draining magic from scores of trees for at least two hundred years. I don't know how long it was there before I arrived, but that slab already contained a lot of magic."

"You've seen a god created! Don't ever tell anyone how it's done. The bishop nearly had a heart attack, until he realised that magical creatures only knew gods could be created, not the method." Abel recovered a little, but he didn't like that look. "Don't, Ferryl. The gods would kill you if Creepio didn't get there first."

"Not kill, not if I succeeded. Gods chain and drain other gods, once they have been overpowered. I saw a minor goddess chained once, the second time I saw a heaven made. That's how I know how to do it, because it isn't obvious the first time." Ferryl looked lost in thought for a while. "Your history books call her Nerthus, and have given her a place in mythology. I knew her as a benevolent sorceress who preferred plant magic, but helped with difficult pregnancies and sick children. She travelled among a few minor tribes in what is now Germany, by the river Elbe. They worshipped her as a goddess. When invaders came, backed by sorcerers, she tried to defend her people but they were defeated. I fought as one of her shield-maidens, because I dare not reveal my true-self and magic, but flew free when my host fell. I hid on a nearby hill, among the treetops, and saw."

The silence went on a long time, but Abel didn't interrupt. Either Ferryl had emotions a long time ago, or finding emotion had coloured old memories, because he'd heard real grief in her voice. He jumped a little when she finally spoke, caught by surprise even if the words were soft. "As the enemy closed in, their priests, sorcerers, sought to catch and bind her. Surrounded, her warriors dead or dying, she took her only escape. She dragged the magic and life from the nearby forest, every animal, magical creature and plant, and made her heaven." Ferryl looked upwards, lost in the memory. "Once a heaven is started, the new goddess can use it to drain any nearby magic, even through a shield. That is the one sure way to kill a sorcerer, even if he is inside his woodland. His trees would also be drained, despite any glyphs, to add magic to the heaven. If I had stayed nearer to Nerthus, that would have been my end as well. Many enemy priests were too near. Their shields failed and she drained them, but the rest ran forward as she collapsed. Nerthus caught hold of the link before they reached her, and her essence was drawn into her heaven. Safe."

Ferryl drew a deep breath and let it out in a long shuddering sigh. "That was the second one I ever saw. It taught me a terrible lesson. Death, or binding by a mortal sorcerer, might be better than being a goddess." She turned to Abel, a single tear in the corner of one eye. "Do not be tempted."

"Not a chance. I'm not god material."

"She shouldn't have been goddess material, not enough worshippers. Though sometimes I wonder if one is enough to make a heaven, just not enough to give a goddess the power to survive. That night the heavens warred, lightning and thunder but without rain. One bolt of lightning struck her discarded body and it breathed. Nerthus had been defeated by a stronger god, and forced back into her body."

"How do you know?" Abel bit that back too late.

"The priests who collected her knew, and they talked. They shouted and sang, triumphant, because now she would help their conquest. They took her away to chain her, magically, so their god could feed on her magic until she faded. Every prayer to Nerthus would give her a trickle, which would be stolen, again and again until her last worshipper died."

"That could be centuries, because people still remember many of the old gods. Or maybe not, maybe remembering isn't enough." Abel almost whispered, horrified by the thought of an immortal being chained up and bled of magic, century after century.

"I crept close and listened to them celebrating, talking about how long she might serve their god. One worshipper, that's all it takes for a goddess to survive. The worshipper must think of the goddess's symbol, her sign, and pray. Not formal prayer, just a wish to connect, intent is everything. The sign is what makes her heaven. That's all it takes, that sign and the intent, enough magic, and believers. That's also how I know, because both the god and goddess cast their own sign to make their individual heaven. It wasn't a cross, even though his worshippers use one now. I don't know how their god managed that." Ferryl shook her head in disbelief. "Nerthus must have truly believed in herself, been sure she was that sign, that it encompassed everything she was, before casting it up into the sky for all to see. That sign is the birth of a heaven, but then intent must shape what form it takes before a goddess takes up residence. I often wonder what her heaven might have been, because she had very little time to imagine it."

"That's another strike, because I'd never be able to imagine a whole heaven. Does that mean the Christian God imagined angels and all that, or that his heaven is something else? What did he cast if it wasn't a cross?" Zephyr interrupted before Ferryl did more than shrug. A car had pulled up outside the gate.

*　*　*

One glance between the trees showed that Mz Fisher had arrived, a little early, and had brought reinforcements. Ferryl put a hand on Abel's arm as he moved to show himself. "Wait, let's see what they do."

The next few minutes consisted of a growing argument, fuelled by frustration, as the three newcomers all tried to open the garden gate. The voices grew louder until Abel could hear them. "It's the barrier. They thought they could get through."

Ferryl nodded, intent on the voices. "I know, I've been listening. Sorry, I have been shaping the wind to bring the sound to me and forgot you couldn't. They've been trying to force each other to open the gate. Mz Fisher seems to think if two of them keep encouraging or ridiculing the third, they'll be able to overcome the suggestion."

As Abel and Ferryl watched, the other two took hold of the reporter and went to shove her at the gate, then changed their minds. Mz Fisher rounded on them. "Why did you stop?"

"Because it's pointless. Why risk injuring yourself when you hit the gate, just to get into an overgrown garden?" The man threw out a hand, pointing. "I've always trusted you but look. How could the interior be intact after all these years? Any books in there will be rotten, or mouse nesting."

"According to you, there's up to five teenagers looking out of those windows. Those boarded up windows." The grey-haired woman shook her head in disgust. "I shouldn't have let you talk me into it. Whatever the explanation is, those kids got the idea from somewhere else. Probably they just saw ghosts, same as we did."

"Then where did this book come from? You checked, and every original copy even close to this condition is exactly where it should be." Mz Fisher brandished what had to be Pride and Prejudice. "How else can those kids know what each creature does, without years of study? How did they manage to keep specimens in captivity to study them?"

"Not in there. I can't see a single ghost in there." The man spun round towards Mz Fisher, anger in his voice. "Though you tell me they aren't ghosts, even if you agreed they were."

"Forget it. Take us home and we'll look into it on our own. We'll talk to the children ourselves." The grey-haired woman turned to the car.

"That's our cue. We don't want them charging about asking questions, or spouting whatever our discreet reporter told them." Abel started forward, raising a hand and his voice. "Hello Mz Fisher. You forgot to mention your friends when we arranged to meet." He kept walking forward, slowly and steadily, ignoring the babble of questions about how he got in there and about the lack of ghosts. "I see you brought the book back. Did you want to borrow another?"

All three shut up, two of them turning to look at the book. Mz Fisher looked hopeful, then guilty. "Could I? I'm sorry, but I've known Jerry and Eleanor for years and spent hours watching ghosts with them. I wanted to be sure you hadn't hypnotised me, to stop me getting back in." She glanced at the gate, then the house door. "I've been back twice, once at night, and even though I'm determined to go in I change my mind."

"Now we keep doing the same, and I've never met either you or that young lady so it isn't hypnotism. I'm Jerry and I'll tell you right now, I've been studying ghosts for years without coming up with some of what's in your game." The man checked himself. "I usually have better manners. Hello. I'd shake hands but?" He gestured helplessly at the gate. "That shows up perfectly normal on infrared, and I tossed a pebble that bounced off normally. A pebble tossed over the top seemed to go in there, then I noticed it laid at the bottom of the gate. What happens if I throw a rock big enough to break in?"

"It misses, falls short." Ferryl moved to the gate and put her hand out over the top. "Hello, I'm Ferryl Shayde." She shook Jerry's hand. "We can't bring three in, not without preparation, so we'll be talking in the church. It's Sunday so there's no workmen. You'll be able to argue and rant if you need to."

Neither Abel nor Ferryl would tell the trio why they couldn't come in, so in the end all three had to accept it. Abel sent them on ahead in their car, to the church, and walked through the village with Ferryl. Neither of them were sure where this was going. If Mz Fisher brought these two to be convinced, that might help. If not, all three would forget today at the very least.

*　　*　　*

The three were waiting outside the lychgate, inspecting it. Jerry pointed at the stone pillars supporting the roof. "We have our first question. There could be many more, because I travel the country cataloguing ghosts while Eleanor heads a study group."

"Seven of us. We experiment, trying to attract ghosts to divine their purpose or if they want something. So far food works best, especially rotting food, but only for some and none of them communicate." She rolled her eyes. "Which you managed to work out in a couple of years. Forgive me if I sound tetchy now and then, but this is my life's work."

"We'd love to see your research, because there may be creatures we've never seen. They'd go into the game, so anyone seeing them would know what to do." Abel smiled at her, impressed by Eleanor's sheer dedication. "Kelis is in Germany, so she might find new ones there."

"So why is Eleanor finding the church gate unpleasant? I'm a little uneasy, but Fish has no problem with it. Ah, sorry, Mz Fisher." Jerry glanced apologetically at the reporter.

"My father's fault." The brief smile looked nostalgic. "He said that since I was the shortest Fisher, my name should be shorter. I have known Jerry and Eleanor long enough to drop any formality." Mz Fisher turned back to the gate. "I really can't feel anything."

"At a guess you go to church regularly, Jerry goes now and then or not at all but considers himself Christian, and Eleanor is another religion or an atheist." Ferryl watched them exchange glances, but none of them argued. "The hex used to be stronger, to stop the heathen vandalising the churchyard. It's just gentle dissuasion now, and doesn't stop someone who is really determined, or drunk, or high on drugs."

"A lesser form of your garden." Eleanor braced herself and marched through the gate, relaxing on the other side. "The feeling has gone." Her eyes roamed over the building and graves as the rest filed through. "Won't that be awkward for a refuge?" Her hand shot out to point. "There, a predator flyer, inside the churchyard." She leafed through some papers until she found a creature booklet from the Bonny's Tavern game. "Fae? Catches and drains magic from faerie or…. Does that one sting?"

"No, but they'll all avoid us anyway." Abel took Ferryl's hand and asked Zephyr to connect them. Mz Fisher and Eleanor noticed spooky-phone but Jerry didn't. "Take them inside. I'll ask a goblin to wait outside the door in case we need one." He hung back as the rest went in, then waved a gargoyle down off the wall. When Abel went inside, a garden ornament squatted down by the door to wait.

The first part of the discussion centred on ghosts, quickly settled by Abel sending them out into the church proper. There the visitors saw brownies and piskies, which scuttled off to hide when Abel came out. Abel offered Tavern hexes and after testing them, Eleanor and Jerry gratefully accepted two each to keep 'ghosts' out of food. Jerry preferred them to crosses which he used, reluctantly despite being nominally Christian. He didn't understand how the influence of a cross could vary, the whole thing smacked of blind faith. Abel explained church magic in some, but not others, and he decided he'd use a mixture of crosses with the Tavern hexes to study the differences. Eleanor confessed to being sorely tempted to use a cross to keep her food and bed clear, but didn't as a matter of principle. Now she seemed quite upbeat at proof that something ungodly deterred ghosts. She wanted to test a variety of other religious symbols, to see how they compared to a Tavern hex.

Despite conceding the Tavern explanation covered everything known, the new pair were reluctant to call the creatures anything but ghost. For now at least, though Eleanor modified the names to fae-ghost, pictsie-ghost and brownie-ghost. Eventually she also met a goblin-ghost, which really threw all of them when it spoke. A ghost denying that it was a ghost left Jerry and Eleanor a bit glassy-eyed, and Mz Fisher a bit flustered, so Abel refused to show any more proofs.

Despite the revelations, neither of the two newcomers completely let go of their ghostly convictions. Both wanted time to think about the whole idea, and investigate, but agreed to keep quiet about what they'd seen. Jerry announced he would continue his travels, to try and find discrepancies between the Tavern explanation and evidence. Eleanor wanted to talk to her study group, and perhaps bring them to see Abel. She pointed out that if the Tavern had the true explanation, her group wouldn't have a hobby anymore. Some of them might ask for a job.

Abel smiled, and admitted he needed someone to help explain creatures to aware people over thirty. Ferryl pounced, asking for a list of everything they'd found out about ghosts, if possible, and Eleanor showed her some notes. By the time the trio left, Abel considered the meeting a win overall. Mz Fisher agreed to visit the three adults who'd contacted

Bonny's Tavern about seeing creatures. She'd hedged until Abel passed her a bundle of cash to cover her expenses and a reasonable fee, providing she gave him receipts for the expenses. Being a businessman had started to rub off, or Eric and mum nagging for paperwork.

Though that only dealt with three of the emails. The Taverners had visited nine teenagers in the first somewhat frantic ten days, most of them local, and the minor Taverns had dealt with another dozen, pretty good considering what a shock they'd been. Unfortunately emails kept coming in for Ferryl Shayde, so Jenny still had nineteen on her list. With luck that would go down, because now the Taverners had started getting organised.

*   *   *

Abel sneaked out of bed early the following morning, but not as early as his mum. He finally passed inspection and set off, finding Ferryl raring to go. The first appointment lay in Dumfries, two hundred miles away, and neither had ridden more than twenty in one run before. After taking one look at a busy main road, both opted for minor roads. That cut down on speed, but it let them stop when they liked. The trip turned out to be a lovely way to relax after the dashing about and all the interviews, because neither of them even looked at a phone. A couple of breaks for coffee and a snack later, the pair pulled up on the outskirts of town to call their first potential Taverner.

The phone call directed them to a local public park. Even as Abel parked his bike he could feel the magical markers claiming it for a sorcerer, so Abel and Ferryl kept well clear of the trees. An earnest, bespectacled youth made a beeline for the pair of leather-clad teenagers as soon as they walked through the gates. The first job had to be warning the lad, Stu, not to touch any trees, especially in parks, not now he'd awakened his magic. Stu insisted on proof. Walking towards a mature Oak started his feet itching, turning to painful pins and needles, very sharp ones, when he persevered. Stu got the message and backed off.

Once the real explanations started Abel for one wanted to laugh, but that wouldn't be fair. Stu expected to be able to cast glyphs straight away, as soon as he'd been given the trick. He seemed downcast when he learned it could take months, but cheered up again as Abel tossed a Tavern hex towards a litter bin and he saw the creatures avoiding it. Stu took half a dozen hexes for now, for his bedroom and to protect food. Meeting Zephyr convinced him the whole magic part must be real, because he saw the spooky-phone and then the shimmer. He looked worried when Abel put up a veil and demonstrated a dancing leaf and rippling gravel on his palm, but careful observation showed that nobody nearby could see. Ferryl waved at passers-by and danced about to prove she was invisible.

An hour later, Stu headed for home clutching his starter pack, including a lead bar already full of magic. Abel and Ferryl would call back in two days to check on progress. The youth had cheered up once Ferryl drew a Tavern shield on his arm, and he could feel the magic when he stroked it. Now he seemed very confident about casting his first glyph. Despite all the warnings, Stu took some convincing that he shouldn't tell anyone else. He especially wanted to tell his psychiatrist that the hallucinations were real. Abel and Ferryl fervently hoped Stu could persuade the shrink he'd been miraculously cured, and stop the visits, otherwise the shrink might eventually need a shrink.

The next leg took another three hours steady riding, across country to the outskirts of Middlesbrough, another relaxing scenic trip. The appointment would be the following morning, so after a meal the pair booked into a small hotel. Abel didn't understand Ferryl's little smiles as they went in, or the wider one, almost a laugh, when he paid for the two rooms with his Pendragon bank card. Once he'd dumped his bag in his room, changed out of his leathers and gone back down to the bar, Abel had to ask what she'd found so funny.

"I'd wondered about the rooms." Ferryl still had a little smile. "Some boys have more than one reason for a trip with their girlfriend."

It took Abel a few seconds, but not many. "You expected me to get one room?" He could feel the blush already, just lurking. He'd sat in Ferryl's room, cuddling, but....

"I thought you might ask." Her little smile didn't give any hints.

Did Ferryl expect him to? "What would you have said?"

Ferryl's smile didn't alter, giving nothing away. "I'd have asked if we'd reached the bottom of the bucket list, the first one."

"Have you?" Abel thought about it, of all the things Ferryl had talked of doing, and they'd barely scratched the list. "No, we've barely started."

"There's plenty of time for a new list when we've finished with this one." Ferryl leant over and kissed him. "That's for not assuming." A wicked gleam came into her eyes. "Or using my true-name to insist." She burst into laughter as Abel's blush rose up in its full crimson glory, and hugged him. "Sorry, I couldn't resist."

Though Abel wondered about that conversation, just a little, when he finally went to bed. He didn't feel ready for that with Ferryl, or did he? He liked her company, and the hugs and kisses and joking, but more? If he decided he wanted more, and tried, and Ferryl said no, would that spoil what they had? Abel had never had a normal girlfriend, without magic, so what was normal? Did Ferryl expect something more, was she used to more from living in other bodies? She was a gorgeous seventeen-year-old, and he really might be tempted but…. Abel finally recognised the but part. But that body was only a loan. He really liked Ferryl, her personality, so if that had been her real body? Not a discussion he wanted with anyone, let alone a sorceress. Abel finally drifted off to sleep, reassured by knowing that if Ferryl wanted something different, a thousand-year-old sorceress would find a way.

Ferryl thought about the conversation as well, but she didn't expect anything. She would move this relationship forward just as fast as Abel wanted, because it would all be new, not physically, but emotionally. She'd been in bodies that were married, both male and female, a really good disguise when the church hunters closed in. The relationships had meant nothing to her, but physical interactions such as kissing felt entirely different with these new emotions. She had started to look forward to kissing and hugging, especially when they were alone, more than anything in her sketchy memories. Moving on to more physical contact would be a very interesting experience.

From tonight's talk Ferryl felt it could be a while before Abel finished with this bucket list, or wanted more than cuddles and kisses. She wasn't sure why, but thought she might need someone else for the next stage. Even so, twenty, fifty or a hundred years of waiting would be a small price for her life and this new knowledge, the feeling of emotions.

*　*　*

A phone call the next morning confirmed the meeting place, and how to recognise the next potential Taverner, Anniyah. Abel had barely sat down when he found out she'd missed some details. "Trouble?"

Ferryl eyed up the three teenagers coming into the café, one of them carrying a Bonny's Tavern booklet. "She didn't mention friends."

"Zephyr, please check for recorders, phones or cameras. Turn them off but no damage." The trio had no trouble finding Abel and Ferryl, because both were in their leathers. One of the girls, the wary one in the middle wearing a high-necked top and headscarf with a jacket and trousers, saw Zephyr's shimmer. She followed it with her eyes as it sank into her companion's jacket. "No harm intended, but we want to be sure who we are meeting." Abel kept his eyes on the girl and spoke to her, but one of her companions answered.

"You're meeting Anniyah, but we've come with her in case there's trouble. She's not supposed to be in town on her own." The darker girl, taller and wearing a short dress over thick tights or stockings, eyed up Abel and Ferryl. "We recognise you two from the website, so that's the first worry out of the way. We thought it might be a scam."

Anniyah put her hand on the girl's arm. "It isn't, I promise. I can tell already."

"How? There's enough public types conning kids out of money and then there's sects. Plenty of people know your problem, Anni." The third girl, heavy-set with jeans and a polo-necked sweatshirt, kept her voice down and glanced around. "This is public enough, but you reckon they'll take you someplace private."

Until now the girl in the middle, Anniyah, seemed quiet and subservient, but now her eyes flashed and her tone sharpened. "It is not my problem. It was something unexplained." Her voice softened as she looked at Zephyr, flowing back into Abel's arm. "Now I know the explanation."

Zephyr reported in. "The other two girls had left their phones on, and one carries a recorder but I turned it off."

The girl in jeans glanced at Abel, then back to her friends. "How? He's barely spoken."

"Remember the Bonny's Tavern characters? Wind Chaser?" Anniyah kept her voice very low. "I just saw his tethered sprite. I told you, Enise, the whole thing is real."

"Bullshit." The girl, Enise, opened her mouth again then glanced round before speaking to Abel. "Can we sit here a bit and talk? Before going someplace private? We want more information." She put a hand on her pocket.

Abel looked at her hand. "Yes, of course, but if you want a real talk don't turn on the phone or the recorder." This Anniyah had obviously talked about creatures, at length, and equally obviously her friends were worried about her. Now Anniyah had seen Zephyr she'd tell her friends in detail, here or later, but Abel didn't want it recorded.

As the three sat down, the taller one put her hand in her pocket and pulled out her phone. "How did you turn this off?" The other girl checked hers, and the recorder, and scowled.

"I told you. He's got a tethered sprite, like in the game. It searched us. Now shut up while I talk." Anniyah put an apologetic hand on her friend. "Sorry, but I've dreamed of this. Not this, but being right."

"Not too much talk, not here. Would you like a drink or something to eat?" Despite Ferryl's hand telling him it wasn't a good idea, Abel didn't mind sitting here for a while. He could keep the conversation quiet and fairly innocuous. All three shook their heads.

The shorter girl took out her phone. "I've got to call my brother. He's up the street." Enise looked a little guilty at the startled look from her friends. "He doesn't know why we're meeting you, but he'll keep his trap shut. I asked him to follow us because women get in trouble sometimes, when we're off the estate. Not always, just if the wrong bunch of yobs see us."

"Our parents worry, with us being girls. The yobs used to give me more trouble cos I'm darker, but now its Anni and Enise. I tell 'em, me mam's as English as they are." The tall girl shrugged, then eyed Ferryl and nodded gently. "I'll bet you get it as well."

"Not really, but we live in a little village where everyone knows everyone. So why not meet us on the estate, wherever it is?" Ferryl reassessed the girls' skin colour and hers. "Where nobody would notice you."

All three girls pulled disgusted faces. "Because there's a few idiots there who would take offence to Wind Chaser here." Enise smiled to make the name a joke. "Not to you, Ferryl, but they'd want to know why you're letting a white bloke hold your hand, that sort of rubbish."

"And if word got back to Anniyah's family, that she was meeting strangers and one was white, they'd probably ground her until she's safely married." All three broke into smiles as the third girl continued. "All right, not that bad but they'd be worried about what people would think and who you are. A wizard might not be a good answer."

"Phone your brother, or ask him to come in if you like." Abel stifled the giggle but couldn't stop his smile. "The Tavern don't care about colour. We accept goblins and they're green, and dryads and they really are all shades of brown, wrinkly and miserable."

"Silly sod." Enise didn't believe Abel about goblins, but she tapped a short message into her phone. "I've told him you're the right two, and you don't need to groom anyone because you've got a girl." She grinned and shrugged, completely unrepentant. "Not the girl part, just the not-a-groomer-type. Not that I've met one but those on the telly are older." Her phone buzzed within seconds so she read the reply. "He's more worried about where we go from here." She looked up at Abel. "Where? Do you have a room or what?"

"Choose a place, a public park would be good." Abel saw the alarm on Anniyah's face. "We'll hide under a veil, the magic version. You won't notice, but nobody will be able to see you." The girls glanced at each other, uncertain. "Don't worry, it really is safe, though Enise had better tell her brother we're ducking out of sight."

"There's a shelter with a seat, but my brother will still worry about yobs so he'll follow us to the park. I'll tell him he can watch from the back if he wants, where he can't see inside. If he shows his face and embarrasses me, I'll embarrass him with his girlfriend. Sisters have ways." Enise for one seemed to be relaxing, while Anniyah kept her eyes on Abel's arm where Zephyr had disappeared. Moments later Enise laughed. "He's going to find someplace uncomfortable to sit, and I owe him big-time."

The taller girl sighed, and put out her hand to shake. "If we're doing this, I may as well introduce myself, Zarah. My dad's from Syria and my mam's English. I look black like mam but get crap because of dad as well."

"Enise is Turkish, and I'm English, but we're both lumped in with Pakistanis or Indians, except by them. Is religion a problem? Do we have to worship something, like Wicca maybe?" As Anniyah shook hands she started looking worried again.

"I'll explain in the park. No problem at all, I promise." Abel understood now, or near enough. Housing estates like theirs, where most of the population were coloured minorities, were on the TV now and then. The residents could be insular, though nobody gave them much trouble. There again that was according to the news, which didn't notice magic and reported a horde of creatures as a broken gas main and hornets.

*   *   *

Walking to the park, Abel noticed some unfriendly stares. It amused him when some glared at Ferryl in her leathers, because that face could be any colour she chose. A striking face, so some youths were watching Ferryl and her leather for an entirely different reason. Halfway there, Zephyr reported that she'd spotted the brother, keeping well back. As promised, once in the park Enise took them towards a wooden shelter, enclosed on three sides with a bench around the inside. Abel stopped well before reaching it. "Do you two want to know for certain, or not? Anniyah is going to see some magic and start her training, and I reckon she's going to tell you all about it once we've gone."

"She'd better. We've been listening to stories about things in our meals for two years now, so if they're real I want to know!" The taller girl, Zarah, pointed at Enise. "So does she. We've had to put up with enough crap about being friends with loopy here, so if it's right I want payback."

"You can't tell anyone. I promise to explain, but first you've got to believe." Abel couldn't help his little smile. "I could produce something really spectacular, but this park is claimed by a sorcerer and he won't be happy. Ah, I'll repeat the warnings later, but don't go near trees after today."

"Anni doesn't anyway, she reckons trees hurt her." Enise looked at the trees, then back at Abel. "I've never had trouble."

"No, but soon you'll want to learn magic, and then they'll hurt you. If you learn enough, in time you'll get a tree that doesn't hurt and you'll hug it as often as possible." The walk across the park towards the shelter passed in jokes about tree-huggers, nervous jokes. "Enise and Zarah, if you want to know for sure, stand here where you can see into the shelter. When we disappear, walk slowly and steadily forward and into the shelter until you see us again." Abel saw both of them open their mouths to start asking questions. "I'll answer afterwards."

Anniyah stayed quiet for the first three of the fifteen steps to the shelter. "Really disappear?"

"Yes, but the shelter won't. We could hide the shelter, but Enise's brother would notice." Anni sniggered nervously as Abel continued. "I'll say this privately, but you can explain to your friends later. Your colour or your religion, how much you do or don't believe, makes no difference to magic. Good or bad is how you use it. If you train as a Taverner you have to agree to that, to accept that your fellow Taverners might look different or not agree with your beliefs."

"My friends don't agree with me now. I can do that, I think. What religion are you?"

"Heathen, according to a vicar, and Ferryl is a cat worshipper. She purrs to them." Ferryl smiled back at the curious look and produced a perfect cat purr. She still greeted any new cats they met. "Do you want to stand or sit? You won't feel anything, I promise."

"Stand. What should I do? Do I chant or make a symbol?"

"Look at your friends, at their faces, and have a good laugh." Which Anniyah did, giggling when Abel cast the veil because both looked poleaxed. Enise started forward first, looking very determined while Zarah took her time, examining the shelter very carefully as she came closer. Once they'd walked into the veil, and could see their friend, Zarah insisted on leaving and coming back again to check. Abel explained they could only do that until they activated magic, then walking through a veil would pop it. He had to prove that, letting one of them stand outside while Ferryl popped the veil by leaving it, then recasting. Anniyah went outside to watch that, and reported she could see blurs through a shimmer.

The next hour turned out a lot like that, doing things more than once, except that once he'd explained about her being a real sorceress, Ferryl took over. Abel left the shelter briefly, taking a short hike while Ferryl drew a Tavern sign on each girl. After that Anniyah could feel her magic, so Ferryl started on glyphs.

Anniyah's two friends couldn't see the glyphs fly, but could watch Abel and Ferryl make the leaf dance and the dust ripple in mid-air. Both insisted on trying, even though they couldn't feel anything in their arms, but Ferryl felt sure that Anniyah wouldn't take long to move a leaf. Watching their friend flutter a leaf, someone they knew, would encourage the pair to try harder. They all knew the creatures even if two had never seen them, because Zarah had bought the Bonny's Tavern game. She'd taken the creature booklet for Anniyah to look through, and since then they'd all tried the meditation with a leaf. From Anni's reaction her friends hadn't taken it very seriously, but they'd definitely changed their minds now.

Once they'd escorted the trio back to catch a bus home, Abel and Ferryl talked over teaching Anniyah to veil as soon as possible. Despite the joking, all three girls were worried about being seen practicing by relatives, or berated by strangers if they left their estate. Hopefully it would all work out, and the three of them would establish the first Middlesbrough Tavern.

The next meeting went much better. This teenager lived in a village in the Yorkshire Dales, but met them on the outskirts. The lad worried about magic versus the church, but seemed satisfied when Abel hung a Tavern hex next to his cross without anything bursting into flames. With all the rolling countryside and moorland on his doorstep, there'd be plenty of places to practice, especially now his new hexes sent the magical creatures scampering away. The church cross wasn't quite strong enough for the whole village, so he had a few creatures in his food and bed, but the hexes would sort that out.

As Ferryl and Abel rode away they were feeling quite upbeat, which might have been tempting fate just a little.

A Bigger Pond

Another night, in another small hotel, then once again Abel and Ferryl were meeting someone in a public park. Once again Ferryl inspected the boundary, claiming it for some local sorcerer, and looked at the trees from a safe distance. She was attempting to catalogue the differences in the glyphs each sorcerer used, and their effect. This one preferred aching in the joints as a hint. A teenager arrived at exactly the right time, and headed straight for them. Abel let Zephyr fly free, and the lad squinted but definitely saw her. "A bound spirit?"

That threw Abel, because spirit wasn't the game name for her. "Not a sprite?" Before Abel could say more Zephyr's voice burst into his head.

"He has a tether! He just used it."

Moments later Ferryl's hand confirmed it. "Towards the entrance, the man feeding pigeons. The tether goes there."

There wasn't much point in beating around the bush, not now the supposed new recruit had used a sorcerer description. "You are a tethered apprentice, not a newly-awakened game player. Please ask your master to join us. The pigeons aren't really hungry, and it would be more polite than lurking."

The apprentice didn't answer, but the elderly-looking man put the bag of feed in his pocket, straightened and headed towards them. He stopped by his apprentice. "Not your fault, Leonardo." Abel noticed a little wince at the name, so the teenager hadn't got used to it yet. The sorcerer turned to Abel. "I've seen you on the television, Abel I believe. Is that all?"

Abel didn't even start to answer, because Ferryl had let go of his hand after passing a message. "Show the ring." She took a step forward and bowed, just a tiny one before announcing herself. "You will have checked, I am sure, but perhaps not properly. I will introduce myself first. Ferryl Shayde, unbound and untethered sorceress, bodyguard to Abel, Master of Pendragon Enterprises and Master of Castle House. I am much older than my employer, so I have less tolerance. I also have diamonds in my bones and can self-heal very quickly."

The last two were a way of telling the sorcerer the apparent schoolgirl had probably lived more than one human lifespan, and become magically adept. The bow seemed more like sorceress good manners than admitting any inferiority, because the sorcerer returned the bow, exactly. "Aesop, sorcerer, and I also have diamond in my bones. Let us hope we don't have to compare self-healing, especially as you are stood in my park."

Abel turned his hand a little, and the sorcerer took note of the ring. "Definitely not, because that would be a very public firework display and annoy a certain archbishop. He doesn't need much of an excuse." It wasn't hard to smile, because Abel had just seen the wary look at the word archbishop. Creepio had a reputation. "Since we came to help someone who had discovered magic, and this young man doesn't need help, we'll be on our way. There are a lot of others to visit."

"But not in this part of Bradford. You will stop awakening teenagers here, and will not come to meet any who contact you." A hand swept around, no doubt to indicate his demesne. "Your Tavern is not welcome here."

"The Tavern only appears where you are neglecting the people living in your demesne. That means you aren't dealing with magical problems, so the area is unclaimed under the Accord. You can hardly complain if someone else tries to clean the place up." Abel launched into explaining about only helping areas that were neglected, because they didn't make money for church or sorcerer, while smiling and trying to look helpful and friendly. "Bonny's Tavern is on sale, country-wide. Teenagers will buy it and play, so they will see the pictures and some will recognise them. I am hoping to soften the impact on them and you."

"Your allegedly innocent game will awaken teenagers, or show them they are awakened and not just hallucinating. Then according to you you'll teach them magic, and let them put free hexes all over some grubby council estate or tower block. My paying customers will not be impressed." Aesop's brow furrowed in thought. "I doubt everyone will agree with your interpretation of the Accord, or your solution. You offer to leave the estates alone if one of us deals with the creatures. My solution is to stop your Tavern from interfering. You will tell me if anyone living in Bradford phones you."

Abel recognised the same old sorcerer chest-beating attitude, though this seemed a little more civilised. "They are phoning me at home, in my demesne not yours."

Aesop suddenly turned very uncivilised, he didn't even hesitate. A huge veil shimmered into being around all four of them. "Or I could stop you now."

Ferryl interrupted, and she had never been polite. "Perhaps you forgot the bodyguard part, and that you would have to deal with me first? Even if you succeed, fifty or sixty Taverners will come here to complain. Then this area is added to Castle House demesne, because even if you kill Abel you don't have the bloodline to claim it." Ferryl nodded towards the young man. "You aren't short of apprentices, so why argue?"

Aesop opened his mouth to reply, but hesitated. He didn't answer Ferryl directly, turning to Abel with a puzzled frown. "You really are the blood heir to Castle House? Why didn't you have the decency to warn this young man, when you arranged the meeting? You could at least turn up in a car with three or four apprentice bodyguards. Riding around on a motorbike, dressed in scruffy leathers, makes it look as if you're some apprentice who has barely learned not to burn your own fingers. Then you spring a full sorceress bodyguard on me!" Abel was confused, because now the sorcerer seemed to be complaining about manners and appearance! "I heard a rumour of forty apprentices, but discounted it once I saw you. Now I must reassess. Why so many and why do the Council allow it? Is it because of Castle House?"

"There's a score more since you heard that, though they are all trainees, not apprentices." Ferryl glanced down at the state of her leathers and slapped some dust off them. Despite what Aesop said they weren't scruffy, but had definitely got more than a bit grubby. "We are riding around to try and meet everyone who contacted Bonny's Tavern, because most Taverners are too young to drive. There's another nineteen possibles, mostly in villages where no sorcerer will care, but we are having trouble getting to them all. That's why everyone has split up like this. In a month there'll be more prospects, but we'll have five or six more drivers making the initial introductions. The month after there could be a hundred or so prospects, and we've no idea when the phone calls will stop." Ferryl hardened her voice, and her face. "None of them will affect your business, but you will not harm any of them."

"You are very confrontational, considering you are in my park. Even so, I must remember that I invited you. Actually my tethered apprentice did, which is the same under the general rules for such things." Aesop looked from one to the other, or at their puzzled faces. "You don't understand the rules?"

"We've seen the Accord, but didn't know there were more." Abel had started reassessing, fast. "If we've broken them I apologise, but I had this sorcery business thrust on me. I found out I am Celtchar's heir, survived the first test, and found out what to do next." He shrugged, glancing at Ferryl and hoping she got the hint to back off. Holding hands or private messages through spooky-phone might give the wrong impression. "Since then I've been attacked twice but managed to win. Now we are trying to sort out the next problem. Ferryl Shayde really is a powerful sorceress, but she has been out of circulation for some time."

Ferryl obviously didn't feel the same about one thing; she moved back a step and took Abel's hand. "Not powerful enough to fight a strong sorcerer in his own park, where he will be able to take magic from trees. That isn't necessarily enough to win, but I don't have my wits yet. Aesop will know many more glyphs than me, and probably the counters to mine, so I would lose. If he really is a senior sorcerer, even a hundred Taverners would be moths in a bonfire." She sounded embarrassed, apologetic, and definitely worried. "I have never really met with senior sorceresses. They used to stay in their fortresses, not walk around towns. The lesser ones used to revert to bluffs and threats but I didn't hear of many actual fights. Creepio seemed to confirm that, and I'd no idea there were unwritten rules."

"Will Ffod bop work?" Zephyr didn't sound keen.

"No! Sorry Zephyr but don't risk it. Stay in the tattoo until we leave, please." Abel didn't want his puff of wind blown away by mistake.

The sorcerer had been looking the pair of them over, debating on something. "At least you have apologised. Very well, accepted. Please note that such meetings are normally held in the neutral zone, near the town centre. Even so, as I said, my asking you to meet in my park automatically confers safe conduct. I may have been a little abrupt; even with your attitude your titles deserve more respect. After all, what are we without them?"

"Thank you, we really didn't understand. Would you mind telling us how to find this town centre? There's no sign of anything like that in Stourton. Pendragon held the monopoly there, while the only other sorcerer, Redwolf, just keeps a house there so he can relax away from his business." Abel glanced at Ferryl, but her hand told him to keep going. "I've been busy since the takeover, sitting exams at school, so I haven't even met my new neighbours in Sheffield."

"Exams? Really?" The laugh came so naturally it had to be real. "Your sorceress as well?" He laughed again when Abel nodded. "I'll know who to call when my computer breaks down." Aesop seemed to find that very funny, still chuckling when he turned to Ferryl. "How did he force you into school if you aren't tethered?"

She seemed to have relaxed as well, or tried a different sort of bluff. "I enjoy school, and being a schoolgirl is liberating. This way I'm learning a huge amount about how the modern world works, very quickly, which is a good thing. Otherwise I might think an aeroplane is a dragon, and start throwing glyphs."

"Oh yes, though I know exactly what those drones are but I still accidentally zap one now and then. That takes less magic than veiling." The sorcerer sobered, looking back at the two motorbikes with a small frown. "I really would advise coming in a decent car, if you have one. Didn't that jumped-up little cur have an armoured Bentley?"

Despite the description Aesop had to mean Pendragon, though now Abel realised he was Pendragon to the sorcerous world. "Smashed and burned. We retrieved the gold and the rest went to a scrapyard. The best of the other cars are a very flashy Range Rover, a Volvo convertible and a BMW SUV. I prefer the SUV if there might be trouble, so my friends can come with me."

"Smashed and burned? Impressive, and enough to believe at least one of you is truly dangerous." His eyes showed he'd chosen Ferryl for that accolade. "The minimum escort for a serious sorcerer is three apprentices, one trained as a bodyguard. Since only two children on bikes turned up, my usual companions waited in the car. Use your Range Rover, then any extra friends can follow on motorbikes." Aesop had decided to have fun, judging by the trace of sarcasm in that part. He looked around, curling his lip at a nearby park bench covered in graffiti, and tutted in exasperation.

"I hadn't really expected to be standing about out here long enough for an actual discussion. It's not exactly comfortable, but I don't suppose you'll want to sit in the car with me?" One look at their faces answered him. "Very wise."

"We could arrange to meet you again, if you wouldn't mind? A proper meeting in the neutral zone? Is there an accepted place?" Anywhere would be better than here, in Abel's opinion. Ferryl reckoned she'd lose even without the bloke's apprentices, and then he'd wipe out the Taverners if they came for him! The whole master plan had to be reassessed.

"There is, but I'd rather not advertise I'm dealing with you. Definitely dealing because even if you are barred from the towns, you'll have these Taverners of yours in every village. Dozens of them, capable of filling a hex but not strong enough to be a threat, ideal if I need extra help." At one point during the ensuing nit-picking Abel wondered if a fight might have been easier. He finally conceded that any potential apprentice who contacted the Tavern would meet their local sorcerer. The sticking point turned out to be allowing them to leave afterwards, untethered, to meet a representative of the Tavern. Aesop wanted to pick the strongest, not take those who chose to go back and accept a tether in return for the pay and conditions.

The sorcerer finally agreed the newcomers could choose the Tavern if they wished, if Abel paid him. That final concession took some serious bargaining, settling on five day's-worth of free hex-filling from any Taverner who reached that stage. Aesop also wanted to fix a rate for hiring any nearby Taverners as temporary hex-fillers, using their own magic. Luckily Ferryl's hand reminded Abel not to mention trees. The sorcerer would assume the Taverners were giving up most of their daily magic, and agree a price based on that. In return Aesop agreed to an extra. He'd remove the tether and send any apprentice who didn't make the grade to the nearest Tavern, uninjured. According to the sorcerer, the usual retirement package for failures consisted of stunting or killing them.

When Abel suggested having Woods and Green check the contract for him Aesop nodded, not put off in the least. "I expected that, after seeing them advertised on the front of your game. My own solicitor is unhappy."

"Why? I've never seen anyone advertising magical legal services, so it isn't poaching."

A mischievous smirk cracked Aesop's negotiating façade. "I think he's annoyed because Woods and Green thought of it first." The sorcerer started speaking a couple of times and rethought, then came out with it. "Which is a good point, because I'm obviously the first sorcerer to make a deal. I should take full advantage. To save you some time I could negotiate a similar contract with the rest of the sorcerers in Bradford, in return for free hex-filling based on the number of acceptances. I am considered the senior sorcerer here, so they will listen to me." Abel had no problem with the idea, but only if Aesop got him the same deal they'd just agreed. Cue more nit-picking, because they started with wildly differing ideas of how many hours a deal would be worth.

Aesop seemed to have lost his impatience while he negotiated, but didn't waste time on socialising afterwards. He left immediately, in a Rolls-Royce that pulled up by the park entrance. His new apprentice, Leonardo, didn't get a lift, walking off into the town on his own. Ferryl heaved a sigh of relief and hugged Abel hard, before suggesting a sit down and a strong coffee. Both agreed it had to be in a very public café, in the town centre.

One coffee became a meal, because they could talk without speaking and there was a lot to discuss. Phone calls from the other teams had mentioned meeting sorcerers, but so far the Taverners had taken names and promised Abel would be in touch. Now Zephyr contacted Ginny, while Abel called the office and told Eric to pass on a message. No more meetings in parks, because the Taverners hadn't been invited by the sorcerer so they'd be trespassing. Everyone should arrange to meet prospects at their homes, or in a very public car park, square or café in a town centre. Just let newcomers have hexes and the basic instructions and promise to be in touch again. Then everyone should come home for a full explanation and instructions. Abel didn't mention Ferryl's chances in a real fight, or the moths in a bonfire idea. He didn't want rumours flying about.

By the time Abel and Ferryl had eaten, Eric called back. Two teams were already heading home early, because some of their contacts didn't turn up or answer phone messages. Another pair had been told to clear off when they'd arrived to meet a prospect, very rudely but they'd kept quiet and left. After talking it through, Ferryl and Abel decided to revisit the first three potential Taverners as promised, instead of heading home. Two of them would need a new place to meet, somewhere not a park, and all three should be warned.

*   *   *

Stu, the bespectacled beginner, met them in a café in the town centre. He seemed despondent he wasn't already fluttering his leaf, and even more so when Abel explained how some sorcerers felt. Abel went through the practice again, verbally, several times very quietly which wasn't easy in public. While he had a break, Ferryl described how long it took Abel to learn the first part, even with a magical being in his arm to help. That reassured Stu the lack of progress wasn't his fault, and he promised to keep practicing, but only in his bedroom for now. Ferryl gave him an extra lead block full of magic, topped up the first one, and left him staring determinedly at his Bonny's Tavern instructions.

As expected, the second visit to Anniyah, Enise and Zarah wasn't quite that simple. Ferryl had phoned even before meeting Stu, to warn them they'd be meeting somewhere away from the park. By the time the three young women arrived in the same café, they'd worked out an alternate meeting place with one proviso. "You, Ferryl, could you really squish some yob that gave you trouble?" Zarah kept her voice low, glancing towards the door.

"Yes, though I would prefer to do so in private to keep magic a secret."

"Private isn't the problem. There's an old garden with a fountain and some bushes, a scruffy overgrown place, normally a bad place for girls to go on their own. Hah, it's a bad place for most people. It should be deserted in daylight, but even so we'd usually keep well clear." Zarah looked from one to the other. "Dealers use it to sell drugs, pills and speed and all that shit."

"What about you, Wind Chaser? Can you look after yourself?" Anise's assessment didn't think so. "There'll be two brothers this time, near enough to hear me yell if there's trouble. Actually, Yaman insisted he stayed with us, but I got him to agree to staying out of sight and hearing unless I shout. I told him you'll do if I need a bodyguard." She hesitated, eyeing Abel and obviously embarrassed about the next bit. "He wants to

247

meet you first, just to see if you can keep me safe long enough for him to get there."

"Use wind glyphs to stop a punch, or trip or throw him. Something that won't hurt him but looks like you've been trained."

Abel chuckled at a sudden thought. "One brick?" Ferryl chuckled as well so he turned to Anise. "I can show him something very special, martial arts special. A brick wall would be best?"

"Really? This I gotta see. I'm warning you it'd better be good, he's not kidding." Though Anise had already taken out her phone and started tapping. The walk didn't take long, and this time Anise's brother didn't try to hide when he followed them.

The garden, on the corner between two streets, must have been the pride and joy of some town planner many years ago. The neighbourhood had gone downhill, the fountain had stopped working, the gates had been taken away, and nobody had weeded or trimmed for years. When the five of them stopped by the gateway, Anise's brother kept coming until he reached Abel. "My name is Yaman. My little sister reckons you can keep her safe but I'm not so sure, so either prove it or I come to this meeting." He carefully inspected Abel and Ferryl while shaking their hands. "Though she's right about one thing, you're that kid selling the game on the internet. Did you really design it?"

"Me and my friends. I understand why you are worried, but it's important that I speak to these three privately. I think I can reassure you, if you give me a minute." Yaman gave a short nod, not convinced, so Abel stood with his back to the low brick wall. He put his hand down and tapped a brick. "See this brick?" As Yaman and the others nodded he fed magic into the glyph and slapped the wall, then looked down. Not as neat as Ferryl's version, and his palm stung a little, but most of the brick had shattered and blown out into the garden. "Now imagine I'd slapped you."

"Bloody hell! That's got to be some sort of special karate thing." Yaman glanced at his sister with a little smile. "It's like I keep warning you, don't be fooled by the harmless-looking ones." He pulled out a phone, turning back to Abel. "There'll be two of us, one at each entrance, in case there's any druggies sleeping in there. Any trouble, slap whoever starts it and yell." He lifted the phone and started talking, but Abel didn't understand a word.

"Come on, he's just laughing about that little kid on the advert being a lot tougher than he looks." Anise tugged Abel's arm and the group headed down the cracked path. The little gazebo in the back corner had seen better days, and wouldn't keep out rain, but the seats looked sound enough. Ferryl gestured and a short, vicious gale cleared out the leaves, litter and discarded needles.

"When will Anni be able to do that?" Zarah turned to Ferryl with a big grin. "Can you do the brick thing?" Ferryl nodded so Zarah slapped one of the posts holding up the roof, about head height. "When can Anni learn to bust something like this? Just as practice of course."

"It's the same glyph she's practicing, but very advanced. Ferryl taught me." Abel pointed at the clean seats. "Clearing away the rubbish is a sort of halfway, the Mary Poppins stage, or the Mickey Mouse version if you try too soon." At a thought, Zephyr flew off to check the rest of the garden. "I've asked Zephyr to check around to make sure we won't be disturbed. While she does that you can tell us how you've been getting on with the practice."

Anniyah watched the shimmer leave, then picked up a stray leaf Ferryl had missed. "Can you put the veil up first, please?" As soon as Abel cast the glyph she held out her hand. "Watch this." Her triumphant tone should have been enough warning, the leaf jerked up and off her palm! In some sort of déjà vu, Abel and Ferryl had to explain to Enise and Zarah that it could take them weeks to manage the same.

"I'll never do it. I can't even feel anything from that lead bar, though Anni reckons she can suck bits of magic from it." Zarah scowled at the lead bar, then her friend. "It'll take forever because we can't find anyplace to practice. We can't leave the estate without one of Enise's brothers following, which is reassuring but, well, she's already been caught practicing once."

Enise looked guilty. "I should have known better. I've got five brothers and I'm the only girl so they worry about me. Luckily I could show him it's part of the game instructions, but he wanted to know why I'd drawn the glyph, the swirly thing, on my hand." She hesitated long moments, glancing at her friends but they weren't saying anything. "Could you let me have half a dozen copies of Bonny's Tavern, to sell? On sale or return? I'd get the full price and pay you, I promise?"

"Her brothers looked up the game, Bonny's Tavern, on the internet." Anniyah picked it up as Enise stalled. "Yaman recognised your pictures from seeing you on your last visit, and wanted to know why his sister had met the game designers. She said she'd offered to be a local saleswoman."

"I'll bet he loved that idea." Abel glanced over his shoulder, but today's watch-brothers were staying safely out of sight as promised.

He'd meant to be sarcastic, but the three girls didn't notice or didn't care. "Yes he did, which is why he agreed to her meeting you again. All her brothers love it, and even promised not to tell her parents until she makes her first thousand pounds." Zarah rolled her eyes as Ferryl and Abel stared, flabbergasted. "Enise's brothers are always trying to set up some sort of business washing cars, selling junk at markets, cutting lawns and hedges or selling out-of-date food from supermarket skips, that sort of thing. They're dead proud of little sister for getting a big businessman to listen to her!"

"I'm sorry. It was the first thing I thought of. But then I really thought about it." Enise didn't look completely sorry, more like hopeful. "I don't fancy cleaning offices or working on a production line when I leave school, and that's if I'm lucky and can get a job. You need people to sell Bonny's Tavern, and I'm still at school with your target customers. My brothers would watch out for me, and make sure nobody nicked any."

"We thought it might work out better if more people played, and someone else starts seeing things." Anniyah didn't seem against the idea either. "Though maybe Ferryl should come on her own another time. Maybe not on her own, not with some of the oiks round here." A sudden smile wiped away her serious expression. "Ooh, I forgot you're a real sorceress. I could take you to where you could slap some real stinkers?"

"We aren't supposed to cast glyphs in public, so it would be best if Ferryl, or anyone else, avoided trouble. We've got other Taverners who can visit, ones who won't stand out on your estate. A couple will turn up now and then to carry on your training, but you'll need someplace private to practice. The next ones won't know how to slap like that if there's trouble." Abel had been considering the sales idea, but realised a big flaw. "You won't be able to sell to white kids, not if they can't come on your estate."

"No problem, most people don't care that much. Even the weirdos ignore what colour a customer is, as long as they've got money. A few white kids might not be keen on coming right onto the estate, but we can hand over the goods at school, or a café. With a bit of luck, if it all works out, we can use Zarah's place as a sort of shop. Her dad never puts his car in the garage, and it's near the edge of the estate. Their street is mixed anyway, all colours, and so are some of the families." From the way Zarah and Anniyah nodded, the three of them had already put some serious thought into the idea. "We might even sneak in some practice in the garage."

"Not much though, because Enise's brothers will want to see how she's doing. They'll be counting the stock every ten minutes."

Enise laughed at Zarah. "And your dad will be just as nosy."

"Can't you teach me to cast a veil?" Anniyah looked around them, though she couldn't actually see Abel's veil from inside it. "How good do I have to be with the leaf before I can manage one?"

"A lot better, and you'd also have to find a spot where nobody would walk through it by accident. Give us a moment please." Abel took hold of Ferryl's hand and Zephyr connected to her. Despite her wide-eyed look, Anniyah didn't comment. "The actual selling idea is a bit hit and miss, but we wanted a local Taverner willing to mentor newbies? Anni can move her leaf, so she can already demonstrate to newcomers and she'll get better with practice."

"We haven't thought about the practice part, and now we know parks might be off-limits. Our betas practiced while playing the game, even if they didn't realise at first. Right from the start there were small groups who could meet, and the same with the relatives who were given beta copies. If someone is the first player in their area we can give them contact numbers, but it will still look odd if they spend ages meditating to play over Skype." Abel could feel Ferryl's mental amusement. "Unless they all become salespeople and commandeer garages."

"I'm not sure if we can do it, legally. Employ schoolkids." Abel still didn't legally own his own business, not outside the magic world. "Though if I buy twenty copies of Bonny's Tavern at the usual rate for retailers, for cash, then give them to Enise? She can pay me when she sells them, and keep the profit. It'll give those three a really good excuse to keep meeting up in private?"

"They can have more stock when a Taverner visits to help with the training. It'll even be a good excuse for them to meet whoever we send." Ferryl's hand gripped a little tighter. "That could work elsewhere, anyplace kids need to explain meeting a stranger on a regular basis. Look at how protective Jenny's dad is. There'll be other parents who feel the same."

A loud stage cough interrupted. "I can see the spooky-thing but Enise and Zarah can't. Are you talking about the veil, because we can find a place? One where nobody will walk through it." Anniyah shot a glance at her friends. "And none of Enise's brothers will trample us. We can't use it now because anyone walking past would see us."

Abel smiled and nodded. "We were discussing veils and Anise's brainwave. We'll try the sales idea, but I can only let Anise have half a dozen games to start with. Sell them and I'll send more, but whoever delivers will want the money from the first six. You'll all just have to be careful practicing magic, because Anniyah won't be able to cast a veil for some time yet. Take it slow and careful and you'll get there."

"Lead block." Ferryl pointed to the one they'd just given Anniyah, full of magic. "How are the goblins hiding in the shrubbery, if anyone gets near?"

Abel ignored the stares at the casual mention of goblins, thinking through Ferryl's idea. "The old uses magic to activate a glyph, then sits it on a lead block full of magic. Good idea." Abel reached into his pocket. "After all Kelis's training, I carry a marker pen." He turned back to Anniyah and tried to look confident. "There is a way. Be very, very careful not to do this when anyone is looking at you, because you'll pop out of sight." Three teenage girls leant eagerly forward, transfixed as he drew on a page from his little notebook.

"A dotty circle? That's magic?" Zarah wasn't impressed, and neither of the others looked confident.

"This glyph won't activate as it is, just a circle of dashes, because I've left a small break in this line. Draw it accurately on a piece of wood or a pebble, and join up the broken part, only once because you can use it again and again." Abel held his hand over the drawing, palm down. "You'll have to push magic first, into the pebble, exactly like when you activate the air glyph on your palm. As you do, imagine the circle slowly spinning anti-clockwise. You have to really mean it, intent matters. Then put the pebble on top of the glyph we'll draw on the lead bar full of magic. The veil will last as long as the magic does, or until you remove the pebble and walk away."

Zarah promptly looked around until she found a flattish pebble for Abel to draw on, one that wouldn't roll off the block. She wanted Abel to draw the glyph, to make sure it was dead right. Ten minutes later it might have been a good thing the gazebo wasn't anywhere more public, and that veils dampened sound. The cheering and squeals of excitement when Anniyah briefly activated her new glyph would have definitely brought both Anise's brothers running. "Yes, I can do two magics!"

"Not really, that's a cheat. You are supposed to imagine the drawing and the speed and direction of rotation and you'll find that's a lot harder." From Anni's face Ferryl didn't think she cared if it was cheating or not. "Now remember, don't let anyone see you disappear or we can't teach you anymore. I mean it, one hint and the church and sorcerers will come and stop you. You can't even let Anise's brothers see." It took a while and several repeats before Ferryl had any effect on the three huge smiles.

Eventually, since they couldn't see the veil from inside, the three agreed that one would always stand outside to be sure it worked. The watcher could join the other two without popping the disguise. By the time both the others activated magic, which would pop the veil, Anniyah should be practiced enough to be certain. To help with that, Abel left four lead bars of magic. The others wouldn't be able to use them yet, but they'd be trying really hard now.

Yaman looked puzzled by how excited the three girls were on the way out, until Anise punched the air. "Yes! I'm in business. Only a few to start with, but we've got to persuade Zarah's dad to let us use the garage."

"We'll clean his car for free if he does, just the outside?" Yaman turned to Abel with a big smile and stuck out his hand. "If you ever need a car cleaned, or someone to deliver games, or extra salespeople, give me a ring. We could get you a stall on the market?"

"It'll have to go through Anise, though I suppose she might give you preferential treatment." Abel and Ferryl left while Anise was still explaining, just before the other brother reached them. As Anise had said, nobody would be nicking anything from her.

After leaving Middlesbrough, Abel and Ferryl talked the whole idea through. They left their last three spare lead bars with the last trainee, to help him practice though he couldn't move his leaf yet. At least he wouldn't fall foul of a sorcerer, but Abel warned him not to tell the local priest unless he wanted to actually become one. After talking it through again at every stop on the way home, both Abel and Ferryl were sure. Anyone with a problem finding privacy would get the same help, once they fluttered a leaf.

Like most plans this one had provisos, two very big ones. It depended on the Taverners being able to cope with the number of new magic users emailing Ferryl Shayde, and on them avoiding trouble with sorcerers.

Neither Abel nor Ferryl Shayde had any inkling that miles further south, a group of Taverners were already running into trouble. More trouble than any of them could handle.

*   *   *

As Abel and Ferryl headed gratefully home along scenic byroads, a group of four Taverners, in Cambridge, were relieved their journey down a traffic-choked A1(M) was over. They'd only got this one newbie to introduce to the rules of magic, then they could go home. Shannon parked the Volvo convertible very carefully, because despite all her joking about speed machines she worried about denting it. Too slowly, by the time she'd turned off the engine Rachel had unbelted and stood up, trying to see further into the park. "Nobody. No dog walkers or bird feeders, and no teenager looking nervous but excited. Definitely nobody carrying a Bonny's Tavern creature booklet."

"Give us a moment Rachel, that's a big park and I think the instructions were a bit more specific." Warren stood up to look as well. "She'll be out of sight until we follow that path. We should back off, like Eric said, because the place is definitely claimed. I can feel it from here. I suppose all the parks are taken."

"Park? A Common according to the map and that about describes it.

I thought we'd get somewhere a bit posher in Cambridge, near a college, though I suppose whoever claims it doesn't care about anything but the trees. Nor about this industrial estate next door, though at least the name of the road doesn't describe it, Garlic Row." Rachel jumped out over the door instead of opening it. "You agreed, none of us want to make this journey again, so we get it over with now. She's not answering her phone so we can't cancel, and we don't want the lass standing about in there all day. After all, three of us are adepts so we're not exactly helpless." She rolled her eyes at Warren, who obviously disagreed. "One quick look won't hurt. We'll get a better view once we get out from among all these factories and stuff, and if she isn't there we'll leave, okay? Come on Cecilia, Shannon will want to tuck her pretty car up and give it a big kiss before we leave it."

"I'm definitely putting the roof up, and I'm still not keen on parking here. There'll be lorries delivering to these places." Shannon stayed put as with a whine the soft roof began its slow climb out and over the car.

"Stop teasing Shannon, Rachel. And careful in there, even if the place is called a Common it's got plenty of trees for cover. Eric said we'll be trespassing, so we don't want to trip over the owner." Warren held out the small rucksack. "Here, if you've got enough energy to jump out you can carry the hexes and lead bars." The teenagers bickered good-naturedly as Shannon locked up, and as they walked along the short stretch of road into the Common itself.

"There, acres of grass, as common as it gets. The trees are just round the edge. Though I'll bet nobody puts their goats on here these days." Shannon stopped and pointed as she came around the bend in the path. "That must be our new Taverner, just under the trees. She can't have activated her magic properly, or standing there would hurt her."

"Or blind her! I've just tested a tree. Getting anywhere near felt like needles pricking my eyes, or what I think it would feel like." Rachel waved to the tall slim girl holding a small booklet, but she didn't respond. "Why doesn't she move? Surely she recognises my costume."

"As Little Red Riding Hood?" Warren ducked away from the threatening hand. "A red cloak with a hood does not K'ress Bloodclaw make. You need the black leather as well."

"Not likely, mum would kill me! Or I'd break my neck falling off the high heels. The black shirt and jeans are as close as I dare get, but not today because mum chucked them in the washer. That's funny, she's still not moving." Rachel raised a hand and waved again, raising her voice. "Hello, are you looking for Bonny's Tavern?"

"That's far enough." As the four teenagers stopped, surprised by the firm, clear, commanding voice, the girl in front of them morphed into someone looking very much like the game character K'ress Bloodclaw. Her imperious glare, long sleek black dress with a slit up one side, and crimson cloak with a high collar would have won her any competition. The shimmer of a veil surrounded her, hiding the transformation from casual sight. "You, boy, you are responsible for this?" She held up the booklet, definitely from a Bonny's Tavern game pack.

"No. That is, we all are in a way, but Abel, Rob and Kelis designed it." Warren looked around, in time to see an impeccably dressed man and woman stroll out across their escape route. A veil surrounded each one. He turned and another two veiled apprentices, they had to be, were coming from the trees further into the Common. "We came to meet a young woman who thought she could see creatures. To help her."

"No, you arranged a meeting in my demesne, on ground reserved for my magical use, without any sort of approach, or explanation, and definitely without permission. Which of you is the senior apprentice?" Her eyes fastened on Shannon. "You look the oldest, but still no more than a hex-filler."

"We are all trainees, not apprentices. Look, I'm sorry if we upset you but we didn't know...."

The sorceress cut Shannon off as her veil expanded to cover the teenagers as well. "No apprentice? None of you are tethered?" All four shook their heads and Rachel opened her mouth to answer but didn't get chance. "That is downright insulting. Oh well, I'll keep the car as compensation." With that she raised a negligent hand and four glyphs smoked out towards the Taverners!

Shannon and Rachel shielded without a second thought; they'd both practiced long and hard since the fights. Warren grabbed a startled Cecilia's hand. Luckily the sorceress hadn't wasted intent on fast glyphs, so by the time the magical missiles arrived he'd slammed up a shield around both of them. The glyphs hit, and four acid green splashes fizzled for a few moments before evaporating. Rachel raised her hand, a glyph boiling into life but Warren got there first. "No! This is her property. Don't start a fight."

"Very wise." The sorceress took a step closer to a tree, within touching distance. "Three shields but not tethered? Are you newly freed, the sort who lost their mistress?" She shook her head, obviously trying to work out the puzzle. "That glyph would have killed anyone unprotected, even if they had a ward, and then you four would have joined your deceased friend in fertilising my trees. As it is, all three shields are strong and very stable for the speed you created them. Either throw that glyph, little girl, or banish it!" Her momentary annoyance at the glyph still in Rachel's palm vanished in a smile, one with a lot of anticipation. "No, throw it, I insist. Let's see what sort of damage you might have done."

"All right, but Abel said we weren't to start a fight so which bush should I flash-fry?" Rachel really wanted to blast something. Deceased friend? This bitch had killed an innocent teenager and just tried to kill four more! Then called her a little girl! As the sorceress pointed, Rachel concentrated on the glyph, tightening and strengthening her strike. If the cheeky bitch wanted a demo, she'd get one. The glyph lashed out, with plenty of intent to make it much faster than the ones thrown at the Taverners. The inoffensive bush flashed into flame and then ashes, leaving a smoking black stump sticking out of the bare earth. Beyond it a swathe of grass browned and smoked. "Oops, a bit overdone." Rachel flicked out a dozen small growth glyphs, re-growing the grass. "The bush might be past help."

"Rachel! Stop it now!" Warren didn't care about the sorceress hearing, he had to stop Rachel. He knew how hot-headed the fifteen-year-old could be, and this time she could get them all killed.

Despite putting her hand on the tree, the sorceress didn't seem worried. "No, that's what I wanted. I prefer to see what I'm dealing with and those growth glyphs were interesting. Not just the skill, it's the casual throwing away of magic. But first, let's just make sure you don't try to run. I get the feeling you are the chivalrous type, young man." The hand against a tree might have looked negligent, but the surge of magic and the glyphs weren't. The earth boiled up to form a wall well over a metre high around the back and sides of the Taverners, before moving in to force them into a line. Smaller walls grew between the three shields, which left Warren and Cecilia together. Some of the earth came from a two metres wide strip right across the front, leaving a deep trench.

The Taverners tried to push back against the earth but the sparks and cracks in their shields, and the drain on their magic, were too much. Rachel went further, throwing a mix of a windhammer and the destructive version of the earth glyph. Earth cracked and blasted backwards and some dissolved into dust, but more soil piled up and it all kept coming. When the earth banks solidified, the Taverners could see each other, the sorceress and her apprentices, but were neatly penned in. "You can't climb with globe shields, and you'll never maintain a shield around two of you while jumping over the trench. You can escape if you wish, young man, but you'll have to leave your girlfriend."

"Friend, not girlfriend, but I won't leave her. Taverners stick up for each other." Warren meant it, but Cecilia's death-grip probably meant he couldn't anyway. "It's all right Cecilia, we'll explain to this lady and then Abel, Zephyr and Ferryl will deal with it all."

"The archbishop won't like it if you kill churchgoers." Cecilia had finally managed to speak, but even then she didn't sound confident.

Less so when the sorceress laughed. "How will he know? One heap of ash looks much like another. Why are you even here if you are one of his God-botherers?"

With a quick glance at Cecilia, Shannon moved to the edge of the trench to get the sorceress's attention. A look down showed the trench was at least two metres deep. "Cecilia is a beginner. She can only just manage air, but came along with us as part of her training. The Tavern allows any faith. I carry a cross and a Tavern hex, and still attend church." Despite the circumstances a tiny smile touched her lips. "We have refused to join the archbishop's Church Militant, but he still gave me a blessing after I killed a woman."

"Killed? You?" A series of glyphs hit Shannon's shield and it glowed and spat sparks. Most hit near her feet as she danced back a few steps. "No, you are defending not fighting back. Put your clothes out." A shocked

Shannon looked down to where her jeans and shoes were smoking. Concentrating on pulling vapour from the air, to wet them down, calmed her down enough to ask why she'd been attacked. Too late, the sorceress hadn't waited for questions. Her attention had switched, and was now firmly focused on Rachel. "I would have put you down as the killer." Her eyes narrowed and she nodded gently to herself. "Yes, if I'd done that to you, you would have been throwing glyphs right back at me. Who did you kill? Someone who called you a little girl? Hah, yes, I thought that annoyed you the first time."

Rachel tried really hard not to get mad, because the sorceress obviously meant to wind her up and could read her reactions. She'd promised not to do anything stupid, but had already lost it enough show off a bit. "I didn't kill anyone personally, but I helped with three apprentices when Pendragon attacked. And one of Boudicca's. Shannon killed a traitor, ran her down, and rammed a sorcerer with a minibus, then helped me with Boudicca's apprentice. I apologise if we have offended, but please let Cecilia go at least. She can explain, otherwise there'll be fifty or sixty Taverners looking for us, and two sorceresses."

"I heard about the sorceresses. A youngster from Germany. And the other is bound into a schoolboy." The sorceress made a throw-away gesture with one hand. "I'll need to dig a big hole, or the ashes from sixty would be too obvious." Her face hardened, and her whole voice and stance looking more threatening. "None of you are going anywhere yet. I'd already be scattering ashes but you interest me, little girl. For a moment I thought you'd fooled me, but you aren't a sorceress in a young body, or under a Seeming. Those glyphs and your shield are too strong for your age, but they aren't strong enough for someone old enough to change her body. More than that, you have the instincts of an older sorceress, and very little hesitation. If that boy hadn't spoken, would you have thrown that first glyph? A glyph strong enough to kill?"

For long moments Rachel tried to decide which was best, but then realised the sorceress already knew. "Yes. Some of us have been in big fights against magic users or creatures. Several were badly injured, and others were briefly tethered. I swore that would never happen to me."

"Not if I give you the choice, a tether or I'll kill these three?"

"No, because then you'd use me to tether them. I saw it happen to others, including my brother. He hurt my brother to get me to take a tether, but I said no. The sorcerer is dead now." Rachel knew her satisfaction at that showed in her voice, she couldn't help it. She braced herself and fed magic to her shield, but didn't form any glyphs, not yet. "So if that's your idea, get on with it."

"Feisty! I like you. You won't take a tether now, but if you survive today your attitude will get you into trouble. If the trouble is too much to handle, ask for Pandora. Others will tell you, I treat my apprentices well but they must be strong and willing to fight." Pandora turned to the others. "I'm still undecided, because although you were beyond impolite you really are just school-children." She licked her lips very slowly, almost hungrily. "Strong children, or three of you are. Consider this your final examination. If you pass, my trees won't be fed and you can take my message to this Abel." She gestured again, one hand still on a tree, and glyphs scattered. Earth flew up in arcs and settled into a dome-shaped cage of rock around all four Taverners. "You, the religious girl, the one who can shield and pull water from the air. Can you throw ice?"

With a quick glance around at the cage, and the apprentices who were now spaced out cutting off any escape, Shannon nodded. "Yes, though I am better with just fire or air. My name is Shannon. This is Warren, the beginner is Cecilia and Rachel is the one in the red cloak. The cape is a costume, because we all play characters in the game. Do I throw the ice at the cage, or a tree, or an apprentice?" Despite her attempt at sounding confident, Shannon saw Pandora's eyes narrow as she said "apprentice."

"You claim to be a killer, so hit my apprentice. That one there, Pride. The others are Wrath, Envy and Avarice." As she spoke Pandora pointed to each of her apprentices in turn. "He is proud of his shield so dent his pride, Shannon." Shannon looked at the apprentice, and although he sneered at her she hesitated. "Would it be easier if I asked him to throw something really nasty, at the choirgirl?" Even as she shook her head Shannon began to build her glyph. She wasn't good enough to make strong ice, but she could maybe add some dust as it flew over the wall, toughen it up a little? For long moments the glyph grew, while Shannon concentrated on the man's sneer and let her resolve harden. Intent mattered, and she wanted to put a real crack in his shield if possible.

The glyph flew, the apprentice looked startled, and Pandora laughed.

"Pride? I should rename you Arrogance! She raised a spark, a definite spark. Maybe a tiny crack?"

Pride looked really worried by that, more than any damage to his shield warranted. "No, not a crack, not even a spark. Just a bit of a glow because I didn't take her seriously. She's only what, eighteen or nineteen?"

"Target, target, target." The other apprentices shut up when Pandora glanced at them, though her tether must have allowed them to mock.

"One week." She turned to the baffled Taverners, patting her hands together gently. "Well done. He really didn't try as hard as he should, a mistake that let you raise the spark. I liked the earth, it definitely helped and showed a little complexity, but even so one of my senior apprentices shouldn't have been troubled." Her smile, and the ones from the other three, were a stark contrast to a very worried Pride. "Any apprentice showing a weakness in their shield plays target for the rest. You'd be surprised how much Pride will improve after a week of that. Now, the chivalrous one, Warren isn't it? What character do you play?" Her wind glyph plucked a booklet from the ground beside her, the list of standard characters, and she leafed through it.

Pandora seemed to be sort of playful, but deadly playful, so Warren went along with it. At least the sorceress seemed to like Rachel, even if the reasons worried him. "Shayde Warrior, a mix of magic and martial arts. I prefer fire or earth to the water glyph." Warren looked hopefully around the apprentices. "Or judo with no magic?" The other three Taverners kept quiet because Warren usually played Nik Smartish, a Warlock thief.

"No, no, no, that's not how it's done. I don't suppose you have trained with a knife or sword?" Pandora turned the booklet to show a picture. "This shows knives and a sword, and a staff?"

Now Warren wondered if he'd made a mistake. He'd thought Pandora would sneer at a thief, and he took the same karate lessons as Justin so he could play the part if necessary. "It's just a game. We never even expected to find magic, just started testing it and then suddenly, pow!" He hesitated, then decided to go for it. "If you let us go, I promise to start sword training?"

"This isn't a negotiation!" Warren thought he'd blown it, but after a moment Pandora smiled again. "Earth and wind I think, because I've already seen a very respectable fire glyph. First I want to see you try and crumble the cage, just one bar. If you can affect it, I'll let you throw earth at Wrath. You won't get a spark, but I can read the magic drain down the tether." At a gesture, earth surged behind her, covered in thick grass which wove itself together then turned into something that looked like chequered red and black cloth. Pandora sat in the instant armchair and leant back, turning a little and crossing her legs. One leg came out of the slit in her dress, half-way up her thigh, and she laughed at Warren. "Don't let me distract you. That's one of the first lessons male apprentices must learn. Come on, concentrate!" She leafed through the booklet again.

Warren had been startled for a moment, but the girls' costumes in the Tavern included miniskirts, leather shorts and netting so he wasn't really distracted. Now he inspected the cage, trying to reach into it as he'd done to sort earth. Rob kept saying matter was like the pixels in a colour picture, mix to suit, but Warren still thought of Lego bricks. Everything built of different colours and shapes, and some shapes and some colours needed changing. Though no matter how he tried, the surface resisted any attempt to alter it. Warren's magic felt past the hardened outer layer, not easy, and the centre wasn't quite as tough. Still compacted into rock, but there were spaces, tinier and fewer than in a handful of earth but he began to sift.

Warren had no idea how long he stood there, his attention concentrated under the surface of the rock, sifting and shifting and compacting. Someone spoke but he'd got into it now, slowly moving the spaces and softer bits together, scrunching some of the edges away from his part. That made the rest tougher but Pandora said to affect the cage, not break it all apart. Sweat dripped from Warren's nose and he dashed it away without conscious thought, lost inside the rock, sometimes only moving one grain at a time. Eventually he'd done enough, or as much as he could. Warren took a deep breath, and opened his eyes to see everyone watching him. He stretched himself, carefully because his neck muscles in particular were painfully tight.

"Too tough? Oh dear, you've failed your exam."

"Not yet, because I thought I should stay in character. Mixed magic and martial arts?" Warren knew he'd never break the crust with a glyph, Pandora never meant him to. She'd suffused the surface layer with magic, stopping him altering the structure, while it had been hardened to where even a hammer might have bounced. Now Warren took several deep breaths, finding his centre as the instructor told them, came up on his toes, spun and kicked. His heel struck where he'd been working, hitting a thin sheet of very hard rock over a shallow hollow backed by softer fragments. "Yes!"

"How?" For a moment Pandora came partway off her seat, then she settled back. "Now look, you've got me all excited. That's not a good idea, I sometimes have to kill someone to calm down." Her apprentices didn't seem to think that was a joke, so none of the Taverners laughed. Glyphs floated out, caressing the pillar and the small hole, drifting inside to inspect the rock. "Clever, I must remember what you did and be more careful with my tests in future. Not a terribly difficult feat for a sorceress, but impressive for a child. My apprentices could do the same, but they might not have thought of it. Now hit Wrath."

Warren had been ready, waiting, because he knew that would come. It would take time to solidify a lump of rock but he already had some shards from the cage, harder than anything he'd ever make. One wind glyph sent a blast towards the apprentice, picking up grass, twigs dust and pebbles to dash them against her shield and blind her. The other wind glyph scooped up the pieces from the pillar and drove them in a tight group, like shotgun pellets, right through the rest!

The dust cleared and Warren's heart sank, because Wrath sniffed in disgust before turning to Pride. "Hard luck Pride, you're still in the barrel this week."

"But he did better than expected. No spark or even a glow, but the sudden extra surge, the additional drain when that hidden strike arrived, surprised you." Pandora turned back to Warren and nodded gently, ignoring the glare from Wrath and the smirks from the other apprentices. "Complexity in the face of superior skill and power, not the forte of junior apprentices. Which is a pass mark. Very few people startle Wrath and live, congratulations Shayde Warrior. Now we'll just test your would-be Pandora." The sorceress held up the booklet to show the picture of K'ress Bloodclaw, all red cloak, skin-tight leather, high heeled boots and attitude. "It seems I have a fan! Who told your artist about me?"

All four Taverners looked at each other, because the answer might not go down very well. The comment about Warren living had seemed to get them off the hook, but now? Rachel raised her head defiantly. "K'ress Bloodclaw is based on Kelis, one of the designers and the artist. She hunted down a giant fursomnium dressed just like that, and all the lads wanted her as a character. Her usual character is K'liss Windcatcher."

Pandora leafed through the booklet, her eyes narrowed, then she relaxed. "So she doesn't normally dress like that?" All four shook their heads. Oddly enough, and reassuringly, Pandora seemed more interested in a proper description of Kelis than killing anyone. By the time she had determined that Kelis was a tall, very slim seventeen-year-old and nothing like curvy, the sorceress seemed almost jovial. "Good. Just tell her, no long black dresses or I may come and sue her for copyright." Her smile died as she inspected Rachel, who started to worry again. "Now what should we do for your test?"

"I could just hit you with my best shot, and you could laugh and send me home?" Four strained laughs were echoed by four real ones from the apprentices.

Even Pride forgot to sulk, though he hadn't fully recovered. "Or I could hit you with my best shot, and we'll see if you survive." As the silence continued he started to smile, just a little.

"No, because you are the target this week, Pride. You aren't allowed to fight back. If you didn't break her shield, I might only allow you your naturally absorbed magic for the next week. That wouldn't help your shielding, would it?" Pandora smirked at the mixture of glee, curiosity and relief from those facing her. Pride turned sheet white and absolutely didn't want to play anymore. "I accept, little Pandora. I'd better touch my tree in case you really are a sorceress, and have managed to fool me." Despite all the laughter from the apprentices, Pandora made a great show of putting her hand on her tree. "Now what was it, Rachel? Hit me with your best shot?"

Rachel tried, really tried because even if it didn't get through she wanted the bitch to feel it. Pandora had killed a teenager and used her ashes to feed the trees, then wound them up, let them down, tweaked her apprentices, took the piss and generally had fun. It would be ice, Rachel decided, but properly hardened with rock in the centre and on the tip. Condensed ice, the earth glyph could make it really hard. Even then she needed a diversion, something like what Warren did, but a surprise attack wouldn't work. Rachel had been watching as Pandora played, and even apparently relaxed on the chair the sorceress stayed poised, ready to lash out. The Tavern's youngest adept poured magic into her construct, knowing Pandora would be assessing it even as she built it. She used a lot of magic, nearly all there was in her belt, but Rachel kept some back. Not much, just enough for the surprise, a shield in case this wasn't enough, and maybe one feeble fire glyph.

"Ready?" Rachel nodded, the ice spear hovering while she still worked on compressing the centre. She ignored what had to be a faked opening for a surprise attack when Pandora turned to Pride. "Pay heed, because I doubt this one will throw a straight ice spear. I may ask the others to test whatever it is." Rachel ignored that as well, it was all a part of Pandora's act. "All right little girl, let's have it."

Rachel didn't need the final gibe to help her intent, she already wanted to pin the supercilious bitch to her chair. The spear accelerated, powered by a huge windhammer, but as it did Rachel flicked her other hand. A line of bright yellow flowed across the grass, aimed at Pandora's feet! As it closed in, catching up with the ice spear, the ice split into two. Half dived to strike where the line did, turning yellow as it dived, while the other flashed bright red as it drove home at head height. Rachel staggered back two steps and sat down hard, then hugged herself. The backlash from pushing the windhammer hurt, really hurt, and it had absolutely no effect on Pandora. In some sort of daze she watched Pandora's glyph coming at her. She'd failed.

*   *   *

"No!" As Warren called out a fire glyph and a windhammer, his and Shannon's, tried to intercept Pandora's attack but were too late. Green gunk fizzed and spat as Rachel's shield flared, briefly, and held! She pulled every last dreg from her storage belt to boost her shield, then tried to stand but her legs simply couldn't. Even so Rachel stuck her chin out and glared at Pandora, refusing to beg, and the sorceress laughed!

"Well done. The shield is your pass mark, little Pandora. A free lesson in survival. If you had put everything into the strike, you deserved to die. The combination of strength and attempted diversions in your attack were adequate." The sorceress stood up, giving an airy wave of the hand. The grass and earth of the chair, and that around the Taverners, rearranged themselves to leave the ground looking more or less unchanged.

"You are letting them go? What about the car?" Avarice really was well named, while two of the others looked surprised.

"They passed my tests, and I promised. It would be impolite to make them walk home, though I will want one small souvenir. Your red cloak, please, little Pandora." Rachel glanced helplessly at the other three. Was this another twist, let them go then start again? "Just the cloak, little one, to remind you. You really did throw a very strong and clever best shot, given your age and skill levels. Even so, you are not ready to challenge sorceresses, or even my apprentices, and you lack manners. When you have learned how to act in company and gained some control of your temper, and learned more glyphs, come to see me. Make a proper appointment, apologise and show you have grown, and you can have it back."

"Put like that, Rachel?" Warren shrugged and Shannon came to help her up, so Rachel took her cloak off. She took the opportunity to drain some magic from Shannon's belt.

Rachel used some of the magic to help her walk over unaided, even if it was more of a stagger, and tried for a smile as Pandora held out her hand. "Look after it, please?"

"Oh yes, I really will. I've never had fans before. Now get in that delightful little car and go home before I decide to keep it after all. Or you." The sorceress leant against the tree to watch the four of them leave. They didn't make an impressive sight. Cecilia had Warren's arm over her shoulder because he'd hurt his foot kicking the rock, and he had a banging headache and sore neck from sifting rock. Shannon's jeans and shoes were charred, and she had to half-carry Rachel most of the way because the last throw had really strained the youngster's muscles. Just before getting into the car Rachel stopped, stood up straight and pushed Shannon's hands away. Using the last of the magic she'd taken from Shannon, she cast a Seeming on her dress. From the back it now looked like a short red cloak. Delighted laughter rang out behind them, as Rachel collapsed into the car and curled up on the back seat.

"I'm sorry. I wasn't any good at all, and stopped you from escaping."

Warren patted Cecilia gently on the shoulder. "Not really. I reckon she'd have liked running prey, or maybe setting her apprentices on catching us. Though after this, you might want to go back to the church?"

"Not a chance! People like her must be stopped, and the church won't do it!" Cecilia took a moment to calm down, giving an apologetic smile. "Not that I did much. We'd better call in and warn everyone. Just in case someone else ignores Eric's warning."

"I'd love to, but Pandora had a final joke." Shannon held up her phone. "Junk, burned out." A quick check showed that all four phones were dead. "We'll call from a phone box."

"Just to tell Eric to pull everyone in until we've spoken to Abel. We need Ferryl and Zephyr to give Pandora a good hard slap for starters." Warren straightened his leg, very carefully, he'd jarred his knee as well. "I hope that witch charm works on this."

"We're going to have to confess we ignored what Eric told us, and apologise. That'll be fun. Even then, Ferryl and Zephyr might not be able to do anything about Pandora. She didn't seem too worried, even at facing sixty like us." Rachel hugged herself, trying to get comfortable. "I ache, all over. Now I know how Ferryl felt pulling that car, and I didn't even scratch the bitch."

"Sleep if you can. Here, take some magic." Shannon passed her belt. "On the bright side, nobody hit the car with a lorry while we were gone." Nobody laughed or even smiled, then or on the long drive home. On the way they talked and all of them agreed, they wouldn't explain properly until everyone could meet. That way no Taverner would hear a rumour and think they could get payback, and die.

* * *

Ferryl and Abel might not have known about Pandora, but their reception on reaching Brinsford wiped away all thoughts about sorcerers, veils or garage sales-children. Rob stood in the garden of Castle House, frantically waving his arms as they slowed down, literally hopping from one foot to the other. Abel pulled up and took off his helmet, to hear Rob shouting. "I've been waiting here for ages! It worked, the trap, but it got away. Not a troll, but a troll hole. Maybe. Why don't you answer calls?"

"Because I might crash if I answer phones while riding a bike?" The meaning of the first bit got through. "Melanie really did see a troll? How do you know if it got away?"

"How about putting the bikes in the shed, hiding under a veil and going to look. Carefully because your mum might see through a veil, and then she'll want a blow-by-blow account of the trip." Ferryl pushed her bike through the garden gate. "We should put in a proper drive and a big gate, with a garage for Kelis's car. Or the Range Rover if it's still not claimed when she passes her test."

"No driveway yet, or there'll be too many questions about how we got permission, then how come I inherited the place. The same reasons Kelis is sticking with the car her mum bought her, rather than swap for one of the captures." Abel followed Ferryl through the gate. "How urgent is this, Rob? Can I get these leathers off first? We've got to find out why some teams came back early, and talk to everyone about how they approach sorcerers."

Rob sighed in exasperation, but deflated a little. "I suppose you could go home, have a bath, see your mum, meet the Taverners, and look the day after tomorrow because there's not much to see. Just a hole in the ground, a bit over twenty centimetres across, where something went through. Then it escaped, because there's nothing in the pit underneath." He gestured in the general direction of Stourton. "Or I suppose you could nip into town and find out why Rachel, Warren, Shannon and Cecilia are being secretive. They won't talk about their meeting until everyone is there, but want everyone brought back home immediately."

Abel looked at Ferryl and she nodded. "I reckon they met someone like we did. At least they are all safe, so there's no need to change the instructions. I agree with getting everyone home, but those visiting a village should still do so."

"A couple of days won't matter. We need to talk to everyone at the same time." Abel called Eric to make sure the Taverners understood the instructions, while Ferryl let Rob know what had happened. Not all of it, she skipped around how helpless she'd be against senior sorcerers. As Abel put his phone away, Ferryl finished explaining about Anniyah and the veil.

Rob wasn't even slightly impressed by the veiling idea. "What if some idiot shows off? A beginner might not be able to resist. You know, to mates. Now you see me, now you don't?" His familiar smile came back for a moment. "I probably would have, right at the start, if it wasn't for you, Kelis and Ferryl threatening doom and disaster."

Put like that, Abel realised he'd probably got a bit carried away. "All right, we'll think again. Maybe assess the individuals."

Rob had followed them to the hut and now he sat down and relaxed a little. "So what went wrong? I noticed some parts of Ferryl's version were a bit sparse, so I assume they were bad?"

"Yes, but it wasn't the actual meeting. The problem is telling the other Taverners, or confessing really." As the pair of them shed their leathers and heavy boots, Ferryl filled in the gaps, admitting her weakness when facing real experts. "The Taverners think I'm their ace. Now I've got to own up to not having enough glyphs to fight someone like Aesop, but I can't explain the reasons. The Taverners mustn't learn about my lost wits, or that it was me in that hole for two hundred years. I vaguely remember knowing some very complicated glyphs, but not the glyphs themselves or the memory of how to use them."

"Don't the memories give some hint of the actual glyph?"

Ferryl tapped her thigh. "When I put in the wit showing me how to make gold, it held vague memories of manipulating huge quantities of earth. The wit with shields on told me there are advanced glyphs that will break them, and others to strengthen shields or weapons. There's no detail, none at all. It's like the glyphs Creepio saw, the ones for the ogre. I don't know them until I have the wit, but then I also remember how to manipulate them, expertly."

"But what you know has been enough, and glyphs like the one Creepio saw warned him you might know the rest." Rob frowned, working through what Ferryl had said. "You seemed to think that was enough."

"It was, when I thought the real sorcerers were still in their fortresses." Ferryl sighed in resignation. "The Taverners saw me deal with Pendragon's apprentices, then Valdar and his apprentices. If Aesop is a really old sorcerer, he would have done all that without getting a scratch. I'd better warn everyone I'm only a second class sorceress. They'll all have to be more careful."

"Don't tell the Taverners you don't know many glyphs, or word will get out to all those senior sorcerers. Even Redwolf might decide on payback. We need to be very careful because Redwolf thinks you are old, but the Taverners think you are our age. Maybe not our age, because some of them must be realising you fight too well for a teenager. Self-healing is a big giveaway." Rob settled down, the troll hole forgotten for the moment, and the four of them tried to work out a story. Ferryl wanted to tell a very abbreviated version of the truth, it would be easier for her, while Zephyr suggested that her own limitations should be explained at the same time.

Eventually the whole business had been beaten to death without any nice neat conclusion, as usual. "Right, let me finish my drink and we'll go and see this hole." Abel raised his can of cola in salute. "After I've topped up from a tree. You don't truly appreciate unlimited, fresh tree magic until you've gone four days without any."

*   *   *

While stood under a tree, topping up his magic, Abel came back to Rob's greeting. "Since we aren't going to be dashing off to town, what did you catch in the trap?"

"I told you, nothing."

"Didn't it trigger my glyph to seal the top with magic?"

"Yes Ferryl, but that didn't stop something smashing a blothering great hole in from the side, underground. It had to be inwards; I can see where the side collapsed. I strengthened that to nearly rock." Now Rob looked even more despondent. "I can't even get a proper look, not without breaking your magic block and taking away the rest of the earth covering. Then there'd be a great big hole, which I'd have to fill in straight away in case dad or mum looked over the back fence and saw it."

"Is the tree there yet? The dryad seedling might have seen something." Though Abel could see the answer on Rob's face.

"The day after tomorrow, I got a text." The next bit cheered him up. "Kelis will have fun, explaining her new tree when she gets back. She forgot to tell her mum before zooming off to Germany."

"Eek. How do you know?" Abel knew there'd be something else to explain as well. "Kelis's mum can see creatures, so we'd better warn the dryad seedling."

"Kelis received the warning text, about when her lorry will be coming, and called me in a bit of a panic. I've told her to make up her own lies and text them to her mum, but I warned Chestnut you'd be wanting the seedling in a few days. You ought to talk to Chestnut. It's a bit twitchy about something."

Fifteen minutes later three teenagers stood under a veil, carefully inspecting a small round hole in the grass outside the back fence of Rob's house. A shimmer had dropped through the hole to look inside. Abel glanced towards the house, and a bedroom window. "That hole is a bit bigger than you said, Rob, but still too small for a human. It's a good job nobody looked over your fence. Where's Melanie?"

Before Rob could answer, Zephyr answered Abel. "Out with Ginny and Diane. Ginny cancelled her trip after I warned her over the tether, so she's been taking them on outings. Right now the children are allegedly visiting your mum at work, to get some work experience in an office, but are actually taking pictures of Carsington Water. Other Taverners can show the pictures to parents to prove where they've been." That made good sense. The reservoir was only a couple of miles from Stourton and a good alibi for a day out.

"Me, Shannon and Rachel are allegedly taking Diane and Mel to a zoo the day after tomorrow, your mum's suggestion. The two of them would have gone with Ginny to take pictures to alibi us three adepts, but now all trips are off so the right people will actually go. The pictures will still come in handy, and on the way back everyone can spend time practicing glyphs. She seems to be getting a real kick out of knowing about magic, your mum I mean." Rob gave up pretending to be patient "Well Ferryl? You and Zephyr have been hand-waving or hovering for ages. What happened?"

"Just what you said. Something magical came, heavy enough to break the trap and magically strong enough to ignore the boundary hexes. The trap worked perfectly, except something else broke it from outside." Ferryl bent a little, peering through the hole at an angle. "Something very strong, magically or physically, and almost immune to magic. Going by the size of the hole and the broken earth it was the second type, a baby troll, just as you guessed." She held out her hand towards the hole, again, and scowled in frustration. "I don't recognise the magic traces from whatever fell in, nor the marks in the loose earth at the bottom. It threw glyphs to try and break out, but I cannot remember a magic user fitting Melanie's description."

"That's it?" Rob threw out an arm, pointing dramatically towards his house. "That's my little sister's bedroom window, right there. I'd like something a bit better than unknown magic-using skinny-thing! A toadstool according to Mel!"

"I doubt it will come back now, not here. It might still spy on Brinsford, but it's had a scare. A big one when it couldn't break out without help." Ferryl still sounded thoughtful, working on the problem. "I'm trying to remember what might be getting help from a baby troll. Something the adult troll trusted, that's certain. Trolls don't usually have allies, as far as I remember, but we've already seen adolescent trolls working with leeches. Practice your earth crumbling, Rob. You'll need it if we meet the adult." She muttered to herself, quietly so the others couldn't hear.

Abel looked at Rob and mouthed 'I need my wits,' but for once Ferryl didn't actually say it out loud. "What about the hole?" He glanced at Rob's house, then each way along the edge of the field. "I doubt your dad will come looking again, and there's no reason for anyone else to walk along here, but if they do it'll take some explaining."

"I'll fill it in now Ferryl's seen it." Rob began to build glyphs. "If I gather bits of field from over a wide area it won't show."

"Take the top off first, please, without dropping earth in the hole. I want to examine the pit and the tunnel. We might get an idea of the direction it went." Ferryl shook her head when Rob pointed in the obvious direction. "Trolls, even babies, aren't stupid. They set off in a random direction, then head for home once they are clear."

Even after Ferryl broke the magical seal, and Rob removed the thin layer of grass and earth, Ferryl couldn't identify the magic user from the traces. Eventually she jumped down into the hole. Moments later she looked up at Rob and Abel with a big smile. "Trolls usually collapse the tunnel behind them, to stop anything following, but I think the baby must have panicked. It might have turned for home before remembering." She bent to look into the tunnel, a small spark drifting from her hand and disappearing into the dark opening. "A person would be a tight fit, but a Zephyr wouldn't?"

After some dire warnings about watching for traps, because the troll had a magic user with it, Zephyr drifted into the dark. Abel reported back as she slowly and carefully followed the winding tunnel, until she reported a sharp bend. The tunnel ran dead straight for a while until it ended in a jumble of collapsed earth. That led Rob to wonder where the rest of the earth went, from all the tunnelling. A short lesson from Ferryl explained how rock trolls had one magical talent, compressing or loosening earth and rock and holding it in place. The soil would be compressed into the tunnel walls, but when the troll released the magic the soil expanded to refill the hole.

Meanwhile Zephyr had tried to get through the collapse and failed. Unfortunately Zephyr couldn't tell which direction the troll had gone, not from underground, and she wasn't sure if digging upwards would bring the whole tunnel down. Abel asked Zephyr to come back for a phone. With luck the satellite signal would reach underground.

"No need. Ffod can do this. I remember magnetism from when I wiped out your music trying to see it in the machine. You said it was magnetism, so I looked on the internet while you slept. I can magnetise, move the insides of iron to line up so they will find north." Zephyr must have been inspecting the earth as she explained. "I am working back, sensing into the walls like when we make earth into rock. Got it! I have iron! Rusty bits. Ffod casts fire to melt it and make a needle! Compass needs a needle."

Abel tried to keep the others informed, catching up a bit as Zephyr concentrated on her needle-making. Rob kept interrupting, asking what Zephyr had done to the music on Abel's player and how often she surfed the web. Abel had barely got up to date when Zephyr started 'talking' again. "No need for water, a puff of wind casts wind for floating." Abel felt another tiny tug as she pulled more magic. "It is wobbly. Maybe I did not get the parts lined up, inside the iron?" Zephyr sounded despondent, but not for long. "Yes! It moves! Ffod throws a twenty for perception! If that is north, and the tunnel leads to the left of the needle, it is almost west. Oh, but the needle has two ends, which is north? I am sorry, Ffod has failed." Zephyr sounded truly despondent, especially after all her excitement over coming up with a solution.

"Good enough, Zephyr, because you've narrowed it down to due east or west. Come on home before the tunnel collapses and traps you." Which Abel had been worrying about, even if Ferryl seemed confident the walls would hold.

"I can blast through with air, because my tether will show the way. Earth cannot stop my tether, unless I split into too many little Ffods and lose myself." A big relief for Abel, though it explained why intervening houses and trees never seemed to affect his communication with Zephyr.

Rob looked off over the farmland above the tunnel, then turned with a big smile. "Ask Zephyr if the big turn is left or right!" When Zephyr confirmed the sharp turn was to the left he pointed towards the Copple's farm. "The tunnel went that way, west up the Brinn valley."

Ferryl turned to look the same way. "A troll will want to make her home in solid rock. What is beyond the farm?"

"More fields, but the ground rises either side and turns into real hills with some low cliffs, and the fields are really narrow. Eventually the Brinn really does have a valley, a rocky one. There's sheep up there but I'm not sure who owns the land. The Pennines aren't real mountains this far south, more like big hills, but they're solid rock."

"That's near enough to narrow the search. We can look for signs up the valley, to narrow it down until we can find the lair. Going by the other creatures sent to spy on Brinsford, the sooner we find these strangers the better!" Ferry turned back to the tunnel in time for Zephyr to come shooting out.

"Home again! I am faster following my tether. Look, my needle!" Everyone admired the thin length of iron floating on air. Even if it wasn't really a needle it was pretty good work for a puff of wind in a tunnel.

Ferryl used wind to blow herself up out of the pit. "Now we'd better fill this in. Don't use Zephyr to help you, Abel. You need the practice with earth glyphs before searching for a troll." As they gathered earth for the hole, carefully solidifying the fill so it didn't slump afterwards, the three of them discussed troll-hunting. Ferryl wasn't confident, not with mountains to hide in. Despite being mostly magic inside, the rock crust on its skin meant a troll had very little magical signature. With luck its magic-using ally would be easier to trace.

None of them had a decent plan for tracking the creature before they split up to go home. After that Abel found himself too busy explaining the trip to think of much else, editing as he spoke to avoid telling his mum about casting glyphs using pebbles, or stroppy sorcerers.

Later, in his bedroom, Abel called Warren, Shannon and Rachel, but nobody wanted to talk about it until they had him, Zephyr and Ferryl present. Shannon admitted they'd had a big scare. A call to Eric confirmed that if any other Taverners saw any hint of a sorcerer, they would run, and in any case everyone should be back tomorrow. There were two pairs out of touch, but they were probably looking for a phone box. Other sorcerers enjoyed burning out phones. If the missing couples called in tonight, they'd be back by lunchtime. Meanwhile Shawn would ask Bertram and

Veren about the neutral zone in Sheffield, again, and hopefully bring a map to the meeting. Terese would know, but Abel wanted to find out what had happened to Shannon before involving his solicitor.

Eventually Abel drifted off, though not before his usual nightly musing about tiny magic sparks. They were a lot more restful than thinking about tomorrow.

Slave Mistress

The morning dawned bright and sunny, but Abel couldn't relax and enjoy it because of the upcoming meeting. Despite Zephyr asking down the tether, Ginny couldn't find out what had upset Shannon and her group.

One couple had called in overnight, from call boxes because their phones mysteriously died, and were on the way home. Two Taverners, Les and Penny, were still missing and hadn't called in, which might mean a real disaster. An hour later they phoned from a call box, reversed charges, and reported they'd be home by lunchtime. Neither wanted to discuss details on the phone, but Les, the driver, wanted to know what the car insurance covered. Since Les had taken his own car, Eric had the Sheffield office checking. Late morning Ginny reported. She'd been to pick the pair up from the railway station, because their car had been thoroughly burned.

Despite the morning being allegedly restful, Abel, Ferryl and Rob were wound up and raring to go by the time Eric picked them up. Ginny couldn't play chauffeur, because she was allegedly at the zoo. Jenny wasn't very happy about the reasons for the meeting, but was relieved at getting away from home. Sitting in her dad's office, hearing everything second-hand, was driving her crackers.

*   *   *

The number of cars in the park outside the gym warned Abel, but even so the sheer number inside surprised him. Definitely more than sixty Taverners, a quick count came to over eighty! Most of the new Taverners were from the Sheffield demesne, some of them brought to Shawn by Veren and other local sorcerers including Capone. The seven new locals Abel knew about before his trip had become a dozen, all from Stourton and the nearby villages inside Abel's demesne.

The babble died back as Abel came in, dropping to almost silence before the questions started. Abel wasn't completely surprised when Shannon, Eric, Shawn and a few other adepts tried to quieten everyone down, though Rachel and Claris pitching in came as a pleasant surprise. Claris noticed Abel's look and pointed to her security uniform, smiled and shrugged. By the time Abel had reached the practice cube, most people were waiting more or less quietly. Rob leant close to whisper that, if the Taverners didn't like what Abel told them, he'd stood in the glyph-casting target area.

Shannon more or less insisted on speaking first, and started her recital more or less calm and factual. Rachel wasn't calm, she spent the time pacing up and down, scowling. Shannon had only reached the part where Pandora told them she'd killed the possible Taverner, and fed her ashes to the trees, when several people looked ill and two bolted for the toilets.

Everyone paused, waiting, but Les, the one with the burned car, felt he should explain. "One of those in the loo is Penny. She came with me on the last trip, to Gloucester. We went into a park, before we got the warning, and found GO AWAY written in capitals on the grass, and two Bonny's Tavern rulebooks. The letters were made out of lines of heaped ashes. Penny poked through them with her foot, trying to see what had been burned because it was too much for two game packs." By now several others were looking ill. "As we came back to the car we were surrounded, a sorcerer and four apprentices, and our phones quit working. They veiled the whole area, then burned the car. Not just set it on fire, they kept hitting it again and again, stoking the flames, then damped it all down when nothing else would burn. We were guarded by apprentices for two days until Hamilcar, the sorcerer, decided he didn't want two more apprentices. His apprentices dumped us at the railway station with tickets home, so we took the hint and got on the train." From his look, Les wasn't far from a dash to the toilets. "Even so, we hadn't thought of the ashes being human. Penny got her shoes covered, and had to use tissues to clean them."

"If we hadn't shielded really fast, and if Warren hadn't grabbed Cecilia in time, we'd have all been ashes. The bitch didn't even warn us!" Rachel glared around then at Ferryl. "I want you to go over there and fix her good. See how she likes having to hand over her fancy cloak!"

Ferryl glanced at Abel, but he wanted to hear all the rest first. "Later Rachel, let Shannon finish." Rachel backed off, but she took up pacing again and muttering to herself. From the looks, a good few wanted Ferryl to do something. "Shannon?"

To Abel's relief, Shannon continued and her story explained Rachel's outburst. Once she'd done, others wanted to tell about contacts who stopped answering the phone, or their own phones stopped working. One lass had turned up but with a sorceress, and already tethered. Others had messages from sorcerers and sorceresses, anything from go away or else through to names and contact details for Abel to get in touch. By the time the last had finished, everyone could see the pattern. Almost all the demesnes or active churches were in towns, where many sorcerers objected to Tavern interference. The churches seemed to rely on their crosses to protect their area, because nobody met a magical priest.

Abel started by telling everyone about the meetings with Anniyah, a bit of light relief with some lessons for the future. He moved on to Aesop, and the new contract, definitely welcome news. As he retraced the actual meeting, several people were casting curious glances at Ferryl. She ignored them, waiting until Abel finished.

*   *   *

Absolute dead silence fell when Ferryl took her turn. "You are all wondering why I didn't challenge Aesop to do his worst. He would have put a hand on his tree, any tree, and then I would have had trouble getting Abel out alive. I can't go and get Rachel's cloak from Pandora, or march into Hamilcar's demesne and torch his car. Not won't, I simply can't." She stood silent, waiting patiently for the storm of protest to die back. "I know you are angry, and so am I. One day there may be a chance to reply, but every sorceress acted legally. If Pandora or Hamilcar visit, and we can get them close to Abel's trees, then there'll be a reckoning. Even then it might be a bad idea."

The babel died enough for Rachel's "why not if it's legal" to be clearly heard.

"You are all wondering why I didn't challenge Aesop to do his worst. You heard what Pandora did, how casually she sculpted earth and changed grass to cloth without any real effort. Using that amount of magic leaves even an old sorceress a little weaker, which is the real reason she touched her tree." Ferryl really didn't like admitting the next part, the strain showed in her voice. She'd discussed it with Abel, and this was the least she could make public. "If enough sorceresses came for payback they might win, even if I'm touching a tree. I'm not old enough

279

to survive that sort of attack, so we daren't start a war. Now you all know why nobody else fancies it."

"You must be as powerful as those others, because you can heal yourself. I thought that meant you were old?" Warren stopped dead, thinking about that. "How old are you, Ferryl?" Some of the Taverners were suddenly very thoughtful.

Ferryl took Abel's hand. "I know we talked, but maybe I should tell them the whole truth right now." Abel didn't want to answer through Zephyr, or everyone would think there must be a problem, so he kissed her cheek. That should do, because they'd agreed a schoolboy couldn't have a thousand-year-old girlfriend. "All right, here goes." With a big breath, Ferryl very obviously braced herself for the reaction. "Older than you think, but not some ancient crone with a new body."

"Yeah, we all know Abel likes us older girls." The ripple of laughter at Jenny's joke wasn't much, and quickly died.

"I came to magic very early, much earlier than most. You all know that using magic is impossible until puberty?" Several agreed or nodded so Ferryl pushed on. "I started before I was ten, younger than most." That part was true, because Ferryl had learned magic very quickly after quickening, becoming sentient. "My father wanted me to be strong, so I received my first lessons immediately and concentrated on wind, then healing. As a result I never had what you would call a normal childhood. Within years most wounds were survivable, but if I am hurt too deeply or badly I can't fix it." Also all true in a way. If an attack wounded Ferryl's true-self she'd concentrate on healing that, and if necessary let the body die. "I never had proper schooling, so I really am learning when I attend lessons." Ferryl paused, concentrating on a way of telling her story without revealing the real facts or timeline. Even Abel didn't know how she came to be, and when.

A voice asked what many must be thinking. "You really learned to heal in a matter of years? I thought that was very advanced."

Ferryl didn't have a chance to answer, because Rachel did it for her. "Of course she can. So can you, or me, any of us. I'll bet I can heal a wound inside of ten years. If I forgot about other glyphs, and concentrated on healing, it'd take a lot less. Any takers?" Nobody answered as she glared around. "No, because we get loads of extra magic and lessons, just like Ferryl. Though now I'm curious just how old Ferryl is. Well Abel, have you gone for older or mature, cougar or crinkly?" At least that came with a little smile.

"Oh no, I'm not giving away my girlfriend's age. Though I'll say I've seen the real her, before the makeover, and I'd have been able to take her home to mum." That got a quick look from Jenny, but was true though Abel wouldn't have introduced the Leech victim as a girlfriend. "Just remember the important part. Ferryl isn't old enough to have practiced lots of different glyphs. She is a bit like us, very advanced in some ways without going through the usual training."

"I can vouch for her having to swat for exams, so she hasn't got years of knowledge tucked away. The healing thing explains her magical strength, because Ferryl can store magic in diamonds set into her bones." Rob, serious for once, nodded slowly as he saw various Taverners remember how Ferryl hadn't asked anyone to fill her belts after the Valdar fight.

"Though even that is new, because she carried magic in lead bars and belts to start with." Una had seen Ferryl using lead blocks for extra magic, and then a belt like Abel's. "That means she's too inexperienced to tackle someone like Pandora, who could be several centuries old. Centuries learning more and more glyphs, practicing them and storing them for future reference."

"Hey, good point, why don't you learn all the glyphs in Castle House? Someone mentioned a library." Tobias smiled and looked around the rest. "I'll spend all summer there, and then let's see Pandora get nasty again."

"We've looked, and those we can read are training books. Many of the glyphs are relatively harmless, unless you want to carve wood or take up weaving? What they do is teach control, because without that a dangerous glyph will kill you. A wobbly wind glyph isn't so bad, but others can turn a wall or a person to dust if they aren't cast properly." Ferryl looked pointedly at several Taverners who were struggling with the earth glyph. They could harden earth, but trying to alter anything still left them with dust.

"I'll vouch for that. Just remember if you get that far, whoever teaches you isn't joking." Warren turned towards Ferryl. "Now can we get back to the real problem? If one of us upsets someone like Pandora, we've got nothing to stop her."

"Yes we have. Firstly, if she comes here it's open season, and she doesn't know just how strong any of you are. She'd have trouble breaking any adept's shield if they're connected to a tree, and won't be able to top up anyplace." Ferryl held out a hand as if to cast. "With one hand on a tree I can hold off one sorceress, even an old powerful one. Then the rest of the adepts get a hand onto bark and finish her and her apprentices, because even simple glyphs backed by a tree have awesome power. Pandora won't risk it."

"Why did she do that if she's so super-scary? Put a hand on a tree I mean." Rachel's hand came up as if to cast her own glyph. "Was she bluffing!"

"No, just practical. I told you, using that amount of magic would drain the diamonds in her bones, just a little. By using the tree instead of her own magic, Pandora would still be fully topped up if real trouble started." Through his hand Abel could feel Ferryl relax a little as the Taverners got down to what to do in the future, and how to deal with trouble if it came calling, rather than her age. Abel knew the subject of Ferryl's age would come back, but probably in quiet, private questions or jokes about older women or cradle-snatching.

By the time the meeting broke up into dozens of conversations, everyone knew the way ahead. The first job in any town would be to locate the neutral zone, and then leave polite messages outside the parks. Ferryl would teach the adepts to form messages that could be seen, but only by those with magic. Meetings with new prospects must be in public, or out of town altogether, until Abel could rent neutral premises. New trainees in towns would get a lead brick, to keep them from raiding the bushes someplace for magic. Out of town, if the trees were claimed by a mixture of dryads and more than one sorcerer, the area wasn't in a demesne. Then each strong hedgerow or sapling could be drained of just a little magic.

Anyone meeting a sorceress would ask if Abel could contact them to discuss the spread of the Tavern, and hint that negotiating might be profitable. Abel would start on the list of sorcerous contacts to date, alternating friendly invites with the others. He'd definitely be in a car. The argument over which one wasn't settled, but he'd have bodyguards.

More phones went on the shopping list, a lot of phones, cheap ones to carry on trips. Presumably the mystery breakdowns were a sorceress hinting, deterrence rather than an actual confrontation.

Eventually Abel, Rob, Ferryl and Jenny left the rest to their arguments, promising to listen to any comments and suggestions. Not tomorrow though, everyone needed a day at least to let tempers settle. Rachel might need a year.

Abel had a good excuse for leaving, he had an appointment with Terese at Woods and Green. He told her about Aesop, and she promised to confirm the contract, then asked about the rest. When he asked about old sorceresses and unwritten rules, Terese arranged for Dryad Woods to deal with the rest of Abel's queries. Once Terese left, Woods confirmed that his junior partner assumed Ferryl was an old sorceress, so she would know all about the stronger glyph-casters. Terese couldn't detect Ferryl's true form, which is why she hadn't warned Abel at the first meeting.

On reflection Woods could understand Ferryl's mistake, because there had been a slow, quiet revolution in the sorcerous community. Over the last two hundred years, as industrialisation grew, many of the more powerful had become less insular. They had moved into towns, where most of the business lay, probably encouraged by the difference between modern facilities and old, draughty fortresses.

The neutral zones came about as an answer to modern business concentrating all the sorcerers in towns, a way for magical rivals to meet without elaborate preparations. Stourton once had one, the High Street, but when the town became a monopoly, that lapsed. Locating neutral zones elsewhere relied on finding the identifying glyphs, though many locals didn't make it easy for visitors. The part of the town centre overrun by creatures would be a good hint that nobody claimed it. Some individual businesses would be protected, because everyone competed for business there, including the weaker sorcerers. Finding a senior sorcerer might be difficult unless Abel found a message wall, literally, the side of a building in the neutral zone used for magical messages.

Abel tried to come up with a solution, but he couldn't get round one restriction. The master had to make each deal personally. Once a few more sorcerers had met him, Abel could deal with minor matters through a tether, but not through a trainee. Woods thought Veren might be accepted as a messenger, to set up meetings or for preliminary negotiations, because a vassal wasn't much different to a tethered subordinate. By the time Abel staggered out, clutching Terese's list of amenable sorceresses and sorcerers, he'd decided one thing. Veren would definitely be trying to negotiate, just to make a dent on the workload, and Ginny would be doing the same. If Ginny didn't admit who actually held her tether, she could act for Abel when meeting anyone but senior sorceresses.

Abel, Ferryl, Rob, Jenny and Zephyr held their own impromptu Tavern meeting, in Castle House, to find a way to help Abel. They organised the list of visits, but apart from acting as bodyguards that was the best four of them could do. Ginny, included for part of the discussion via her tether, agreed to negotiate, or play messenger to try and set up meetings. Nobody mentioned she didn't actually have an option. At least Jenny cheered the rest up before heading home. She'd be here tomorrow to see Rob's tree planted, with her very jealous little sister.

*   *   *

The arrival of Rob's tree the following morning kept most of Brinsford amused, as well as Jenny and Diane, because of the size and all the machinery. Rob's mum still seemed unsure about her unexpected present. She hadn't mentioned liking Red Maple until her son asked for her favourite tree. Next thing she knew, he'd bought her one! Terri had just got used to the idea of a young tree, a sapling, when a big, definitely mature one turned up on a lorry with a crane, a digger and a team of men to plant it! If she'd had any warning the answer might have been no, but when the workman knocked on the door everything was sat on the field out back.

While the workmen removed grass and a section of flower bed, Melanie climbed onto the lorry. She sat there and watched as the big machinery swung into action, carving a neat pit in the corner of her garden, occasionally putting a hand on the new tree and giggling. She had to stay back as the machinery switched to lifting and positioning the tree, then filling in around the root ball. Melanie switched to teasing Diane, though only about having an instant tree because most of those watching weren't magical. Once the ripened seedling had been carried here in a chunk of wood, Melanie would have her own dryad, right in her back garden. Diane had already confessed to being green with envy, and trying to work out where she could have a tree planted at home.

The workmen had assured Terri, Rob's mum, that they'd put everything back. Two hours later they'd done a pretty good job, though the flower bed had to curve round the trunk. The surplus earth had been put in a truck, the fence rebuilt, and the machines were even erasing their own tracks from the field. As the workmen watered everything in, and explained the tree wouldn't look its best until next spring, Abel's phone rang.

A text from his Mum said she'd had a call from Jess, Kelis's mum, something about a tree? One that would arrive in an hour or so? By the time Abel and Ferryl reached home, Abel's mum had arrived from work! "Come on. Kelis texted her mum to say a tree would arrive today, and to talk to you and Ferryl, then stopped answering calls. Jess thought it was a joke, but the delivery firm just called." She rounded on Abel. "Is this a magical thing?"

"Yes, but the short notice is only Kelis forgetting to mention it before leaving for Germany. She was supposed to call her mum and confess, but we didn't realise it would be here today. The firm probably arranged them both while all this machinery is here for Rob's tree. Both trees are here to power the protection around Brinsford. Magical batteries, like I explained? If Pendragon Enterprises were doing it, it'd cost the villagers a fortune." As expected, the prices the firm charged for a few drawings on a building diverted his mum, long enough for her to calm down.

Though she soon got back to her main worry. "Will Jess see anything extra, more creatures, enough to send her barmy?"

"Not now, not for a while, and then just one that lives in the tree. We'll explain to you first, and let you see it." Which meant getting Dryad Chestnut to talk to Abel's mum without freaking her.

Abel got a pass for now. "In that case, I want you pair to stay away. I'll tell Jess it's to do with creatures, and she'll have to ask Kelis when she gets back." His mum looked quite smug as she set off. "Jess believes whatever I tell her about them, though this is definitely going to cost you. It's about time I saw inside that house." Abel watched her go, trying to come up with an answer, but he had a feeling nothing would work this time. On the bright side, there'd be a repeat of the circus in Rob's garden, complete with the spectators, so Kelis's mum would have to keep reasonably calm.

*　　*　　*

Instead of joining the circus, Abel turned towards the village green. "We'd better ask Chestnut how it feels about meeting my mum."

"According to Rob, Chestnut wanted to see you anyway." Ferryl walked along, deep in thought, but stopped short of the green. "Maybe it's time to explain Castle House to your mum, properly. It isn't any stranger than hexing a house or guarding a village, just more powerful glyphs. Toad might be able to explain exactly why you can inherit, but your mother can't."

"Maybe, if we can avoid the full master part. We'll ask the rest for ideas. Now let's get one problem sorted before facing any others." Ferryl didn't seem worried, but nothing seemed to bother her since she'd made her confession. Abel walked across the grass to the tree, glancing around to make sure nobody saw him cast the veil. "Greetings, Chestnut. I have a favour to ask, at a later date so I have not brought honey."

"There is a sad lack these days." The words were right for Chestnut, but the tone and delivery were quiet, subdued. "You may wish to speak to another dryad, because I must break a bargain."

"I'm sure there is a good reason?" Abel tried to lighten it up. "If I go elsewhere I'll have to persuade the dryad to talk, then listen to all the complaints about magic users, then haggle for hours."

"Doubtful, almost Master of Sorcerer's Keep. Look around." As Abel turned a little he caught the shimmer of a nearby veil, and Ferryl gasped.

"They are all out of their trees, the other five dryads on the green. So is the one in the old Yew in the churchyard. Veiled against the villagers, but they all want you to see them for some reason."

Abel didn't have chance to ask. Still in that quiet, almost apologetic way, Chestnut explained. "They have come out so you will have options, because all of them are willing to uphold my bargain for me. Some are laughing at me."

"What bargain?" Abel looked around the wrinkled, twiggy shapes but couldn't tell if they were laughing or angry, much like the creaking noises their trees made. "Why would they offer to step in?"

"Seedling! Dryad Chestnut has no seedling for you." Startled, Ferryl blurted it out loud, and her hands over her mouth were much too late.

The rustling overhead carried on for a few moments before Chestnut spoke, still very hesitant. "Truth, but not quite truth. I have a seedling, but I misunderstood the timing, how soon you would want one. It is barely sprouted, not yet ripe enough for a tree. That takes time, another three or possibly four of your weeks at least." The not-wind through the leaves made a very human-sounding sigh. "So I have not fulfilled my offer, and payment is forfeit. The others will all find you a seedling, though you must still wait a while. It has been a long time since a sorcerer and a dryad trusted each other, and I have broken that trust."

"Hey, just a trainee, remember. I came here for a favour, which a sorcerer would never do." The leaves and branches rustled a little but only in the wind. Abel racked his brains. There had to be a way to get Chestnut off the hook, because a month didn't matter. The trouble was, with all the rest watching Abel couldn't just laugh the whole thing off. From the reaction, keeping bargains must be very important to dryads, more important than he'd ever thought.

"Not a seedling, just word of one."

"What do you mean, Zephyr?"

"I remember your porkies for you, as we agreed, but I remember much more. You asked if Dryad Chestnut would tell you when a Horse Chestnut dryad had a seedling ripened, because you had a tree that needed one. There was no bargain to supply one."

Abel quickly passed that to Ferryl, through Zephyr, and asked if it would be enough to save face. Ferryl didn't think long. "Not to save face, because no dryad would accept anything less than a genuine way to keep its word. It is a point of honour, to underline that the sorcerers were the ones who broke all the bargains. If you never specifically asked for a seedling, and Dryad Chestnut didn't offer one, the only bargain was to tell you if one was ready. Was payment specifically agreed?"

Zephyr had the exact wording. "Only a large payment for a small answer."

"Which is perfect." Abel put on his best surprised face, though he'd no idea if Chestnut could read expressions. "But you just fulfilled our bargain. I asked for news of a Horse Chestnut dryad seedling, and you have just told me one will be ripened in four or five weeks." He sighed dramatically. "I never specified the payment, just a large one, which was foolish because now you will punish my carelessness. I know honey will not be enough, so I offer a home for one of your seedlings. Is the payment sufficient?" He almost held his breath waiting for an answer, because both of them knew exactly what had been implied the first time.

Dryad Chestnut didn't reply straight away, but the trees belonging to the other six dryads rattled their branches and leaves drifted down. Abel wondered if they were angry at missing the chance, but didn't care. None of them had even spoken to him before, whereas Chestnut had become as much of a friend as a cranky, suspicious dryad could be. Eventually the branches above Abel swayed gently, rustling a little. "I forgot how devious humans can be. The payment is accepted. Though perhaps I am lucky you are still a trainee, rather than a sorcerer who might have laughed at tricking me out of a free answer. How will you protect your tree in the meantime?"

"Hexes, Tavern shields. I'll take them off when the seedling arrives, though I'll tap a little magic to power the Tavern hexes on a few posts." Oops, Abel realised he'd missed that part. "Providing the seedling accepts."

"Its memories will suggest that is a good idea. Perhaps more, if you agree. There is talk of dryads bearing Tavern hexes, so that the protection can be stronger. Though you could make it stronger if the trees have no dryads at all?"

"But I prefer dryad eyes to stronger glyphs, because I can trust them to see through veils and tell me if sneaky sorcerers come sniffing around. It would be even better if I could have both in one place at least, maybe two places because the seedling in the Red Maple may agree to do the same." Abel looked around at the other dryads, still watching. "Are they annoyed? About not getting the chance?"

"No, but I believe they are ready to make a decision. One we have been discussing for some time. Please wait."

Abel made himself comfortable, not sure how long this could take. Someone might have a better idea. "Ferryl? What decision?"

"I have no idea. Dryads usually decide for themselves, not as a group. That is their weakness, they don't trust each other." She turned, looking around them. "Six big trees, seven with Chestnut, all many hundreds of years old." She twisted a little further. "Maybe eleven with the other churchyard Yews, because the oldest one seems to speak for them all. That is a lot of magic. Whatever they agree, don't argue."

"Blimey, not likely." The pair silently discussed if the three Willow dryads would be included in the whatever, or the ones in various gardens. None of the other mature trees, such as those in Kelis's old garden, were anything like as old as these eleven. Abel fretted over his mum seeing a dryad, but Ferryl thought she should meet goblins as well. Talking, reasoning creatures might actually be reassuring, rather than the apparently mindless ones she saw raiding rubbish bins in Stourton or grazing in fields.

A rustle brought Abel's attention back to Chestnut, just Chestnut. A quick glance showed that all the rest were back inside their trees. "It is agreed. Whispers on the wind claim you have paid debts that were not truly yours, and freed bound dryads, and given them true contracts. A seedling promised a Red Maple tells of a dryad saved with great difficulty, and homed, yet still paid for guarding its new woodland. If you prefer dryads in your boundary trees, wearing Tavern hexes so that you can strengthen the defence, we will all offer them. The churchyard Yews must wait until the church frees them, but hope they will still get the opportunity in trees elsewhere. The wearing of the hex, and dealing with intruders once the seedling is strong enough, will be payment for the gift of trees, if you will agree to the bargain." Not-wind sighed gently. "No need for Woods and Green, we will accept your word."

The last part took Abel's breath away for a moment. Dryads didn't trust magic-users, ever. From the way her hand gripped his, Ferryl caught that part. "But I will make sure Woods and Green put it in Castle House records, as a contract, because even if I become a sorcerer I will not live forever." If Abel died and someone else, someplace, had a drop of Celtchar's blood, the new master might be a really nasty git.

"Truth. If all our agreements are completed, what favour did you want? Just remember, I have had little honey of late." Chestnut seemed to have recovered its usual mercenary attitude.

"Truth, though honey might not be necessary. My mother may have already seen a dryad." Abel chuckled at his next thought. "Meeting one might actually be a bad idea. Unless she met the Willow dryads, they are very friendly?"

"And cheap. But they are children, and will give a bad impression. Your ancestor has not seen us, we hide from her and the one with the dog and gun. Meeting an old, sensible dryad would make a better impression on her, well worth the price." Abel and Chestnut set into bargaining, not too intense because Abel would go up to a large pot of honey. Chestnut never asked for more, and sure enough that ended up as the price.

Better still, Chestnut stayed on its best behaviour the following day, when Abel veiled a very suspicious mum and produced his pot of honey. She wasn't surprised by the dryad's appearance, because of the game artwork, but Chestnut's manners made a big impression. Abel warned her other dryads were grumpier, not something he'd ever expected to say about this one! After that Abel agreed a series of meetings, spread out because he still worried about the effects. She would meet the Willow dryads, then Dryad Sycamore and the goblins, and finally have a proper talk with Zephyr. Abel put the visit to Castle House right at the end, which his mum accepted while still excited about meeting Chestnut.

There might be two mothers at some of the meetings, because Kelis's mum could see creatures in the fields now and wanted a full explanation from her daughter. Kelis had better spend the two days before she arrived home preparing her answers.

*　*　*

The two days dealing with the tree planting, and then his mum meeting dryads, turned out to be a sort of holiday for Abel, albeit a short one. By teatime the second day both Ginny and Eric had contacted Abel, wanting him to be available for answering Taverner's questions. As Ferryl commented, so much for Abel being the absolute master in his demesne. She sounded a little waspy when she said it, because the Taverners had another set of questions just for her. Rob's fan club contacted him directly, hoping to jump the queue, while others thought Jenny might have better answers.

The biggest potential problem died down, without embarrassing

Abel or Ferryl, when Rob and Jenny swore that Abel told the truth about Ferryl's original age and looks. There would be a lot of 'older woman' jokes in Abel's future, but he'd had them with both Jenny and Claris. In a way the Tavern seemed to welcome having a slightly older sorceress, because that meant a stronger, more experienced one. For her part, Ferryl promised to work even harder to get stronger. Meanwhile she started reading the books in the library, because training glyphs might be better than nothing. She wouldn't be able to read them all, not unless she found a wit with more languages.

Even while they asked questions, the Taverners were getting ready to set off on their travels again. Contacts in villages were given top priority, while the objective in every town would be finding the neutral zone and hopefully a message wall. Someone suggested using cafés with hex protection as meeting places, because the staff might be less likely to react to overheard snippets.

Lists of sorcerer meetings were drawn up, though all of them would be agreed in advance, so technically Abel didn't need protection. Even so, Aesop seemed to think all sorcerers should have bodyguards, for appearances' sake, so at least a minibus load of Taverners volunteered. When Abel pointed out ten might be considered a threat, Taverner paranoia insisted he took four or five at least, though they'd settle for three if Ferryl was one of them.

The number of bodyguards led to Abel's mum finally putting her foot down. She must have been talking to Bertram. If her son would be meeting other businessmen, he should take the best car, the Range Rover. By the time everyone finished organising his life, Abel felt more than ready to meet sorcerers, any sorcerers.

At least Veren, Abel's vassal, came to Stourton rather than him having to visit Sheffield. She brought the list of junior sorceresses she would try to negotiate with, so that Abel could give her precise instructions on what to agree or offer. Veren really did act like a minor subordinate, un-nerving for Abel because she had to be in her forties. The sorceress also promised to find out exactly where the Sheffield neutral zone might be, and who were the really big local sorceresses. She'd known there was a safe area, but had never needed to know more. Bertram hadn't heard of the neutral zone, or specific major sorcerers. Abel's corner of Sheffield really was a backwater, full of small barely-sorcerers who each controlled a few trees.

The Taverner teams spread out again, but this time they'd go to one destination, meet anyone local, and come home. No more extended road trips.

Abel kept his first visit to a day trip, because Terese's list and the one from the Taverners had one nearby name in common. Better still, an apprentice to sorceress Daorban, Mistress of Trentham, had given the Taverners a phone number. Bertram called her senior apprentice, and arranged a meeting in the car park of Trentham Gardens in Stoke, reassuringly public. Siobhan, the apprentice, hoped the Tavern could suggest a way to deal with the numbers of newly awakened teenagers. Encouraged, Abel arranged a second meeting in Stoke, with a Cheval Mallet who had sent a message to stop trespassing. With luck, if Abel could sign up this Daorban, then Cheval Mallet might reconsider.

Despite the preparations Abel had to answer phone calls within minutes of setting off. Veren wanted his approval on the prices offered to supply a sorcerer with hex-fillers, and had possible sales for some of Valdar's goodies. When Shawn phoned to discuss the detailing on the new BMW, Abel passed the job to mum. Nobody but Bertram, and Abel's solicitor, had realised that the car burned by Valdar would be replaced under the insurance.

*   *   *

This time Abel travelled in definite luxury. With only four seats in the Range Rover he ended up with Petra as a driver and Warren riding shotgun, and Ferryl in the back with him of course. Rachel volunteered, and tried to insist, but taking a stroppy fifteen-year-old might lead to the sorcerer or sorceress underestimating Abel's companions. On the way to meeting Daorban, Ferryl and Abel debated over asking for information about sorcerers in general. A lot depended on how the meeting went. The sorceress might turn out to be a polite homicidal maniac.

That seemed less likely, when the figure flanked by apprentices turned out to be a homely-looking fiftyish black woman. Daorban's title meant her demesne must include Trentham Estate, and the huge area of trees, a lake and gardens, and a golf course suggested a powerful sorceress. All the strong sorceresses Ferryl ever heard of looked young and glamorous, while sorcerers opted for either handsome early thirties or the old, bearded, white-haired traditional look. Now Abel wondered if he was meeting another new sorceress like Veren, because although well-dressed, Daorban wouldn't stand out in a crowd.

The apprentices with her included one teenage girl who looked very nervous, unlike the other three. Ferryl caught hold of Abel's hand. "That sorceress is a lot older than she looks! Look at the apprentices, definitely older than Daorban so her appearance is deliberate. She has learned to self-heal, and probably a long time ago if she is strong enough to hold this demesne." Abel reassessed, because the man and two women looked to be in their mid-sixties, so they could be as old as eighty and very experienced apprentices.

He also realised that despite asking to meet in her demesne, and all the trees nearby, Daorban wasn't standing near any of them. "Who has shields, Zephyr?"

"One apprentice, the man, is showing a globe shield. He is using it to shield the youngest apprentice." The pair were stood close together, but didn't look like a couple.

Ferryl heard Zephyr's reply through spooky-phone. "She must be a new apprentice, which seems odd for a meeting like this. Keep your shield below the skin, where it can't be detected. The sorceress will be doing so, and senior apprentices like those might be able to do the same." That made sense, because although Warren couldn't manage that yet, other adepts like Petra could. Ferryl let go of Abel's hand to take two steps forward. "Greetings. I will introduce myself first, to avoid unpleasant accidents. My name is...."

Abel watched as Ferryl issued her usual introduction, phrased as a subtle threat but she'd toned it down a bit. She might have reconsidered after Aesop, or maybe because this was an arranged meeting. He bowed very slightly when his titles came up, and Daorban did the same when one of her apprentices introduced her. As soon as the introductions were over, Daorban looked very obviously at spooky-phone. "That has to be communication, but not a tether. Does it work with anyone?"

"Anyone magical, and magical creatures. Probably with those not aware of magic, but I'd rather not do that." Abel daren't even let Zephyr connect to his mum, not yet. "No need for a tether."

"I heard that, from your apprentices. They called themselves trainees, and Taverners. Very polite, but not exactly subservient, even to a sorceress in her own demesne. That might be unwise." Since her tone seemed light, not really threatening, Abel kept his the same.

"The Taverners might have a different attitude, because many of them go to school with a sorceress, and me of course. Though if someone does take offence, they are stronger than their age would suggest." He gestured towards Warren and Petra. "Warren and Petra, for instance, both have strong shields. Not only that, but we've found that not all sorceresses are very strong."

"The newly freed, and the accidentally free? If their mistress dies before training is complete, many senior apprentices try to become independent sorceresses. Most of them fail, either dying or being re-tethered." She turned a little to look at her apprentices. "Though even if they complete their contracts, few apprentices are a threat to a real sorceress. Seventy-five years of very slow training is enough for competence, not expertise. Since this is a most unusual situation, would you mind proving your claim? I would like to test the strength of your apprentices' shields." Her big smile looked natural and friendly. "I will offer the same, an opportunity to assess my apprentices? Negotiating with the unknown is nerve-wracking."

Abel answered the smile, automatically, while thinking hard. There didn't seem to be a threat here, and something like a shield didn't give much away. Both his friends were wearing three belts of gold blocks, so the drain wouldn't be too bad. "Something simple, and non-lethal." He looked around. "And private."

"Definitely that. The church can be touchy, and other sorceresses like to take advantage of any excuse to penalise a rival." She looked at Warren and Petra, assessing them. "Publicity is one of the things we must talk about. There is an old factory site in my demesne, derelict and overgrown with weeds and bushes. If my apprentices chase out any squatters, that will be private enough. What happened to the armoured Bentley?"

Abel smiled because that car must have been really well-known. "Something big and nasty, and fatal. We melted the gold out of the scrap."

"That would have been a shock for him. Such a small demesne would never have warranted a vehicle like that, but he inherited it along with the core portion of his master's holdings. If I call for my vehicles, will you follow us?" She noticed the reaction from Ferryl. "The drivers are beginners, barely casting wind, so your trainees will not be overwhelmed."

"It doesn't work like that. Ferryl deals with the apprentices, all of them. We just hunker down and duke it out until she's done." Petra smiled happily at the startled look on Daorban's apprentices. "Then once she's finished, we can all concentrate on the sorcerer. It's worked three times so far."

The sorceress seemed amused rather than threatened, or even wary. "This is why I'd rather talk first. I wouldn't want to have to train up new apprentices." Two cars pulled up, an immaculate old-style Mercedes with plenty of chrome and a very ordinary estate car, and Abel's first reaction was that he hadn't been too badly out-posed. Only one driver got out, to open the door for Daorban. Petra, with a big smirk, opened Abel's car door.

*　*　*

Abel sat in his car outside the abandoned factory for fifteen minutes, while Daorban sent four of her apprentices inside to chase squatters. She kept one senior apprentice and the nervous girl with her, and stayed in her car as well. Just to be sure he wasn't being suckered, Abel sent a free-flying Zephyr to flit in the shadows and check for unannounced magic users. There weren't any. Once the old buildings were clear, an apprentice melted the chain on the big gates and the three motors crunched over broken glass and debris until they were out of sight of the road.

To Abel's surprise, an apprentice took a small folding table and eight collapsible chairs from the back of the estate car. "Since we are being civilised?" Daorban smiled, gesturing to a flask and cups. Petra produced the ones she'd brought for the journey, and the two groups sat facing each other. "To get right to the point, we suddenly have magically-aware teenagers coming out of the woodwork. Sooner or later some reporter will notice."

"Why suddenly? The teenagers must have been aware all along, seeing creatures, or they'd not recognise the pictures." Some Taverners had suggested sorcerers killed off unwanted magic users, but right now Abel had one who seemed willing to talk. "What usually happens to them?"

"Sorceresses pick them over and take the strongest. Some of us try to help the rest, blur memories a little, take the edge off the fear and confusion, but we can't stop them seeing magic. Many of the aware turn to drugs or drink, then end up in mental institutions or jails, or learn to keep their mouths shut." The sorceress hesitated, then pushed on. "Before long drugs and alcohol are a bigger problem for them than the hallucinations. Many of the aware die young, but it's difficult to be certain because that is true of drug users and alcoholics in general. Some sorceresses kill any that become too visible." Daorban leant forward, fixing Abel with a curious look. "Now instead of hallucinations, they are claiming to see the magical beasts in your game. What are you going to do about it?"

"Panic? I didn't expect so many, not until they'd tried the meditation exercise from the game. Even then only those who were close to finding magic should be affected." Abel looked round at his friends, but they all looked as shocked as he felt. "So that's it? Tethered, killed, or hard luck and let them rot? Anything I do has got to be better."

"It's the publicity that will cause the trouble, because nobody pays attention to a drunk hallucinating. Now, with so many pointing at your game and agreeing on descriptions, something has to be done." Daorban sat back a little, her voice sounding much softer. "What can we do? I have twice as many apprentices as most, for the size of my demesne, but I can't find work for more. I can't even train them all properly, or I will break the Accord and the local sorcerers will call in the Council."

"If you all drove sensible cars, you could afford more apprentices." Warren shut up, glancing apologetically at Abel.

"Some sorcerers with a smaller demesne than I, ride in a Rolls-Royce. A sorceress's car is our way of publicly showing where we stand in the magical hierarchy. Even so, it comes down to numbers." A little smile touched her lips as she eyed Warren. "If I had more than twenty-four apprentices, four strong and four weak seniors, with sixteen who can only cast wind or barely passable fire, my neighbours would feel threatened. Then they would probably combine and attack. So what would you do with all these teenagers, Warren?"

After a quick look to check with Abel, Warren launched into explaining the Tavern mission, to put at least a witch or warlock in every village or housing estate that hadn't got one. Daorban didn't disparage the idea, asking practical questions about financing and how it would be controlled and organised. Eventually she sat for a while, thinking hard, before turning to Abel. "That could work, because they aren't traditional apprentices. You expect them to get ordinary jobs so you won't be supporting anyone, or not totally. Offering them magic from your trees, a favour you can withdraw, is an interesting idea. You can build up as many trainees as you like, unless an alliance comes to Stourton and wipes you all out before you get stronger. To stop that you need allies, now. Established sorceresses. What have others said to you, about your Taverners running around their demesnes?"

"You are the first official meeting. We've made one agreement with one sorcerer I met on the road. He gets to pick over anyone who calls us, but they get the choice of accepting his tether or joining us. We keep off his business, and he lets the Tavern deal with the unprofitable areas. He wants to hire Taverners if he's short of apprentices, just to fill hexes." Abel smiled at the next bit. "He's on commission to sell the idea to his neighbours."

"Clever, but it wouldn't work here." The sorceress didn't seem happy about that. "Hiring hex fillers is a way of recruiting them to strengthen him. They will free his official apprentices to put pressure on his neighbours, perhaps steal more business. He may change his mind once he sees how many Taverners there are." Her voice sharpened, as did her look. "Are you satisfied with that arrangement?"

"No, but I accept it because I won't get anything better." Abel knew sorcerers would always tether apprentices, and neglect areas of their towns.

"I want to be absolutely certain about what your trainee said. None of your Taverners is tethered or bound?" When Abel explained about Ginny, and Veren being a vassal, Daorban accepted the reasoning. "So it could be said you are encouraging a multitude of independent, relatively weak magic users to find their own niche. No power base, no alliance except an agreement to help each other if attacked. Any Taverner may leave at any time and will simply cease to have further training, access to additional magic, and the help of other Taverners. At any time, a Taverner can give up magic or join the church or a sorcerer?"

"Yes. It's all voluntary." Abel started to explain but Daorban stopped him.

"Before we go any further, I really would like to test your trainees, as potential allies rather than enemies. There have been some developments in the last few days, something I could do very little about. If your trainees really are capable of facing up to other apprentices, there may be some options." The sorceress eyed up Petra and Warren. "But how to test them without risk of injury?"

Alarm bells had gone off in Abel's head, reminding him of what Redwolf had tried to get him into. "I don't want to get into a war."

"No war, but maybe a show of strength. Unfortunately they would have to be capable, just in case the other party objected." A little smile played over Daorban's face. "I promise that if you don't think it is in a good cause, I will not take offence."

"But before we get to that, you need the results of the test." Ferryl had been eyeing up Daorban's apprentices, and now she joined with Zephyr in making some sort of lightning-fast silent appraisal of the magic they carried. "There is a way, Abel. None of those apprentices carries enough magic to break Petra's or Warren's shield with one strike. The apprentice's shields will stand a return strike, easily because they will be more adept. Nothing tricky, just a plain ice spear." When Abel passed on the suggestion, the sorceress agreed.

Two of Daorban's apprentices threw their best ice spear, which caused sparks and some deep red cracks. Both recipients reported a definite drain as their shields recovered. Petra and Warren returned the favour, and were gratified when they also managed to produce sparks and a few tiny cracks. After a very quick bumping of shields, Daorban talked to both her apprentices before turning to the Taverners.

"I am impressed, because my informants are certain none of you have been aware more than three years. Your shields are very tight, so providing you remember to always retain enough magic you can stand toe to toe with many senior apprentices, and some junior sorceresses. I can see your inexperience in your strikes. You both build plenty of magic into the glyph before releasing it, but the results would be even better if you learn to tighten them, concentrate the effect." She bowed slightly, with a little smile. "My apologies. I mean no offence, but I would prefer any allies to be as dangerous as possible."

The sorceress needn't have worried, both the Taverners were paying close attention. "We don't mind, we're used to teachers and either Ferryl or Zephyr giving us advice. All the Taverners are trying to learn as fast as possible, and Ginny already told us all we need to work on economising." Petra glanced at Warren then bowed to Daorban, just a little one. "I don't know if that's right?" Warren belatedly copied her.

"Mine was an apology, but very small bows are also the equivalent of a handshake or polite greeting. After all, hand gestures can be misunderstood, and actually touching a hand can be painful. Now I know you can protect me, perhaps I can recommend somewhere for a meal?" The sorceress turned to Abel. "A place we can sit and talk in comfort?" Abel tried for a little bow, but Ferryl sniggered through his hand.

*   *   *

In some sort of light-hearted détente the whole party headed for a restaurant, emptied for their party because Daorban sent a message to an apprentice via tether. During the meal the apprentices and trainees sat apart from Daorban, Abel and Ferryl, at the other side of the room. Daorban made a very clear twisting motion at her shoulder to show she wasn't listening. The apprentices and trainees soon had their heads together, talking quietly.

"Order what you like because we won't be charged. The benefits of buying my own restaurant." Daorban definitely seemed to relax, probably because of all the defensive hexes Ferryl and Zephyr spotted on the way in. "Perhaps you could start with expanding on that explanation of your Tavern, Abel, how easily members can leave and why you might eject them?"

That wasn't hard. Abel ran through the now-familiar list of crimes and penalties, and explained how he expected some to be tempted away by the apprentice lifestyle. As he reached the end, Daorban commented that there didn't seem to be any serious punishment. Abel disagreed. "Losing access to extra magic will be a big blow. There is also the option to kill or tether, but only for a really serious betrayal involving the injury or death of innocents. We don't believe in stunting, that's disgusting, and tethering is mind invasion, worse than putting a collar on a slave."

He didn't expect the huge, beaming smile. "You have no idea how much I agree with you. That's why I asked to meet you, though you should tell your trainees to be a little more discreet. Do you know what my name means, young Abel?" When Abel shook his head her face straightened and Daorban sat up straighter. "Slave, specifically a female slave, the sort that once wore the collar you mentioned. My village sold me to a sorcerer two hundred and twenty-nine years ago, aged fourteen, because the shaman preferred male apprentices. I barely remember my place of birth. The sorcerer wanted a curiosity, a black girl apprentice, a savage from the heart of Africa. I followed him around wearing a gold collar and chain, dressed as his idea of a barbarian, a savage. He taught me to control my magic as a party trick."

Daorban paused for a drink, and glanced down at herself with a little smile though it soon faded. "When I reached eighteen, he decided he liked my appearance, so I should stay young and his idea of beautiful. He taught me to heal myself, long gruelling hours of being injured so my master could use the tether to guide my attempts. After a very painful six years he allowed me to heal all the scars, and then insisted that I alter my appearance as instructed." Daorban stopped, taking another drink and waiting a moment before continuing. From her look, some scars hadn't healed.

"I'd expected you to look younger." It was out without thought, and then Abel almost held his breath in case he'd offended her.

"Ah yes, most sorceresses enjoy being young and beautiful again. I spent too many years making myself what my Master considered attractive, changing myself to suit his whims. My appearance is deliberate, to show my opinion of all those pretty faces." The quiet smile crossed her face again as she glanced at Ferryl. "No offence intended."

"I look like a schoolgirl, which means I can attend classes and be there to guard Abel. Over the years my appearance has changed many times, for my own convenience, and some of them were definitely not attractive." With her own quiet smile Ferryl added, "And now I sometimes find myself acting like a schoolgirl. Holding hands and kissing on doorsteps is oddly appealing."

With a quick glance at Abel's slight blush, Daorban pointed out that she'd never tried that, so perhaps one day? "Though I should finish my explanation, so that you know who you are allied with. After fifty years as an amusing ornament, I'd also learned enough magic to be useful and defend myself. My master had another idea. At that time neither the law of the land or the Accord considered slaves to be people. The seventy-five year rule, intended to stop sorceresses training apprentices as bodyguards for several hundred years, would never apply to me. He set out to make me more dangerous than all but the strongest of sorcerers, and stronger than any if we fought together. First he tightened the controls so that I could barely think of harming him." She stopped again, her face drawn with remembered pain, and took a drink and a short break. This time Abel left her in peace.

"A succession of trainers taught me to fight, while my master taught me to be immortal. He took me to Brazil, to the new diamond fields, where I stole genuine diamonds for my bones and gold for ornaments, magic stores. He could afford to simply buy what he needed, or he could have taught me to make them, but my master enjoyed watching me kill innocents. My next lessons were how to remove the flaws in the diamonds, because flaws affect their ability to store magic."

This time Daorban paused because she could see Abel glance at Ferryl, who nodded to confirm the news about diamonds. As Abel turned back to her, the sorceress continued. "Once I had diamonds to hold more magic, my fighting training intensified. As my instructors became more and more skilled, I learned to heal faster and faster because they didn't pad their blades or pull their glyph strikes. A hundred and fifty years after putting on her collar, the beautiful savage, walking behind her master on a chain, had become more powerful than any apprentice and many sorcerers. The non-magical world abolished slavery, but not mine. Emancipation spread but still I wore a golden slave collar, filled with magic to help protect my master. The only difference was the chain leash, though I still wore it in private or among other sorcerers."

Abel thought she'd finished, or as much as he'd be getting, but when he opened his mouth Ferryl squeezed his hand. "No, she has more to say. I doubt she meets many people like you, who think of the tether as slavery. She will want you to know how she broke free."

Both Ferryl and Abel jumped as Daorban's harsh laughter burst out. "Nothing could protect him from an old German bomb, undisturbed for years until building work started. It detonated without warning, shattering our shields. No bodyguard could stop the concrete block that crushed him instantly, before he could recover." Sheer glee danced in her eyes at that memory. "I almost died as well but had enough magic, and stayed conscious long enough, to recover." Brisker now, she finished the tale. "He had let me see his secrets, because I would never be free to take advantage, so I took over his main demesne and all property in England and Wales. The other apprentices understood they could not challenge me, though I let them share out the Irish, Scottish and American property. Since then I have tried to find an alternative to the slavery of the tether, but the sorcerer community will not allow it."

The burst of laughter had stopped all talk at the other table, and the apprentices and trainees had listened to the last part. "They will never allow untethered apprentices, unless they are not truly apprentices." From her shining eyes the senior of Daorban's apprentices, Siobhan, liked that idea. "My tether is very light, and I knew what it would be before I took it, but even so." She looked guiltily at her mistress. "Though my mistress is known for being foolishly generous."

"Would you like me to remove the tether, Siobhan?" The glee came back into Daorban's eyes for a moment. "You could join the Tavern?"

The dark-haired, heavily-built woman took time to think that through, seriously. "No, not yet. I will wait until there are a thousand Taverners, too many for even the Council to kill without a very public war. Then who could object if a sorceress took off a tether, and her apprentice asked to become her trainee?" She turned to Abel and Ferryl, trying to explain. "My mistress needs someone to watch her back, and the best way to do that is on a tether. Better still, nobody pays attention when apprentices talk about their masters or mistresses. Nobody can question us without permission, because we are not responsible for our actions. It is no secret that a few sorceresses, all younger ones, want to abolish the tether, but there are others who are more discreet. My mistress lets me keep secrets, ones the tether would reveal if she looked, but none of her apprentices knows enough to justify a purge." She had clenched her hands now, trying to contain her sheer excitement. "We all thought any real progress, building up enough strong sorceresses to be able to come out in the open, would take two or three hundred years. It might have taken longer, until enough of the old guard died, but now?"

"Calm down Siobhan. We could still face a purge if you are careless. I would be obliged if you could give this young man's trainees a few names, without telling me of course. I would be honour bound to report any conspiracy among sorceresses to the Magic Council." The glee still lived in her eyes as Daorban held out her hand. "Are we in accord, Master of Castle House? Do you believe the tether must be abolished?"

Abel didn't hesitate, he took her hand and shook. "Or not quite, but only as a punishment. A jail without bars as an alternative to death?"

"Done. May we live to see it."

"Done. Who are your solicitors?"

Ferryl seized Abel's hand, though he'd already seen the alarm in Daorban's eyes. "No! Not a word to Woods or Green! One breath of conspiracy and they would have to report to the Council, though I think they will avoid it as long as you are careful. Remember, Terese Green took great care to clarify that Taverners aren't tethered or bound, or apprentices." Aloud she turned to Daorban with a smile. "He's new to this, and has never had to deal with the Council."

Sheer relief made Daorban laugh. "Lucky boy, though the old farts haven't been so bad this last hundred years or so. They can't agree on a chair, so they can't make binding decisions. Except one, because they don't want another like me. Slaves must be released after seventy-five years, the same as other apprentices. It isn't in writing yet, not until there is a chair, but keeping a slave too long would be a fatal mistake." Abel had a quick update on the Council, and how it had to have a chairperson powerful enough to force the other Council members to obey rulings they didn't like.

Individual sorceresses disagreeing with the Council wasn't a crime, but if they suspected a conspiracy the Council could use a truth glyph on a suspect. The Council were careful not to over-use their power, in case that actually caused a war, but refusal once they'd asked was an admission of guilt. Abel started worrying again, but Daorban told him the truth glyph needed a unanimous vote, including the chairperson. Even if that finally happened, no single sorceress knew enough names to prove a conspiracy.

The discussion about the Council moved onto some less than complimentary details about a few of the members, and how most of them never even attended meetings. Pandora had a seat, and her senior apprentices were well known for being accomplished killers. Oddly, Daorban thought most of their victims deserved what they got, and wondered why Pandora cared enough to kill a harmless teenager. Abel also found out he would be paying a tithe to the Magical Council. The amount would be somewhere in the office paperwork.

*   *   *

By now they'd worked through their meal, in Abel's case a medium curry that tingled his tongue without actually removing skin. "So now do we find out about this situation you've got, the one that might mean my friends needing shields?" Abel still wasn't keen on that idea.

"A particularly unpleasant neighbour, called Mallet, has come up with an answer to your Tavern. I had heard rumours before we agreed your visit, but the situation has deteriorated since then." Daorban stopped when she saw Abel's and Ferryl's expressions. "You have met him?"

"No, but we were supposed to be meeting a Cheval Mallet, later." Abel looked at his watch. "Maybe not, because we've been here a lot longer than I expected. I'd better put him off until tomorrow. Considering his message that won't go down well." He looked up and saw the question on Daorban's face. "The message told me to stop trespassing, go away, and if that wasn't good enough he'd explain face to face. I chose to meet Mallet, hoping for some sort of truce, that he'd let me rescue anyone he didn't tether."

"Maybe you should put him off two or three days, because Cheval Mallet is the situation, and a problem for both of us. You won't get your truce, because he responded to your Taverners by rounding up anyone in his demesne with a hint of magic. He'll tether the best, then sell or stunt the rest." The sorceress's face tightened. "That is his right, but since then he's become a bit more ambitious." Daorban raised her voice a little. "Goldie, would you tell Abel what you told me, please?"

The nervous young apprentice came to their table, and sat on the proffered chair. "I only know what the man said. He stopped me on the street, asked about what I saw, and wanted me to point to pictsie and a hoplin. When I did he took my name and address, and promised there'd be someone round to collect me the following day, to take me to a meeting. He told me to keep quiet and not tell anyone else, but make arrangements to be away from home overnight if I wanted answers." Goldie glanced towards Daorban, but she nodded to carry on. "When he'd gone, Siobhan came over and asked what he'd wanted. She suggested I waited in the café across the road, to meet her sorceress and get a different offer. It was public, so I waited." She touched her shoulder. "I accepted this because it means nobody else can touch me."

"Would you rather be a Taverner, Goldie?" Despite Daorban's gentle voice, Goldie jerked in alarm.

"No! You said I'm safe on your tether, and I can stay at home and finish school before I train. I don't want to leave."

After both Abel and her sorceress reassured her, Goldie re-joined Petra. "Siobhan recognised one of Mallet's apprentices, out of his demesne. With that and Goldie's story to warn me, I started looking and found out about the rest. The meeting place is an industrial unit on the edge of the neutral zone, just inside the border of Mallet's demesne, and it's more like a harvest. We don't know exactly how many Mallet has gathered but more arrive every day. Yesterday he made his announcement, that he'd fixed the problem of all these youngsters talking about magic. He'll stunt any that aren't worth tethering and selling, which is cruel. They'll still see creatures, but can't be trained to throw glyphs or even fill hexes, because they can't focus their magic. In the past such people moved to the villages, but it's years since I saw a witch or warlock looking for a weak youngster to train."

He still wasn't keen on a fight, but Abel liked this idea of Mallet's even less. "So you want us to help you break them free?"

The sorceress looked really bitter, but resigned. "No, because if you brought your Taverners to free them by force, the other sorcerers round here would probably pitch in on his side." She shrugged, unhappy but resigned. "Since your Taverners can shield, I thought they could hang around near the place and stop the volunteers going in. It would take a very public demonstration of magic to remove them."

Abel could see an easier solution, since Daorban knew where the kids were kept. "Can't the police go in? An anonymous phone call, blue lights, tipped-off reporters with cameras and all that, and the kids are out. The Accord would stop him using magic on the coppers so the whole thing would look like perverts or a con. The captives would scatter or be locked up for questioning, but he'd never trick them again."

"It wouldn't work. Mallet is tethering the new arrivals, so they'd claim they'd gone to a voluntary meeting. He'd call them back in as soon as the dust settled. Mallet releases a few every morning, though they are always back the following day. We followed some, which is how we know they're tethered. Every single one went home and announced they were leaving, or picked a fight and stormed out." Daorban sounded utterly dispirited, all her recent happiness gone. "Mallet will probably make the ones under sixteen email, or phone their parents now and then for a while, then they'll say they don't want any further contact. If any parents keep trying to find their children, he'll kill the parents or sell the child in another city. Worse still, the idea will spread because he'll make a lot of money."

"Surely he hasn't caught them all, every possible magic user?" Ferryl sounded puzzled, because there'd been no evidence of hordes of possible apprentices. "How did he identify them all?"

"Mallet hasn't taken any more from my demesne, because my apprentices very obviously shadow his if they trespass. He won't have got them all, even in his own demesne. He's just picking up anyone who has been talking about either the right sort of hallucinations, or claiming to see creatures from your game. They are the ones who will attract publicity." The sorceress wasn't just dispirited, Abel could hear an undercurrent of real anger. "I don't even know how many Mallet's apprentices took from my demesne, before Siobhan spotted one."

"Could you capture the building?" Ferryl sounded a lot happier than anyone else. "Not for long, and preferably without Mallet knowing."

The sorceress thought about it for a few minutes. "There aren't many guards, and only four or five of Mallet's apprentices, and not all of those can shield. There's no need for more, with the occupants all tethered. If we attacked and killed an apprentice, we'd start a war. The only way would be to knock out the unshielded apprentices, then hit the others hard enough, and often enough, that they daren't drop their shield even for a second. We'd have to be careful not to actually break it, or their tether would connect. We'd need several decent glyph throwers to keep each one suppressed, and the whole thing would have to be over in fifteen minutes."

"Why only fifteen minutes? We've got at least thirty glyph throwers who can manage a decent fire glyph." Abel smiled quietly, remembering Ginny teaching the Taverners to tighten their glyphs. "They'll keep the attacks just strong enough so those apprentices wouldn't want to get hit, so they'll keep their shields up."

"Under fifteen minutes, Mallet will think his apprentices are just shielding to talk without the Master listening. More than that and he'll know there's a problem. Though we'd still be left with all those tethered kids, and the only way to free them all quick enough is to kill Mallet." A savage smile briefly split her face, and then disappeared. "I'd love to, but the local treaty would kick in, and we'd be in a war with the other three senior Stoke sorcerers."

"Can we snatch one of these new recruits, a tethered one? Just for an hour or three?" Ferryl's smile looked predatory now, and Abel didn't need the sudden interest inside his tattoo to understand. Zephyr and Ferryl had only inspected Pendragon's tethered bird for a few minutes, but that had been enough to eventually learn its secret.

"Of course, they walk off down the street without any sort of guard. If a total stranger hit them over the head with a club, so the tether went dead?" Daorban smiled just a little, a welcome return of humour. "Pour half a bottle of booze down them before they wake up and leave them in an alley. A little touch of confusion so he can't force them to remember what they were doing, and he'll assume the kid got drunk to try and work up courage for leaving home. The only risk is if Mallet's watching when you snatch them, but that's unlikely because all those tethers must be a huge strain. He'll barely use them. Why?"

When Abel asked her to, Zephyr flew out to hover while Abel explained. That stopped all discussion, until he'd explained that he couldn't train another wind spirit. The sorceress had immediately assumed Abel must be a real-life version of Wind Chaser, the Tavern character, and wanted

307

him to train one for her. When the real planning started, Abel truly appreciated having staff, because he didn't have to be polite to Mallet. He made a phone call to Sheffield, asking Bertram to reschedule the meeting for three days' time. Bertram didn't even ask why he had to make the call at two-fifteen exactly, and insist on talking to the sorcerer himself.

There'd only be one chance to make this work, so the sorceress and the Taverners set into making sure it did.

*   *   *

Finding a victim wasn't hard. Daorban already had her weaker apprentices watching the industrial unit, and following any of the newly tethered when they left. At two-sixteen Abel's phone rang, and Shawn confirmed that Bertram had Mallet on the phone. That should keep the sorcerer occupied, too busy to bother monitoring a teenage boy walking down a street.

Petra immediately made the call to Ferryl. Ferryl felt her phone vibrate and tapped the lad walking in front of her on the back, quickly pulling him round to hug him. The youth slumped, fast asleep as she put her arms around him and used wind to keep them both upright. One of Daorban's very ordinary cars pulled up alongside, and in seconds the kidnap was over.

Back in the abandoned factory, Daorban insisted on watching, but confessed she had no idea what Zephyr did to investigate the tether. Abel explained that Ferryl put her hand on the spot on the lad's skin to help Zephyr connect, because using Ferryl's human skin would let the spirit make better contact. Actually, Zephyr had wrapped around Ferryl's hand so they could silently discuss how to break the tether.

After an hour, Abel began to worry, until Ferryl winked at him. "It's harder without the tether being active, but Zephyr has the key. She is testing, not actually removing the connection but loosening it, making sure there are no hidden surprises."

"We won't be able to hold the place long enough, not if it takes an hour for each." Daorban sounded frustrated, ready to try anyway, but Abel put on his best confident smile.

"Zephyr de-tethered ten teenagers being held under guard, within minutes, without the watching apprentices even noticing. Don't worry."

Though he'd missed a vital piece of information. "How many has Mallet tethered?"

"I told you, we don't know. There's at least thirty, but Mallet is poaching anyone he hears about, not just from the poorer areas that are claimed but not really monitored." The worried look developed just a little smug. "Because I have so many apprentices, I can spare enough to follow Mallet's once they leave his demesne. We've made it more difficult for him, and impossible in my demesne, but his people have even made trips to Manchester and Birmingham to collect teenagers." Daorban went back to watching, and fretting.

Fifteen minutes later the youth woke up, more or less, with half his bottle of whiskey all over his clothes and enough splashed into his mouth to explain why he felt woozy. By the time he gathered his mazzled wits, the car that deposited the kidnapped apprentice had long gone.

When Abel arrived back home and discussed the visit with his mum, he stressed how nice it had been to meet a helpful, friendly sorceress like Daorban. He hoped that would stop her worrying.

*   *   *

At least three Taverners, adepts, didn't know about Daorban or Mallet, not yet. Abel would wait for Kelis to finish explaining trees to her mum, and for Una and Justin to have a peaceful evening back with their families, before throwing this at them. Justin wouldn't get long to relax. His sister Rachel would want to give him a blow by blow account of her meeting with Pandora. Abel had set the meeting for three days' time just so the returnees were rested and ready to go. If the rescue went wrong, he wanted Kelis's diamond power and Una's sword on hand.

Abel didn't get to see Kelis until the following morning, though Ferryl had been called upstairs from her room to help explain the tree to her mum. At least Ferryl had been primed by Abel's mum, so she could guide the conversation away from anything that might push Mrs. Ventnor into a breakdown. When Ferryl came round later, to see her boyfriend, he found out the landlord had been blamed for the tree. Kelis made a quiet comment to Ferryl about expecting the sticky stuff to deal with any queries. She had to mean queries to the letting agency, so she'd finally worked out Abel owned the flat and shop.

Abel fended off all queries in the morning, insisting Kelis had more time with her mum, because he'd prepared for today. The six of them, Kelis, Rob, Jenny, Ferryl, and Abel with Zephyr, needed time to catch up. Selling Bonny's Tavern left Jenny out of touch with the magical side, they all had questions about Germany or Abel's visit to Stoke, and anyway the Taverneers missed each other. They had become used to almost living in each other's pockets for months, as had Zephyr, both because of magic and while setting up Bonny's Tavern.

Now Ginny picked them all up, but got out at the Stourton office and Jenny took the wheel. Despite passing her test, Jenny still wouldn't claim a car for her own use. She simply didn't think she should get that sort of special treatment, and made sure the other Taverners knew. Taking a car home to her village would mean it being unavailable for glyph-fillers, which quietened down a few of those still trying to score their own wheels.

Today someone would get a treat, the Range Rover, because the five Taverneers wouldn't fit. Even though it was 'only' the BMW, Jenny took her time driving because she still hadn't had that much practice. All five, six with Zephyr, were really curious, because this would be the first visit to one of Abel's land packages with a definite house on it. Stoneham Manor couldn't be anything else. A casual inspection hadn't discovered any accommodation in the other woodlands they'd visited. During the drive Kelis brought them up to date on Germany, or as much as she would admit.

Abel for one thought he'd hear "what happens in the Black Forest stays in the Black Forest" from both Justin and Una, judging by Kelis's grin. Outside of that part, the trip had been mixed. Emst, his cousin and Laurence would be dealing with any minor problems, short-term, soon to be helped by a niece. Emst had been playing Bonny's Tavern with friends and relatives, and felt relieved Kelis had come over to help both him and the potential sorceress over her first few days. The two Germans, and Laurence for another couple of weeks, would do their best, but wanted some of the more adept Taverners to take a holiday in Germany to help out.

The shooting lodge in the forest had become Emst's Tavern, but only for Emst's acquaintances because it belonged to his family. Kelis had rented two small, long-empty shops in cities, luckily in the city centre, for new magic users to visit. By the time she left Germany she had candidates for running them, but not until Emst gave them the okay. After listening to all the problems with sorcerers, Kelis offered to bring Emst up to date on the extra rules and dangers. Providing Tavern premises in Germany wouldn't be a big problem for some time because the German launch had been low-key. So far, Emst only had seven contacts to deal with. Oddly enough, the first few seemed willing to wait once he sent them Tavern hexes.

Kelis showed off her prize, a long slim dagger called a misericord, supposedly used to finish off a downed knight in armour. She'd already hexed it and filled the blade with magic. Una now had a real sword, one with a fancy wraparound hilt suitable for Robin D'Ritche, while Justin had accepted a slim blade that only reached from his waist to his knee. He thought it suited his Shayde Warrior costume better than a longer one. The hunting lodge had dozens of swords and daggers on the walls, so Emst had insisted the three Taverners were properly armed before heading home. Laurence had already shown off his rapier so Emst now had a hexed sabre, and strict instructions about keeping quiet. Despite the excitement, Abel wasn't so sure about sticking a dagger in anyone. He'd settle for whacking anyone like Valdar with his hexed baton, or a glyph.

When Kelis tried to discuss housing, and people throwing filthy money about, Abel promised to talk about it later and kept his fingers crossed. All the conversation died away as the satnav warned them they were getting near. Jenny drove through a little village, two miles along a lane, and pulled up by an old driveway. "Where are the woods, the trees?" Jenny peered around, disappointed. "The trees down that driveway are old, really old so the old misery will have glyphed them. Ooh, not all of them. There's a couple of replacements down there, younger trees, but definitely mature and only young compared to the rest. Will they be protected?" With that she turned up the drive, past an overgrown sign claiming it led to Stoneham Manor.

Jumping out of the car, Jenny headed towards the two trees in question, but carefully. The rest followed but soon everyone except Abel stopped. As he kept walking he heard Kelis sniff. "Sticky stuff and trees.

Oh to have the right relatives."

"What sort of glyphs are there in these trees, Zephyr? I can't tell because the old trees aren't affecting me either." Abel knew there'd be two sorts of glyphs, but he'd expected to be able to tell the difference.

"Jenny is right. The two younger ones have Terese's glyph, so they were planted after Celtchar died. There is no sign of the house, but there are magic feeds from some of the trees, running along the driveway." Zephyr must have been analysing the effect of the glyphs. "I think I can show you the difference. Put your palm out, like Pendragon when he tested the barrier at Castle House." Abel did so and concentrated. After a few moments, his palm tickled a little and he could feel something. It wasn't uncomfortable, just watchful and perhaps accepting. "I had to help a little. Now the next tree." This one, an older one, didn't take as long and welcomed Abel without reservation. The feeling was faint, and the difference hard to spot even with Zephyr showing him. Abel didn't think he would have ever noticed without Zephyr's help, funnelling them through his tattoo one after the other.

"Why doesn't the Terese glyph seem to recognise me? The others, the old ones, certainly do."

"The old trees recognise your bloodline, Celtchar's bloodline, a familiar feel. The newer one recognises your right, but is not tied to your bloodline. I think."

Ferryl must have connected to Zephyr. "I couldn't have shown that, not through my hand. Can you feel the difference Abel?"

Abel tried, without Zephyr helping which meant he had to concentrate harder to pick up the effect. "I've got it now, thank you Zephyr." Abel kept going, putting his hand on a younger tree and imagining the glyph Terese showed him. "Here Jenny, put your hand on this one. It feels fine to me."

Jenny approached, cautiously, then quicker when she didn't feel any nasty tingling or itching. She put her hand on the tree. "Hey, can you do that with any of them?"

Kelis's voice sounded from right behind Abel. "Just the newer ones, I reckon, until you get to be the real master. Well that's mission accomplished, you can use this one for the nearest Taverners."

"You'd better try as well, all of you, then we'll call the local Tavern and get whoever Petra recommended to come over to be introduced." Abel kept his hand in place as each one touched the tree for a moment.

After putting her hand on the bark Kelis turned to look all around. "The house is a bust. It must have fallen down. Maybe there's ruins in the undergrowth?" Now they'd come far enough up the driveway, everyone could see where it ended. The walled area full of tangled trees and undergrowth looked a lot like Castle House gardens, but without a big old house in there.

Abel didn't answer for a moment, because when Kelis touched the tree to get her permission, he'd felt it. Now he wasn't sure if he wanted her to ask for permission to touch all the trees, or not. Once Rob and Ferryl had put a hand on this one, he moved to the other newer tree, feeling just a bit guilty about the tingle when Kelis touched the bark. "We ought to go up past the gardens and look for the woodland. That's supposed to have a proper barrier, a keep out type but non-fatal, with dryads to back it up." Abel checked his sheet of paper to be sure. "The dryads have proper contracts now, so we shouldn't have any problems."

Jenny had all the phone numbers, and soon contacted the local Taverner who'd been judged most trustworthy. She promised to take a taxi, if it meant she'd have extra magic for practicing. That would take a while, so Jenny drove further up the driveway. A hundred metres short of the gardens, just before the driveway split to go around each side, Abel felt a definite zing and everyone gasped. Suddenly, right where it should be, on the other side of the uncut hay that was once a lawn, stood the house. A big house, a true mansion or stately home, and not even boarded up. Woods had said the houses were frozen, preserved, but Abel hadn't realised exactly what he meant. The long, four-storey, stone-built structure didn't have a sign of weeds, and possibly no dust. Even the carriage parked at the bottom of the sweeping steps only needed horses and a driver.

Everyone got out of the car and stood looking for a few moments, flabbergasted. "Crikey." Rob couldn't even come up with a fanciful curse. "That looks ready to move into."

"Yes, I thought if Kelis keeps on about sticky stuff and the shop, I'd ask the landlord to kick her out of the flat." As Kelis turned, Abel smiled at her. "Then I'd tell her mum this place needs a live-in housekeeper, all found. Because the owners are always away. D'you reckon she'd go for it?"

"Don't you dare!" Kelis turned back to the house. "You'll never be able to afford to keep it anyway. It must cost a fortune in upkeep."

"Not really, not if it shuts down while he's away. Blimey, when I get my own place I want that glyph. No dusting." Jenny started walking towards a small gate set in the low stone wall around the garden. "That's not fair. It's telling me to keep out."

Abel walked forward and, just as Woods had warned him, the place wouldn't let him in either. "Sorry Kelis, you're stuck with Brinsford." As she opened her mouth he pointed at the fields behind her. "Though if you change your mind once it's available, I bet the income from renting these fields out there covers any running costs."

The others burst out laughing but Kelis deflated, losing her indignant attitude. "You'd do it as well, wouldn't you? Idiot. The worst part is, mum would go for it. She's worrying about getting work." With a little embarrassed smile she stepped forward and hugged Abel hard, then took a step back again. "That's sorry for being a cow. It's just that you really are an idiot, of the nicest sort. You've already bought the shop for me and mum, and tried to give me a blooming great house in Sheffield and a Range Rover. I kept on about filthy money to put you off giving me anything else, or you'll end up broke. My bad. Are we still okay?"

Abel took a few moments, trying not to show how absolutely lovely that hug had felt. "We always were okay, Kelis. I thought I'd fooled you about the shop."

"You did, until I realised that when you offered the tree you never mentioned asking the landlord. Because you didn't have to, did you?" Abel shook his head, smiling happily. Kelis really wasn't upset about the money, just being daft about sharing.

Rob and Jenny stopped laughing, staring from one to the other. "You mean he really bought the shop?" Rob looked completely thrown. "But you said he couldn't have. Even if it was very convenient and all that, you'd worked it out."

"She's only just realised, from the tree thing. Though back when Abel insisted he was sharing his inheritance with us, he was a bit sparse on details." Jenny turned to Abel and pointed at the house. "So just how many of these have you got? You kinda skipped around invisible mansions, or how many acres of farmland you are renting out."

"I still don't know. There's no descriptions for them, just that there's accommodation in some locations. All I got was that list of places with an acreage, some of which would be woodland, and a notation if there's a place to stay. I don't get any more because I can't access them anyway." Abel shrugged and pointed to the large, imposing stack of stone blocks and huge, small-paned windows. "According to Woods, some places are more like caves or barns. I reckon whatever it was in the other places we visited stayed hidden, somewhere in the woods. There'll even be a cave or something similar in Millponds Nature Reserve, or maybe that old forge counts."

Ferryl had been walking along the barrier, hands up to feel it while Zephyr shimmered alongside. "Celtchar used a variation on what I designed for him in Castle House gardens. If you want to break this we probably can, Abel, though the house may be better protected." After thrashing it over, everyone agreed it wasn't worth risking a serious backlash. Abel would get the keys officially, as it were, if one of them could work out how to open the next door in Castle House. And the next, and the next....

Instead Jenny drove them round the side of the gardens to where the driveway forked. One fork led to large gates giving access to the back of the big house, but the other one headed for nearby woodland. As Abel got out of the car a shield shimmered into existence just inside the wood, and a dryad came out of its tree. The three dryads in residence monitored the barrier, each of them connected to the magic in scores of mature trees, and would combine to destroy anything magical trying to break in. Non-magical workmen came to remove dead trees, and had dug some up lately. Ramblers and naturalists were tolerated, though they soon felt uneasy and left. The dryad seemed to enjoy that part.

Abel touched the dryad's tree, each of the Taverneers touched a perimeter tree, and they all had free access. There was no negotiation and barely any communication, so Terese must have been very specific in her instructions. The rest of the wait became a relaxing stroll, surrounded by peaceful woodland and a swooping, happy Zephyr. Doubly happy, because while Abel had been touching the trees on the drive, she had eased out of her tattoo, just far enough to make contact and be granted access.

On the way back to the car, Abel showed the others the acreage shown against the entry for this place. Judging by the size of the woods, large but not a forest, a good bit of the nearby farmland really must be his, and rented out. As Kelis pointed out, he could have ex-girlfriends living all over the country. If he had too many houses, there'd be volunteer girlfriends when word got out. She'd obviously recovered from her shock.

The appearance of the mansion as they drove back towards it didn't surprise them, but the sheer extent of the out-buildings were still a shock. Despite looking very carefully, nobody could see anything alive in there, a relief because a long line of split doors were obviously stables, and there was a large pen and several kennels. That led to Jenny offering to move in, if Abel ever needed a housekeeper. She used to help out at a stables in return for rides, and here she could finally have her own horse.

Even dealing with the Taverner, once her taxi arrived, didn't dent anyone's relaxation. There were dozens of trees along the hedgerows between fields, so Abel simply asked the lass to choose two newish ones and gave her access. She listened to her instructions about filling lead bars for the other four locals, to help their practice, still wearing a big silly smile after her first belt of tree magic. Abel paid the taxi driver to wait as long as necessary, because the lass didn't want to let go of 'her' tree.

As Jenny aimed the BMW towards home, the happy smiling face waving after the Taverneers underlined what was at stake. If Mallet had his way, the best of the teenagers like her would be tethered. The fate of the rejects would be even worse, traumatised and stunted after being forced to leave home. If Mallet's system worked, and made a profit, Abel felt sure there were plenty of sorcerers who would adopt it.

With that in mind the rest of the trip home became a planning marathon, to make sure Abel had covered everything. A half hour walk around a small zoo, to get pictures for Rob's, Kelis's and Jenny's alibis, gave them a short break. Nobody enjoyed it much. Unlike the zoos Laurence had chosen last year, the pens looked too small with too much concrete and not enough greenery. The birds and animals seemed listless, either bored or depressed. Kelis in particular wanted to nip back at night and open a few pens, to release the birds of prey.

Though first there were at least thirty teenagers who had to be released from their cage.

Snatch Squad

The planning came in handy the next morning, because all the Taverneers could answer questions. Abel went to the gym for the day, partly because he'd been neglecting his training but also so he could meet whoever he liked in privacy. As promised, Eric had put in an office just for him, with thick concrete walls and floor for privacy, and protection. Jenny had more or less taken over the other office, filling the walls with big maps covered in coloured pins and lists of contacts.

Both offices were needed today. Taverners on road trips were arriving back early, keen to discuss the mystery operation, but Abel also had other magically-inclined decisions to make. After working out the costs, he phoned Terese to organise five adult trees for the yard at the back of the industrial unit. They would be a quick source of magic, if anyone tried to wipe out the Taverners as Daorban had suggested. Some village trees would be arriving within days, but elsewhere the local Taverner still hadn't found a small plot of land or wheedled permission from parents.

Una and Justin came by, entertaining everyone with tales about Germany and teasing Kelis about what they'd promised to keep quiet. Once everyone had admired Una's new sword, a real one, she demonstrated her new skills. Several Taverners were interested, even though they weren't aware of its magical properties. There weren't all that many real swords available in the UK. Most of them were in museums or stately homes, which led to certain people exchanging glances. They'd just realised Celtchar's houses probably held the equivalent of an armoury, possibly already enchanted.

Eric phoned to confess that the logistics just didn't add up, so for the first time Abel didn't have enough vehicles. He couldn't just hire a couple of buses, because Abel knew his mum would see the paperwork eventually. Several older Taverners set off to hire minibuses, for cash, while Abel called Daorban. She was already ahead of him and had just the thing for the main event, a forty-seater coach. During the afternoon several Taverners took trips to zoos and parks, taking pictures so the rest could claim to have been there tomorrow. By the time the pictures were being distributed the rest of the transport had been arranged. Eric had spoken to Veren and she'd offered three cars with drivers.

*   *   *

The sound of rain on his window woke Abel the following morning. That wouldn't help the Taverners who'd told their parents they were going to a zoo or park for the day. Despite that, Abel only had three cancellations by the time his mum used the Tavern minibus, now fully repaired, to pick up Rob, Ferryl and Kelis on the way to work. Mum knowing about magic definitely eased the logistics at times. Jenny had already been picked up by Una, rather than ride in on her moped as planned. Another four Taverners phoned in because they'd had trouble persuading parents that they didn't mind getting wet. Luckily those tended to be the younger ones and the most adept of those, Rachel, made it. Her parents had been quite pleased her brother would be taking her to a museum, somewhere Rachel genuinely wanted to go. After inspecting Justin's new weaponry, she wanted to look at a variety of styles for herself.

Despite it only having four seats, Abel would travel to meet Mallet in the Range Rover, for the poser factor, with more bodyguards following in the big BMW. That would be later, because as Abel arrived in Stoke those two vehicles were already making a slow, very obvious trip around the ring road. The windows were tinted so the ten Taverner passengers, all beginners like Cecilia, could pretend to be the main event.

Abel and his friends were travelling anonymously, in a minibus, heading for an entirely different meeting. He'd come dressed in a suit, for the meeting, but covered it with a long cheap mac. Rob wore jeans and a hoodie in case he ended up wrecking more clothes in a fight. Despite the risk of damage a good few Taverners came in costume, but kept them covered up with coats or sometimes plain cloaks. Abel had been downright gobsmacked when Kelis turned up in character, complete with dagger, but she told him this Mallet bloke needed to learn who he was messing with. The talk about being careful with sorcerers hadn't worked, because Kelis was furious. By the time the minibus pulled up next to Daorban's coach, Abel thought he'd talked her out of pushing Mallet into a fight with forty Taverners. Nobody could be sure exactly how strong he was.

Daorban phoned to confirm her Mercedes had met the Range Rover, and would pretend to guide it to the meeting with Mallet. Meanwhile

Abel's convoy, headed by the minibus, followed several of her anonymous cars and the coach to within two streets of the real target. The Taverners unloaded, those in costume checking they'd covered them up properly before following Abel and Daorban. The sorceress did a double-take at the three Volvos with older drivers, ranging from late twenties to early forties. "Apprentices, loaned by my vassal. They'll stay here." Abel didn't want to rely on Veren for the actual raid.

Daorban did another double-take, at Abel. "Her apprentices? How old is this vassal? Later, right now I want to know what's happening ahead."

"Take a peek, please, Zephyr."

The shimmer slipped out of Abel's arm, untethered, to drift through shadows and along gutters until she had spotted all the lookouts around Mallet's captives. Easing past the non-magical guards, Zephyr slid between the sheets of cladding and into the industrial unit. Once she'd located the big room with the press-ganged recruits, Zephyr sank slowly down towards one who'd curled up in a sleeping bag. Softer than a butterfly's breath, a tendril of not-mist drifted over her skin to find the tether. Zephyr tested it carefully, without actually disturbing the bond, and this one seemed to be exactly the same as the one she'd inspected. On the way out Zephyr checked the location of the apprentice on guard inside the building, and the best way to reach the targets undetected, before flitting cautiously back to Abel.

The next five minutes crawled past, because this part had to be timed and synchronised. As Daorban stood up and the shimmer of a veil swept over her, up on the bypass the Mercedes in front of the Range Rover indicated. The three decoy cars turned onto the next off-ramp heading into town. A veil swept over Ferryl and she followed Daorban, led by a flying shimmer. The two sorceresses followed Zephyr along a twisting route, so none of Mallet's apprentices spotted the veils, until they came out near the two security men at one end of the building. Once again, they paused. Daorban started forward at a signal down the tether, so Ferryl followed, each one closing in on a target. Neither man had a chance. As the veil enveloped them, from behind, they blinked briefly out of sight. The veils moved on after removing any weapons, leaving two sleeping men.

Back with the rest of the party, Siobhan smiled and stood up. "Time to go. The two guards are down. Ferryl Shayde will try to get inside, to stop the apprentice there from contacting Mallet. My mistress is remaining there to cover her escape if it doesn't work." Forty-nine grim-faced would-be rescuers, thirty-eight of them Taverners, split up and headed for their positions.

Abel wasn't very happy about this part, because both Ferryl and Zephyr were inside that building. First Daorban, then Zephyr, were adamant it was just an industrial unit hired for the job, with no magical defences except door alerts. Mallet didn't need any more protection, because tethered victims couldn't be rescued or get away, but Abel still wasn't happy. He settled in where he could see the front door, determined that if an alarm started he'd break in regardless of any plan. From the looks on Kelis, Rob, Jenny, Una, Petra, Justin, Warren and Eric, he wouldn't be alone. All around the perimeter, the anonymous-looking Taverners stayed out of sight but prepared their glyphs. Despite various people's expectations, Rachel kept calm and didn't kick off early.

While the others crept forward, Ferryl altered the elements in a cladding panel, softening the metal enough to bend it out of the way. The sorceress slipped through the gap, into the storeroom scouted by Zephyr, and the pair pulled the metal back down. Zephyr checked the corridor, Ferryl tripped the lock, and the pair were loose inside the building. Following her ephemeral scout, Ferryl made her way silently and unseen to where an apprentice watched over the captives. He wasn't there! Zephyr flitted off to look for him, because he had to go down first.

Outside the tension mounted. A silent message down Daorban's tether sent the Mercedes and Abel's two cars on a detour from the route to Mallet's meeting, eating up a few more minutes. Daorban waited impatiently, wanting to go inside to help, but Ferryl might need her escape route kept clear. The warrior sorceress had wanted to lead the main attack, but only she and Ferryl could be sure of knocking out the guards with sleep glyphs without causing permanent damage. In front of the building, Abel touched his baton, still folded up inside the holster under a Seeming. He'd need glyphs first, to smash that door down.

Deep inside the building Zephyr hurled out of a side-passage, thankful she couldn't get breathless, and shot out a spooky-phone. "In the toilet! Coming now." Ferryl flattened against the wall, close to the corner, and formed the glyph. She hoped this didn't scramble the man's brains, or kill him, but only because Abel would be disappointed. Zephyr agreed with her reason for trying this way, even though killing the man would be easier and much more certain. Zephyr had a fire glyph building, for if the stunning didn't work. Even if the apprentice could shield, he would never have the chance to cast the glyph.

The man sauntered up to the corner, started to turn and a soft "boo" brought his head round. As he stared at the softly glowing ball floating in mid-air, a big yellow smiley with two burning green eyes, something tapped his head and crippling pain dropped him to the floor. Welcoming darkness took the pain away.

Ferryl pulled her hand back, shaking it as she healed the burns. "He had a strong ward, so I had to drive the glyph through. He'll have a terrible headache, but might recover in time." The glowing ball became an almost invisible shimmer. "Off you go, Zephyr, I'm healed now. Give me a minute to gather the glyph and power it, then work as fast as you can." The shimmer dropped down and stretched out, flowing off along the angle between floor and wall.

Ferryl leant back against the wall, pulling magic together and building the glyph bigger and stronger, bigger than the plan needed. She was supposed to knock out everyone inside, but she wanted to reach the armed men outside. Then there'd only be apprentices to deal with, and no chance of a stray bullet. For long moments the magic gathered and her intent hardened, until it reached a critical level. With a soft exhalation, Ferryl finally released the glyph, staggering as the magic flowed outwards.

In the big hall every person slumped to the floor. Zephyr, already poised to go, flew quickly forward and sent out ten tendrils. She daren't try more, in case she lost track. At least she would have enough magic this time, because she wouldn't need an ogre. Ferryl Shayde would be guarding the corridor outside, and no mere apprentice would get past her!

Outside the building four guards slumped to the floor, while the other two staggered and held their heads, totally mazzled. Air glyphs hit both, knocking them down and Taverners rushed forward to make sure they were out. Mallet's weaker apprentices staggered as the glyph struck, so the strongest automatically slammed up their shields. The other two were hammered by a storm of wind glyphs, knocking them down and pummelling the pair into insensibility. Small fire glyphs struck the remaining pair of shields, a steady stream of them. The attackers weren't trying to break the shields, just make it impossible for the apprentices to drop their protection to use their tethers. As every other guard went down, Taverners and Daorban's apprentices spread out around the last two to keep up the steady assault from all directions.

Abel didn't see any of the attack. Once he saw the guards drop he turned and, followed by the others in the so-called diplomatic group, legged it towards the vehicles. Not far, because Daorban had felt the mazzlement glyph and called for the drivers down her tether. As Abel and his group scrambled aboard the minibuses, Daorban ran up, complaining about physical exertion being dangerous for a woman her age. From the way she moved, Abel felt sure the sorceress could run him into a grease blob. Three of her apprentices joined the Taverners and the vehicles took off.

*   *   *

A few minutes later the three decoy cars, led by the Mercedes, took another turn off the direct route to the meeting, causing confusion among Mallet's shadowing apprentices. While they tried to decide if it was just a precaution, to avoid a possible ambush, the cars turned into a side street. A full veil slammed down, leaving only bare tarmac in sight! Frantic messages passed along the tether to Mallet, but he couldn't react. If his apprentices moved forward and broke the veil, they would be arms-length from at least two annoyed sorceresses. Worse, Mallet daren't look concerned with three other sorcerers watching his every move. He wondered if this Abel had heard about the reception, and chickened out.

Mallet tried to contact the apprentices at the holding pen, but he couldn't even reach the ones without shields. That meant it was deliberate, they were inside the shield of a senior apprentice, probably discussing the catch and if they'd get one. He didn't mind apprentices dodging the tether now and then, but all of them being out of touch was careless, and once they reconnected he'd punish them for the insolence. Before Mallet could have second thoughts, about if they'd all dare go off-tether together, an apprentice contacted him about Abel. The cars had reappeared and were heading straight towards the meeting. With a smile he wondered if this newbie's nerves had called for a toilet break.

Inside the Range Rover, Kelis wriggled in the front seat, trying to arrange her cloak without strangling herself. Rob, in the back, struggled out of his hoodie and into his latest attempt at Rokk'n Rolla, a long grey leather coat. "Did it work?" Jenny still hadn't sorted out a definite costume beyond frills and flounces for Bonny the Barmaid. Just as well because she needed all her attention on following the Mercedes, now carrying Daorban and four apprentices. One of them was a Taverner, because Siobhan had stayed behind to supervise. When Abel had asked if she wanted to borrow a fourth who could shield, Daorban had grinned nastily and chosen Tobias. He'd made a valiant effort since Easter and could hold a decent shield, and Daorban wanted to see Mallet's face when he saw her with a black apprentice. A rare sight in England because until recently, in sorcerer terms, what few there were had been slaves.

Abel had time to think about all that, because he'd only had to check his shoes were shined and his tie straight. Now his mum knew the secret, he could at least keep his suit at home. Before he could start worrying again about how much his mum knew, or should know, the Mercedes pulled up outside Keele Hall on the Keele University Campus. Abel had been expecting the place to be closed, but it wasn't. Despite the holidays there were plenty of people enjoying the woodlands and wide lawns, not all of them possible students. As he watched, wondering how to keep a meeting private, a young woman approached the cars and Jenny wound down the window. "Your entrance is this way ma'am. Please park in the reserved spaces and go through that wooden gate."

As the fourteen-strong party disembarked, Abel missed Zephyr. She would have nipped over the fence to check everything out. Everyone filed through the gate into a small gravelled area, screened by tall bushes, where a smartly-dressed man was waiting. Now Abel missed Ferryl, because she would have known if he was on a tether, or shielded. Before anyone had a chance to speak, the man bowed, briefly. "Greetings. My Master has found a location that is public, away from his trees so nobody will feel threatened, but hidden from casual view. We will not be disturbed by the visitors. Please veil before leaving the screen of bushes, and follow me to the large marquee."

"Ooh, a circus tent. Lucky we've brought a clown." Jenny winked at

Rob, their usual joker, and he obligingly turned his shoes bright yellow, just for the blink of an eye.

Rob turned to Abel with a smile. "Maybe it's a rave. We should have brought a Rock'n Rolla." A flicker of a smile from the apprentice made Abel wonder if Mallet's people had studied the game for hints. He looked harder at the tent, wondering what might be hidden.

"I'm sure if you want music, it can be arranged once the introductions are over. The barriers around the area and the no entry signs should ensure privacy. The marquee is a Seeming, there is nothing else but a veil so everyone inside can see if danger approaches. Please don't be alarmed by the others attending the meeting. Since this concerns all of Stoke, my master took the liberty of inviting the other three significant sorcerers. They have each brought four apprentices, of course, so there are no objections to all of your party attending." That had to be a dig at Abel turning up with Una, Warren, Petra, Shannon and Justin, all in costume, in addition to Kelis, Rob and Jenny.

"Lead on, please. We'll be right behind you." As the apprentice nodded, Abel winked at the tense set of Kelis's face. "I should have dressed to impress as well."

Her face relaxed a little. "An old leather jacket and a balloon isn't exactly impressive." As she stalked past to take the lead, bodyguard position, she swirled her cloak and added "idiot."

Meanwhile, Daorban looked intrigued, hesitating for a moment to speak quietly to Abel before veiling. "This should be interesting. At least it won't turn into a fight, not right out in the open with the gardens full of people. It's a good job I came with you, Abel, because Mallet's invitation didn't get to me."

Abel smiled, because both of them knew Mallet wouldn't have sent one. "I would have insisted." He stopped talking because the route went too near to the ordinary visitors. Even muffled by a veil, disembodied voices wouldn't help the secrecy part very much. He wondered about how they'd get through a big veil without popping it, but the apprentice lined them all up just short of the shimmer. A second veil sprang into being behind them, and the one in front disappeared. The party walked through the non-existent Seeming of a barrier and the wall of the tent.

From inside all that showed was a pale green shimmer in the air, and all the people enjoying the gardens. Abel had never been inside a Seeming, and wondered if the colour was deliberate or a by-product. Once again he missed his two magical companions.

Daorban had one thing dead right. If a war broke out among the picnics and sunbathers the non-magicals would have a front-row seat. Any stray glyphs wouldn't be stopped by a mere veil, or Seeming, and would smash the Accord. "I have strengthened the veil so even if we shout it shouldn't be heard." Mallet, looking a typically smart mid-thirties, sounded tremendously pleased with himself. "Daorban, how nice of you to come. I understand you made some sort of agreement with this young man, but didn't include us. Our colleagues are considering unmaking it."

"You have no idea what the arrangement is." Daorban didn't seem rattled. "It might be how to divide your demesne? Though since it only included my demesne, I'm not sure how you intend undoing it." A faint thread of threat ran through the last part, and the other three were suddenly alert. "I'd better do the honours, since you failed to."

Before she could speak Kelis strode forward. "I am Kelis, the senior trainee to the sorceress Ferryl Shayde, personal bodyguard to Abel, Master of Castle House and Pendragon Enterprises. Neither I nor my trainer is bound or tethered, so we will respond to any threat without waiting for instructions." Kelis spoke to them all, except at the end when she turned her attention fully onto Mallet. "Cheval Mallet, I presume?" For a moment Abel thought the sneer would set the whole thing off. Real anger crossed Mallet's face for a moment as he looked up at that sneer, definitely up because Kelis had come dressed to kill. Covered top to toe in black leather, with her heels and hair bringing her up to at least two metres, she looked every bit the bodyguard or maybe assassin.

She turned, swirling her crimson cloak, and stalked back to stand just behind Abel's shoulder. He bit back a smile, because she'd glued false fingernails to her black driving gloves, trimmed to points and painted to match her cloak and lipstick, the only colour apart from black. Her misericord dagger hung in full view.

Dead silence followed for a few seconds, until Mallet broke it. "A trainee bodyguard? What use is that?"

"Enough to stop you long enough for her trainer to get here. Unlike you, I asked for a test before making assumptions. That trainee will kill any of your apprentices, maybe two, but it isn't her job." The big smile on Daorban's face didn't make it to her voice. "Abel's bodyguard has a unique approach. The other apprentices hold off the other sorceress, while she kills off the opposing apprentices. All of them."

"It's a good job she's not here, then. Come on, Mallet, introduce us or I'll do it myself. You can tweak his bodyguard when she gets here." With barely a pause the sorcerer made a tiny bow. "Greetings Abel, and Kelis, an absolute pleasure. I am Johannes Liechtenauer, sorcerer and swordsman. Please call me Johan, it saves time." As he finished his eyes flicked to Una, and he nodded very slightly in her direction.

Mallet quickly introduced the other two before they could speak up. "I believe you came to negotiate on behalf of all the young people who have recognised the creatures in your game, Bonny's Tavern." That came with a definite sneer. "Since they were attracting attention, I have dealt with the problem. You have no further business in Stoke."

"You've attempted to tether them all, without their permission, and intend selling them off or stunting them. Aren't you even interested in another solution?" Abel tried to keep his voice steady, but this guy seemed to want to be a pantomime baddie. "Daorban seemed to find my alternative acceptable."

"But she is well known for wanting to save all the poor little kiddies, even those who can barely blow out a candle. This tidies up the problem. I make a profit, and these three can buy a strong new apprentice without having to search for them or test them." His voice hardened and his apprentices lost any relaxation. "More to the point, this is not your demesne."

That spurred Daorban into speaking up. "But you have been straying off your demesne, haven't you? Into mine for a start. I have a young apprentice who was approached in a public street by one of your apprentices. You." She pointed at one of Mallet's apprentices. "If Siobhan hadn't been nearby and seen it, she would have trotted off to your prison."

"Exactly, off the streets and out of trouble. Now you'll go on about breaking up families and all the other tiresome sob stories. Apprentices have to break links with family, so the sooner the better." At least two of the others were nodding at that. Mallet turned on Abel. "You are trying to poach. Stop it and leave."

"But if I'm poaching, it's all out in the open. I haven't stolen kids off the streets from some other sorcerer's demesne, and then offered to sell them to him or her." Abel saw the other three glance at each other, startled, so he'd been right. They didn't realise. "Worse, what happens when a sorcerer in Manchester realises you went poaching there, then finds the stolen youngster tethered to one of these three?"

"Rubbish and I can prove it. They can ask the merchandise." Who would be on a tether and lie, Abel realised. Or maybe Mallet would never let these sorcerers see anyone from their own demesne. The Tavern could scupper that, if Zephyr had been successful. A puzzled look on Mallet's face might be him trying to check on his merchandise, or the apprentices at least.

Diverting him would be easy. "Is it really your demesne if you don't look after it? In the Accord it says you are responsible for the people under your control, not that you should let them go crazy or take to drugs and drink."

"Of course it's my demesne. Try and take it and you'll soon find out."

One of the others, a large, muscular man in a pinstriped suit, jumped in. "Any potential magic user in my demesne is mine."

"So deal with them, rather than let him take the strongest and sell you the dross." Abel smiled instead of spitting at the arrogant git. "My way they phone me, and my people meet them and stop them shouting about visions. You don't have to go looking, they'll come to meet us. If you want any as apprentices you make them an offer, and if they agree you tether them."

"Not a chance."

"Shut up Mallet, I'm interested. Aware children can be troublesome sometimes. This way they turn themselves in, and he didn't mention me having to pay anyone." The red-haired woman, a young looking, slim sorceress wearing a green cloak that matched a tight-fitting version of an old-style military uniform, turned back to Abel. "Though what's the part about if they agree? I choose, surely?"

"You have the right, but in return for rounding them up I ask you to only take volunteers. There'll be plenty who choose a tether over working for a living." Abel didn't get a chance to finish.

"After he's stolen all the strongest." Mallet wasn't giving in yet. "According to that, you aren't mistress in your own domain, you have to beg them to take the tether."

"Not beg, just ask, and I get plenty of volunteers that way. Maybe more enthusiastic ones as well, who don't use the shield to cut themselves off so they can talk in peace." A saccharine-sweet smile accompanied that, before Daorban turned to the other three. "Listen to this young man. He won't tether them himself, even the rejects. He'll even take some out of the city, and all of them will find non-magical jobs. That means they aren't competing with us for magical contracts. I've made an agreement to hire some if I run short anytime, for filling hexes." Bedlam broke out with Mallet trying to shout Daorban down, or extol the profits if they sold the surplus, while the other three couldn't agree.

Abel soon realised one wasn't against the idea, but he liked seeing the others argue. The swordsman used words like weapons, a quick jab now and then to sting someone or make a point. One particular jab struck a very sore point. "You say you will stunt the rest. How do we know you won't keep them, Mallet. You might train them hard for a year or so, to throw wind or maybe fire. Then one fine day you've got more fighters than all of us put together."

Just for a moment Mallet glared at Johan, and a glyph began to shimmer in his hand. The red-head immediately raised both her hands, palms towards Mallet, and his glyph died. The previous shouting rose in volume, with Mallet denying any sort of plot to extend his demesne.

A soundless flash of light shut everyone up and presumably, like Abel, they all shielded. "Good, now I can hear myself. This is my meeting, so you will listen." Mallet pointed at Abel. "From that garbage he just spouted, he has no apprentices so no power. Those trainees are schoolchildren, even that supposed guard, so let's see just how useful they are." A tiny shower of glyphs went up into the air and drifted down.

"He's just checking shields, I've seen it before." Abel looked back and up at Kelis and murmured, "Perhaps we can show him a little control?"

Kelis smiled and turned to murmur to Rob, who passed it along the line. Abel wasn't quite sure how good the other Taverners were at altering shields, except his three friends, Una and Petra. Everyone's shields, including Mallet's, lit up with a light blue glow. Abel promptly shrank his down to within a few centimetres of his clothes, pulled it inside his skin, then let it come back out again. Out of the corner of his eye he could see other shields altering, but not how many.

Johan, the swordsman, pursed his lips. "A little more than schoolchildren, and tethered or not, they are obedient. May I speak to them please, Abel?" Abel nodded, curious. "You, the young lady with the sword, the real one. I don't know your name but can you use it, properly?"

"I'm Una. I've been taking lessons, but until recently I only had a re-enactment version." Una sounded wary.

"Real lessons? Are you tethered?" Una must have shaken her head. "I would be really interested in offering you a position as an apprentice."

Now Una sounded decidedly unfriendly. "Sorry, I don't like the idea of a tether."

"A pity, but if you ever change your mind, or just want to spar?"

"Not now Johan. This is business!" The larger sorcerer looked and sounded exasperated. "There's more to life than waving a pig-sticker."

"I don't know, I dressed up like this just to tease him but he's more interested in her weapon." The sorceress ran her eyes along the Taverners, coming back to Kelis. "I really must try that look as well."

"Of course I'm interested, most modern youth just don't want to take the time and effort to learn to use a sword properly. Finding a fan who is also more than competent with glyphs is a real treat. Abel, I agree to the same terms as whatever Daorban negotiated, on one condition. Una spars with me once a month, at a place of her choosing, with bodyguards if she wishes." Johan bowed a little towards Una. "Non-lethal, though true sparring may bruise her a little."

"Accept it Abel." Una laughed, probably at the expression on Mallet's face.

"Too late, I've already tethered all the potential apprentices in or near Stoke, so your agreement isn't worth spit. If you want new apprentices in the foreseeable future, you'll buy mine." Mallet smiled triumphantly for a moment before his head jerked up. "What is that!" Several hands went up, palms out and glyphs swirling into life.

"Hold fire!" Abel grinned, just as triumphantly, as a multi-coloured firework blossomed in the sky above Keele Hall, a big old mansion house. As all the non-magical visitors looked up and oohed and aahed, and a shimmer dropped down towards the veil, he turned to a startled Mallet. "Better do the double shuffle with the veil to let her in, or it will pop." Behind the sorcerer an apprentice cast a small glyph downwards as Zephyr zoomed closer and hovered. She hesitated, then flew towards Abel.

"Since nobody looks startled, I think you timed that right and the veil held. Now what wanted to get in so urgently?" The sorceress's eyes narrowed as Zephyr disappeared into Abel's sleeve. "I thought your wind spirit was tethered?"

"Obedient though, like the apprentices. Sorry, trainees. Perhaps the system works, but I'll stick to tethers for now." The big sorcerer turned to Mallet. "All the potential apprentices in the area? Are you telling me Daorban is right, you've been poaching?"

"Yes, he has but I'll bet he's been careful. Personally, I don't believe he's tethered any of them. I reckon it's a bluff, then if you went for it he'd make a big profit." Abel looked at the three guests in turn, trying to ignore the jubilant recital in his head. "If you object he turns them loose and denies everything."

"That would suit your style, Mallet." Once again the swordsman hit perfectly, stinging his target.

Both baffled and angry, because he still wouldn't have heard from his apprentices, Mallet rounded on Abel. "You are calling me a liar?" He stopped for a moment, then continued with a nasty smile. "I should challenge you to a duel. You or that freak next to you, your bodyguard."

Abel could almost feel Kelis coming to the boil, but before he could calm her down Daorban cut in. "If anyone is challenging it should be me, or these other three, challenging you. If you've taken our people, tethered or not, that is poaching. I'd like to check all those you collected, for anyone from my demesne. If you were stupid enough not to tether them they can tell us where they're from." The sorceress had understood Zephyr's firework, and Abel's jibe about the tethering. As she turned she reached up to tap her shoulder, so Daorban had dropped her shield enough to use a tether and would be getting the full story.

"I do not duel. I have a bodyguard for that." The mere idea of a challenge from Daorban had shaken Mallet, badly. "I'll let you see those I tethered, so that won't be necessary."

"But that's not what I've heard. Siobhan just found forty-one people aged between fourteen and nineteen wandering down the street." The sorceress turned back to Mallet with a smile that should have drawn blood. "She's put them in a bus and is on the way, because they all want to join Abel's Tavern. According to them, they are from all over Stoke and some really are from Manchester and Birmingham."

"If that's true, perhaps I could challenge first. Then when your bodyguard is dead we can get to the main event." This time Johan the swordsman wasn't jabbing. He'd thrust straight for the heart. "We've all been hoping to see you and Daorban face off one day. I doubt she'll use a bodyguard."

"If these youngsters have strayed due to a misunderstanding, I'm sure we can clear it all up. But if they are tethered...." Mallet stopped dead and shock wiped out his sneer. "How!" He wasn't talking to anyone present, though he recovered enough to whirl towards Daorban and croak, "You?" The shock and bewilderment faded and his face straightened. "If the children really are coming here, then I call on the Stoke treaty. I have been attacked and my property stolen."

"The bus has just pulled into the car park." Rather than being worried, Daorban's expression suggested the cat had found a whole cream jug.

"Shut up until they get here, fool." The largest sorcerer looked Mallet up and down. "I'm sure you thought you'd tethered them, but if you did we'll soon know. If they've hired enough specialists to break forty tethers we'll hear about it, and there'll be evidence if it was done that quickly." He turned to Daorban and shrugged. "If you really did attack his apprentices, then regardless of the reason you broke the treaty."

"Who attacked your people, Mallet? Name an apprentice. Apart from Siobhan, all the truly dangerous senior apprentices in Stoke are here."

Johan still looked as if he fancied killing someone.

"I can't, they were all strangers in jeans and hoodies or long coats. Dozens, maybe scores of them." Mallet's eyes went to Abel, then the line of Taverners behind him, and the revelation hit him. "You did it, you sent your apprentices, you're the only one who has those numbers."

"Sorry, I can't order anyone to do anything. They're all free agents." As understanding dawned on every face, spooky-phone shot out across the gardens, and Zephyr reported the first Taverners coming through the gate. Daorban confirmed that Siobhan had grouped several rescued teens under a veil, and they were on the way. As their Taverner escorts appeared, resplendent in their costumes, Mallet had to admit they didn't match the descriptions of the attackers.

Siobhan led the group across to the marquee and waited for the veil to move. One look told Abel the ten freed teenagers had been chosen with care. The youngsters all seemed more angry than frightened, and they were very, very certain what had happened. As they each recited how they'd been approached and told to go to a meeting, a place to learn about the strange creatures, Mallet started shooting nervous glances at the other sorcerers and sorceresses. At least one witness came from each demesne, and better still, each one pointed at the apprentice who recruited them.

Just for a moment, Abel thought the others would risk attacking Mallet, public or not, but Daorban diverted them. Instead of breaking the Accord, Mallet's three guests accepted an invitation to see the rest of the youngsters still on the bus. The score of gaudily dressed Tavern players in the car park and bus attracted plenty of public attention, but with a little veiling distracted the usual visitors from the rescued teenagers.

An exhausting half-hour later, everyone but Mallet and his apprentices had made their way out of Keele Hall gardens. Mallet had agreed to meet his four local peers in due course, to discuss penalties for poaching even if he hadn't actually tethered any of the captives. He'd steered well clear of talk about challenges and duels, once it became clear none of his apprentices were badly hurt.

Just as well, because Daorban kept trying to get Mallet to challenge Abel again, now that Ferryl had arrived. The sorceress had announced her name and job in her usual manner when she arrived, and Johan had burst out laughing. The red-headed sorceress had offered to keep Mallet busy while Ferryl killed his apprentices, just as a demonstration, and didn't seem to be joking. To rub it in, Kelis stopped by Mallet before leaving, so close he had to tip his head right back to meet her sneer, and told him she didn't like people who picked on kids.

*　　*　　*

Kelis lost the sneer and the attitude once she got back into the car. "It's not really a win. Some of those kids won't go home again, and some might not be welcome if they try. From what they said a few really burned bridges, probably goaded by that tether."

"Those already living on the street, trying to find ways to stop the visions, will be better off. I'm more worried about the same thing happening all over the country." Rob had taken off his leather coat. "I'm drowned in sweat, mad as hell, and never even got to squash a cockroach."

"It isn't that bad." Jenny didn't seem as downhearted. "I've been talking to Siobhan. Daorban's apprentices will pass the whole idea, and rescue, along to the apprentices of sorceresses who don't like the tether. Unofficially, of course. They'll talk to others who feel the same, to make sure everyone understands the message." Her smile widened a little. "They'll give Daorban the credit of course, both to take the heat off the Tavern and because she really is one scary lady so everyone will believe it. Once the sorceress community stop laughing at Mallet getting his apprentices beaten up, and his captives untethered, they'll try to avoid the same thing."

"Will sorcerers care about apprentices being beaten up? Will Mallet, because he didn't actually lose any?" Abel shrugged, then threw his hands up because that wasn't enough. "He got away with it apart from a few fines."

But Kelis had cheered up a bit. "I never thought about the ridicule part. Daorban and Johan were really laying that on, now I think about it. Some won't laugh. That sorceress really meant it about Ferryl killing Mallet's apprentices as a demo." She turned round to smile at Abel. "They'll be real fines, heavy ones so they'll sting because those three were definitely unhappy, unhappy enough to sign up for our deal. Especially that swordsman bloke, he really came round once he realised Una could use that sword. How weird is that?"

The whole day had been weird, they all concluded. The thought of all those teenagers trying to explain going missing, for anywhere from one to seven days, didn't help anyone's mood. At least Daorban had promised to advise them all, to help with excuses. Some, the later arrivals, would claim they'd got carried away playing Bonny's Tavern with a big group and hadn't realised how long it had been. Other captives had never heard of Bonny's Tavern, not until the Taverners woke them up and herded them onto the bus.

Mallet had scooped up every teenager he'd heard about, those talking about having visions or hallucinations. Some would claim to have got drunk, or taken something unwise to explain their sudden desire to leave home. Oddly enough, their previous erratic behaviour while they'd struggled with visions of creatures would make a few lost days more understandable. Several were already drinking heavily, or experimenting with drugs, to banish the visions or just to forget them for a while. For those living rough, a decent bed and knowing they weren't crackers should be an improvement.

There'd be reports to the police, and to the media no doubt, but Daorban promised to arrange magical diversions. Better yet, Mallet had grudgingly agreed to pay for any cover-up. A few stories might circulate, about stupid children frightening parents, but they'd only be word of mouth and seem like isolated incidents. Abel had offered all the freed teenagers a copy of Bonny's Tavern, because now they all wanted to join up for the protection. Playing the game would explain why they were all carrying Tavern hexes, given to them to warn of any further attempts at tethering. As a bonus the creature booklet would identify the magic creatures, and hopefully make them less frightening.

*   *   *

As the sound of the last vehicles died away, Mallet heard more approaching. Only three, his somewhat battered and bedraggled apprentices from the industrial unit had finally arrived. He left Keele Hall to meet them in a side street, where he could cast a veil and give them hell. As he wound down, and the tether-induced pain faded from their faces, Mallet caught sight of a figure lurking nearby. The edge of a broad-brimmed black hat and the swirl of a black cloak brought a scowl to his face. That arrogant young whelp had left a spy, still dressed in his ridiculous cartoon clothes.

Mallet turned to go, dropping the veil as everyone climbed into their cars, and passed instructions down the tether. The strongest of the disgraced apprentices, the one who had been inside and the one guarding the door, could earn some forgiveness by taking care of the watcher. Killing a Taverner wasn't much of a consolation, but it would do for now. Mallet knew he'd have to be careful how he did it, because Daorban had made it clear she only needed the slightest excuse to challenge him. As his car drove away, the sorcerer saw the black-dressed figure peering around a corner to watch him go, and smiled nastily.

One of Mallet's cars stopped briefly, just around the corner, to let the two apprentices out. He activated their tethers, relaxing by listening to their thoughts as the pair slipped into an alley that would bring them out behind the spy. Nobody should play games with a sorcerer on his own demesne. As his car travelled further away, Mallet followed their progress as his apprentices veiled and cut through two back yards. When they came out into the street, the spy had his back to them. Mallet hammered the order down the tether. "Kill him!"

Four strong, tight glyphs flew at the black-cloaked figure, who turned to show the ridiculously large cross hung on his chest. Mallet felt his apprentices' disbelief and alarm as their glyphs fizzled out, barely sparking, and the tall, slim man smiled. The tethers were cut as both apprentices slammed up their shields, but not before Mallet cried out in shock and pain when pure white light blanked out his vision. He waited until the spots before his eyes cleared and tried the tethers. Still down, so that cartoon vicar must be putting up a fight. A vicar the apprentices had thought looked well past his teenage years, Mallet suddenly realised. Two cars slowed, turned, and most of Mallet's apprentices sped back towards the fight.

Meanwhile the two apprentices blinked to get their eyesight back, one on his knees holding his head and whimpering. Ferryl had left him with the equivalent of a bad migraine, so the bright light felt as if it had set his brain on fire. The other peered at his opponent, leisurely walking towards them while glyphs grew in his hands. The whirling white circles looked like the hoops thrown at a fairground, as a stream of them looped up and dropped towards the apprentice's shield. As they landed on top, each one expanded, slipping down around the globe. The first one tightened again at ankle height, then the rest spaced themselves to hold the whole shield in shining white bands, right up to level with the apprentice's neck. The black-clad figure pulled in his fingers to form fists, the bands contracted, and the shield collapsed. With a despairing scream the apprentice died as the glowing rings cut him into sections.

The apprentice on his knees peered up at the priest, eyes squinting in pain. "What was that?"

"St. Michael's halo. The penalty for attacking a member of the church." The vicar raised his hands again and glyphs swirled into being. "Your turn now."

"I didn't know." The glyphs grew and the apprentice realised that wasn't going to be enough so he dropped his shield. "I surrender." He felt his tether connect and knew with sickening certainty that Mallet would force him to fight, then the tether cut off again! Although the apprentice didn't realise, because his eyes hadn't recovered enough to see the faint lemony shimmer, Creepio's shield had expanded to include him.

"You throw yourself on the mercy of mother church?" The apprentice nodded, tears of pain still trickling down his cheeks. "You must relax, while I break your tether and connect a different one. Where is it attached?" With a sob the man pointed at the place, one hand still holding his head. As Creepio reached for the tether point his eyes narrowed in curiosity. "What is the matter with you?"

"A glowing yellow cloud, a ball, hovering. Smiling. Burning green eyes. Then pain and blackness. Will this hurt?" Creepio's shield vanished just before his hand connected, and the apprentice screamed and collapsed.

"Of course. Redemption always has a price." The archbishop stood over the comatose apprentice, pulling off his cloak and hat and stowing them in a bag hung from one shoulder. "A cloud this time, a yellow ball not an ogre, and it knocked a warded apprentice clean out?" As his cross shrunk to its usual size a Seeming hid the bag. Air glyphs plucked the apprentice from the ground and dropped him over the archbishop's shoulder, then moved him a little to a better position. The churchman strode off down the road without a backward glance, deep in thought. This little scheme worked best if Abel's merry band had wound the victims up first. He'd have to keep an eye on where they were going next, for more than one reason.

Despite considerable research, he still couldn't work out exactly what lived in young Abel's tattoo. It definitely wasn't a captured wind spirit. Any such creature, especially one without a tether, would have killed rather than stunned. More to the point, a wind spirit wouldn't have been able to create an ogre with claws solid enough to score timber, nor break through a ward, so exactly what had young Abel found? The archbishop had rejected it being a bound sorceress, as some had claimed, but now he'd had the report from the bishop. A bound magical being who was also a sorceress? No, the being could stand the church magic inside a cathedral, so it wasn't the bound remnant of a magical creature.

Engines sounded, closing rapidly, but the archbishop didn't increase his pace. His hand moved to cast a glyph. By the time Mallet's apprentices hurled round the corner, and screeched to a halt by the dismembered body, Creepio and his captive were invisible even to magical sight.

Back in his car, Mallet hunched a little, trying not to show the crippling pain that had shot through his tether connection. One apprentice had connected long enough to show his fear, pain and confusion, then cut off. The tether opened again, briefly, to deliver vicious pain, but now it had cut off again. "Eyes front! Drive!" The driver jerked his eyes from the rear-view mirror, back to the road, and Mallet closed his eyes and tried to relax. Even before the reports started to come in from the other apprentices, he knew, deep inside, both his men were dead. Finding out one body had disappeared posed a question, though now Mallet had a bigger worry.

If Daorban had set a trap he could recover in time, train up more senior apprentices, but maybe the intruder had been a real churchman. If so, from the result it could only be a certain archbishop, and by attacking him Mallet had broken the Accord. Or maybe not, was the sorcerer held to account if an apprentice attacked? Did the church invading his demesne mean the attack was legal? Mallet daren't even ask a solicitor, in case they notified the Magical Council.

* * *

Daorban, and the Taverners, were too busy trying to sort out rescued children to even think of setting traps. More than half the released teenagers in Stoke went home the same day, many of them in cabs paid for by Daorban. Over the next few days a steady trickle of Taverners travelled to Stoke to help Daorban and her apprentices with the rest. The temporary lodgings the sorceress found gradually emptied, as the occupants made their peace at home, or moved into flats, or in with friends.

Daorban helped Abel to purchase a small industrial plot, in the unclaimed town centre but on the edge of her demesne where it shouldn't get any hassle. At least this sorceress told the Taverners the exact boundary of the two zones, one each in Stoke-on-Trent and Newcastle-under-Lyme though everyone just called the combination Stoke. Abel made arrangements to site a large second-hand mobile home on his new plot, a clubhouse where the Stoke Tavern could meet. The decrepit warehouse on the plot would come in handy as a place to practice magic, because all the founder members of this Tavern were aware.

Despite already having thirty-one members, the Stoke Tavern wasn't that popular in some quarters. Many parents blamed the game for their child going missing, though an open invitation for any parent to call and meet the players mollified a good few. The rules on the wall helped, stressing that school work came before Tavern work or play. Taverners from Stourton, supervising the new members, assured any visitors the home Tavern hadn't realised what the youngsters had been up to. Within the week some parents were helping their kids to clean up the site, and the street outside. About a quarter of the teenagers wouldn't be visiting for a long time, not until their families had got over the shock. The four from Birmingham and Manchester were put in touch with other new Taverners in their home cities, so they could meet up.

Six of the new Taverners didn't feel safe in Stoke, and couldn't or wouldn't go home, or had already left before Mallet found them. Abel made arrangements for those to move to Sheffield, into Valdar's two apprentice houses, to keep them off the streets while they learned how to deal with their magic. Veren offered to help, without tethering any. The vassal sorceress had been impressed when she heard about Daorban, while Daorban had been intrigued by a vassal who wasn't a desperate youngster as she'd first thought. The practice of accepting vassals had fallen out of favour as the nobility declined, replaced by straight conquest or tethering.

Eventually all the new Taverners would have to decide what to do with their lives, though in some cases that would be after they broke a serious addiction. Ferryl's command voice helped, along with belts of pure tree magic when the addiction bit deep. Una visited Stoke several times to help out, and went for her first sparring session. She took Shannon as a bodyguard, coming back a little bruised but happy. Johan and Daorban started sending any aware teenagers to the Stoke Tavern clubhouse. A few even arrived from other demesnes, though not from Mallet. Johan assured Una the other Stoke sorcerers wouldn't approach any Taverners about apprenticeships for at least six months, until the whole affair had blown over.

Abel hoped the initial rush, as Bonny's Tavern slowly spread and frantic teenagers emailed Ferryl Shayde, would be over in a lot less than six months.

*　*　*

While the magically-inclined youth of Stoke worked their way through their problems, a gradually increasing number of teenagers elsewhere in the UK saw the Bonny's Tavern artwork and sent that email. The next few weeks turned into a series of trips by small groups of Taverners to meet confused, frightened or jubilant teenagers, and try to set up training and if possible a Tavern. The increasing number of non-magical players helped with that, with small groups asking for an official Tavern sign to set up their own. Many of those were using a room in their house for meetings, which would work unless any of them discovered magic.

In the towns, where practical, Abel sent someone with cash to rent cheap premises. That gave the local players somewhere to meet others and compare notes on setting up, and the first few began to play death-matches between local Taverns. Luckily Rachel's Tavern had already asked for that, so there were rules. The rented premises gave any magical Taverners somewhere private to meet instructors, and practice, but that still left too many scattered players. Magically aware or not, those could only play by Skype. Bonny's Tavern in Stourton tried to put each one in touch with the nearest players, while the players themselves were trying to solve their problem by recruiting friends.

Abel spent his time racing around to meetings with sorcerers, but the numbers asking to see him rose faster than he could meet them. He also had to find time to meet the better of the new recruits to give them access to a tree. That should have waited, but there weren't enough adepts to chase all over the country handing out extra magic. Where he had no woodland, but the local would-be Taverner could find a suitable plot of land, Abel reverted to the village tree system. Even his allegedly spare time grew less and less, because mum pushed on with working through her list of the magically disturbing. She was determined about getting into Castle House before school started.

Another chore could only be carried out by Ferryl and Zephyr, using magical sight, which meant Abel as well. After some fruitless searching, the first traces of troll had been found. The signs were in the right direction, towards the mountains, but they'd been magical traces so only two entities could see them. A bit at a time, Abel, Ferryl and Zephyr began to track the troll up the valley of the Brinn. Zephyr took to flying up the valley at night, high up, looking for unusual magical activity. An outside chance, because the night fields were alive with magical creatures grazing or hunting. Abel might have given up, but he remembered the previous times magical creatures had spied on Brinsford. This time he'd be prepared.

*   *   *

In all the chaos Abel, and his friends, had forgotten one person. Or actually three people, as Kelis reminded Abel when she brought him a parcel from Eleanor's study group. The box contained copies of all their notes about ghosts. "I just flicked through these when they arrived, but mum wanted to know what they were. Now she knows about creatures I thought she'd find them funny. She found this." This was a note pointing out most of the contents were obsolete, but the study group would take time to come round to that idea. Could the Taverners arrange a meeting and a demonstration? "And this."

Abel opened the sealed envelope addressed to him, and scanned it. "It's a report from Mz Fisher, the reporter. I'd forgotten all about her." He passed Kelis the neat, precise accounts of meetings and the reporter's expenses to date. She had visited four people, all over fifty, and reassured them. In three cases she'd explained that the game designers could also

341

see ghosts. In her opinion those three weren't ready for the truth. She had one candidate for conversion, an odd way to describe learning about magic.

"We could combine the two, the study group and this bloke. They could compare notes and would have comrades in confusion?" At Abel's look Kelis stopped, but she still had a grin. "Come on, after all the doom and gloom this is light relief."

"Or not." Abel passed the last sheet of paper, a short letter from Mz Fisher. She explained she could accept more names, but only a few at a time. She had her other work, which had picked up after her last article. Could she talk to Abel and his friends again? After the last meetings she had started a new series of posts and newspaper reports, about ghosts and afterlives, and had more questions. "Have you heard anything?"

"About ghosts? Not a whisper, but it isn't on my usual browser history. Flobberclomps! Why won't people talk before shooting off and adapting the master plan?"

"I remember someone pointing out a certain bloke had to learn who he was messing with, after swearing off leather for life." To Abel's surprise Kelis blushed a little! "Are we likely to see more of it?"

"No! Well maybe, if we need an impression. It's actually quite practical, though I'll need shorter heels for fighting. And you can stop smirking!" Ferryl tried but it wasn't easy. "Anyway, we were talking about reporters."

"Your leather was reported? Where? In Germany?" Abel's smirk got an outing as well when Kelis wouldn't answer.

None of them smirked when Kelis found the first article by Mz Fisher. She hadn't debunked her ghosts, but she claimed to have a better understanding of their purpose. "Not really, she's adapted some of what we said about real ghosts and heavens, but applied it to creatures. I suppose that covers anyone seeing our artwork, and she's already told three people our artist used ghosts as models." Ferryl narrowed her eyes in anticipation. "I could drop round and explain her mistake?"

"No, because it's a neat way to explain sightings of creatures. Except now I think about it, we'll have séances emailing Ferryl Shayde for a guest appearance." Kelis glanced at Ferryl, but she wasn't playing that game.

"What do we do? Apart from sending Zephyr to rustle the curtains and knock on tables?"

"Let her run for now and hope she doesn't get too ambitious. After all, she's been writing articles for years, and at least this way she might do some good." Abel pointed to the papers he'd given Kelis. "Those expenses aren't too bad, and our Mz Fisher was right, her name and reputation got her an interview without any publicity. I'll call her and give her some more names, and arrange to send her money."

"Email her, the address is here. I'll put Eleanor off for now, until we can work out what to show her friends." Kelis repacked the papers. "I'll ask mum to keep reading, and tell me if anything looks interested. She's enjoying being useful."

"She'll be more useful once the church refuge opens?" Abel almost held his breath, but Kelis had finally accepted someone had to organise the place, and her mum lived just up the street. "At least the charity side is still getting enough money."

"Because of the fees from the hex filling, fees that should now go to Pendragon Enterprises. Mum is saving you a few quid, or will once she learns the basics of working with stained glass. She really enjoys helping out with the church windows, and has signed up for a course. She wants to try and sell some, eventually." Kelis obviously liked that idea.

Rob pointed at the receipts. "Now if we can just find a load of extra work for the business, to pay for all the rentals."

Kelis shook her head and smiled at Abel. "I nearly said then we could stop using your money, meaning selling the loot, but the business is yours as well. When you end up bankrupt and living in abject poverty, I'll let you share my gruel." Her smile widened at a memory from when Abel offered her a place to stay. "Or sleep on my settee, though it'll be crowded with two." Ferryl smirked but Abel blushed, so Kelis left well satisfied with the result. After that Abel really did try to remember to look out for Mz Fisher's next article, but the sheer volume of Tavern work swamped him.

Progress might slow up fairly soon, or Abel might need Kelis's settee. Not quite that bad, but more and more trees were needed and transport had become a major expense. Abel put any new requests on hold. The new magic users would have to manage with a trickle of extra from hedgerows for now. The money from the sale of the odd-shaped coins found in Castle House provided a welcome financial boost, but most of the best valuables were gone now.

More of Valdar's and Pendragon's treasures went on the market to keep the money coming. Abel kept eyeing up the sovereigns in the dragon room, hoping to get through another door in Castle House before he had to use them. Not quite yet, the security business kept solvent while the magical side made a profit, which put off the final reckoning. He hadn't asked yet, but Abel began to worry his balance at Woods and Green would run out as well.

At least he'd been finding friendly sorcerer or sorceress faces at some meetings. Some were on Terese's list, but from the hints the friendliest might have been set up by Daorban's apprentices. Three of those each sold Abel a tree in a local park, for Taverner use when he hadn't any woodland nearby. He travelled in the Range Rover, often with Petra as a driver because she still worried about scratching the paintwork. Kelis came to any meetings that sounded contentious, though she didn't wear the leather again. She still claimed that had only been worn to bluff Mallet, to back him off until Ferryl arrived.

*   *   *

The steady progress couldn't last, and it didn't. Warren didn't beat about the bush when Abel walked into the gym after his latest trip. "You'll be needed in Dumfries, as soon as possible. Stu is refusing to fill lead bars or help out with the new Taverners. He seems to think you can't stop him taking magic from his tree, so he'll keep the magic for himself and be as strong as a sorcerer."

"Not only that, he's been trying to persuade his shrink the creatures are real. He keeps trying to get the man to float a leaf." Sarah sounded more despondent, maybe because she was supposed to be mentoring Stu. "He thought it was funny when I told him it would send the psychiatrist crackers. Reckons the bloke can cure himself. I warned Stu about the Accord, but he thinks he's fireproof because he's in the Tavern." The psychiatrist part reminded Abel exactly who Stu was, the first teenager on the motorbike trip with Ferryl.

Before anyone else could speak up Ferryl dived in. "Has he burned in a ward?"

"Yes, and he's had a Tavern shield tattooed on his arm. I don't know which Taverners he's been talking to, but he thinks he only has to show it to back off any local apprentices. He thinks the Tavern shield is what gives him access to the trees, it's why he's had it tattooed." Sarah sounded even more depressed as she continued. "The protection is true to an extent, because Abel has an agreement with the locals so they leave Taverners alone, treat them as apprentices."

"But one of the conditions is the Tavern doesn't cause trouble. Okay, give me a moment please." Abel held up both hands and shook his head as Warren tried to speak again. "Please, let me talk to Ferryl and Zephyr." He tried to ignore the expectant faces. "Ferryl, is it the Tavern shield? When I give access to Celtchar's individual trees I mean, because where we've used the dryads they read the true-self."

"The Tavern shield has no effect on hexed trees, the glyph from Terese is what gives a Taverner access. Stu will cause trouble if we banish him. From the sounds of it he's stupid enough to think he can challenge a sorceress. I can magically stain his skin, cancel the tattoo? That will stop him using it as protection from apprentices. Then one will use him as tree fertiliser."

"In spite of a ward?" Abel thought that protected magic users.

"Without training or extra magic, or a shield, even Veren's apprentices could take him. If it comes to banishment I can mark Stu, even if he won't give up his magic. Get him close to a tree, one I have access to, and I can do it slowly without any real injury. Otherwise I'll have to be faster, more brutal, to break through his ward. That will injure him, quite badly. What I can't do is stop Stu or anyone else accessing a tree. You'll have to ask Terese about that."

Abel sighed, because he had hoped it never came to this, and looked around at the rest. "I'm going to stop Stu's access to trees. Refusing to fill the bars, keeping all the magic, is grounds for shunning. If he won't accept that, the rules are clear. I'll banish him, but according to Sarah he'll pretend he still belongs to us and probably upset some sorcerer or the church. Ferryl will fix that, mark him so he can't pretend he's still in the Tavern, but we need him near a tree. Once Stu loses access to extra magic, and training, he'll never be able to persuade the psychiatrist."

Right now Sarah couldn't see any happy endings. "What if he floats a leaf for the bloke? I'm not sure why he hasn't. That would be a real problem, Accord-style problem."

"Then someone like Creepio will kill Stu and spread his ashes, and the coppers will want to talk to the Tavern. At best it'll cost a fortune to cover up. I hope you've got another vase to sell, Abel?" Warren looked hopeful, but his face fell when Abel shook his head.

"No, though we aren't actually scraping the barrel yet. There's still some of the loot to sell, and what's left of my income from my legacy. A big cover-up could blow the lot." Abel realised everyone had made an assumption. "Will he meet me?"

"Yes. I told you, he thinks he's fireproof. He's telling anyone who'll listen that you'll try to persuade him to toe the line, and offer concessions, which will prove he's right. We've had a few more mutters here and there, new recruits who complain about having to work filling lead bars to earn their magic." Sarah scowled, tapping the 'gold' belt she'd earned. "If some of them got one of these, they'd be straight off to the pawnbrokers."

"You've got to sort Stu now, Abel. If possible, get some of the others there to watch." Kelis paused, then a wicked smile split her face. "That's it. Contact all those who really have a problem with the rules, and invite them to discuss it with you. They'll think Stu is right and you want to deal. Meet near Stu's tree." Her smile faltered as Ferryl slowly shook her head.

"Not unless we can stop Stu accessing the tree. Nobody thought of this, how to stop access short of chopping down the tree or killing the offender. Terese probably expected you to do that, kill anyone you want to stop." She sighed, and put her arm around Abel. "You keep trying to be the good guy, and spread all the benefits, but some people just don't deserve it." As she hugged, Ferryl's hand touched Abel's neck. "I'll deal with it. A sudden disappearance, or I can mazzle him to where he can't remember what a tree is."

"No! There has to be another way. Let me ask Terese." Abel didn't need an answer, he could see it in Ferryl's eyes. "I mean it. Please, I don't want to hear he's suddenly missing."

"You will anyway, if Stu annoys the wrong sorceress. Whoever it is might even cancel their agreement." Ferryl let go, turning to the others. The discussion went around several possible ways to stop Stu, but the rules already covered it. Shunning for refusing to follow Tavern rules, then banishment if he refused. The problem was, none of them really wanted to banish a Taverner. It seemed too much for what Stu had actually done up to now, but shunning wouldn't work if he didn't think anyone could stop him getting magic.

Worse, there were other Taverners who wanted to deal with him themselves, which would lead to anarchy. Despite all of them racking their brains, every solution relied on Abel stopping access to one of his trees, for one person. The only practical ways were to cut the tree down, or let Ferryl magically stop Stu drawing magic. Now Abel wished he'd asked Terese for a glyph like the locksmith had created for Pendragon's trees, with unique keys.

"I'll talk to Terese as soon as I can, and then deal with Stu. I've got the message now, no more nice guy Abel." Abel didn't even try to smile as if he was joking, he wasn't. Stu, and those like him, posed a real threat to the whole idea of the Tavern. It might be exasperation, or maybe he'd just lost some patience, but Abel had stopped worrying so much about causing Stu some pain. The Tavern meant real hope for too many teenagers. One greedy kid couldn't be allowed to wreck the whole thing.

Abel knew there were outside threats to the Tavern, from those who didn't agree with the whole concept. He could even sort of understand why most sorcerers were cruel and arrogant, and seemed to spend so much of their time bickering or showing off. It had to be all those centuries of absolute power. What really baffled him was why someone inside the Tavern would insist on messing the whole thing up. They didn't have to belong, it was voluntary.

Stu had been seeing a shrink for hallucinations before the Tavern came along, and really wanted to join. Once he hit the knack, Stu had rapidly mastered casting a glyph although he had little control, not a problem when draining a tree or filling bars. Now, within weeks, he'd started acting like the real sorcerers and thought he could have it all without rules! Abel turned away from the others, to find some privacy and think.

"Now let me work out exactly what to do, to avoid either burning a tree or mazzling Stu into idiocy."

He came face to face with Jenny, who had been parking the car. "I can live with either of those, but my vote is to save the tree. I'm well known for preferring flowers." True enough, her plant glyphs were improving faster than anyone else's, to where she'd inspired a new game character. Verdant Bounty roamed the byways spreading bountiful harvests or strangling nasties with branches and roots. Now Abel had to repeat the problem and the various suggestions, but once again the discussion over how to do it went round in circles.

Abel held up his phone. "Okay Warren, that'll do for now, until I've spoken to Terese. Will you ask Eric and Shawn to check with the other teams, make a list of any other problem Taverners?" After a quick call, the Taverneers went to see Abel's solicitor, more preferential treatment. Ferryl sat on Abel's knee for the short trip, illegal but it meant Rob, Kelis, and Jenny could cram into the car as well.

The meeting didn't last long, and didn't really solve the problem. Or rather it did, but Terese's solution was a glyph to cancel the permission for everyone but Abel. That was at least practical, but meant Abel had to give everyone else using that tree access to a different one. At least there weren't many at the moment, but arranging to meet them all would disrupt everyone else's arrangements and practice. "I'll do that in the future, only give access to one person per tree. Then I'll need a flipping list of which tree and which person, which is why everyone has the same tree."

"I remember your porkies, but that list might get too big. You could write them down and put them with the dragon head, the same as the other list?" A whoop of triumph echoed silently in Abel's head. "We could put a dryad in the tree, then it could stop Stu but let the rest take magic!" Zephyr connected spooky-phone to tell the other Taverneers her suggestion.

Ferryl reminded Abel that moving to a new tree was difficult, and painful, for adult dryads, and a seedling wouldn't have enough control. The idea still had promise, and Zephyr and Jenny came up with an alternative that led to Abel having a long talk to Chestnut. The dryad didn't even bargain, it wasn't allowed to teach Abel, or any human, dryad skills. Abel sat under a veil for half an hour while Chestnut thought about it, and came up with a solution. The dryad didn't bend the rules, because that wasn't allowed, and would only help out if the six oldest village dryads agreed.

Their first condition was that Zephyr flew free to touch the churchyard Yew, to prove she was a magical creature, unbound, and that Abel couldn't read her mind. After that, and a mere forty minutes of silent dryad argument or discussion, Chestnut gave Abel the second condition. Zephyr must swear on her true-name to never reveal what she had been taught. The price would be Zephyr revealing her true-name, though only Chestnut would know it. Abel hadn't even known she had one, but Zephyr didn't hesitate. After her lesson from Chestnut, the puff of wind pointed out that she doubted Abel, or any human, would even understand the instructions.

Over the next few days Zephyr spent a lot of time in Dead Wood, off her tether and out of sight of anyone but Dryad Sycamore, practicing.

*   *   *

A week later, seven days in which Stu had reputedly become more certain he couldn't be barred from tree magic, the Taverneers left the Range Rover in Stourton and drove off in the BMW SUV. It would have been a happy trip any other time, all six of them heading out together again, but most of them spent the journey worrying about how hard Stu would resist. Ferryl and Zephyr weren't worried, but knowing that neither had any qualms about burning and scattering the problem wasn't helping Abel's peace of mind.

The view when Jenny finally pulled up went well beyond any of their worst fears. Stu stood with his arms folded and chest out, with two other teenagers backing him up. A group to one side, at least a score, definitely seemed to be encouraging him, while a larger number to the left looked moments from throwing glyphs. Two lines of Taverners from Stourton, adepts, were keeping the two groups in place.

As agreed, Ferryl, Kelis, Jenny, and Rob got out of the car first. "Silence!" Abel had heard Ferryl magnify her voice before, but even so he jumped a little. Stu certainly lost his cool for a second, then recovered. "You will show some respect when the Master of Pendragon and Castle

House is present."

"Why? What will he do?" The voice came from the crowd encouraging Stu, anonymously.

"This?" Rob gestured and a dome of earth surged up, big enough to hold a person. That wasn't in the script, but neither were all these people.

Jenny had ditched the script as well. "Or this?" Grass crackled as it exploded into growth and braided together, weaving a similar dome.

"Or possibly this?" Wind swirled and strengthened, a brief cloud formed and then a tall, slim waterspout tore up a swathe of grass before collapsing and wetting the whole group. Kelis held out her hand again, ready for a repeat. Silence fell as Ferryl raised her hand. Inside the car Abel had really started to worry, this wasn't according to the script!

"Stay in here. Kelis wanted an option for if there was open opposition. Nobody will be hurt unless they are very stupid." Zephyr's voice didn't seem too worried about the possibility. "Stu and his group want a confrontation, so there is a new script. You must be a true sorcerer today, so that the newcomers can see exactly what they will face elsewhere." Abel listened with mounting unease as Zephyr outlined plan B, but he could already see that plan A had crashed and burned. Those idiots really believed they only needed tree magic to challenge real adepts. It didn't help that he had to agree with Kelis's reason for not telling him. Abel knew he would have refused, because he'd have never believed Taverners would act like this.

While Abel listened to Zephyr, Ferryl set his stage. "I have two options for you." A bush turned to ash in a burst of heat, but then a faint pink globe formed around the group of hecklers. Several called out, or maybe they did because no sound escaped. Ferryl turned to the rest, including a warier Stu. "They can hear, but they will not interrupt again. The fire option is for Stu, and anyone with him, who will not accept the judgement of the master."

"Yeah, burn him. He's a disgrace." The youth raised both hands and mouthed a silent apology as Kelis turned his way, hand raised.

Abel waited a moment, but that seemed to be enough so he opened the car door and got out. He really felt pleased about his habit of picking trees that weren't in public view. Not that it would have mattered, he realised as he stood up. Petra stood with her hand on a tree, one he'd given her access to when she drove him to give Stu his tree. She glanced upwards. Abel's eyes followed and he saw the faint shimmer of a veil covering everyone, including the cars and a couple of trees each way. He listened as Ferryl introduced herself as if to another sorcerer, then introduced Abel with his full titles. The girl with Stu already looked a little less certain. "Now I must ask, do you two stand with Stu and share in his punishment?"

"Punishment? There's been no trial? I thought we were here to negotiate?" The other teenager with Stu looked towards his support group, but of course no-one could answer him. Ferryl raised her hand but Abel interrupted.

"No, Ferryl. I will answer." Abel didn't want Ferryl to flatten the lad for a question, and he had to explain for the rest anyway. "There is no trial. Stu has broken the rules of the Tavern by refusing to fill bars in return for his extra magic. He can accept being shunned, or he will be banished. Now, right here. So do you stand with him?"

But it wasn't the youth who answered. The girl glanced nervously at the two domes and then towards the pink bubble before she spoke, and wasn't even slightly aggressive. "Stu said you can't stop him." The girl looked at Stu, still trying hard to look unimpressed, then once more at the pink bubble, the domes and torn grass, and the ashes of the bush. "It was bullshit, wasn't it? Sorry Stu but you're on your own. It was too bloody good to be true anyway." She slouched off to one side.

Una met her, and offered her a rucksack. "Your backlog of lead bars. When Abel has finished, you apologise to him, and he will decide if you are to be shunned. Either way you will take no more magic for yourself, and will not practice glyphs, until all the bars are full." The girl had barely opened her mouth to object when Una very obviously put a hand on her sword hilt. "I wouldn't even need magic. Once you've caught up you can leave the Tavern if you wish, but you will fill these bars first." Once she'd handed over the rucksack, Una turned towards Abel and gave him the tiny bow for a sorcerer. She must be learning, along with sword fighting.

"Well? Are you backing Stu or backing down? You had plenty to say before the car arrived?" At least Rachel had held off for a while. Now she sneered at the teenager still standing with Stu, which might have made up his mind.

"I'm with Stu. I've got a Tavern tattoo as well, so you can't stop me taking magic from the tree. Not this one, mine's near York. Stu will fill bars for me to get magic if I visit, and I'll do the same for him." He glared at Rachel who turned away with a satisfied smile, so she'd probably wound him up on purpose.

Abel didn't care because he'd realised just how far some were planning to go; they wanted to make their own rule-free network hiding behind the Tavern tattoos! He suddenly felt a lot better about what he'd come to do, and plan B. "When I've dealt with Stu, you will come with me to York, and will be rejected by your tree. If you accept your shunning, and keep the rules in future, you will be allowed to stay in the Tavern. No second chances."

Just for a moment Abel thought it would be banishment, but the lad hesitated and Stu didn't. He tried to get back to his own agenda. "What if he doesn't go? You haven't got police or anything else, and the Tavern is all about being kind. No picking fights to get payback from some arse, or nicking a few sweets with air glyphs."

"Ferryl, please hold Stu firmly but helpless, with wind. Kelis, his friend please." Neither had chance to do more than look startled, then wary as breezes wrapped around them. Both teenagers struggled briefly as the air thickened, until they were held almost immobile. Their wards didn't react, because the glyph didn't attack them, just created a shell to stop movement. Ferryl wasn't done. Stu bobbed up into the air and hung, suspended nearly a metre up. Moments later Kelis giggled, and Stu's ally joined him.

"Where do you want them, Master?" Ferryl sounded completely impersonal, her voice clear in the dead silence that had fallen over the spectators.

"Just there for now, please. Stu, while you remain a member, you or your friend will carry out any reasonable request from the Tavern. If you are being punished, the reasonable part doesn't count, you will still obey. When you are put down, I want you to approach your tree and draw magic. I want everyone here to see that I haven't set this up in advance, so they understand whose tree it is. Then I will bar you from it. After that you will drain your magic into metal and I will pronounce sentence." Abel meant the length of the shunning, which would definitely depend on how well Stu behaved in the next few minutes. "If you refuse your shunning you will be banished, and Ferryl will mark you. If you resist she will still drain you and mark you as banished, and cancel out your Taverner tattoo, but it may hurt you. Put him down please Ferryl."

Stu looked shaken, even after he'd been released, but still wasn't conceding. "You can't take my tattoo. It can't be done without leaving scars, and anyway my shrink has seen it."

"Silly boy, it's magic. Your shrink will see what he's allowed to." Ferryl pointed to the tree. "Take some magic. Fill up if you like, because you'll be giving it back straight afterwards." She watched with a little smile as Stu approached the tree, cautiously and then confidently.

Behind him his friend rotated in the air so he could see. "I need a string so I can tow him about." Kelis winked at Abel as the watching Taverners, the pro-Tavern group, laughed. She nodded towards them, and lowered her voice to just above a whisper. "Some of those were looking like a lynch mob, they needed a laugh." She walked up and down a little and the helpless teenager bobbed along after her. Rob and Jenny helped with the distraction by dismantling their domes. Rob made his earth dissipate in little ripples, while Jenny's grasses turned into a score of braids that coiled up before dying. Neither took long, but Stu still had a hand on the tree and Abel's heart sank.

Even while pronouncing sentence Abel kept hoping, but if he'd filled up Stu still meant to resist. Maybe the hints had been there at the beginning. Stu had been annoyed he couldn't throw glyphs straight away, and resented having to learn how. If he hadn't been the first in Bradford, and learned to fill lead blocks really easily, maybe someone would have realised how he really felt? The teenager certainly seemed to have recovered his confidence now he'd got plenty of magic. "I'm not being marked. I'll leave the Tavern." Stu shrugged nonchalantly, though the pose faltered when he looked at Ferryl. Abel assumed her face promised severe pain at least. "I'll fill up when I need to, or kill a couple of hedgerows, and my tattoo will get me accepted at any Tavern. They'll let me have magic from a lead bar if I say I'm just passing through." His confident look at his supporters expected cheers, but he'd forgotten the bubble. Even if Ferryl had let them be heard, none of them looked keen on joining the floating teenager.

First things first. Abel would deal with the leaving part in a minute. "Tree, you will not supply magic to anyone but me." This part had to look good, so even the adepts from Stourton wouldn't know how it was done. "Try to touch the tree, Stu."

He tried, pushing past the first discomfort, then Stu spun round with his mouth open in shock. "How?" He pulled up his sleeve and relaxed, glancing contemptuously at the two bars Shannon held out for him to fill. "Hah, fat chance I'm giving up my magic. I knew you couldn't take the tattoo, so I'll still get magic elsewhere."

"Tree, imprison him."

If he'd been fast enough, Stu might have got out from beneath the branches in time. As it was, by the time he'd tried to understand what Abel meant, heard the creak and rustle, and looked up, he was too late. The branches on the entire tree arched out from the centre and their tips drove into the ground. As the glyph poured through them the twigs and shoots thickened and others sprouted to fill the gaps. Stu peered out from his leafy prison, shocked and now definitely frightened. "Let me out! You can't keep me here." He tried to grab the branches, then recoiled and rubbed his hands along the phantom itching in his arms.

"Yes he can." Ferryl had turned to the group under her pink bubble, though the pro-Taverners were leaning forward to make sure they heard. "With all the magic in that tree Abel could cast a veil so nobody could see Stu, or a Seeming so the tree looked normal. The tree would keep it going until Stu's bones finally crumbled into dust. This tree, all the Tavern trees, belong to the Master of Pendragon and Castle House." She flung out her arm towards Stu. "You were told that sorcerers are too powerful, that you shouldn't annoy one, and now you can see why. The only person who can release Stu now is Abel." She turned round to face Abel. "This Taverner defied you. What is your sentence?"

"Three months shunning, and permanently barred from tree magic unless I decide otherwise. Stu, you have not earned magic by filling lead bars. Drain your stolen magic and give it back." Shannon looked cautious as she moved close enough to throw the lead bars through the branches to Stu. Not of the youth, she kept glancing from the tree to Abel and back. Abel waited until Stu threw back the bars and promised he'd let all the magic go. "Tree, release him." With a creaking and groaning the branches wrenched themselves free of the ground and moved back into their original places. The thickened twigs and shoots, and the extra growth, browned as magic drained away. Moments later they fell as a rain of dead leaves, dry, rotting twigs and shreds of wood. Apart from one long thick branch, the tree looked as if nothing had happened.

Stu dived out from under the tree, glanced back and then moved even further away. "Forget shunning, I told you I'm leaving and you can't stop that. The Tavern is voluntary."

For a little while, when he saw Stu's face after the branches imprisoned him and then when he'd accepted the lead bars, Abel had hoped it was all over. Now he didn't need an act to sound serious, he was. His problem was keeping it formal, and trying not to show how bloody frustrated he felt. "If you refuse a shunning you are banished. You will be marked as untrustworthy, so other Taverners will know."

"No chance, I told you. I'll leave but no marking. My ward will protect me from your girlfriend, and anyway she daren't take the tattoo. I told the truth. The psychiatrist saw it, and my mum and dad. It'll leave a scar so I'll tell them you did it. If you disappear me the police will investigate, and there's all these witnesses." Stu kept shouting reasons why it couldn't happen as Ferryl walked towards him and held out her hand. He began to back away, then realised he'd be under the tree. A quick glance each way showed Warren, Una, Justin and Rachel waiting, two each side, each with one hand raised and a glyph swirling.

"No pain if you don't resist, and no scar. If you fight, I don't care how much it hurts you because I've got my orders." Ferryl took a quick step to catch hold of Stu's arm with one hand, holding it tight when he belatedly tried to yank it free. She raised the other into the air.

Abel gestured. "Tree, supply magic for Ferryl Shayde." The one tree branch that hadn't returned to normal bent so she could grasp it. He ignored the startled glances from the adepts, and the gasps and a couple of startled yells from the spectators. For a few moments the tableau held, then Stu began to wriggle, then struggle and complain. Ferryl held on, implacable, as he hit her and yelled when his hand blistered, held on until he begged, then cried, then screamed. A good few of Abel's supporters and even some the adept Taverners looked worried now, though others obviously thought Stu deserved it. The five Taverneers knew the real reason for the pain, so none of them had any sympathy.

When Ferryl let go of the tree, then Stu, letting him slump to the ground, she told everyone. "Stu lied to a sorcerer. He claimed he'd given up his magic, but he'd kept most of it. I had to overcome that to affect his tattoo, because his ward resisted." She pointed down at the sobbing teenager. "No ward can resist the magic of a whole tree. I could have overcome it in seconds, but that would have burned off his arm. Those were not my instructions." Ferryl's voice had stayed calm, level and impersonal, but now her voice cracked out at full volume, startling everyone else. "STU! Stand up!" Abel, and probably everyone else, felt the pull as Ferryl used her command voice. Despite having a ward, Stu shot to his feet and stood still, gently swaying. "STU! You will not take magic from any tree, bush, metal, or anywhere but from the air. Do you understand?"

"Yes." Stu's voice came out toneless, with all hint of defiance quenched.

"STU! You will not tell anyone what happened here today, only that you stole from the Tavern and were banished. You will not enter any Tavern property, or speak to any Taverner. Do you understand?"

"Yes."

"STU! You will not speak to anyone about magic, or magic creatures, except to say they are all imagined. Do you understand?" Ferryl's voice hammered the instructions home, utterly relentless, and Stu nodded helplessly.

"Yes."

"You will apologise to the Master of Pendragon and Castle House, and then you will allow a Taverner to take you home. That is all."

Stu actually staggered at the last word and almost fell, then cowered away from the schoolgirl. His eyes, still wet from his tears, swivelled to find Abel and he fell to his knees and started apologising. Abel stopped him after a couple of minutes. He wasn't sure if Ferryl had set a time limit. "Show everyone your tattoo, Stu."

Abel had begun to worry, even though he knew why Stu had been hurt, and wondered if there'd be any scars. Now, as the youth pulled up his sleeve and turned, everyone could see that Ferryl hadn't touched his skin or the actual artwork of the Tavern shield. Even so nobody would mistake Stu for a Taverner, not with BANISHED across the lettering and a cross over the flower. The red marks actually glowed, but Ferryl explained before any of the puzzled looks turned to questions. "That is magical stain, so only those awakened to magic can see it. If any of you want to test that, I will give you a little something to take home. Show it to anyone you like, ask them to read it." Earth lifted and spun into a ball, then smeared into a disc between her hands and hardened to rock. Ferryl was having fun, even if her face looked severe and uncompromising. She used her finger to write MAGIC on one side in glowing red letters, then offered the stone disc to the ones who'd come to support Stu. A click of her fingers and the bubble popped, but nobody wanted to shout or even speak. In the end one of the other group took Ferryl's demo, to use as a mouse mat for a laugh.

"All done now, Zephyr. Time to come home."

"Good, it is damp down here with the worms. Nobody interesting to talk to, and if I had eyes I might be frightened." Zephyr sounded happy, despite spending the whole meeting underground.

* * *

A week ago, while the Taverneers were trying to work out how to bar Stu in the most spectacular way possible, she'd reminded them Celtchar's defences considered her a part of Abel. Only when on a tether, but that meant she might be able to act as his hand on a tree. A quick test proved it was true. During the next week, the biggest job for Zephyr had been learning how to instruct a tree to act like that. It had taken her many hours of relentless practice to perfect the dryad method, to encourage a tree to change rather than using force. Sheer magic would have managed something similar, but the tree would have been splintered and twisted and wouldn't have been anything like as impressive.

Even the original plan called for introductions and some talking when Abel first arrived, to give Zephyr time to sneak down Abel's trouser leg and burrow under the ground. She'd searched for a good thick root, and spread herself round it to get a good contact, then waited. Abel couldn't hear her thoughts through the tether, but Zephyr could hear Abel and the tree glyph responded to her instructions. From then on, she moved the tree as told and turned the magical access off for Stu, then back on for

357

Ferryl to use. Zephyr didn't even have to draw magic from Abel, she had a whole tree full to play with.

*   *   *

At least the whole mysterious powerful sorcerer thing seemed to have worked. The belligerent group had lost their attitude, and with luck they'd either leave the Tavern without any fuss or stick by the rules. Either way nobody there today would be relying on either their ward, or a Tavern shield, to protect them from a sorceress. That had been a deliberate lesson, a survivable demonstration of real sorcerer power before one of the trainees ended up as ashes. The supporters, those who came to see Abel deal with Stu, were well satisfied by the result and absolutely loved the show.

When Kelis got round to him, the floating teenager promised he'd stick by the rules in future, and serve his shunning. Kelis kept him in the air until he'd agreed, then set him down nice and gentle. She warned him, any more problems and he might become a permanent ornament outside her house, covered by a Seeming of a big red balloon. He didn't get a chance to change his mind. According to the Taverneers, Abel had to leave now, to let the adepts sort out the transport and answer questions.

That meant Abel went to York, followed by a car driven by a very nervous young man who didn't go near his tree. This lad didn't even want to check he'd been barred. He accepted two months shunning, emptied his magic into lead bars, promised to be good and went home.

Abel would have to arrange new access for those using the York tree, probably the same way he'd done it in Dumfries. The week had been enough for Terese to arrange for five trees to be planted on Abel's land, but not given the Celtchar protection glyph. After some serious discussion Petra was given five glyphs, versions of the Pendragon permission. While everyone else had been waiting for Abel, she'd cast one onto each of the new trees. After the demonstration, Ferryl had met each of the five locals who used to fill lead bars from Stu's tree, and drawn one glyph on each.

On the way home, the other Taverneers agreed that despite Stu's defiance, the whole day had gone better than expected. A triumphant Zephyr accepted her due praise, although she agreed that Ferryl's command had also played a vital part. A ward should stop a command, but Ferryl confessed to cheating to get around that. Since Stu resisted, she kept pushing gently against his personal ward until he had hardly any magic left. The gentle part meant that despite the pain she hadn't physically harmed him. The shouting, and his name at the start of each command, hammered the words through the remnants of Stu's protection. As she'd said about sorcerers being invulnerable in their forest, there's always an exception.

Despite some serious questioning, Ferryl refused to give any more examples, except for admitting she couldn't stop a hell-hound. Any defence she'd known must be on one of her missing wits, the shards of bone containing her years of accumulated magical knowledge. With luck, in time, she'd find out how to deal with one.

Trial by Sorcerer

To Abel's surprise, some of the sorcerers he met after the banishment had heard about Stu. Some thought he'd been too soft, some found the solution funny, but they all seemed reassured that Abel had control. Una let Abel know, eventually, that the Taverners had deliberately informed a few apprentices, just to prove the Tavern had some discipline. The idea was to encourage any sorceress who had a complaint to talk to Abel, rather than revert to the ashes method.

Generally, the Taverners were impressed, and triumphant because 'their' sorcerer had produced a real magic show, though the adepts also wanted to know how Abel had done it. Tree power left a lasting impression. Una wondered just how bright her sword would glow if she had her hand on a tree, because Petra's super-veil had really impressed her. Petra wanted to make a tree dance, but Abel told her absolutely honestly he couldn't tell her how. When several people asked her, Jenny admitted she didn't have the first idea how to make plants act like that. Privately, she confessed to really wanting to find out.

The way he'd controlled the tree also helped Abel when meeting sorcerers, though he never realised until Daorban mentioned she'd heard about the incident. The Taverners who saw the banishment, especially the new ones, were happy to talk about it to anyone who asked them. After some cross-checking, quite a few sorceresses were reassessing Abel's magical expertise. Daorban confessed that she didn't have that amount of control of plants, flexibility without any damage, and didn't know of anyone who had.

Abel just hoped he never had to live up to his new reputation, unless Zephyr and Ferryl were there to back him up.

* * *

The poser part of sorcerer meetings worked even better from early August. On the ninth, Abel's mum asked him to come and look at the repaired BMW, to see if he approved of her colour choices. When he arrived at the office his mum told him it was waiting at the gym, which seemed odd. As the Range Rover pulled up, and he got out, Abel already approved. His mum had gone for a two-tone blue, not too dark so it wasn't even close to black. A large group of Taverners were admiring the car, but parted to let Abel have a look, laughing and making jokes about family influence.

Abel had thought his friends were out visiting elsewhere, but Kelis and Rob were back early. Jenny had come outside to join in. She spent a lot of her time in the small office Eric had now built for her in the gym, rather than work from her dad's home office. She preferred privacy while fielding questions about Bonny's Tavern, helping ordinary players set up a local Tavern, or dealing with yet another new potential magical recruit.

"Ginny is coming." Zephyr sounded excited, which seemed strange until Abel turned towards the car park entrance. As he stood there, mouth open in shock, the Taverners started cheering.

A two-tone blue Bentley swept into the car park and pulled up, and Ginny got out. "Your car's fixed, boss. Do you want a spin in it?" Abel looked from her to his mum, still speechless. From the look of Kelis's and Rob's huge grins, Jenny's giggles, and all the other laughter, everyone else had known.

His mum came forward and hugged him. "The insurance company phoned, asking if you wanted the same armoured options on the Bentley as the original. I asked what Bentley, then if they could email the list. Armourcorp sent a really polite young man with a thick brochure." Her smile wavered a little. "I want to talk to you about why the last owner needed armour, but if he did, so do you. I also looked in the insurance files after they called. They paid out a lot of very expensive medical bills at the same time as you had that allegedly minor accident. I added a few extra extras because his armour obviously didn't work well enough, and put the Tavern shield on the personalised bits."

"We should have taken the money. That thing must be worth a fortune." Several fortunes, Abel felt sure.

"It is. Once I saw the armour plating options I tried to work it out, and with all the other extras and adaptations that thing is worth half a million quid. I thought you'd probably take the cash, but for some obscure reason that isn't an option. Bertram looked into it and the vehicle must be replaced if it is destroyed, something to do with a gryphon. You could sell it?" A big smirk crossed her face. "If you can find someone who wants an armoured Bentley with Tavern signs all over it, and the back seats narrower and re-arranged to seat four? I knew you'd want to take Jenny, Kelis, Rob and Ferryl with you sometimes." She gave him a quick hug. "Since it's a new car I was asked what registration you wanted. They meant personalised numbers. I said ABC 1 for a laugh, but the man said that wasn't a problem. Now you're stuck with it, Abel Bernard Conroy."

"In that case you'd better take the keys to the BMW, just so the family cars match." Ignoring her protests, Abel allowed his friends to push him into the Bentley. Since it wasn't made to take everyone who wanted a ride, there were soon youngsters stood on the extending boarding steps and sat on the bonnet. Not that the extra people made any difference to the Bentley as it drove slowly around the industrial estate. According to Ginny it drove like a racing car, or a racing tank. Eventually Abel went home in his mum's car as usual, though this time she agreed to keeping a set of keys for the new BMW. Only as a company car, she'd still leave it Stourton overnight for the Taverners to use, but Abel settled for that. His mum would get used to the idea a bit at a time.

Despite feeling very conspicuous, Abel enjoyed his first trip in his new wheels. He went to Stoke to take a delighted Daorban for a drive. She insisted they drove through Mallet's domain, with the windows down to make sure his apprentices saw both the car and her. According to her, Mallet had been very subdued, and rumours abounded that he'd lost two senior apprentices in a mysterious fight.

Abel also made a point of taking Terese Green for a ride in the car. His solicitor didn't seem surprised it had been insured, though she laughed about the premiums going down. The insurers thought the Master of Castle House was less likely to be attacked than Pendragon.

The assessors meant magical attack because with the armour plating, including concealed rams front and back, no ordinary car accident would have any effect on the Bentley. Ferryl and Zephyr added to the protection. The pair of them spun a skein of glyphs into something resembling an art form, using every protection glyph they'd lifted from anywhere else, what Ferryl could remember, and any glyphs from the practice books that could be adapted for protection. Once Abel melted enough lead to fill the big empty box beneath the boot, and spent half a day filling it with magic from trees, it would take another platycroc to make a serious magical dent in the car or passengers.

Now all Abel had to do was avoid platycrocs.

*   *   *

The Bentley meant more sorcerers took Abel seriously, but the list of appointments still grew faster than he could meet them. The protection in the car reassured him when he received a different sort of invitation, to a sorcerer trial. The sorcerer in question would conduct the trial, rather than be the subject of it, but offered Abel a chance to speak for the defendant. A teenager had been carrying out public demonstrations of magic on street corners in Oxford. Under the Accord that was a capital crime, but the youth had claimed the protection of the Tavern. The local ruling sorcerer, and others nearby, were intrigued, and offered Abel a chance to explain. They'd even reserved rooms for Abel and his party.

Planning went out of the window, because the sorcerer, Uror, would hold the trial the following day whether Abel attended or not. A quick search on the internet showed that the venue, the Macdonald Randolph Hotel in the middle of Oxford, wouldn't be a trap. Located opposite the Ashmolean Museum, just metres from the University of Oxford Colleges and close to the famous riverside and boatsheds, any firefight would be very public. Abel replied, promising he would be there in the morning but declining the offer of overnight accommodation. None of the five fancied spending the night surrounded by strange sorcerers and their bodyguards.

The notation 'Dress Formal' caused some consternation because neither Ferryl nor Ginny knew what it meant. Eventually Kelis made a quick phone call to Siobhan, Daorban's senior apprentice. Formal just meant bring four senior apprentices, but Abel should dress well, something better than jeans or sweatshirts. Kelis said Siobhan laughed when she advised suits rather than full Taverner costumes, though cloaks wouldn't look out of place. All of them should wear an obvious weapon, something more dangerous than the batons. The other sorceresses would wear anything from robes to modern suits, with at least a dagger though most preferred a sword. Jenny offered to stand down if Ginny would be more help, but the apprentice had never heard of a trial. That suited Abel; he preferred having his friends watching his back and offering advice.

Zephyr would keep Ginny up to date on what happened through the tether, to stop the other Taverners worrying.

After using the internet to show his mum the hotel, Abel had to promise to take her there sometime because she really fancied the spa. He didn't tell her he'd be going to a trial, just a meeting of security firms to sort out what areas they'd be operating in. From the look she knew there must be more to it. So far she kept to the Stan system, don't push too hard because she might not like the answer.

The trip down didn't take long using motorways, though Jenny wasn't comfortable steering the big vehicle through the Oxford traffic. She'd worried about parking, in case she scraped another sorcerer's car, but the hotel had valet parking. A footman assured Jenny that the woman would be able to drive the Bentley, if someone opened the door to allow her access, because she had no trace of magical ability. Since Zephyr assured Abel that the car in front had been wreathed in magic, and a hotel driver had just taken it away, he agreed. If Uror's guarantee of safe conduct wasn't kept, losing the car would be the least of his worries. As he walked up the steps Abel noticed several people staring at his party, but at least as many were looking at the Bentley. That car really must have been well-known. A footman showed Abel and his friends into what must be the dining room, full of small tables though they weren't set for a meal.

Most of the tables were occupied by what must be sorcerers and sorceresses with their apprentices, at least a hundred and the numbers were still growing. Some really did come in long, flowing robes, the majority wearing various types of historical clothing, almost all of them with a cloak, even some of those in modern suits. Their apprentices were sometimes dressed in matched outfits similar to their sorcerer, while others were dressed plainly, perhaps to emphasise their master's garb. Weapons ranged from variously sized and decorated staffs to a variety of edged weapons from dagger through swords, including a short-shafted spear-come scythe. As they'd been told, swords were popular, though most of the weapons had gems or gold embedded in them, so were presumably enhanced.

Abel's weapons, the set from the Pendragon room, had some decoration even if the glyphs wouldn't activate for some reason. The rest of Abel's party wore unadorned swords and knives, their Tavern glyph concealed under a Seeming. A frantic phone call had led to Justin loaning his longknife to Jenny, while Rob had the sword and dagger found in Valdar's house. Kelis thought her misericord dagger would be enough. Ferryl declined the offer of Una's sword; she reckoned the only person able to use the thing should keep it. She still wore a sword, because half a dozen Taverners had now managed to buy or beg one and were happy to loan them. Every one of the five hoped they wouldn't need to use the weapons, or they'd be dead ducks.

Enough sorcerers wore modern suits to let Abel fit in, though he'd be conspicuous anyway. His party were seated at what would be the front of the proceedings, going by how everyone had arranged their chairs. A waitress offered a selection of drinks, none alcoholic, and light snacks. Since all the rest would be using tethers, Zephyr connected Abel's party while they surreptitiously inspected the others.

"Why are there so many?" Kelis kept her voice down, but sorceresses could probably hear her.

"I've no idea. They can't all be from Oxford, unless there are a lot because of the Universities." Abel nodded back to a woman dressed in exactly what Ferryl had suggested a bloody-handed sorceress should wear, red and black. She smiled before looking Kelis up and down and nodding politely. That seemed to be the seated equivalent of a bow. Kelis's smartest clothes were her Windcatcher dress and cloak, but not in character because she had her hair down and very little makeup. For a moment Abel wondered if the woman might be Pandora, but she seemed too friendly. Even so, one of her apprentices should be called Arrogance. Several other people caught Abel's eye and nodded slightly, and a few smiled, though others avoided his eye or frowned. Despite most of the guests taking a good look, and some speaking to each other, none of them actually spoke to the Taverneers.

Rob leant forward, speaking quietly and urgently. "Mallet is here! I thought this was a local trial? How come Daorban hasn't been invited?"

"Zephyr, use the link. Ask Ginny to phone Daorban and ask." While Zephyr told the rest what she'd done, Abel answered aloud for all the listeners. "I've no idea. Maybe he wants a return match with Kelis." The flicker of a smile, from a bearded old man dressed in velvet, might mean that story had spread. Abel couldn't see any other sorcerer from Stoke, but now he recognised Aesop from Bolton, several others he'd made deals with, and a couple who'd refused point blank. "Zephyr, tell the others, it's not just a trial. It's some sort of setup to do with the Tavern."

Ferryl's hand agreed. "Though not a trap. The way some of these are glaring at each other, if a fight starts it will be a riot." She had been inspecting the room, openly in her role as a bodyguard. "We have friends, but not the sort who can say so. At least three of Daorban's conspirators are here. You wouldn't realise but their apprentices talked to your bodyguards." Before Abel could react she squeezed his hand. "Calm down. If you knew, and the Council ever agreed to investigate you using a truth glyph, they'd all die."

Abel didn't have chance to try and guess, because the doors opened and a man dressed in something close to a Beefeater's uniform introduced Uror. The sorcerer himself, a big thirtyish man with a neat pointed beard, wore a breastplate and what must be military uniform based on the same look. That included a sword and a red cloak. Abel could see where Ferryl got her ideas about sorceress dress; over a third of those present wore red cloaks.

The young man walking between two Beefeater-style apprentices might already be tethered. Skinny and unkempt, he walked jerkily, as if someone else operated his arms and legs. Abel saw his eyes jerk around from face to face, so it wasn't total mind control. Uror and his entourage took the vacant table, while the accused stood against the wall. Uror's bodyguard announced himself, and his master, then indicated every table in turn. The introductions took up most of the next hour. Abel hoped Zephyr could remember who everyone was because he lost track, though he noticed they were from all over the UK. Ferryl's turn came last but she gave them the full bit.

"Very informative, Ferryl Shayde, but be warned that many of these bodyguards would be classed as sorcerers or sorceresses in their own right. You may not be the strongest here." Uror wasn't challenging, keeping his voice bland with just a hint of condescension. "Despite some investigation, nobody here can find any evidence of a senior sorceress leaving Germany recently. We recognise you are strong, but not the extent of your skill."

"But I never told anyone I left recently, just that I came from there.

Perhaps you should look back through the list of those who have disappeared in previous centuries." Ferryl kept her voice bland as well. "If there is a challenge, please state who I will be fighting, and I will provide all the proof the rest of you need."

"It's more that some have been wondering. One in particular, but he apparently turned down an opportunity to challenge you directly." The flick of his eyes and just a trace of malice identified Mallet. "Or your trainee. In the interests of clarity, I should explain that your master, Abel, has been introduced last because of his youth and lack of apprentices. It is no reflection on the status of the Master of Castle House." Uror turned just a little to look directly at Abel. "The strength of the senior apprentice is the usual ranking method in meetings. Your bodyguard does not even say you employ her, and your use of untethered trainees means you are technically unaccompanied. The reality might lead to a re-assessment of our methods."

Someone called out. "Not a chance. If he won't tether an apprentice, he can wait until last."

"Being last doesn't bother me at all. It gives me a chance to see who everyone else is, and I'm sure Ferryl will take note of the order you rank the apprentices." Abel pointed at the youth, standing stock still though his eyes were still jerking from one face to another. "Nobody introduced the accused."

"He is not significant. You are of much more interest, and the reason there is a trial. It has become clear there simply isn't time for you to meet everyone who sent an invitation. Since we rarely come across something that threatens to alter our accepted ways, I invited senior sorcerers or sorceresses from twenty towns and cities, and several other interested parties, to discuss the matter." An undercurrent of muttering sounded, as if a good few of them weren't happy for one reason or another. "I understand you have made agreements with some, so this is your opportunity to reach a wider audience." He clapped his hands together, turning toward the youth. "Though as you say, we have a trial to deal with first."

"How does a trial work? Sorry, but as most of you must know, my magical education is a bit hit and miss. Is there a jury?" Abel jerked his head round at the wave of laughter from the rest of the room.

"High and Low Justice means I decide, and under normal circumstances this reprobate would be fertilising the roses by now. His claim of protection from this Tavern is ridiculous, because you have no jurisdiction in my demesne. He is still alive because this seemed a good way to get you here to answer questions. The trial is over, the sentence is death and there is no appeal." The mild, almost affable delivery disappeared as Uror leant forward to fix Abel with a glare. "Unless you think I don't have the right to pronounce sentence?"

"No. That is exactly how I deal with Taverners who clearly break our rules." Abel held Uror's eyes, wondering how to phrase the next part, but Ferryl's mental voice cut into his thoughts.

"Careful, you must not challenge him. This is a trap, but not a physical one. They want to cross-examine you. The accused was already condemned."

"Can they make me answer questions, with that truth glyph?

"No, but leaving could be considered a retreat, a sign of weakness." From her 'voice' Ferryl didn't like that idea. "Everyone attending will be offended, and those who object to the Tavern will push for confrontation or outright rejection."

"How about if I refuse unless they release the youth?" Abel thought that the lad looked terrified enough. If he survived today he'd keep his mouth shut in future.

"Uror won't go for that. He'll insist on punishment and probably on carrying out his sentence. Include his fate in any discussion?" Ferryl didn't sound too sure, but that was enough for Abel.

Uror waited patiently, despite the silence, and Abel realised that sorcerers were used to others having silent conversations down the tethers. He forced a little smile onto his lips. "I understand the Accord. If you ask around, I have never claimed any rights in any demesne but my own. Though if I have no jurisdiction here, I'm not needed for the trial." Abel looked around the room, noting how many were definitely unhappy at that idea. "That seems unfair, considering how far some have travelled. I came here for a trial, you want to discuss the Tavern, so why don't we combine the two." Abel's smile widened just a little. "A minor concession on each side."

Uror ignored the muttering from elsewhere in the room. "What sort of concession?"

"You will lift this young man's death sentence and discuss alternatives, during which I will answer questions about the magical version of Bonny's Tavern." Abel kept his voice calm, hoping Uror didn't realise how much he wanted to keep the lad alive. "What is his name?"

The sorcerer glanced dismissively at the youth, who now had his eyes fixed on Abel. "I don't know, and until I agree it is irrelevant. Are you disputing my right to kill him for a blatant act of public magic?"

"Not at all, but I dispute your right to bring me here under false pretences so you can satisfy your curiosity." This time Abel couldn't raise a smile, he was stifling a look of horror as he realised Uror hadn't bothered to ask a name.

"He's got a point, Uror, it wasn't exactly good manners." The sorceress in black and red who had nodded at Abel, smiled at him this time. "The Master of Castle House may be a child, but his titles demand some respect. You should definitely be polite to the Pendragon name, since the dragon seems to have regained some of its bite."

"Pandora, always so polite, so careful about upsetting others." From Uror's sarcastic tone, and the laughter from others in the room, Pandora must be far from polite. The sarcasm vanished as he turned to Abel. "Though she has a point. My apologies, Master of Castle House. Master of Pendragon as well, an older title that may no longer be irrelevant now the two have combined. I have been careless of my manners, so I concede some small redress is in order. The youth can live, stunted or tethered to a junior apprentice. I'll decide after I test him."

Abel didn't answer for a moment, shocked to find out this really was Pandora because he hadn't heard her name announced. The reality was confusing. She seemed both sociable and polite, though her dress and cloak really did shriek K'ress Bloodclaw to any Taverner. The sorceress waggled her fingers in a little wave to Kelis, and Abel suddenly realised that Kelis's reply would start a fight. "Smile, tiny polite nods, don't scowl and Kelis, do not speak! She's done absolutely nothing here to warrant insults, and we don't want a fight."

Ferryl touched Abel's hand, under the table. "Perhaps this is how sorceresses act in a group, to stop fights breaking out, or it may be a trap after all."

Abel passed that on through Zephyr, then turned back to Uror. The lightning fast mental communications had only been a brief pause to everyone else. "I accept the apology, and if that is your sentence the trial is over so we are done." He started to get up. "Though my offer is still open?" He paused, without actually getting up though Ferryl, Rob, Jenny and Kelis stood. "You still decide the sentence, but I trust you to take some note of whatever I say."

An anonymous voice called out from behind Abel. "Go on, it'll be a novelty if nothing else."

"I'll take the lad." Chatter died back as this sorcerer continued. "If he's already managed that leaf fluttering, he's mastered casting glyphs. Teaching new apprentices is usually unprofitable, but after that meditation nonsense he'll be able to fill hexes from day one." The background muttering rose as other sorcerers discussed that idea.

"It seems my guests really do have something to discuss, Master of Castle House. We have a deal. After all, as has just been pointed out, he is already through his initial training so killing him would be a waste." Uror turned to the lad. "You may speak to answer my direct questions. No pleading, no additional information. Do you understand?"

"Yes." Abel recognised the youth's monotone, and the mental tug as the sorcerer spoke. Uror had him controlled through the command voice.

"Your name."

"Steven Clarence Horsely." The lad's eyes were flicking from Abel to Uror, but his voice remained a monotone as Uror extracted the relevant details. Steven had seen creatures since he was fourteen, three years ago. He'd failed his exams, and couldn't keep a job because he got drunk and smoked pot to drive away the visions. Once Steven saw the game advertised, and recognised the pictures, he contacted the manufacturers. The Tavern had called him back on his stolen phone to explain how to do the leaf thing. Once he could do it, and found it worked on things like phones and coins, Steven thought he could earn money by doing tricks. Yes the Tavern lady told him he shouldn't tell anyone, or show them magic. But he was broke, and out of pot and beer.

Abel agreed that was a clear breaking of the Accord, but a minor one. A fine should be enough. A fine paid in hex-filling, though Uror would have to feed and clothe Steven or he wouldn't survive. Uror retorted that he may as well tether him as a real apprentice, and give him a new name. That way the tether would break him of any addiction, by refusing to let him indulge. By now the rest were joining in. The discussion broadened to the Tavern country-wide, and the potential apprentices now contacting Abel.

Various sorcerers were pleased to find another way to round up the strays, though the reasons varied. Learning that some sorcerers carried out a sweep every few years to thin down the numbers came as a shock. They sorted out the strongest, then killed the rest, but resented the time it took and the cost of hushing up mass disappearances. Others mazzled anyone talking about creatures until they could barely speak. Many of them complained about the wasted time or the cost of dealing with the problem, whereas Abel seemed to be offering a free alternative. Most still wanted the pick of the catch, without the apprentice getting a choice, but were willing to consider alternatives. Abel offered them an incentive, a big one considering the comments about losing money during initial training. The Tavern would teach any volunteer apprentice how to fill a hex before their tethering.

A group headed by Mallet were totally against the idea, offering to carry out the sweeps and sell any decent potential apprentices. A similar number were quietly supportive, claiming that voluntary apprentices worked best. Eventually a majority accepted that a certain number of the new magic users would want power and wealth without the constraints the Tavern put on its members. Those would accept tethers, knowing that in seventy-five years they would be released to do as they pleased. Free initial training seemed to be winning over a good number of them; sorcerers really were stingy.

"What happens if an established Taverner decides they want to leave, accept a tether and stop following your rules?" From the look, and several earlier comments, this sorcerer knew all about the Tavern. He seemed supportive, so Abel wondered if this was a deliberate feed. If it was, he could definitely use it.

"They lose their access to additional magic and training from the

Tavern, and their Tavern mark, and will no longer be welcome in our premises. That's it." Abel felt sure he knew what the man wanted, because the sorcerers were currently discussing whether to wait until a discovered Taverner could fill a hex or choose the strongest immediately. "The ex-Taverner will be stronger than apprentices the same age, better trained."

"They'll want to negotiate access to trees. Once we taste magic fresh from the bark, nobody really wants to give it up." Jenny's trademark innocent smile and giggle brought answering smiles from a good few sorcerers.

"I do that sometimes, allow mine to fill up from a tree as a special reward." This sorceress's gaze swept around the room. "This discussion needs to be more private."

Several didn't seem to see why, but others agreed and so did Uror. "Agreed. Please muffle your apprentices." All around the room apprentices placed their hands flat on the table in front of them, their faces stilled, and they closed their eyes. Uror looked over Abel's table. "That is a little difficult. Right now the apprentices can see nothing, say nothing, and hear nothing, a command sometimes called the three monkeys. We don't want apprentices knowing what we talk about next, but your trainees can't be muffled."

"But these trainees are also my friends, and know everything that I do."

"It is about tree magic. Or maybe how fast Taverners train."

As Zephyr finished, Ferryl's 'voice' sounded in Abel's mind. "They are worried their apprentices will learn about the Taverners, about how fast they learn. If a Taverner elsewhere tells them, it can be passed off as boasting."

Abel asked which. "Is it the speed of training that has to be kept secret, or the Taverners' access to additional magic?"

"Both are ridiculous, and should be stopped." This old-looking, bearded sorcerer in robes, carrying a staff, looked disgusted. "Apprentices should be kept in check. Personally I'd go back to the days where we killed most of them after seventy years, rather than releasing them to become potential threats. Young sorcerers have no restraint." Before Abel could react at least half the room burst into laughter.

"I'm surprised you didn't bring along a goblin for the fireworks."

"Or a hell-hound and a chimera for a prize fight."

"A chimera? He'd bring a Cheshire cat."

"Where are the dancers? Couldn't you get any of the Eleven drunk enough?"

"He won't even pay for a potted dryad, stoned on honey."

From the way the rash of comments were made anonymously, and the look on the old sorcerer's face, Abel assumed he must be too strong to upset face to face. Uror obviously didn't want the sorcerer annoyed, because he quickly brought the subject back to the speed of training and tree magic. Abel explained, with his friends helping, though they downplayed the speed of progress. Once the sorcerers understood that Taverners progressed as fast as they were capable of, Abel sensed a small shift in the mood. From the questions and calculating looks, some Taverners would be receiving tempting offers once they were truly adept with fire. The calculation would be to get them before learning to shield, to avoid the Accord rules on seniors. Already knowing the basics of self-healing would be a bonus, making the new apprentices more durable.

Eventually the apprentices were released to rejoin the discussion. Some were definitely curious while the looks from others, after a few minutes, might mean their sorcerers brought them up to date. Unfortunately a small number of sorcerers, led by Mallet, were still absolutely adamant the whole scheme wouldn't work. Mallet himself poured cold water on the idea, or ridiculed the Tavern, at every chance. Although not as unpleasant about it, the old sorcerer with the staff supported Mallet's group. Unfortunately, his opinion seemed to carry a good deal of weight with older sorcerers.

The subject came back to Steven, still stood like a slightly trembling statue. Uror tried for Abel training him up, then handing him back to pay his fine, but Abel wanted that to be voluntary. A huge debate started up, on whether Steven would ever volunteer. Nobody had tried that idea, training someone before tethering. Someone suggested a fixed term of a few years on the tether, then releasing Steven and giving him the option of being re-tethered. Uror really considered that idea, because Steven could pay his way on the tether, filling hexes rather than training. While Uror debated whether he could make re-tethering an attractive proposition, because Steven might be strong enough to keep, several of those present started a discussion on the cost of removing tethers.

"No cost for some. They even take the tethers off other sorcerer's apprentices. Watch out for these Taverners. Once they're in your domain they'll steal your best prospects and then your apprentices." Mallet stood up and pointed at Abel. "He stole forty from me."

Kelis and Mallet had exchanged several glares, especially when he tried to dismiss the Tavern as incompetent amateurs. Now Kelis stood, pulled herself up to her not inconsiderable height, and produced her very best sneer. "From what I heard, a sorcerer thought he'd tethered them, but he was so incompetent they all wandered off down the street." A ripple of laughter went round the room and Mallet flushed scarlet.

"Liar! You and that so-called master stole them, removed the tethers. Forty of them. Without a trace!" As Kelis stood there shaking her head pityingly, Mallet finished with a triumphant "I challenge you!"

Ferryl shot to her feet. "Accepted. Kelis is a trainee, so I will fight as part of her lessons." She turned to Kelis, totally serious. "Pay close attention. This may not last long."

Uror looked from one to the other. "Mallet, I am not particularly pleased about this. You were invited as the senior sorcerer in Stoke, not to use it as an opportunity to settle a private grievance." A little smile touched his lips. "Though since you challenged an independent trainee, and a bodyguard who isn't covered by the agreement, I must allow it. This will be an excellent opportunity to assess Ferryl Shayde as a bodyguard." Uror's smile strengthened a little, with just a hint of mocking. "Considering the strength of your apprentices, and the apparent strength of Ferryl Shayde, your champion might not be much of a test. Unless you will be fighting personally?"

"No chance, and it will be a better test than you think. One that will definitely kill that alleged bodyguard. I have hired a new bodyguard for this visit, only hired so he wasn't announced." Mallet turned and pointed dramatically towards the doors. "My bodyguard is Dupont."

Abel only knew one Dupont who fought, and only because he'd been in the history books and a film. He asked Ferryl through Zephyr. "The real Pierre-Antoine, Dupont the duellist? He'd be two hundred and fifty years old now." Abel realised that wasn't impossible if he'd been magically aware. "He was a really good swordsman."

"I've never heard of him."

Mallet still looked triumphant, until Abel shrugged and said, "Who?" As Mallet stared in disbelief, then malicious glee, several others gave Abel the bad news. Dupont wasn't the real French duellist, but he'd been apprenticed to a fan. This Dupont had trained with blade and pistol until he would have probably slaughtered the original, even without using his considerable magical skills. Ferryl listened without any expression until the tumult died down.

Uror eventually called for silence and turned to Ferryl. He looked deadly serious now. "My apologies, Sorceress Ferryl Shayde. This meeting was not meant to be for the settling of old grievances. I will expect reparations from Mallet, before he leaves. Though now the challenge has been issued and accepted, we have a duelling room below the hotel. You are allowed to choose the weapons and options."

"What does that mean exactly? I don't duel, I kill my opponents." Ferryl sneered at Mallet. "I've never had to hide behind rules."

"To be honest, I sometimes think the rules are to make the fight more interesting for the spectators. They also cut down on the number of dead sorcerers, but that might not be as important as being able to see the blood. The rules deter a strong magic user, for instance, from challenging a good sword fighter, since the challenged will choose minimum magic, no healing and blades." Uror glanced at Mallet, still frowning. "Dupont's master had him trained as a duellist, and he continued fighting after being released, so he has no particular weaknesses."

"He has the same weakness as everyone else, he can die. Please explain my options." Ferryl still sounded dismissive about Dupont, though polite and respectful to Uror.

He bowed to her, more than the tiny polite one. "My apologies, I rarely have to give the detail. As the challenged, you have the choice of options. Shields can be dispensed with, or kept within the skin, outside clothing or full globes. Healing can be restricted or forbidden during the contest. The variety of glyphs can be restricted, though both contestants use their full magical strength in whatever way is allowed. There are a wide variety of blades on offer, or black powder pistols, because personal weapons are not permitted. Any combination is allowed although blades or pistols must be involved to some extent. The spectators expect blood." He glanced down at her plain sword, then his eyes met Ferryl's. "Duels are to the death."

"What is this Dupont supposed to be best with?" Ferryl's expression never flickered, remaining casual, aloof, barely interested even when Abel begged her, through spooky-phone, to stop posing before it killed her.

"I believe he prefers swords, when he has the choice. He is rarely challenged so I can't be sure." Uror had hardly finished before several sorcerers confirmed swords. "There are a variety of weapons in the duelling chamber, matched to give no advantage. They are not enhanced, though adding glyphs is an option."

"Dupont can choose which swords we use. We will be allowed one glyph on the weapon, personally applied and covered with a Seeming. We will fight five minutes with swords, and under-skin shields as strong as we can manage, which should give your spectators their blood. Then if both can still fight, we will put up standard sized globe shields and take alternating strikes at the other until the duel is over. During the second period we will be allowed to move, but not to use our weapon to parry. No healing until one of us is defeated. If one is unable to take their strike, their opponent will continue. I will allow Dupont the first strike in the second part." Abel still tried to talk Ferryl out of it, through spooky-phone though he could have shouted out loud for all the good it did.

The room erupted, while the man standing in the doorway looked momentarily non-plussed before recovering. He bowed slowly, from the waist. "I accept the conditions." Dupont stood a little shorter than Kelis but not much, and definitely taller than Ferryl. He had plenty of muscle, but the overall effect was of an athlete, an impression confirmed by the way he moved as he walked towards Ferryl. He still looked a little puzzled. "Have we met before?"

"Never. I do not meet assassins twice." Ferryl still had that calm expression, but her words cut through the babble, stilling it.

She'd definitely upset Dupont. "I am a bodyguard, not an assassin. If my employer is challenged, that is not assassination."

"It is assassination when your employer sets out to issue a challenge, to someone he dare not fight himself, and hires you to make sure they die." Ferryl made a throw-away gesture with one hand. "No matter, it will not happen again."

Dupont had recovered, enough to remember all the sorcerers watching and that he had a reputation to uphold. "Because you will stop me with swords? That is a bold move, calculated to sow seeds of doubt, but will have no effect on how I fight. And regardless of how the fight comes about, I always win."

Ferryl brushed past him, to where one of the Beefeater apprentices had opened double doors. "Always? You mean a few hundred years? Wait until you have survived a thousand, and even then you should never say always." Abel followed in some sort of daze. Ferryl would be fighting a notorious swordsman and had chosen to use his favourite weapons. He knew she wasn't any good with swords, because they'd all had a good laugh when Ferryl, along with several others, had tried fencing against Una. Even the few lessons Una had taken meant she'd disarmed Ferryl three out of three.

* * *

With everyone else crowding after, Abel couldn't even talk to the others as the crowd followed Uror's apprentice to a stretch of wall that vanished, to reveal wide steps leading down. At the bottom, Abel and his party were directed one way, Mallet and his three apprentices the other. Three apprentices, Abel had never noticed the number. Not that it would have made any difference, because Ferryl didn't know the duellist so she wouldn't have been warned.

"One moment please, Lord." Abel turned to find Pandora following him. "It seems there is bad blood between you and Mallet?" Missing the sorcerer title and the ghost of a sneer meant she wasn't a fan. As Abel nodded she glanced at Kelis, Jenny and Rob. "He may not be satisfied with killing your bodyguard." Turning fully towards Abel's three friends she addressed them directly. "If your master dies, please consider becoming my apprentices."

"On a tether? No thanks." Kelis stopped at that, with a definite effort.

Kelis's refusal didn't deter Pandora. "Without a sorcerer as protection, many of those present will attempt to tether you. Little Pandora intrigued me, so I spent some time investigating. You three are the strongest, which, considering little Pandora's display, is intriguing." She turned to Abel and repeated the usual little bow, maybe a little more. "I must apologise personally for my treatment of your trainees, Lord. I really didn't believe a youth had been accepted as the blood heir."

Abel nodded in acceptance, because he didn't trust himself to speak beyond, "Her name is Rachel, not little Pandora."

"I know, but I mean it as a compliment. She really will be a strong, fierce sorceress if she survives, and even without the cloak Rachel reminds me of myself in my youth. You do know she gave me the equivalent of the English archer's taunt, the two fingers, before she left?" Pandora had a lovely laugh, especially for a cold-blooded killer. "It has been many, many years since anyone dared to do that. I served my time on a tether, of course, which caged my spirit, but she made me wonder what I might have been if I had never worn one. Please tell Rachel I am taking good care of her cloak, and looking forward to seeing her again in a few years."

Abel didn't know what to say that wouldn't start trouble, but luckily Pandora turned back to his friends. "I am offering positions as senior apprentices from the start, a very good position, with unlimited magic and additional training. In a few years, if you work hard for me, all three of you would be allowed to challenge Mallet. You could decide who killed his bodyguards and who killed him. By then it will be no harder than a practice bout, so you could play a little."

"Why? The magic and training I mean. That isn't the usual package. Why would you offer it?" Kelis wasn't accepting, but seemed intrigued.

"Sorceress Daorban is an exception, because she was a slave, not contracted. She trained as a bodyguard for longer than seventy-five years, in real fights because she learned healing very young. The Mistress of Trentham doesn't duel, she fights, much like your own sorceress which nobody else seems to have realised. You are all very strong for your age, so you have the potential to be stronger than any other apprentice, well within the usual seventy-five year apprentice contract." Her smile should have had more teeth, long sharp ones. "I like the idea of having three like Sorceress Daorban for fifty years or more. There are scores to settle."

Pandora had turned away from Abel to speak to his friends, so he was watching their faces. As the sorceress spoke he could see their answer, and it wouldn't be polite so he butted in. "A very generous offer, Sorceress Pandora, and much appreciated. They will seriously consider it, very quickly, if it looks as if I am about to die." Abel bowed as she turned back towards him. "Now, if you will excuse us?"

Pandora seemed happy enough with that, though Abel didn't trust her smile one tiny bit. Her apprentices looked about ready to kill someone. "The offer is totally genuine. I enjoy being surrounded by beautiful things that can kill." As she swept away with her four apprentices, all beautiful or handsome and presumably killers, Abel held up a hand to stop Kelis speaking.

"Not now. Privately." Seeing another two sorcerers heading his way Abel turned to their guide. "I'd like to get away from the crowd please."

The apprentice led them further along the curving passage until he opened a small door. "Your private box, Lord."

*   *   *

Inside were five comfortable seats, overlooking an arena. The plain oval space with high walls, surrounded by tiers of plush seats, couldn't be anything else. On the arena floor a rack of swords had been wheeled in, all matched pairs. Above the other end of the oval Mallet and his apprentices were taking their seats, laughing and joking. Halfway down one side Uror came through into yet another small box with plush seats, but his also had a lectern and a small gong. The rest of the sorcerers and sorceresses were filing in, glancing up at one end of the arena or the other. "We can't let them do this!" Kelis hissed it but a voice answered.

"You must. I can hear everything you say, to avoid foul play, so please take care. Nobody else can hear until the duel starts."

Abel recognised the voice and raised his eyes to see Uror looking his way. "How does this work? Because if he gets Ferryl killed, Mallet is compost."

"You will have to find another champion, and wait until Mallet has to let Dupont go. The fees for hiring Dupont are excessive, so that won't take long. Then one of you must challenge Mallet. When his champion dies, another of you can challenge him again, and so on until he runs out of people to hide behind. They will be progressively weaker, and you have sixty friends and more every day, the math is simple. Save your champion for when he has to pick up the sword personally." From his voice, Uror seemed to like that idea. He paused, sighed, and continued in a sterner tone. "Alternatively you can assassinate him, but take great care not to break the Accord or let any sorcerer find out. Both sorcerers and the church frown on assassins. Some of both would take great delight in executing you, because your Tavern is causing disruption in a system that has functioned for three hundred years." Below him two doors opened in the arena wall, one at each side, and the duellists came in.

"Why is she in white?" Jenny giggled, then tried to stifle it as she glanced at Abel. "Skin tight white, which has to be causing Abel trouble with his blood pressure. Though if he wasn't a slimeball assassin, Dupont might be giving me an unworthy thought or two."

"So everyone can see the blood." Kelis spoke quietly, but Abel for one could see her bottling up real rage. If this all went wrong, Abel knew he'd have to keep her away from Mallet or she'd go for him. He understood, but Kelis wasn't up to fighting a full sorcerer yet. "You heard what Uror said. He wouldn't want the punters to miss it."

"Punters?" Rob leant forward, looking closer. "They're betting!"

"What are Ferryl's odds? Uror?" Abel calmed, because up at the end of the arena, and probably on the wall above Abel's box, the odds had come up. Ten to one on Ferryl Shayde surviving to the second stage, and fifteen to one on her winning the duel. Dupont's odds were one to five to finish the fight in the first stage, and one to eight odds-on to win overall. "Fifteen to one? I thought it was supposed to be all over?" Abel had seen horses on the TV at a hundred to one, and some won at higher odds than Ferryl's.

"Magic is involved so anyone has a chance. Ten to one means nobody thinks she can even put up a decent fight with swords, not against Dupont. The bookmakers believe her shield might carry your bodyguard through the first part, but her wounds will leave her weakened by blood loss or even crippled. The odds are to try and tempt someone to bet against Dupont." Uror didn't sound happy; maybe he took a cut of the profits. "Did you want to wager?"

Down in the arena Dupont said something and laughed, and Ferryl glanced up at the odds and shrugged. Abel made what had to be a very rash decision. He couldn't go down there and help Ferryl, but he could send a message that he still believed in her. "How do we do that? I don't have my cheque book."

"Wagers must be made with whatever you are carrying, strictly cash because once back on your demesne I couldn't force you to pay. Most sorcerers carry several thousand in gold or gems for unexpected expenses. We will accept banknotes of course."

Abel cursed silently, because he hadn't brought the sovereigns from the dragon room, then had another idea. "Zephyr, warn the others to keep quiet about the gold being magical." He waited a moment until they'd all had chance to digest the message. "I am too young to have diamond in my bone, so I carry magic in belts of gold bars. Each belt weighs a little over eight hundred grams. What are they worth?"

"One moment." Abel saw Uror looking down at something. "Without actually weighing it, your belt's value will be assessed at twenty-six thousand, three hundred and fifty pounds. How much do you want to bet, and on which result?" Uror sounded both cautious and inquisitive. Perhaps he thought Abel wanted to make the best of it, and bet on Dupont.

"I'll bet on Ferryl Shayde winning. Four belts."

"Eight."

"Twelve."

"Sixteen."

"Are you...? Of course you are serious. I'd point out the odds will have dropped if you decide to wager more, but somehow I think that is everything you have. Very well, four hundred and twenty-one thousand, six hundred pounds wagered on Ferryl Shayde to win the duel, at odds of fifteen to one." Uror suddenly chuckled. "I've made a few small bets myself, because you definitely know something I don't. This will give one or two punters a sudden attack of bettor's remorse." At the other end of the arena the numbers flickered and firmed up. Ferryl Shayde three to one to survive the first stage, seven to one to win! Dupont had gone to almost evens on finishing the match in the first five minutes. As Abel watched Ferryl's odds dropped again to six to one. He waved to the faces turned his way.

Down in the arena, the two combatants now had swords and were stood facing Uror's box. Each one put a hand on their blade, then removed it, but whatever they'd cast had been disguised. "Both are pushing magic into their blades. There is little difference in the amount."

"Can you tell which glyph Ferryl used?" Kelis glanced down at Abel's shoulder, at Zephyr, then out into the arena. "I'm going to be stony broke if Ferryl messes up. I've bet all I dared." She put a hand to her throat, where she kept her diamond.

Kelis meant the blur over the glyph in the diamond could be seen with the naked eye, but Abel recognised the real message. What did they do if Uror realised they'd paid in magical gold? He opened his mouth to reply, realised he'd better use Zephyr, then paused and smiled. Down in the arena Ferryl had glanced up at the odds, then given him a brilliant smile and blown a kiss. Dupont had glanced up to see why, and produced a classic double-take. "Zephyr, tell them I thought about what Uror said about repeat challenges, and what Pandora said about me being killed. If Dupont wins, Mallet will keep challenging. First me, then Kelis, and possibly Jenny and Rob. We may as well go down fighting. If Ferryl loses, Kelis uses everything in her diamond to shield and we use our belts to break out of here. If we make it to the Bentley we've got a chance. If I go down, shout for Pandora because that way you don't die as well. In seventy-five years you will be free, and Mallet will be dead." Abel sighed unhappily, and gave an answer for Uror to hear. "My mum will go crackers because I'll have to sell the Range Rover, possibly the Bentley."

"Don't sell the Bentley. Ferryl's ghost might hitch a lift in it to get home." Rob had to mean Ferryl in her shimmery true-form, but Abel thought there were too many sorcerers present for her to get out of the arena. To escape from the body, Ferryl would have to leave most of her magic behind, but it probably wouldn't matter anyway. With so many sorcerers and apprentices in the building, he doubted any of them would get out once Uror inspected the belts. Abel tried to think of something reassuring for Zephyr to pass on, then he ran out of time.

"Everyone please be aware. The sound system is live so anything you say may be overheard." Uror sounded very formal, and had moved forward to stand by the lectern. "We are here to witness a challenge issued by the sorcerer Mallet to the trainee bodyguard Kelis. Since Kelis is only a trainee, the sorceress Ferryl Shayde has accepted the challenge and will fight in her place. Sorcerer Mallet has a bodyguard, Dupont, who will take his place in the arena." Despite starting off formally, Uror's voice definitely made it clear how he felt about a sorcerer who challenged a trainee, then relied on a bodyguard. Several jeers brought a scowl to Mallet's face.

Uror went on to outline the weapons, shields, magic, and the length of time the first stage would last. "Should either duellist break these rules, they will forfeit the contest. Their master, mistress or employer will pay an indemnity."

Abel hoped Ferryl did that rather than die, he'd pay up somehow, but then a voice rang out. "I'll insist on tethering that skinny trainee, so I can teach her real manners." Mallet glared down the arena as Kelis raised two fingers in reply.

Two could play those games. "I will insist on Mallet facing Daorban, one on one, in the arena. No bodyguards. That way Ferryl can put her feet up and enjoy the show." A gale of laughter washed away any reply from Mallet, and it took Uror a few moments to calm everyone down.

"We can't insist on that, though it would be an interesting contest. Briefly." The sorcerer reverted to his official manner. "Combatants, do you understand?" They both confirmed in loud, clear voices. "If either of you are unable to continue, and your opponent withholds the fatal blow, I will ask your opponent's master, mistress or employer if they will grant mercy. If they do, I will drop the white cloth into the arena. If not, the contest will end in death. Take your places. The contest will begin when I strike the gong with the hammer."

*   *   *

Up in their box, Abel and his friends could only hope. They all had faith in Ferryl's fighting spirit, but she'd already told them she couldn't take on real sorcerers. Realisation struck, and Kelis leant close to whisper, "Swords because no glyphs." Ferryl had restricted the contest to her opponent's strengths to hide her weakness, her lack of glyphs! Zephyr passed that on, but knowing the reason didn't make anyone feel better. All of them knew her true-self might get away, but even so she'd never truly be Ferryl again, because she'd leave her wits and some memories in the body. Kelis's hand crept into Abel's, then let go again but rested close, close enough for him to feel an echo of that lovely link. Jenny took his other hand, while Kelis had taken hold of Rob's hand. Zephyr connected them all, but Abel had nothing to say.

Down on the arena floor Ferryl Shayde looked cool, calm and collected, but inside her turmoil raged. She kept trying to put aside all her new emotions, but she couldn't! They persisted, fear for her friends, a deep happiness that they thought so much of her, a pride in their courage, risking so much to send her their support, and a rising fierce anticipation for the battle to come. So many emotions, a mix she couldn't describe let alone identify, rising again as soon as she relaxed so she had to damp them down, again and again. Ferryl had started worrying she'd made a really big mistake. Not one that affected herself, but Abel must have bet heavily to lower the odds so far, and all he had on him was magical gold. The silly, lovely, brave fool had done it for her, to show the crowd she wasn't an underdog, to show his faith. Ferryl had no idea what would happen if the crowd found out, but it might even be fatal. The only way to avoid that was to win.

Once she had learned of this Dupont, Ferryl chose swords so that if she won, nobody would ever challenge her or Abel again. Nobody would ever realise how vulnerable she was while she relearned her glyphs, or found more wits. If she'd lost, it would have been expected and nobody would have made any fuss. Ferryl had read the invitation very carefully. None of the sorcerers themselves could be challenged under the truce, so Abel would have been safe. So would she, because only her host would die, and she could return to Brinsford with a different name and appearance. Not now, because trying to pay his bet in magical gold would put Abel in terrible trouble.

Ferryl felt sure she could survive in her true-form and escape if she lost, so that hadn't worried her. Now it was essential she won, but too late to choose different weapons. Once again Ferryl banished the emotions, the fear of what might happen to Abel and his friends. These emotions were dangerous. She'd been able to suppress them until Abel, and probably the other three from the way the odds fell, had made their move. That sort of unasked, total support had hit her hard. Humans and magical creatures hated and feared her, and sometimes tried to tame or bind her, but nobody liked her that much, ever. But she couldn't afford distractions, because the beginning of this fight would be the most dangerous part for her.

Ferryl had often fought, through her hosts, with magic, weapons, tooth and claw. Her weaponry experience came from melee, in battles, and most often with a shield and spear or axes. She had little practical experience of sword fighting, and none fighting one on one or in duels. That would alter the longer Ferryl fought, and she was a fast learner, but Dupont would be lethal from the first moment. To stand any chance Ferryl had to still her worries, and her pride in her friends, and concentrate on the fight.

The chime of the gong hadn't died away when Dupont launched a first attack. Not full-blooded, just to test her, and Ferryl recognised the move from her newly installed wits. She met it with the classic defence, disengaging as he put in an extra twist to try and snag her blade. After the fiasco, when Una disarmed her three times, Ferryl had been embarrassed. She'd etched several centuries of sword-fighting techniques into her bones, but so far they were theory. There'd been too many other things happening since, so she hadn't actually practiced them.

Dupont moved into the attack again, trying to hustle her but Ferryl skipped aside, using her speed to avoid the point that tried to spike her calf as she did. The duellist looked intrigued, as if she was a puzzle he had to solve. Another attack flicked out, then another sliced in, and Ferryl stopped or evaded each one. After several more attempts Dupont paused. "You have training in more than one school, but only the forms. That will not be enough in a fight." Ferryl just smiled as he moved in, faster and surer this time. The crowd roared as a thin red stripe showed across her thigh, but the edge barely made it through the cloth.

Again the duellist moved in, crowding Ferryl, trying to force her against a wall, but she moved just fast enough to get away. She tried to analyse how this sword-fighting worked, one on one. A battle became a storm, strikes coming from any direction and opponents changing from moment to moment. This would be a dance, a swirling rhythmic duet where each dancer had their own music, but had to adapt to their opponent's. Ferryl became the wind in her pure form, and had danced with hurricanes, so she worked on turning the individual exercises in the wits into a flowing sequence. Not with all her speed, not yet, because if she did and missed then Dupont would never give her another chance. She didn't have to win this part of the dance, just survive without a crippling injury to either arm.

The fighters came together again and again, and now Ferryl had thin lines across one shoulder blade and a bicep and a stab wound in her thigh. None had made it through her internal shield, so none of them worried Ferryl. Her only success, a small, growing crimson stain on Dupont's bicep, brought several calls of "first blood" from the crowd. Not his sword arm, and it didn't impede the duellist as he pushed harder now, faster. Ferryl moved just a little faster once or twice, she had to so her internal shield stopped the blade before it bit deep into her muscle. One thrust went a little deeper, but the damage didn't affect her movement. In return, Ferryl left a short stripe of red across Dupont's thigh, then got her point into his sword arm. The tiny spot, barely bleeding, brought several cheers from the crowd and Ferryl saw Dupont's face set.

The two came together again and as their blades locked, he rolled his hand and hilt over Ferryl's hand, forcing it downwards. She pushed up and tried to disengage, but his blade twisted as he suddenly gave way. Ferryl's sword spun up and across the arena, glittering in the light, and the crowd let out a collective gasp. Above the arena wall a sorcerer's apprentice shielded, and put up a hand to catch it. Dupont's eyes followed the sword for a moment, before he turned back to his victim with a triumphant smile.

She wasn't there! As she felt Dupont's blade twist her sword free, Ferryl started moving. Her hand and the hilt had barely lost touch when she ducked under his sword arm, in the same direction as her sword, swerving around her opponent at full speed for the first time. She took two quick steps and leapt, her fingers snagging the end of the hilt before she struck the arena wall. The sword tumbled free as the pair of them fell to the arena floor, but Ferryl turned her landing into a graceful roll and quickly swept it up, quickly enough to stop Dupont's rush. A massive roar rose from the crowd and some leapt to their feet, cheering.

"She used magic! Nobody can jump and recover like that! Forfeit, I want a forfeit and I want her dead!" Mallet's voice rang out, triumphant, and silence fell as all eyes turned to Uror.

"Ferryl did not use magic. I am not sure if Uror can tell, but I can."

"The leap and the roll are from Acro routines, though Ferryl never made the team. She must have…. Oh!" Jenny put both hands across her mouth and the rest realised. Acro dancing must be in Ferryl's wits, from when she lived in both Jenny and Claris, routines that were driven in by repetition until they became almost automatic. Jenny had nearly blurted out the possession secret! She lowered her hands and giggled. "Though we never bounced off a wall in the middle of an Acro routine."

Rob glanced at her with a little smile. "You should ask Mr. Beresford to put it in. Judging by the crowd here it would be a huge hit." He shut up as he noticed faces turning towards their box.

In the arena, Ferryl waited patiently while Dupont watched Uror for his verdict. Uror wasn't looking at them, his attention fixed on the ceiling. A green light glowed. "No foul. We have an entity who can see magic, and nobody employed magic beyond that in the shields and swords. Fight on."

Dupont looked startled for a moment, then leapt forward. As the swords clashed Uror continued. "I will add the stoppage to the end of the period, to make up the five minutes." At the other end of the arena Mallet stood up, but his apprentices caught hold of him and he sat down again, fuming. Abel felt tempted to wave, but couldn't spare the time from watching the fight.

Dupont wasn't testing now! He'd already realised his first assessment had been wrong, his opponent had actually fought before. He'd come to the conclusion that Ferryl might be out of practice, because as the fight progressed her skill rapidly improved. She had already marked his sword arm, which would annoy the bookmakers, and drawn blood more times than many of his recent opponents. That strike had made him cautious, content to weaken her through blood loss and finish it in the second half. Now Dupont realised Ferryl hadn't been fighting to her full ability, so he couldn't risk trying to cut her slowly into pieces.

He'd really wanted to do that, to repay her for the assassin gibe. Now every alarm went off, as Dupont realised he had to finish this fight as fast as possible. If his opponent wanted to play for time, she had a reason.

There couldn't be any hidden trap in this part of the duel, so he had to make the most of his skill while he could. For the first time in too many years, Dupont knew he might be in real danger. But it was a danger he could deal with, by killing Ferryl Shayde before she could spring her surprise.

Again and again his blade or point sliced or pierced the thin white material, leaving growing crimson stains, but he couldn't get a solid hit to break through her internal shield. Again and again Ferryl Shayde used her speed and agility, moving or twisting fast enough to avoid critical damage. It wasn't all defence, because now Ferryl could feel how the fight ebbed and flowed, deep down in her true-self. She was much harder to hit now, and by pushing to finish her, Dupont left fleeting openings that Ferryl's speed took advantage of. She began to read him just a little, started evading some blows even as they were launched, pushing her human body to new limits and striking back whenever she could. Ferryl felt her muscles twist and spasm and her joints screamed under the pressure, but she drove on through the pain.

A growing number of crimson stains spread across Dupont's sweat-stained clothing, though none of them were deep enough to slow him. There were many more wounds on Ferryl, but despite the amount of blood she seemed faster than ever. The crowd were silent now, engrossed, knowing they were seeing something rare, two supreme duellists in one arena. One had more skill and experience, the other had raw speed and better reactions, one was stronger but the other suppler, and regardless of who won the result would be talked about for centuries.

Dupont knew he'd already taken more hits than he'd accumulated in the last fifty years. No show now, he couldn't afford it because he'd ended up in a deadly serious fight for his life, and everyone could see it. Even if he won, his aura of invincibility had gone, she'd proved he was fallible. The duellist tried to banish the annoyance, knowing he couldn't afford the distraction, but this arrogant woman had dented his confidence and pricked his ego. He dug deep into his experience, dredging up moves that he hadn't needed or used for scores of years, throwing them at her one after the other. She soaked them all up, that cursed speed saving her time and again. Her replies were definitely not in any training manual, but again and again Dupont felt his muscles protest as he avoided crippling by fractions of an inch. Under it all, time and again, he tried to work out who she could be. He shouldn't, he should stay fixed on the fight, but she'd got inside his head.

Ferryl, however, had finally managed to bury her worries, her emotions. Not strictly true, she had replaced all the worry with the sheer glory of the dance. Her wits told her what could be done with a blade, her fighting experience over millennia told her when, and her speed allowed her to make the strike before Dupont could escape it. Not just a dance now, she was the storm against his steel, mixing her fighting experience and instincts with the techniques in her bones. She still took two hits for every one she landed, but she only had to land one properly to finish this now! Ferryl knew she didn't need to do that, just survive, but her old battle reflexes had swept her up, and she went for the kill. Again and again she whirled and spun and leapt, only restricted by the clumsy flesh encasing her.

He wrapped his forearm around hers, forcing her arm and sword away, but she used his arm as a support to tuck her legs up above the slash that would have crippled her. She twisted their locked blades so her hilt hit his nose, and he backed off until his watering eyes recovered, his blade spinning a bright, deadly web that denied her a clean strike. The two white and crimson figures came together again and again, their shining blades slashing and clashing as they spun around each other or collided, then fell back only to launch another attack. Droplets of sweat and blood spattered the floor and walls of an arena silent except for their harsh breathing, the scuffing of their feet and the clash of steel.

*   *   *

Abel for one almost had a heart attack when the clear note of the gong sounded, and both fighters leapt apart. Both rested their fists on their knees, leaning forward gasping for breath as the crowd broke into applause, then cheering, then excited chatter. After a few moments the noise dulled, as Uror cast a glyph so he could be heard. "Are you both fit to continue?" The sorcerer umpire had to ask, but despite the blood and tattered clothing neither looked close to giving up. "Then take your places."

Neither of them hurried, both needing time to catch their breath and collect themselves, to come down from the high. Ferryl limped, not caring if Dupont saw it because she didn't need agility now so he couldn't exploit it. The duellist did his best to look unhurt, but he no longer moved with the same smooth assurance. As the two faced off again, Dupont bowed to his opponent, lower than a sorcerer being polite, gesturing to the cuts on his body and limbs. "It has been an unexpected pain, almost a pleasure."

Ferryl, her clothing in ribbons and covered in blood, bowed back. "I would have preferred meeting you elsewhere, without swords."

"Ready?" Uror waited for two nods and threw a handful of tiny glyphs into the air. Dupont and Ferryl extended their shields to globes, easily seen as they took on a light blue glow. "That is so the spectators can see your shields, and the result of your strikes, and so that if your opponent's shield fails you can offer quarter."

"Kill her. Don't even ask me." This time Mallet's voice wasn't as loud, and definitely sounded less sure he'd get his wish. Abel didn't reply. He didn't expect Ferryl to hesitate if she had any sort of a chance to kill Dupont.

Uror struck the gong. "Strike."

Dupont ignored him, warily watching Ferryl as he raised his sword. "My strike first?" She nodded. He shook his head slightly, but only Ferryl heard the murmured "this is where I find out how I've been suckered." Though Dupont gave it his best shot. Even as he murmured "suckered" the duellist's shoulders twisted as he thrust straight for Ferryl's heart. The crowd gasped, because it was fast, straight, a perfect thrust without any warning and Ferryl made no attempt to avoid it!

Dupont's sword glowed, jerking and then slowing a little as it penetrated her shield before moving faster again. As if in slow motion Abel saw it drive closer and closer to Ferryl's heart while she waited, watching it as if fright or panic had frozen her. She finally moved, but not to dodge. Her free hand came up with blinding speed to grab the blade, smoke and flame billowed up, and cries of alarm rang out. Clear above them all rang a metallic crack, followed by a clang as the blade of Dupont's sword hit the arena floor! The smoke cleared to show the charred remains of Ferryl's hand and forearm, halfway up to her elbow. Dupont looked at her hand, shocked, then down at his sword blade on the floor, and back at her hand.

As he did, totally distracted for the first time in the fight, Ferryl Shayde struck. Even before it hit Dupont's shield, her blade glowed with the magic she poured into it. The point barely slowed, and for only a moment, then it penetrated Dupont's shield and the sword turned cherry red. With the sort of crackling noise nobody wants to hear while crossing a frozen pond, Ferryl's thrust drove in unimpeded. Dupont tried to dodge but too late, by the time he reacted her sword was already through his shield. His hand came up a little as he started to parry out of pure instinct, but even if Dupont still had a blade he would have been too late. Not too late to save his life, because Ferryl hadn't aimed at his heart. Her sword bit into his shoulder joint and through with a popping, crackling noise, almost drowned by the sharp cry from Dupont as she twisted the blade. Ferryl pulled her sword back and stood, waiting, smoke still curling up from her ruined hand.

Dupont staggered, dropped the hilt of his sword and went to one knee. He gritted his teeth, groped for the sword hilt and picked it up, looked at it and dropped it in disgust. The duellist raised his face to look up at his opponent, pain warring with disbelief. "No strike." The crowd went crazy, a mixture of cheering and baying for blood. A good few of them were shouting for Ferryl to kill him, others were just cheering. Nobody seemed interested in mercy.

The clear note of the gong finally quietened them. Uror managed to speak calmly, but he couldn't sound totally disinterested. "Dupont has yielded his strike. Your strike, Ferryl Shayde."

Ferryl watched Dupont as he struggled to his feet, holding his left arm with his right to keep the weight off the ruined, dislocated shoulder. He took a deep breath and faced her, chest out. "Well fought. Strike true." Dupont dropped his shield and a low murmur ran through the crowd. As her blade began to glow, Ferryl looked up at Abel's box.

Abel hadn't been expecting her to wait, and it took a moment for him to realise she'd given him the chance to save Dupont. He leant forward and spoke up, loud and clear, because this time his personal preferences didn't count. "Ferryl Shayde fought, Ferryl Shayde decides."

A little smile touched her face, probably because Ferryl had expected him to go soppy as most of his friends put it, and she bowed very slightly in thanks. She looked Dupont in the eyes, impressed because he hadn't reacted, waiting impassively while she decided his fate. "You are much better with a sword than I am. Such skill should not be lost because of a trick, nor because of a foolish choice of employer. Mercy."

"But I am not the better fighter, which is why I am no longer unbeaten. I will take more care over my boasting, and who I work for in the future. My thanks, Ferryl Shayde." Both looked towards Uror who made a great production of lifting the white cloth, showing it to the crowd and dropping it into the arena. He struck the gong. "The contest is over. You may heal yourselves. All losing bets must be paid before leaving the arena."

With a visible sigh of relief Dupont concentrated on his arm, though he spared a quick glance for Ferryl. He hesitated, but nobody would hear him over the babble of the crowd. "Your choice of rules and weapons were all smoke and mirrors, designed to let you break my blade. How did you stand the pain long enough to do that, and then stay completely focussed afterwards?"

"I missed the chance to kill someone once, because I was in too much pain. I worked on solving the problem." Ferryl's cuts were healing rapidly, but her hand and arm would take longer, longer than Dupont's shoulder. She glanced up towards Uror then back to Dupont, suddenly alert again. "I have just had a disturbing thought. If I challenge Mallet, do I have to fight you again?"

"Oh no, I am technically dead for twenty-four hours. According to the duelling laws I am not allowed to fight you again, ever, or not in a duel." Dupont looked at his ruined shoulder, now no longer bleeding though bone still gleamed in the wound. "I won't be picking a fight with you for pleasure."

"Good." Ferryl turned towards Abel, a big smile on her face because she felt sure he'd have a fit when he heard her. She raised her hands, both the one with a sword and the charred, partially healed one, and the crowd quietened. "I ask a boon of the Master of Castle House. Will you allow me to challenge the sorcerer Mallet, on my own behalf?"

Abel didn't have a fit, because he could still see into the box at the other end of the arena. As soon as Dupont refused his strike, one of Mallet's apprentices had gone to open the door of their box. Now all three and Mallet were frantically trying to pull it open. "Don't let him go, Abel, or he'll ambush you. Or he'll kill some poor kid, a Taverner, out of spite." Kelis glared across the arena. "I wanted to do it personally but we can't wait. Give him to Ferryl."

Which meant if Ferryl didn't kill Mallet, Kelis still intended going after him. That made it even easier. "Okay." Abel leant forward, but before he could answer Ferryl another voice rang out.

"Before we get to that, I'd like to sort out a misunderstanding." In his box, Mallet froze and then very slowly turned around. Daorban stood just inside the room, behind the seated audience. "The fight had started when I arrived, but someone has been filling me in on the details. Sorcerer Uror, why is that scruffy little pretender Mallet here, posing as the senior sorcerer in Stoke?"

"He said he was entitled to represent the Stoke five. There's not much I can do about it now, except tell him he is no longer welcome in Oxford, at any time." The malicious smile on Uror's face knew that wasn't going to satisfy Daorban.

"Alleged Sorcerer Mallet, I challenge you. We even have a convenient arena here. Since that is your champion down there, trying to screw his arm back on, does this mean I get the pleasure of meeting you face to face?" Daorban shouted it loud enough that Mallet couldn't pretend not to hear.

He eyed her for a moment, then turned to Uror. "You promised safe conduct."

The sorcerer turned the smile towards him, still not a pleasant smile. "True. Every sorcerer and sorceress is protected until they leave Oxford, which is why you challenged the bodyguard's trainee rather than the Master of Castle House. Though Sorceress Daorban's challenge still stands."

"But not right now. Let me out and give me my safe conduct. Saying I'm senior isn't a reason for a challenge. She just wants an excuse to kill me." A ripple of catcalls and jeering answered Mallet, because he'd challenged Kelis with less of an excuse. The door opened but a beefeater apprentice stood blocking the way.

"Pay your gambling debts first, please. Then there is the small matter of using my meeting to set up a grudge killing. Your car will be adequate compensation." Mallet didn't even object, though one of his apprentices pulled out a phone. Abel hoped all the taxi firms were busy. The Beefeater stood back far enough for a man with old-fashioned scales and a woman with a tray to start collecting. From his vantage point Abel could see her checking everything with something Zephyr confirmed used magic. Abel's fake gold would have been discovered before he left the box.

A good number of the audience still wanted Mallet to face the challenge, the Bolton sorcerer in particular pointing out anyone else claiming to be senior in his town would be facing him. Others claimed that Ferryl's challenge counted as part of the original one on Kelis, so Mallet should be forced to fight her. Abel didn't care, because he felt sure Daorban wouldn't let up now she'd found a good excuse. Mallet would die when she caught him, which meant that Kelis would be safe. When Rob opened the door a Beefeater stood there, but he only asked where they wanted to go. Abel and his party headed off to find Ferryl.

He didn't get far. Pandora's apprentice must have strained something to get round to Abel's door that fast. "I am Wrath, senior apprentice to the Mistress of Clare, with a message for the Master of Castle House and Pendragon. Congratulations, though she is personally disappointed at not being able to add your trainees to her apprentices." Wrath's look at Kelis seemed happier at the result than the message was. "If any Tavern applicants phone from her demesne, send them to meet Sorceress Pandora. Apprentice Pride will contact your Tavern to arrange for you to meet the rejects, who will include any other magic-aware teenagers she finds cluttering the streets. Her trees will go hungry, providing you will take responsibility for teaching any Tavern trainees to mind their manners."

That meant Pandora would choose who to tether, but Abel didn't think he'd get a better deal. This way she'd send all the rest to the Tavern, which had to be better than ashes. Abel even managed to smile when he replied, because he felt sure Pandora had done it this way so nobody would know she'd made any concessions. "Agreed. Should your mistress have any complaints about local Taverners, she will allow me to deal with the culprit."

"That was expected. Agreed, Lord. I would introduce Pride immediately but he is still recovering from his injuries." With that she bowed, turned and stalked away.

"I don't think she fancied the competition, Kelis." Rob kept his voice down, but Wrath's back somehow managed to stiffen an impossible bit more.

"But was it the beautiful part or the killer, Abel? What do you think?"

The two pink spots on Kelis's cheeks were a warning that Abel had better be careful how he answered Jenny. "Fashion sense, she doesn't fancy the competition."

"Pandora wouldn't allow her to wear leather. How about a furry catsuit, though she'd have to swing her hips a bit more to wag the tail." Luckily Wrath must be out of earshot, because she didn't react even when Kelis sniggered at Rob. The pair began to compete on finding the most ridiculous ways to dress an apprentice. At least that lightened the mood nicely while the four of them waited for Ferryl. The fifth, Zephyr, had already connected by spooky-phone to pass on their congratulations.

Once she came out of a shower and got dressed, Ferryl found herself in a big huddle. For once she seemed to enjoy the personal contact, hugs and pats on the back, just reaching out now and then to snaffle slices of cold roast beef. The meat, and the other snacks, were compliments of the management, to help replace the body mass used to rebuild her still-healing hand. Somewhere in all the congratulations, Ferryl confessed to being out of practice, so it had taken her a while to get the hang of personal combat again. She also explained why she'd practiced being hurt, dulling whatever she felt. If she could have ignored the injury after hitting Pendragon, she could have finished him right at the beginning of the fight.

Silently, through her hand, Ferryl explained the wit full of sword-fighting instructions, and learning to use them. She'd spared Dupont because she'd cheated, no human could dull pain like she could in a host. Zephyr passed everything on to the rest, as the five of them re-joined the rest in the dining room.

When Kelis mentioned Pandora's offer, and the meeting with Wrath, Ferryl had a whole new take on it. "Of course Wrath was pleased I won, because otherwise Mallet would have tried to kill Abel once he left. If any of you accepted Pandora's offer, under the Accord she would have been forced to release a senior apprentice to keep the numbers the same. The apprentice would be cast out to fend for themselves, missing out on the last of their training."

"But those apprentices must be stronger than any of us! Why would she take on someone weaker?" Jenny shook her head, trying to understand, because she'd been included in the offer and was the weakest of them all.

"She would have seventy-five years to train and use you, whereas that apprentice is probably into the last twenty years of her seventy-five. In another twenty years, trained by someone like Pandora, you would be the type of apprentice Daorban became, stronger than some true sorceresses. Pandora will know hundreds of battle glyphs, and as her senior apprentices you would learn most of them." Ferryl glanced towards Pandora, bowing slightly in response to the smile and little wave. "I understand her reasoning, and can even respect the way she took her chance, but I'm really pleased you didn't have to make that choice." The rest agreed, enthusiastically.

*　*　*

Daorban took Mallet's table, after Siobhan theatrically cleaned the seats, and having her there and Mallet missing quietened those opposing the Tavern. Something, perhaps the fight, or blood, or seeing Dupont defeated or maybe Mallet humiliated, had put the assembled sorcerers in a good mood. Even the old sorcerer stopped objecting. He ignored most of the discussion, apparently much more interested in watching Ferryl. His small bow to her when she looked his way seemed to be a signal to some sorcerers, that he'd relented in some way.

A steady stream of sorcerers and sorceresses called by Abel's table to introduce themselves personally, and congratulate him on his choice of bodyguard. All around the room the formality dropped away, with some sorcerers sharing a table. Abel could see and hear deals being made about everything from selling valuables to loaning glyph-fillers. Pandora remained aloof, holding court with a small number of sorceresses and apprentices, though she smiled whenever Kelis looked her way. She might have made a deal with Abel, but the Mistress of Clare had no intention of letting the others know.

Some of the sorcerers asked Abel about the Tavern, but most waited until they were back at their tables before sending an apprentice to talk business. Abel thought at least half of those present agreed to some sort of variant on Abel's proffered deal over would-be Taverners, and would recommend the deal to their neighbours. Possibly half of the rest wanted to talk more before committing themselves, or talk it over with their neighbours once they were back home. According to Kelis, in one of the quiet moments, it came down to none of them wanting to upset Abel's bodyguard.

Ferryl stood by Abel's chair, with a hand on his shoulder so she could talk to him silently if necessary. She said very little, totally ignoring the curious looks or enquiries about what glyph she'd used on her sword, or where she learned to fight. Ferryl looked fully recovered, but confided through her hand that the healing had weakened her a little. She would need serious exercise to get her hand and arm back to its previous condition.

Kelis pointed out Una would be getting company on her Stoke trips, meaning she'd decided to learn sword-fighting. Both she and Jenny were targeted by a stream of apprentices bringing offers or messages from their sorcerers. Abel remembered what the secretary in Sheffield, Bertram, had said. Sorcerers didn't call sorcerers, they had people for it. A high percentage of the apprentices sent with messages used the chance to ask Kelis or Jenny about Abel, or how his apprentices were treated or trained, or who Ferryl really was.

Rob kept out of that, because he reckoned most of them were just trying to work out how to get a knife into Abel's ribs, and he'd say the wrong thing. Abel agreed to him sitting it out, because he thought it more likely Rob would crack the wrong joke to the wrong person. The joker became a secretary, using his phone to record the names of those accepting Abel's proposals, and appointments with others. He mostly just recorded whatever Kelis or Jenny asked him to, but a few apprentices asked him directly if any Tavern members were looking for a change. They promised a very good deal for the right person, an older teen who could already throw fire.

As more asked about appointments, Kelis and Jenny had to explain that Abel could only attend meetings at weekends once school started. That brought some odd looks, but for once Rob restrained his impulse to make jokes and tweak people. That became harder, when several sorcerers and apprentices looked lost after Rob asked for a map of their demesne. He told them to ask junior apprentices, those who could use computers, to send one by email. That way the Tavern could be sure they weren't trespassing.

Even Uror mellowed, confiding privately that he'd bet enough on Ferryl to cover most of his losses on Dupont. With that sort of a hint he'd also bet heavily on Dupont being blooded early and often, at very good odds, and ended up with an overall profit. Uror settled on tethering Steven for three years, then giving the youth a clear option of continuing or joining the Tavern. If the youth turned out to be a strong magic user, the sorcerer would give him extra training and make the offer more attractive. With a little twinkle in his eye, Uror promised Ferryl that he would move her master up the introduction list, high enough so she didn't need to kill anyone. He asked Abel to stay overnight, because several of those present wanted to talk to him or his bodyguard, laughing when Abel declined because their mothers would worry.

*   *   *

As the rush began to ease off, one of Uror's Beefeater types came to ask if one of Abel's party could open the Bentley, so the hotel driver could move it. "No offence intended, but since my friends aren't covered by the safe conduct, I'd rather we stay together." The apprentice bowed to Abel, his eyes looked a little distant for a moment, then a clear tone sounded and most of those present looked towards Uror.

He rose, bowed towards Abel, and smiled. "It has just occurred to me that someone might be foolish enough to challenge another of Abel's companions. Since they are independent, my safe conduct doesn't cover them. Please note that I have extended the safe conduct to trainees Kelis, Rob, and Jenny." A low murmur went around the room, interspersed with occasional low laughter.

Ferryl caught enough to whisper, "They were surprised by Uror naming apprentices, but are finally realising none of us are tethered."

Uror had continued, after a short pause for the noise to die down. "I believe we have all had enough excitement, so another duel could be dangerous for our older compatriots." His smile hardened, as did his voice. "Should anyone be ill-mannered enough to ignore me, there will be a fine. I will then remove their own safe conduct, and bar them from Oxford, permanently. Should any of you challenge Ferryl Shayde, I will insist she has three days to recover before fighting. If she wins, I will not allow her to show mercy a second time."

Rather than anyone looking worried, a ripple of laughter went through the crowd, including some apprentices. Beside Abel, Uror's apprentice cleared his throat. "Lord?"

"I'll go." Rob put his phone away and stood up, nodding towards the half-dozen men and women still clustered around Kelis and Jenny. "These apprentices want to talk, not arrange anything." He left, walking confidently through the crowd behind Uror's man and out of a side door.

When Rob came back, his friends recognised the expression on his face. Rob had some sort of joke, or something very funny, to tell them. As he sat down the others leaned in. As usual, Kelis had no patience. "Come on Rob, spit it out before you burst."

"What?" With a little laugh Rob pretended to cower. "Well, you know how Abel has been worrying about financing new Taverns?" Rob spoke in the barest of whispers, but Zephyr picked it up and fed everything to the rest by spooky-phone. "In all the excitement I forgot my little bet, and I reckon the rest of you did as well." Eyes met in surprise as the Taverneers glanced at each other. "Uror wanted the Bentley boot opened, so his minions could load up our winnings."

"How much?" Jenny barely breathed it, and almost lost that in a giggle. "I've forgotten how much we bet, in pounds."

Rob's voice was stronger now, because it didn't matter who heard this. "A small horde of apprentices just loaded wads of banknotes, well over a hundred kilos of assorted gold bars, bags of assorted gems, some jewellery, and twenty-three bags of gold sovereigns. There's over six million quid, according to this." He placed a slip of paper onto the table, where everyone tried to get a look. "I let the driver in at the same time. She'll keep an eye on the car, because someone might get greedy, and bring it round when we need it."

"Well that's sorted…." Abel glanced round. "A lot of things. What are you going to do with your share, Kelis, now you've got your very own filthy money?" He grinned, making her previous barbs into a joke.

"I could wallow in it, to see if it made me sticky with power as well, like you?" Kelis reached over to mock-punch Abel's bicep. "I'll do the same as you, you idiot."

"Me too." Both Jenny and Rob jumped in to pledge their share, because they knew Abel would put his share into the Tavern.

"In that case, maybe we should run for the hills?" Abel smiled at the interested faces looking his way, some of them a long way from friendly. Now he realised they might be sore losers, not just opposed to the Tavern.

"There's a few apprentices wanting to make appointments for tomorrow, and two of them have offered to pay for us to stay overnight." Jenny might be passing the information, but her tone of voice wasn't keen on the idea.

"The group who want to reject the Tavern are still here, even if there's a lot less now Mallet and the old sorcerer have quit." Ferryl's hand added the rest. "Get out now, before someone else decides they want to play nasty games."

"We wouldn't want that driver to get cramp. How do we call for the car?" Abel had barely finished speaking when one of Uror's apprentices came towards them. That was a big hint about eavesdropping, and a really good incentive to leave, now. Once he'd asked officially, and the woman left on her errand, the Taverneers stood up and headed for the door. Getting out turned into a slow process of explaining their mothers would be worried, or promising to get in touch with various apprentices.

*　*　*

When he reached the door, Abel found himself confronted by the old, bearded sorcerer with the robes and staff, the one who'd disliked any change. "Very well, you are capable of holding your demesne, Master of Castle House and Pendragon. Will you be claiming Celtchar's seat on the Council?"

"Not a chance. I wouldn't know where to start and I've got a lot of learning to do just to run the Taverner network." Abel put together old and Council. "Are you on the Council, er?"

"Sorcerer Beowulf."

"Sorcerer Beowulf?"

The sorcerer ignored the hesitation, and the question. "A very wise decision. I am reassured, most young sorcerers think they know it all. I have also been reminded that even an ignorant youth can act more like a true sorcerer than some who are much older. A stark contrast to many of the modern youngsters. I will not obstruct your Tavern, Master of Castle House and Pendragon, even if I doubt it will succeed. Watching you struggle to make it work will be diverting. So will trying to find out just who your bodyguard is, and why she is so loyal." He gave Ferryl a slow, appraising look. "You are an old sorceress, one who fought on battlefields when axe and spear ruled the day. It showed, even if most of those present wouldn't realise. You would have killed him twice if your sword had been a short spear." He nodded slowly, obviously still racking his brains for a name. "I should know you."

Ferryl smiled and bowed, just a little. "We have not met until today, Sorcerer Beowulf. I would remember." She chuckled, and flexed her healed hand. "I would have killed him even quicker with a Spartan Kopis."

The grunt might have been the closest Beowulf came to a laugh. "Naughty, none of us are that old. Maybe with an axe?"

"Two axes, they are lighter."

"Yes, that matters with your speed, though most preferred one and a shield in battle. If you fought like that, two axes and no shield, I will find you in the old legends and histories, somewhere." He bowed slightly more than politely, and turned back to Abel. "Unlike some of these fools, the elder sorcerers know the only way to get into Castle House is with a blood link. We will not obstruct you. Even if you fail to control it, the heart of the house should be released back into the world. Better yet, you might revive Pendragon's gryphon, enough to release any trinkets it still conceals. Meanwhile I will continue to deal with my own problems, so do not trespass on my demesne." He swirled his robes and marched off deeper into the hotel, so he must be a guest. His apprentices all nodded very slightly to Ferryl before following, one pausing to pass a card to Rob.

As Beowulf left Abel noticed the interested faces all around them. Zephyr sounded a little annoyed. "He cast something to stop them hearing, and probably from seeing clearly. I couldn't work out the flows before he broke it."

The trip home tended more towards a party, with a lot of laughing about the loot in the boot. Ferryl tried to tell the others off for taking the risk and betting with magical gold, but they laughed and pointed out someone was worse, she'd fought Dupont with swords. The journey took longer than expected, because Jenny drove to the Sheffield office first. The winnings, apart from several large wads of notes, were carried inside the gryphon room. With Abel present, the dragon head didn't object to the others. Abel thought he caught a movement, a slight widening of the dragon's nostrils for moment, as Kelis passed nearby, almost as if it could smell her. He watched, but either he'd imagined the reaction or it wasn't repeated.

Visiting a small zoo on the way home dampened some of their excitement. The Bentley stopped off for Rob and Jenny to take pictures for alibis, to explain the trip to their parents. Nobody took many pictures, because they'd found another bad one. This time Rob wanted to nip back and let out a neglected wolverine, probably not a good idea for the surrounding wildlife.

Once Ginny took them all home, Abel found himself having another of those long cuddles with Ferryl, in her room after Kelis had gone upstairs. This time Ferryl didn't want to talk, just sit very close and hold tight. While walking home, Abel tried to work out if that was a reaction to the fight, or if Ferryl might be feeling more human emotions. If she felt more emotions, and one of them involved her boyfriend, did that make her human enough for Abel to ignore her dual nature? After a long cuddle that sounded even more attractive than usual. Abel eventually decided he would wait and see, because he really didn't know what else to do.

*   *   *

As a result of the trial and duel, the list of sorcerers demanding a meeting with Abel shrank to manageable proportions. He still met sorcerers and sorceresses almost every other day, but carefully organised so he alternated the friendlier invites and the challenges. Abel attended two more trials, both of which included meetings with a large group of sorcerers.

Both the sorcerer and sorceress holding the later trials had heard about the duel, so neither defendant faced death. At least one culprit would probably choose the apprentice option once he'd served his time. The teenager had been attempting to shoplift with his less than adequate wind glyph, and seemed interested when the sorceress pointed out stealing with magic wasn't a crime if he wasn't seen. Since the lad learned his wind glyph from Bonny's Tavern, Abel chipped in half the costs of the cover-up.

Everyone attending the trials wanted to negotiate terms for allowing the Tavern to operate in their demesne, so Abel assumed those still rejecting the idea stayed away. Even while negotiating, either the sorceresses or their apprentices would ask about the duel. Ferryl refused to discuss the subject with anyone, remaining deliberately aloof, though she drew her blade if one of the more important sorcerers asked to see it. She had a personal weapon now, the one she used in the duel, a not too subtle reminder to anyone considering a challenge. Uror had sent her the weapon, and its broken twin, allegedly because they were worthless now she'd ruined the set.

Where possible, Abel combined meeting sorceresses with checking out more of his trees, though now he was more careful about giving new Taverners access to tree magic. He found another big house, smaller than the first one but similarly concealed, but the homes on the other plots stayed hidden. Abel really didn't have time to look properly, because any spare moments were spent working up the Brinn valley looking for the troll. Zephyr swore she caught a brief glimpse of a youngster one night, but it tunnelled away, so they were on the right track. Ferryl and Zephyr found magical traces of the mystery toadstools, so the three of them kept searching whenever they could. A burned patch near a collapsed hole puzzled Ferryl, but it wasn't repeated. At least there weren't any more signs around Brinsford, so hopefully the creatures had been scared off for now.

None of the Taverneers had much spare time. Closer to home, a repeated TV clip about cleaning up Leferrier Park increased sales of Bonny's Tavern. The additional players only led to a few new magical Taverners, so hopefully all the local recruits had been found during the launch publicity. Even so, all the villages around Stourton that didn't have an active church would sooner or later need at least one tree, reserved for

Taverner use. The wind had been whispering, because some places also had local dryads willing to negotiate to help power the boundary.

Petra finally got her tree, planted just outside the church boundary in the car park belonging to her uncle's small printing business. Since the church already protected her village, Petra used the tree to protect the small industrial estate, and a new housing estate on the outskirts.

Elsewhere, six million quid had solved the immediate cash flow problems when hiring premises for Taverner practice. In some cases Abel authorised the purchase of a small plot to plant trees or place a clubhouse. He only supplied the actual clubhouse in one case, an old caravan, because even six million wouldn't be enough as the game spread. Woods and Green set a junior on dealing with planning permission where necessary, and shipping trees or sometimes dryad seedlings around the country. Terese warned Abel his rental income wasn't covering costs, so he told her to pay for everything with the winnings. Abel still kept hoping the requests for help would slow down, but as the game spread a steady stream poured into the Ferryl Shayde email box.

At least the new recruits were still struggling with the whole idea, and controlling their wind glyph. These days, an explanation of true sorcerer power, a truly spectacular glyph cast by an adept, and details of Stu's banishment, were all part of the introduction. So far, that seemed to be working. No more recruits had broken the rules, though a few had left, at least two approaching sorcerers and asking for tethers. As school drew nearer, the Taverners concentrated on identifying the right person to put in charge of each local Tavern. Between holidays, the satellite Taverns would have to manage almost completely on their own.

Shannon, Rachel and Cecilia took care of the assessments, zooming around in the convertible to try and decide who could be trusted with extra magic from trees. There'd be fewer problems with removing an access, because any new trees were marked as Pendragon's. That way, individual permission glyphs were drawn on skin, taken from a list Ferryl and Zephyr designed. Kelis and Jenny learned to do so without binding anyone, Rob daren't try, and Abel let Zephyr or Ferryl do the job. Where Abel had to use Celtchar's trees, he only allowed access to one tree. The list in the dragon's room grew until Abel had to file the names, locations and glyphs alphabetically, so he could find them.

Some of the six million pounds helped to cover up several small but potentially awkward moments, when a member of the public spotted an amateur playing with magic. Abel learned to get a price from the church, the Magical Council and the local sorcerers before choosing one. Sometimes Ferryl mazzled a few people and that solved the problem. Despite that, cover-ups were a continual, low-level drain on the shrinking balance.

The situation remained a mess, but not quite out of hand in the UK. The first emails from outside the UK came as a terrible shock.

*　*　*

As more foreign teenagers discovered Bonny's Tavern, through British friends or the internet, some recognised the creatures but weren't in Germany and conveniently close to Emst and his family. A variety of Taverners convinced parents to let them take a road trip in Europe, especially once the adults saw the transport and chauffeur. The Range Rover came in useful for foreign diplomacy, making a good impression when Taverners met sorcerers in Europe and Scandinavia.

The chauffeur for any Taverners going to Europe came as a surprise to them all. Claris had taken a full-time job with Pendragon Security, as trainee security personnel, allegedly because she didn't expect to get the grades for University. Her new uniform, and her profession, reassured some parents. The real reason she took up security work might not have been as reassuring for anyone, especially her mum. The sparring and confrontation training helped her tame her volatile temper, while increased competence with her baton helped her deal with her leech memories. Claris still didn't want to learn magic properly, just enough to charge her baton and throw simple wind glyphs hard enough to relieve her magical itch.

There still wasn't a way of dealing with the occasional emails from outside Europe. As Bonny's Tavern spread across the globe, Jenny sat down for a serious discussion with her parents. She'd made a big decision, to take a gap year before University. Ostensibly Jenny wanted to travel the world, promoting the game and organising local outlets. She would also organise the growing number of new Taverns, groups of players, advertising them locally to boost sales. There were already players in Australia, the USA and Canada, just as Terese had predicted, so the sooner she started the better. The trip should do just that, even if the real reason was to meet the few magically-aware players. Jenny would reassure those seeing creatures, and help them set up a local magical Tavern.

Three other Taverners agreed to take a gap year to do the same, even if, as Tobias pointed out, he wouldn't get into University anyway. As yet the magical players abroad were few and far between, so the four of them, split into two pairs, might be enough. The foreign contacts seemed mollified by promises to visit them, recognising the difficulties in teenagers jetting all around the world unsupervised. Instructions on how to shortcut the glyph activation, by drawing a Tavern sign and the glyph, reassured the newcomers, as did the parcel containing a score of Tavern hexes and repeat instructions. The potential foreign recruits were promised further instructions once they'd fluttered a leaf, live on Skype, for one of the original Taverners to check.

Jenny's parents felt better about the globetrotting once others offered to go with her, just in case she ran into some sort of problem. Laurence's blue blood and business contacts helped, with some relatives and business associates willing to arrange accommodation for a friend's daughter. Even so, the other Taverneers were a little worried about how local sorceresses would react to Jenny's arrival.

*   *   *

Jenny would be better prepared to meet magical trouble, with or without companions, after Ferryl had a long talk with Abel. So far, she'd been able to protect the Taverneers from direct confrontations with sorceresses. She'd only allowed Abel to face Mallet without her, at the meeting in Stoke, because Daorban promised to cover for her.

Realising she might die in the arena, and leave her friends with only basic glyphs, had been a real shock to Ferryl. Now the sorceress broke her own criteria for learning new magic. In a total departure, she taught each of the four friends and a puff of wind one very advanced offensive glyph. Each one learned a different glyph, based on their own abilities and preferred element. The multi-layered, multi-use glyphs were based around that core component with extras from other disciplines, each of variable strength.

Ferryl based Jenny's glyph on plant growth. Her automatic response to the attack in Sheffield had been to grow the hedge to slow up Boudicca's apprentices, and she'd used plants to kill Valdar. The glyph combined plant growth with minerals or trace metals from the soil to create very strong, tough vegetation. With serious intent, variations, and plenty of magic, the roots or shoots could pierce light metal plate, crush ribs, or resist fire, and were durable enough to seriously test a shield. To stress a less than perfect shield, Ferryl taught Jenny to weave the growth into a web, with hardened thorns that attacked over a wide area.

Since he'd always preferred fire, Abel finally learned how to cast Ferryl's red web. That turned out to be constructed mostly of fluctuating fire that would cling and concentrate on any flaw. Solid elements plucked from the surroundings added strength to the structure, allowing it to dig into a shield, and with sufficient intent the web would continue crushing a victim as it cooled.

Ferryl thought long and hard about Rob's glyph. He'd really impressed her with his progress in controlling earth, but she didn't want to eat up too much of his magic. In the end she tried to balance them; the glyph would cost more magic than the others but would be very hard to stop. The colour and strength of Rob's web depended on the earth or rock he formed it from, but also combined elements from earth and air to coat it with a tarry corrosive. The crushing aspects were enhanced, because this web relied mainly on strength to grind through or crumble a shield once the corrosive exposed a flaw.

When Rob asked, Ferryl explained why she used webs. They covered and weakened a larger area of an enemy's shield, without using extra magic, so the opponent couldn't strengthen a single point to conserve their magic. She also taught Rob and Abel the condensed form of their glyph, to hit a weakened portion, though a straight ice shard, tight windhammer or rock spike should work once a shield really started cracking.

Combining her mastery of water and air, Kelis learned to throw a real ice-storm. Numerous ice shards, carefully shaped while still water, were wrapped in braided air that looped and swirled as they attacked, to avoid interceptions. The number could vary from half a dozen large shards, hardened with embedded dust, to the clouds of corrosive ice dust Ferryl used against the fursomnium. The attack could strike simultaneously over an area, or the shards could hit one after the other to hammer a single point. The ice dust, funnelled into a narrow jet, could eat holes on rock.

Even Ffod ended up with her own personalised bop. Zephyr's new glyph produced a dazzling, bewildering cloud of fire-drops, intense spots of heat that swarmed all around and over the target. That didn't take as much magic as the others, relying heavily on fine control of wind glyphs. Ferryl pointed out that if Zephyr could lure the sucker near enough to a bush or young tree, and Abel could spare the magic, she already had a very potent secondary attack. The result of the dryad training had impressed even Ferryl. All the trainees worked hard whenever they could, spurred on by Ferryl thinking they might need this sort of firepower.

*   *   *

In the evenings Kelis and Abel, with Ferryl assisting, introduced their mothers to more aspects of magic. Without Abel's mum's experiences since she was a child, and Kelis's mum's trust in what Chris told her, it could never have worked. Abel's mum stopped the progression several times, when she needed time to sit and think it all through, or because she thought Jess might be getting too close to overload. Surprisingly, the dryad seedling that moved into her garden helped Jess. She would sit under the Horse Chestnut whenever she felt troubled, about her ex-husband and daughter as well as magic, and talk to the tiny creature with the Tavern shield on its front. After the scaled and fanged types she saw everywhere, the seedling looked inoffensive.

Dryad seedlings weren't gnarled, just a slim pale upright stick on half a dozen thin, pale rootlets, though they were more mobile than older dryads so they could travel to find a tree. This seedling's arms had barely begun to sprout either side at the top, and they only had three tiny twiglets on each. Despite that, the frail-looking creature could soon create a decent veil, and had started practicing a shield, both cast through the tree.

Neither Kelis's seedling, nor the one in the Red Maple, saw any mystery intruders. Abel, Ferryl and Zephyr were still working up the Brinn valley, searching for the troll, and were getting towards the end of the farmland. Searching the wilder parts, full of cliffs and gulleys covered in grass and heather, would be a mammoth task. Without the occasional discovery of traces of magic they'd have given it up, but Abel's map showed a definite trail.

The troll and toadstools wouldn't be spying on Brinsford again, not when the mature trees on the village green had ripened their seedlings. The rest of the boundary would soon have tree-powered, dryad-directed cover against spies and intruders. Abel insisted on giving Chestnut a home for a second seedling under the new agreement, because the first tree had been payment of a debt. Kelis still hadn't given up on the dryads in her old garden, though they still wanted trees for six seedlings. Kelis called them greedy, pointing out the meagre amount of barrier the closely-grouped parent dryads could cover.

As August became September, the Taverners really began to believe the worst was over. Keeping everything going while attending school wouldn't be easy, but there were a good few new recruits who had already left education. Abel's biggest worry was his mum, because the day was drawing closer when she'd insist on going into Castle House.

The next book

Ferryl Shayde V

Coming Soon

Abel's World

For those wanting a geographical location - Brinsford is approximately where Parwich and Parwich Hall are in England, while Stourton is about the right place for Bolehill. In Abel's world, both Matlock and Matlock Bath were destroyed in the Middle Ages, by trolls in the nearby cliffs, and were never re-settled. Sheffield is thirty miles north. Carsington Water is Kirk Ireton on our maps, a big reservoir two miles south of Stourton.

Brinsford - A small village in rural England, eight miles from Stourton.

Consists of:

Main Street - With pub and small shop.

Brinn Lane - Off the village green, leads to a small bridge then up valley to local farms - the posh end, where Kelis used to live.

Riverside Close - A dozen council houses - where Abel and Rob live.

Castle Road - The road running past Castle House, connecting Brinsford to the main road half a mile away.

Residents:

Abel Bernard Conroy - 17 - Lives with Mum. Dad died - accident at sea - First Taverneer.

Christine Conroy - Chris - 43 - Abel's widowed Mum, works part-time.

Henry Copples - 17 - Local bully - he is aware of magic creatures but not part of the Tavern.

Jessica Ventner - Kelis's mum, broke, still recovering after her recent divorce from her abusive husband.

John Tyler - Rob's Dad - works in Stourton.

Kelis Ventner - 17 - Abel's best female friend (originally the only one) - second Taverneer.

Melanie Tyler - 14 - Rob's sister - just discovered magic.

Mr. Copples - Local farmer.

Mrs. Turner - Local busybody. Claims she has seen green ghosts in the churchyard (actually goblins).

Rob Tyler - 17 - Abel's best friend - third Taverneer.

Samantha Tyler - 20 - Rob's sister - works at Ireton Reservoir leisure centre.

Stan - Local pensioner and reputedly a poacher - he has a shotgun and an old Jack Russel called Bugsy.

Terri Tyler - Rob's Mum - housewife.

Tyson Copples - 20 - Henry's brother - bully with crossbreed dog Cooch (Cuchelain).

Briarley - Village six miles from Brinsford, seven from Stourton - home to Petra - there is an active church keeping small magical creatures away.

Carsington Water - Reservoir and water sports centre two miles south of Stourton. The local area seems to be part of Castle House demesne but the reservoir is neutral - created after Celtchar's disappearance but surrounded by his demesne so nobody else can claim it.

Castle House - A big, old, rambling house on the outskirts of Brinsford, boarded up and protected by many powerful and dangerous glyphs. Access is guarded by a variety of creatures and constructs. The garden barrier persuades anyone approaching to change their mind.

Abel now has opened the first two doors, and given his friends access. The next locked double doors are at the end of a corridor three metres x seven long, with animal heads on the wall each side, a lioness and a black bear.

Frazer Close - A short Close, near Archer Retail Park, Sheffield, with three houses, one large and rambling, two smaller. They were Valdar's houses, and all have trees in the gardens.

Keele Hall and grounds in Newcastle-under-Lyme near Stoke - including hundreds of acres of woods on the Keele University campus

- the heart of Mallet's demesne.

Kielby - Village seven miles from Brinsford, nine from Stourton, the home of Jenny and Diane.

Leferrier Memorial Park - Public Park in Stourton, magically claimed by Pendragon, now Abel's. The park was donated by a widowed lady, and there is a lake and badly eroded memorial in the centre.

Millponds Nature Reserve - Over 500 acres of woodland in Sheffield, with hiking and horse riding trails, bluebells and daffodils, millponds, and a huge picnic ground. The reserve was donated to the city by a local 'businessman' in the mid-eighteen hundreds. Despite the public access, the trees are magically protected by sentry dryads and their magic is reserved for the Master of Castle House.

Pendragon House - The home of the Pendragon gryphon, an old, stone-built house with life-like dragon reliefs carved into the walls, dragon statues framing the front door, and dragon gargoyles. The house is across the road from Graves Park, Sheffield, which does not belong to the demesne.

St. Agnes Catholic Grammar School - A church school providing secondary education in the Stourton area. Church schools are heavily protected from magical creatures, so their pupils tend to be healthier. Without gremlins in the school equipment, or any biting fae distracting staff and pupils, these schools have a high success rate in GCSE and 'A' level exams. Ex-pupils are therefore generally more successful once they look for work, so they can usually pay more church tithes.

Stoneham Manor - A stately home near Warrington, on land inherited from Celtchar. Abel can access the woodland, guarded from others by glyphs and dryads. The large Georgian mansion is hidden from sight, frozen in time, and protected by an overgrown garden inside a magical barrier that even rejects Abel. The surrounding farmland, also belonging to Celtchar's estate, is rented out to local farmers.

Stourton - A market town eight miles from Brinsford, with schools and businesses that serve the surrounding villages.

Trentham Estate in Newcastle-under-Lyme near Stoke, consisting of extensive woodland, parkland, a golf course, Trentham Gardens, and a lake. The business is owned and run by Daorban's business, and is a valuable part of her demesne.

Stourton Comprehensive - Local secondary school

School year groups: 11 = GCSE year, 13 = A Level year

Mr. Gordon - Headmaster

Mrs. Poole - Deputy Head

Mrs. Svengy - Biology teacher

Carl - 13 - P.upil year 9 - new magic user, the first Taverner to be punished for misuse of magic.

Claris Ellsworth - 19 - an ex-leech victim - she is retaking year 13 after missing school during her leech possession - Taverner but dislikes magic.

Diane Forester - 14 - Jenny's sister, Melanie's best friend - year 10 - she has just discovered magic - Taverner

Fay Shayde - 17 - New pupil - year 12 - the last (or original) of the five Taverneers

Jenny Georgina Forester - 17 - Fourth Taverneer - a retired Acro dancer for the school team - year 13

Justin - 17 - Taverner adept in Stourton, Rachel's big brother - plays as Shayde Warrior - year 12

Kathy - 16 - New game player and Rob's girlfriend - she has just learned magic exists, but hasn't woken her own talent - year 12

Natalie - 14 - new magic user - traitor, now tethered by the church, for life

Petra - 18 - Taverner adept living in Briarley, who plays as a cat-sorceress. The first beta player to discover magic - year 13

Rachel - 15 - Taverner adept - Justin's sister, the youngest adept and leader of the militant Taverners - Plays as K'ress, a red-cloaked sorceress - year 10

Sarah Russel - 17 - Taverner adept living in Stourton, near Elm Park - year 12

Tobias - 18 - New Taverner who dates Kelis - year 13

Una - 17 - Taverner adept living in Stourton - plays as Robin D'Ritche, incl. sword - year 13

Warren - 17 - Taverner adept living in Stourton - plays as Nikk Smartish - year 12

Others:

Aesop - the senior sorcerer in Bradford

Amanda - 18 - Found by the church in the ruins of a leech lair. Infected but the Tavern's bound leech killed the seed. She is now in a church hospital.

Anniyah - Anni - New Asian-English trainee in Middlesbrough, with her two non-magical friends.

Beowulf - Old-looking bearded sorcerer. Very powerful and old-fashioned, possibly on the Magical Council.

Bertram - Secretary in Pendragon Enterprises Sheffield office.

Boudicca - A new sorceress (ex-apprentice whose sorcerer has been killed) with a small, weak demesne in Sheffield.

Cecilia - 18 - Found by the church in the ruins of a Leech lair. Infected but the Tavern's bound Leech killed the seed. She is now in a church hospital.

Celeborn, Denethor, and Galadriel - Pendragon's dead senior apprentices.

Celtchar - A powerful sorcerer, now dead - the previous Master of Castle House.

Daorban - Mistress of Trentham. A 243-year-old black sorceress in Stoke. Her name means female slave, in Irish.

Dupont - A noted duellist. He trained as an apprentice in every weapon allowed in duels between sorcerers. (Magic, and a large variety of edged weapons and black powder firearms) Named for Pierrer-Antione Dupont, the mid-eighteenth century duellist.

Eleanor - Friend of Mz Fisher - a woman in her sixties who can see creatures, but thinks they are ghosts. She heads a study group who are trying to make contact.

Emst - 19 - Laurence's German cousin, who translates Bonny's Tavern into German.

Enise - Anniyah's non-magical Turkish friend. She has five very protective brothers.

Eric - 21 - Warren's big brother, a Taverner adept, and now the manager for Pendragon Enterprises, Stourton.

Father Curtis - A priest freed from leech possession by the Tavern.

Fish - Mz Fisher - An investigative reporter who believes she can see ghosts.

Frederick - 54 - An adult who sees magical creatures. He befriended a dryad in Elmwood Park, which helped him recover from his breakdown. Frederick donated his house as a Tavern clubhouse, then a refuge. Taverner.

Gawain and Paragon - Pendragon's newest apprentices, both ran away.

Guinevere - Ginny - 36 - Ex-senior apprentice to Pendragon, captured by the Tavern, then tethered to Zephyr as a guard and tutor for Diane and Melanie.

Hamilcar - An aggressive and murderous sorcerer in Gloucester.

Jake Forester - Jenny's dad, a local builder and businessman. A director of Bonny's Tavern Ltd.

Jerry - Friend of Mz Fisher - a man in his late fifties who travels around cataloguing new ghosts - actually creatures.

Johannes Liechtenauer - Sorcerer in Stoke, named after a swordsman and is one himself.

Karen - 18 - Valdar's 'housekeeper.'

Kieran - 17 - First Taverner recruit outside the Stourton area. He lives in Hope Valley, in the Pennines - year 12.

Laurence Horatio Sperrick - 18 - Kelis's ex-boyfriend. His family are minor nobility, with a small stately home. The family is not wealthy so Laurence works in the family business, managing woodlands, sometimes in Europe. Taverner.

Mallet - Cheval Mallet - A sorcerer in Stoke, an enemy of Daorban.

Mannan - Redwolf's senior apprentice.

Marianne - Receptionist in Pendragon Enterprises Sheffield office.

Mark - 20 - Neighbour of Petra's, ex-Taverner. A devout Catholic now recruited by the Church Militant.

Master of Park Hall - A sorcerer with an unpronounceable name, a member of the Stoke treaty. A big gruff man, who favours pinstriped suits.

Pandora - A very strong sorceress in Cambridge, a K'ress lookalike who really is a killer.

Pendragon - Local sorcerer who attacked the Tavern and died.

Pride, Wrath, Envy and Avarice - Four of Pandora's senior apprentices.

Redwolf - A Birmingham Sorcerer who has a house in Stourton.

Seraph Angelique Bellamy-Courts - 19 - Wealthy young woman who manipulated pupils until stopped by Ferryl Shayde. She has now left school to manage one of her father's businesses.

Shannon - 18 - Taverner adept - A staunch church-goer and a pupil at St. Agatha's, she carries a cross as well as a Tavern hex - year 13.

Shawn - 20 - Taverner- now the manager for Pendragon Enterprises, Sheffield.

Siobhan - Daorban's senior apprentice

Stephanie Forester - Jenny's mum

Steven Clarence Horsely - 17 - Oxford - on trial for breaking the Accord with public magic.

Stu - A recruit in Dumfries. Abel's first recruit meeting outside his demesne.

Terese Green - Junior (and only other) partner in Woods and Green solicitors. An old, powerful sorceress although she has no title or demesne.

Tess - 20 - Pendragon's housekeeper

Uror - The senior sorcerer in Oxford. He dresses as a late medieval officer.

Valdar - A minor sorcerer with a small demesne in Sheffield.

Verenestra aka Veren - A new sorceress (ex-apprentice whose sorcerer has been killed) with a small, weak demesne in Sheffield.

Vicar Creepio Mysterio - Kelis's name for a peripatetic archbishop interested in Castle House, and the Tavern. He commands the Church Militant in the British Isles.

Zarah - Anniyah's black non-magical English friend.

*   *   *

Magical Entities:

Churchyard dryad: - Lives in a very old Yew tree that predates the church in Brinsford. This dryad and the younger ones in the other churchyard Yews are bound to the church but rebellious. The dryad still resents having a church built near its tree (800 years ago).

Dryad Chestnut: - A strong, ancient dryad living in a Horse Chestnut tree on the village green in Brinsford. It will answer questions for honey.

Dryad Elm: - A lonely old dryad, the only one in Elmwood Park. It lives in a Horse Chestnut, because all the Elms were killed by Dutch elm disease and the other dryads died or left. Has befriended a human, most unusual, and now Frederick has arranged for the Tavern to allow more dryads into the young park trees.

Dryad Sycamore: - A mere two hundred years old, rescued by Abel, Rob and Kelis when its tree blew over in a storm. Now a stone glyph allows it to be the only dryad in Dead Wood, the magically protected woodland behind Castle House gardens.

Dryad Walnut: - Dryad guarding one-fifth of Millponds Nature Reserve for the Master of Castle House.

Dryad Woods: - A small, very old dryad in a large bonsai growing on a rock inside an office building. Woods is the senior partner in Abel's solicitors, Woods and Green.

Ferryl Shayde: - A faded but powerful sorceress, origins unknown, a shimmer in the air unless possessing a living creature. She was imprisoned for 200 years in a pit, until Abel released her. Ferryl is now a Taverner, Fay Shayde, though only four people know she isn't human. She is searching for her memories, her wits, shards of bone inscribed with information that were torn from her last host's body by Celtchar.

Magical Council: - A group of powerful sorcerers and sorceresses who enforce the Accord, negotiate with the Church Council, and attempt to regulate the sorcerous community.

Zephyr: - A created living magical creature. Initially a wind spirit but enhanced, strengthened and taught to have both awareness and a sense of right and wrong. She lives in Abel's tattoo, to replace Ferryl Shayde once the sorceress became strong enough to possess a human host.

Ferryl's World

The world is ruled by Sorcery and Religion, their roles defined by:

The Accord

Modern English Version

In this document, Church refers to any organisation using prayers or religious ceremonies as a source of magical power. Sorcery refers to all other methods used by humans to access or control magic

Magic must remain a secret, hidden from all humans unless they have been awakened. All religions will announce that there have never been any true Witches, Sorcerers, or magical creatures. Any public display of magic must be explained away as natural phenomena or trickery. Magic users or priests advertising that magic still exists, either deliberately or through gross negligence, will die.

Churches and Sorcery will not fight each other. Members of one can only kill members of the other in self-defence or because one has broken the Accord. Forcibly taking control of an area is forbidden, though missionaries and heretics are permitted.

If enough of a population is converted, or loses faith, control of an area may change. The changeover, and other disputes, will be negotiated between two Councils, church and sorcery. Each will have one non-voting seat on the other Council, to observe.

Churches automatically hold sway within the areas protected by their places of worship, taking responsibility for protecting the non-magical and policing their priests. Wars between churches must not include areas held by sorcery, though non-magical soldiers can be used.

Sorcery may claim the rest of the world, shared between the strongest magic wielders. Each holder of a demesne has the right of High and Low Justice over both the magical and the non-magical. Sorcery may have wars, but only using non-magical soldiers. Such conflicts will avoid areas controlled by a Church, and hide any use of magic.

Any unclaimed areas are lawless, though Church and Sorcery will combine if necessary to eradicate serious threats to the inhabitants.

Codicils: By Order of the Magical Council:

Non-magical members of a magic-user's family cannot be targeted. Any such attack will result in the Council Members combining to kill the attacker and every blood relative and apprentice.

Unwarded employees cannot be targeted, providing they wear a hex to show their allegiance. Any such attack will result in the Council Members combining to kill the attacker and every apprentice.

From this date, any newly qualifying sorcerer or sorceress is limited to a maximum of eight senior apprentices, those adept with Air, Fire and Water. Any sorcerer already exceeding that number cannot promote any new senior apprentices unless one is released or killed. There is no limit to the number of junior apprentices, providing they only cast Air and Fire and cannot shield. If the restriction is exceeded, all the apprentices will be killed and the offender will be restricted to two apprentices for the next four hundred years.

From this date all apprentices must be released or killed after seventy-five years, or earlier. This does not apply to apprentices who have already been tethered for over seventy-five years.

The Magical World

Humans may rule, or try to, but there are many magical creatures and most do not acknowledge the right of anyone to control them

Magic: - A power that permeates the air, but cannot be utilised in its raw form. All living creatures absorb magic, but plants are unable to dissipate it. Trees are the greatest natural reservoirs of magic. Animals from insects to elephants will dissipate any surplus in an uncontrolled fashion, unless they are sentient and learn to utilise glyphs and store more.

Glyphs: - Patterns drawn or etched on solid objects or in air or water, or imagined, used to control magic and give it specific purpose. The strength of a scribed glyph depends on the magic put into it, and the medium it is drawn on. Glyphs inscribed in metal are the strongest, scribed in air the weakest, though glyphs imagined by adepts can be surprisingly powerful because of the intent behind them. The effect of a glyph depends on how much magic, skill, and intent is invested in the shaping and casting. The four basic glyphs are air, fire, water and earth. Combined with each other and shaped by intent, they are the basis for glyphs of increasing complexity. If enough subsidiary glyphs are woven into the construct, glyphs can accomplish almost anything that can be imagined. Conversely, a slight mistake can be catastrophic or fatal.

Veil: - A concealment glyph that can be anchored to an object or a person. The amount of concealment depends on the intent and magic poured into it.

Spun slowly anti-clockwise, a veil obscures living beings from unmagical sight, though the magically aware can still see through it and will detect the veil itself as a shimmer in the air. Spun faster it conceals plants, and manmade solids such as metal or glass, faster still dead organics such as wood and leather. The same speed will conceal an object such as a car if the glyph is drawn directly onto it. Spun at very high speed the glyph uses impractically huge amounts of magic but can conceal anything, including even its own shimmer, from magic users. Beings made of almost pure magic can still detect the intense magical activity, but not the veil or what is concealed.

Another identical glyph, spun clockwise at the same time, extends the size of the concealment globe, faster making it larger.

Shield: - A glyph that increases the natural protection covering the skin of all warded magic users. Heat or physical trauma can be felt through the shield while it is next to the skin, though the effect is reduced. The amount of magic used strengthens the shield, and it can by pushed out to cover others and nearby objects. Two shields touching causes both to drain magic from their users, with a spectacular light and heat display.

As a side effect, creating a shield cuts all tethers, spooky-phones, telephone or radio communications. Bindings will hold and shades can be controlled through a shield, but the protection must be dropped to allow them in or out.

A section of the shield away from a threat can be collapsed in beneath the skin, to allow communication down tethers or to free a phone.

*   *   *

Gods: - Most if not all gods and goddesses were originally sorcerers. Once they establish their symbol or mark, and create a heaven, the god's being is drawn into the heaven and their body dies. The god can now draw magic from worshippers, and utilise the magic in their heaven. A god's (or goddess's) power grows with the number of worshippers, as each prayer sends a small amount of magic to the heaven. Souls of believers are drawn to the heaven when they die. At one time there were many gods, but now the old gods act quickly to crush any new ones. Gods fade away as worshippers decrease, but are eternal as long as one worshipper still lives.

Some legends claim that glyphs were stolen from the first god.

Sorcerer or Sorceress: - An advanced glyph wielder who has learned how to prolong their life with magic. They are usually wealthy, live in a well-guarded home and control a wide area, keeping it clear of any large or particularly dangerous entities. Some who call themselves sorcerers are apprentices released early, without adequate training, often when their master or mistress has died. Providing they know enough glyphs, can wield enough magic, and can hold a demesne, they are tolerated but often despised.

Apprentice: - A magically aware teenager (the usual age for awakening), who accepts a tether from a sorcerer in return for training in magic. Apprentices are used to fill protection glyphs for their mistress's customers, using most of their naturally absorbed magic each day. The amount of magic they are allowed to keep for practicing, and the speed they learn new glyphs, varies from sorcerer to sorceress. Some apprentices may serve fifty or sixty years before being given the healing glyph, for instance, while others are never taught it.

Once established, the tether allows the sorcerer to read their apprentice's current thoughts (but not memories), pass instructions, drain magic from them, and control their actions. Memories can still be read if the sorcerer suspects foul play, by forcing the apprentice to think about a time or incident. With concentration the sorceress can treat an apprentice as a puppet, even throwing glyphs though their hands, but this is hard work so most are left to carry out their orders without direct control. The tether can inflict excruciating pain or kill an apprentice, which prevents any disobedience. Senior sorceresses use their access to an apprentice's thoughts to implant imperatives. Those force the apprentice to protect their mistress, and prevent any attempt to harm or betray the sorceress, even with the tether severed by a shield.

Witch or Warlock: - A minor magic practitioner, unable to progress to complicated sorcerous glyphs. With some, they simply haven't the natural talent, while others are failed apprentices. Those are stunted, their ability to channel magic almost burned out down the tether before they are released. Witches and warlocks have a normal lifespan, albeit longer and healthier than the average, a natural result of using magic. Most train a replacement, a village girl or boy who will also support them in old age.

Witches and warlocks develop lesser glyphs, drawn or carved so they need very little magic, often selling charms and hexes to those without magic. Witch magic can also remove or create minor curses, such as septic ear or warts. The profession is dying out, having been driven from the lucrative population centres by the much stronger sorcerers. Even in the countryside and villages, the current disbelief in magic and magical creatures has led to fewer customers. If they are too weak to become apprentices, modern youngsters prefer non-magical jobs that pay a living wage.

Bound Servant: - A being branded with a mark allowing a glyph wielder to control them completely. They will ignore pain or injury, and are hard to kill because they are partially protected from magic by their brand.

Tethered Servant: - A person or creature controlled with a less complicated version of the apprentice tether. They are not taught, nor rewarded, and are never released.

Entranced Servant: - A person controlled by desire. There is no connection, because the victim is completely besotted and will never betray, or disobey, their controller.

If they are ever released, all bound, tethered, or entranced servants deeply dislike or hate their controller.

Creatures Visible to the Non-Magical

Amanatik: - A spined, eight-legged turtle with a metre-long shell. Amanatik are the hunting hounds of the South American Creator Goddess Amana, who rode a giant turtle and had a mermaid's tail. Amanatik have huge heads sporting four long spiral tusks. They reached Europe after following Spanish treasure ships, or as sorcerer's pets. Amanatik prefer seashores, where they wait for their goddess, refusing to accept she has faded from the world.

Blood Leech: - Allegedly the remnants of an old blood magic experiment, blood leeches survive by possessing a human and feeding on fresh blood and the magic therein. As the leech grows, it will pierce internal organs to increase the blood supply, while magical tendrils invade and dominate the host's brain. A single leech may infect healthy humans with seeds, using short-range magical compulsion to subdue their prey. The seeds grow to control their hosts, and create a nest of blood leeches. The originating leech, known as the Firstseed, dominates and is protected by the others. Leeches are connected both by sensing each other's presence and an affinity for the lair, the home of the Firstseed.

Adult leeches prefer pale skinned hosts to shed excess heat. Hosts often wear dark glasses because their eyes show red around the pupils. Most find a willing victim, usually demanding a fixed period of possession (forty years) for the curing of an otherwise fatal illness. Once vacated, the discarded host should be left young and healthy but with no memory of the intervening years. If the leech has kept the bargain they will then live out their lives normally.

Not all leeches keep the bargain, some leaving the host barely alive and often infected with a seed. These also leave the host with full memories of forty years spent hunting humans and draining blood. The host may survive but memories may drive them insane. If a seeded host finds enough fresh blood, another blood leech is created. Even if the host finds a priest or sorcerer fast enough, the seed will poison them as it dies.

Dryad: - A creature that lives in trees, utilising the accumulated tree-magic to protect its home tree and prolong both their lives. Gnarled, bad-tempered, rude creatures, they can manipulate magic to create a veil to hide, or can change their appearance. Dryads will sometimes give answers to questions, in return for honey.

Dryads have a stout woody torso, no neck, and large, round eyes, which are different shades depending on their tree. Chestnuts' are chestnut brown, of course. Their torso matches the bark of their tree. Dryads stand on two short, stout legs without knees, ending in roots that often embed in the ground to help the dryad stand. Their two arms resemble thin branches with long twigs as fingers, but no foliage.

Dryads can work glyphs using tree magic. They protect their tree against rot and disease, and expel creatures that may seriously damage or drain their home. Adult dryads control their tree well enough to drop branches on attackers, strangle small creatures with roots, or hit them with branches. Full control of the roots and branches takes many, many years of practice.

Dryads are asexual, though they can produce very realistic facsimile human features to lure humans close enough to steal a little magic. All dryads can ripen young, but few do so because there are few unclaimed trees. The seedlings are given a basic knowledge of the world, the basic glyphs that dryads can work, and shown how to control a tree. Seedlings move into a sapling before it is mature enough to attract sorcerers or the church, and the two grow together. Both are vulnerable until the dryad learns to use magic, and the sapling matures enough to accumulate surplus magic.

Fraggon: - The true name is unknown, so a trainee sorceress named the creature for its appearance, Frog-Dragon. The long, frilled, many-legged creature has a frog-like head, and looks like a stone guardian when it coils into a column reaching above head height. When it moves, the creature is living stone, both more agile and more intelligent than a guardian. Fraggon may be a rare creature, or an advanced magical creation.

Goblins: - Are visible to the non-magical because they eat large amounts of non-magical food. Goblins eat almost anything humans or animals do, but prefer junk food (or fruit cake) to raw meat. They raid rubbish bins, cat and dog dishes and bird tables, but also eat magical creatures and small animals and birds.

Goblins have been hunted almost to extinction for two main reasons. Firstly their gastric juices and wind are very flammable, making them a severe fire hazard. Goblins sleeping near open fires could explode and set fire to the house if they passed wind. Sorcerers still believe a goblin with indigestion started the Great Fire of London. Some sorcerers once used captive goblins as entertainment at feasts. Guests would shoot burning arrows at tethered goblins, or heat them slowly until they exploded.

Periodic attempts to wipe them out failed because they bred too fast. Goblins often reached plague proportions as their melds (clan, family) keep expanding. Even goblins have no way to limit their numbers except suicide, when their Olds (old goblins) deliberately set themselves on fire.

Periodic hunts scoured the countryside, but one survivor is enough to regrow the meld. Although goblins helped to keep rats in check, for much of human history the fire hazard outweighed their benefits. A goblin infestation sweeping down from the north of England, and wiping out the flea carriers, might be why the Black Death petered out in the Midlands.

The signing of the Accord almost exterminated goblins, because they are very obviously magical and magic had to be kept hidden. After the concerted massacres by both sorcerers and religion, the few remaining melds are secretive, and strictly control their own numbers to avoid notice.

Goblins are dark emerald green, potbellied, vaguely humanoid munchkins. Their two short, skinny legs have fat feet with five fat flat grasping claws, two backwards and three at the front - which can be used for perching. Two long skinny arms end in small palms with four long knobbly clawed fingers, and a very fat, short thumb. The round, bald head has a wide mouth, lots of tiny teeth, a looong thin tongue, round, dark green eyes, and no apparent ears or nose.

Goblins live in melds (similar to a very close-knit, closely related clan). Old goblins are called Olds. Goblin skin crumbles as they get older, until internal gases and juices mix with their magic, erupting in a small explosion. Olds may look for the flame (suicide) if there is a food shortage or the meld is too numerous to keep hidden. When an Old is close to exploding, they leave the meld to avoid killing other goblins.

Batlins - The smallest goblins, with bodies the size of a thrush. Batlins are like other goblins except for large bat-like wings. They live in caves, barns and attics, very much like bats, and usually fly at night to avoid notice.

Ratlins - The size of a large rat, and not as rotund as other goblins. They live in burrows and often steal flower bulbs, or gnaw the roots on living bushes and unprotected trees.

Stonelins - About a metre tall. These goblins disguise themselves with a Seeming, becoming gargoyles or grotesque garden statues or ornaments.

Hobgoblins - Are bigger, tougher and scarier and were used by some sorcerers as guards. Hobgoblins lived in wild places and deep caves, but are now allegedly extinct.

Troll: There are several types, all allegedly destroyed by the church or sorcerers.

Cave or Rock Trolls still exist, hiding deep in the earth. An adult looks like a crusty slug with a pointed head, and is the size of an articulated truck. They have little magic outside of an ability to compress and strengthen earth and rock. This ability allows them to move through solid rock, by compressing the rock outwards leaving a tunnel. Removing the compression seals the tunnel again, stopping pursuers. Trolls accrete rock and earth as they grow, bonding it into their skins as armour, so most glyphs bounce off an adult or only damage the crust. New-formed trolls are about a metre tall, looking like a fat half-worm on end but twisted like a swirl of cream or soft ice-cream (or a dog poop). Trolls emit deep rumbles and vibrations, but there is controversy over that being communication, and if trolls are sentient enough to use a language.

Swamp Trolls and Water (Bridge) Trolls are probably extinct, as they were more visible and killed on sight.

Ice Trolls might still exist in the Polar regions, outside the areas covered by the Accord. There have been unconfirmed sightings by explorers, and from aircraft, but those might be natural phenomena.

Varglin: - The lesser descendants of what were called vargs, the children of the Norse wolf-god Fenrir. They are almost a large wolf, but with sickly green mossy fur, longer fangs and claws, and a ruff of orange porcupine quills. Varglin packs usually inhabit thick woodlands, coming into the open to hunt lesser magical beings, or weak animals.

*　*　*

The following are invisible, unless the human is awakened to magic. Those with enhanced magical sight can see the glow of magic inside the more transparent creatures, created by their life-spark.

Life-Sparks, Ghosts or Souls: - Life-sparks are only visible to those with greatly enhanced magical sight, and some magical creatures. These sparks of magic remain after any entity, magical or otherwise, dies. The life-sparks drift, fading slowly away, or disappear abruptly soon after death.

The churches maintain only human life-sparks are souls, and believers are drawn to their God's heaven. Heathen souls drift and fade, the same as those of magical creatures and animals. Some believe that the sparks of magical creatures can regrow into a new creature, if they come across enough concentrated magic, though the new life has no memory of the old. Because life-sparks cannot be contained, drifting through walls and shields, nobody has ever proved any theory.

A few small magical hunters, such as feral spirits, prey on the sparks, but most of those who can see them ignore them.

Free Spirit: - A semi-sentient fragment of a force of nature that has absorbed a fraction of the life from a dying entity, or is on the periphery of a release of strong magic. A ripple in the water, a flame, a puff of wind or even a pebble can become alive, though not really thinking, and will persist if it finds enough life magic to feed on. The amoeba of the magical world, free spirits are hunted by a myriad of tiny creatures. Wind spirits are mobile and almost invisible, even with magical sight, but earth spirits are visible, immobile, unable to find new magic, and easy prey.

Feral Spirit: - These are free spirits that survive long enough to understand hunger, and seek out the stray magic leaking from non-magical beings. Any who survive long enough, the rarest of feral spirits, learn to deliberately take magic from fish eggs, tiny insects and free spirits. Feral spirits that survive for centuries learn how to drain the magic from larger animals and magical creatures. Although still very simple creatures, the strongest can kill animals the size of humans.

Once again the feral wind spirits are hardest to find, but are the rarest because they have no real defence. Feral water spirits are few, manifest as maelstroms such as charybdis, or possibly saltstraumen and moskstraumen off the coast of Norway. The largest are tolerated, as it is easier to avoid them than destroy them. Feral fire spirits are the most numerous, very obvious but long-lived and difficult to reach, and in the past they have been responsible for such phenomena as the mesas and escarpments of the American West. The feral fire spirit under Burning Mountain in Australia may be 6,000 years old, while the fires under Centralia in America may be a young one.

Even those examples are still ephemeral in nature, mostly magic but with few magical defences. Any strong magic user or large predatory magical creature might drain them, if they can overcome the physical dangers. Completely killing them is difficult, because a small surviving fragment can hide in ripples or a few flames and grow back in time.

The final form, so rare it doesn't have a name, is when a feral spirit becomes truly sentient. They are usually discovered and destroyed at this stage, because their actions are obviously not natural. If it survives to realise how vulnerable it is, such a spirit becomes almost impossible to find and much harder to kill, and may learn to manipulate enough magic to be truly dangerous. The church in particular will use all their resources to hunt down any such creature, once they learn of it.

Beinsnork: - Old Norse for Bonesnake - a metre-long yellow snake with tiny pincered legs, covered in short, sharp triangular blades of bone. They are allegedly the creations of the world-snake, if it bleeds on the bones in a graveyard.

Brownies: - Good ones are fanatically tidy. They live with humans if possible and tidy up dust, cobwebs, dirt on clothes or pet hair for the traces of magic clinging to them. Brownies will leave if humans are either too tidy so there is no food, or too scruffy. If trapped in a house where they can't find a small private place, brownies will actually create a mess.

Catspaw: - A hand-sized beetle with cat's paws and claws and a single sharp spine down its back. They move very quietly and can climb almost anything, so catspaws were often used by ancient sorcerers as a bound servant, sacrificed to obtain information.

Fae: - Faerie-like but leaner, predatory and larger. Some hunt faeries or small insects and are harmless to humans. Others take small amounts of magic from humans and animals, using barbs, suckers or proboscis that can leave itchy marks and be dangerous in numbers. The natural magical food supply for the larger versions is sucked like mosquitoes from unprotected humans, animals or large magical grazers.

Faerie: - Rough-skinned flying creatures in shades and patterns of brown, with long, thin horny wings and a variety of limbs. They absorb magic from grass, leaves, flowers or fruit. Eating a little helps them remain solid, which leaves tiny blemishes on the food. Too many can drain the magic until the plant looks sickly or is dying, and might kill patches of grass. The brightly coloured faerie that preferred blossoms, those giving rise to human legends of fairies, were too visible and were hunted to extinction.

Fursomnium: - Also known as a Dream Stealer or Eater. One of the most beautiful predators on Earth, a pale, luminescent blue cloud containing bright sparks. The creature prefers a place where humans sleep, because human dreams are more complex so they give off more magic. As it grows the fursomnium spreads webs through bedroom walls and ceilings. They can sometimes follow a strong dream back to the sleeper, inducing nightmares to increase the emotions and therefore the magic.

If a fursomnium eats well, for instance if someone nearby goes insane, it can sleep for many tens of years. The ambience and rumours of ghosts in old asylums are often due to the presence of a huge, well-fed fursomnium. A dream shield, often known as a dreamcatcher, can thwart a fursomnium, using glyphs powered by the magic in the gems.

Ganshbaal: - Glittering black nightmare scorpion rats. The survivors of the rats that bore the Indian Elephant-God Ganesh, in his final battle before fading from the world. During that battle, rage and magic transformed them into vicious, poisonous combatants.

Most ganshbaal live in areas that are difficult to traverse, gathering near any paths or trails. That is believed to be in homage to their god, who was revered as a remover of obstacles. Ganshbaal usually keep such paths clear of minor magical pests, but may attack any travellers who worship other gods.

Globhoblin: - A warty, globular creature up to the size of a football, with a variable number of legs ending in clawed feet. They drain the magic from bacteria, maggots and flies on discarded food, but prefer to prey on the helpless like kittens, hamsters, caged birds, chicks and baby animals as well as small, slow wildlife and magical creatures. Globhoblins will also prey on drunks, human babies or the sick, using a stinger to draw magic directly. Despite their size, globhoblin are easily killed by weak glyphs, or banished by hexes, but there are too many to wipe out completely.

Grazers: - A variety of non-flying creatures ranging up to the size of a bison, which feed on the magic in grass, weeds, shrubs and crops. They are often found in farmland, where an infestation may kill or stunt crops.

Grelf: - A magical eel, a fresh-water carrion eater covered in small spines. They are hatched in the bloated carcase of a drowned animal, gorging on the rotten meat, the carrion eaters from bacteria upwards, and each other, to gain strength and become solid enough to survive. Their spines often infected human swimmers, but grelf are rare in Britain now that waterways are being cleaned up.

Gremlin: - A tiny creature whose skin and carapace look somewhat like a toothless old man in overalls. They live inside any type of machinery or electrical equipment, often causing malfunctions. Angry or frustrated humans touch the object, and the gremlin can feed from the leaking magic.

Hoplin: - Little predatory creatures looking like a miniature armadillo but hopping like a kangaroo, with a mildly venomous bite. They hunt in pairs that can drain the magic (and life) from small magical creatures such as thornies, and kill rats, mice, caged birds or a kitten for their magic. Hoplins can be useful for dealing with infestations of rats and mice, but will also eat your hamsters, canaries, pictsies, pixies and brownies.

Pictsies: - Extravagantly jawed tiny predators that often live with humans and their pets, where they hunt faerie, fae, lice, flies, insects and spiders.

Pixies: - Only live with or close to humans, absorbing the magic leaking from the residents of 'their' house or left on clothes. They remove any dandruff and loose hair to store a surplus.

Piskies: - Can be found in the wild, especially around large herds, but prefer gardens or stock pens, preying on the pests infesting animals. They are useful for dealing with ticks or fae, but may cause unexplained accidents if trapped in a house.

Ruttlyte: - Similar to a ratlin but grey, and veined with virulent blue and purple, ruttlyte are the result of a failed attempt at killing and binding a whole meld of ratlins. They are secretive, and like ratlins they prefer flight to fight, but their longer claws and teeth, and tougher skin, make them more dangerous when cornered.

Satan-Steed: - A white lizard two metres long, with red horns, and red jaws like a coachman beetle, usually found in bogs or where old bogs dried up. They are allegedly inhabited by the spirits of those buried alive in ancient rites. Six of these allegedly pull the Devil's coach, or in some mythologies they are the mounts of the Four Horsemen.

Skurrit: - A pack hunter with a long, thin, low-slung half-metre-long body and a variable number of short legs with clawed feet. Their body is covered in long, matted, dirty brown fur, with a light brown bald tail and a nearly bald head and snout, each about 40 cm long, making the whole creature about 1.2 metres long. The small skull has two tiny red eyes, and a long thin pointed snout containing several rows of sharp teeth. One alone will probably run from a cat, two or more might hunt it.

Slimies: - These have a variety of names, none complimentary because the creatures look like dull, greenish slugs with brown scaly patches. The creatures are very slow, so tend to settle on stains or other food sources unlikely to move. Since they absorb the stain as well as the bacteria and their magic, slimies were useful when stains were difficult to remove. They are less popular with the advent of washing powder and bleach.

Thornie: - A prickly creature the size of a mouse, vaguely humanoid, that prefers magic from fruit but will graze from most human food. Thornies infest canteens and rubbish dumps to drain magic from bacteria, flies and maggots.

Wealth Toad: - Sometimes called a Luck Toad. A fist-sized, furred, three-legged toadish thing with three straight, sharp horns. They are not usually belligerent. A luck toad will sometimes use a simple seeming to live in a home as a small statuette, where it will absorb magic when the residents touch or stroke it. Both names were created because the first recorded examples were discovered at new gold strikes.

A profusion of other small creatures exist, grazing or hunting the magic in anything from bacteria, moss and grass through fleas up to rabbits or small dogs. Those targeting spoiled food are actually after the microscopic amounts of magic in either fungi or germs, with any insects a bonus. Creatures also hunt each other. Cats and dogs can see them but not clearly, just enough to avoid them or fight back. Some are beneficial, but aware humans prefer to stop most from fluttering, crawling, hopping or slithering into their homes.

Allegedly Extinct Creatures

Aryadne's Hound: - A man/spider hybrid created by the Goddess Aryadne to serve her. They lived in caves and ate carrion. Aryadne's hounds were well over two metres tall with four spider legs and four spider-like arms on a humanoid torso.

The hounds allegedly died out when Aryadne faded, unable to survive without magic from their goddess, but there are occasional sightings of something similar. Legends of pale creatures living in deep caves, attacking explorers, might be based on old tales of Aryadne's hounds.

Dragon: - There were many types, usually inhabiting specific parts of the globe, but most were killed in the great Dryad-Dragon wars. Sorcery and religion hunted the survivors to extinction. Magically preserved trophies are still displayed by some people.

There are rumours of iuloch, magical vessels containing much of the skill and knowledge of an adult dragon, created at the moment of death as a gift for their young. The traditional receptacle was an acorn, a symbol of the potential within, but very old, powerful dragons needed more space so the iuloch could look like anything portable.

Gryphon: - Sometimes called a griffin, a half eagle, half lion traditionally entrusted with the treasures of kings and sorcerers. The actual creature is extinct, but the object magically bonding a sorcerer to his holdings is traditionally referred to as their gryphon. A small facsimile of a gryphon protects all significant locations.

The oldest, strongest gryphons, hundreds of years old, are capable of defending their home, the magical centre of their sorcerer's demesne. Such gryphons can bind allies to the demesne, to prevent betrayals.

Kalkatrie: - Created by the Greek gods as a tracker. The kalkatrie has a short, flat, pointed beak with teeth, large eyes, a ruff of tiny cockerel-like feathers, two small chicken-like legs with clawed feet, stubby feathered wings and a long, scaled tail. Their sting sends the victims, magical or not, into a deep sleep. They usually slither, preferring to live in tunnels, but can fly or run short distances. The cockatrice legends are probably based on glimpses of kalkatrie.

Ogre: - A six metre tall by three metre wide creature with a tail and tall forked horns, making them look even bigger. They have four thick limbs, each with six vicious talons, and burning green eyes. Descriptions can vary since few opponents survive an encounter. Ogres were hunted by the Church in particular, so now they only exist as bound shades, used as attack beasts as they fixate on any perceived threat. Their square scales can be mistaken for giant's armour.

Skoffin: - There is some dispute if a skoffin is a dragon or something unique. The few, very old sketches show a vaguely draconic or lizard-like creature, semi-transparent, with spines along the body. Two fans of much longer spines may be wings with transparent membranes. The Icelandic creature breathes fire, or the breath can be used to turn attackers into stone. Breathing fire creates charcoal if the skoffin is hunting for food. This creature is probably the source of both the gorgon myth and sightings of basilisk. There are some accounts that claim a skoffin can turn a victim to living stone, still capable of movement and thought.

The Last Paladin: - A mythical figure. Rumours persist that the Last Paladin is female, but nobody can be certain because of the armour. The first recorded sightings were three thousand years ago, and were definitely male. Since then the lone traveller has been given many names, usually translating as the Wanderer or Nameless Warrior. Originally a foot soldier, then a mounted warrior, latterly the horse and rider are wearing crusader armour. The Wanderer, known as the Last Paladin, roams the earth looking for redemption, and may appear to help you if your cause is hopeless but just.

Created Entities

Bound Shade: - A creature with its life-spark magically captured at the moment of dying, embedded into stone, bone, wood or imprisoned in a tattoo. Unless deliberately preserved, there is little of the original mind left except basic reactions. If embedded, the captive soul is forced to create a semblance of life in something dead, and follow inscribed instructions. Those held in tattoos are summoned slaves, animating a temporarily re-created magical version of their body whenever instructed.

Embedded bound shades are usually left as guards, in what appears to be a lifeless plant or plaster figure. Others are used to create novelties such as animated footstools, to amuse a sorcerer or guests. While torpid, such bound shades use up very little magic, though once roused its magic must be replenished, and those left on guard for long periods may prey on anything passing nearby.

Many senior sorcerers carry a bound shade as an additional personal guard. Only the strongest magic users risk carrying large creatures this way, because creating them, and damage to the bound shade, will drain magic from the tattoo wearer. Very large creatures such as ogres and giants are not usually bound into tattoos, because of the amount of magic needed to create the body. The Church Militant utilise huge bound shades by designating extra priests to protect the tattoo wearer and pass extra magic if necessary.

Living Shade: - There is some dispute whether a living shade is created, or is an alternate version of the original creature. A living shade still retains its own life-spark, deliberately abandoning its body to enter the tattoo as a fully voluntary passenger. When reconstituted, such creatures are a true functioning animal, with blood and bone, and will not draw magic from their bearer if injured. Magic is used to heal them once they re-enter their tattoo.

The living shade can pass through a shield constructed by its bearer. Suggestion can influence their actions, but once free they will act as they see fit, usually defending the person bearing their tattoo. With concentration the bearer can get a sense of what they see, which makes them valuable scouts because they are indistinguishable from wildlife. Despite their advantages, few sorceresses carry living shades as they are not connected or directly controlled.

Platycroc: - A unique bound shade, looking like a gigantic cross between a platypus and a crocodile. Fifteen metres from the tip of the three-metre duck-beak to the end of the flat stubby tail, three metres high and a little wider, it has six clawed, webbed feet on short, thick legs. The creature is protected by thick scales that deflect anything but strong magical attack. At the end of the beak is a large, solid lump used for ramming or beating on an opponent.

Once launched the creature will continue battering at an opponent, immune to pain and ignoring damage, until one or the other is destroyed. The platycroc, supposedly a failed attempt at a warbeast, is held in a priest's tattoo and used by the Church Militant.

Stickybangs: - A small short-lived magical construct created by an amateur sorceress, usually cast in numbers. The many-legged creatures cling to whatever they hit. Designed for combating shields, stickybangs suck magic from the target until saturated and then explode.

Stone Guardian: - These are formed from compressed stone, very hard to destroy without magic. The construct is charged with magic and set to guard, often looking like a statue. Once triggered, the magic will animate the stone, repairing any weathering or damage. The animating glyph is carved in the centre of the stone block, a very skilled magical task, and impossible to reach without destroying the vessel.

*   *   *

Names ascribed to various ancient, dangerous spirits.

Pungh Hmmshtfun (Very old type of Hebrew) Breath Stealer

spiritus qui furabatur (Latin) Spirit Stealer

Koška Smerti (Russian) Death Cat

Braeth Huntian (Olde Englishe) Breath Hunter

Background and Charactors
for Bonny's Tavern
a New Board Game with D&D Roots

The world of Bonny's Tavern is semi-medieval, a place where cruel tyrants, monsters, grasping nobles and corrupt churchmen abound. An ancient pact between magic, church and nobility has failed, leaving most of the population, those lacking magic or armies, defenceless. The sorcerers, nobles, church and a variety of magical monsters fight to maintain their power bases, often crushing the populace between them. The best a peasant or small businessman can hope for is to scrape together enough to pay their tithes and taxes, and be ignored. The game quests include clearing monster infestations, finding lost treasures and mythical weapons, freeing heroes or maidens, hunting fugitives, fighting small wars or rebellions, robbing corrupt bishops and barons, or helping the local populace when famine or war wreck their lives.

All game quests start at Bonny's Tavern, which acts as a neutral meeting place for creatures and humans who would normally attack each other on sight. Bonny's half-sister is a mercenary, Robin D'Ritche, which frightens off any low-level ruffians who might risk fighting Champ, the ex-pugilist bouncer. The smith, Fe Hamma, insists on carrying out business there because he likes the ale. Anyone upsetting him won't be able to buy his enhanced armour or weapons, and might fall foul of his enchanted mace. Cackle the Crone wants a place to sell her charms and hexes. If you interfere, be prepared to wake up with a septic ear. Bullseye the Bowman has to buy new enchanted shafts somewhere, while Nikk the Warlock Thief needs a place to sell his plunder, or steal yours if you annoy him.

Stronger potential raiders, magical or otherwise, understand the message and the magic in the Tavern shield, the sign hung outside. A variety of humans and creatures, all dangerous in their own right, find having a safe house convenient. Even the nobles and church stay clear, because potential enemies as varied as a Paladin, a Barbarian hero, a wild hunter and several sorcerers and sorceresses, including a feline with her bodyguard, have agreed to enforce the truce. They enjoy a peaceful pint of ale, or a good meal and a bed without fleas.

Characters:

Players can choose another name and sex when adopting a character. The standard types are not all human, and advanced players may choose different racial characteristics for their chosen character to enhance their skills.

Not all characters can be adopted by players. Bonny the Barmaid or Champ supervise the game, much as a DM (Dungeon Master) guides a game of Dungeons and Dragons. There are a wide variety of monsters, entities and ephemeral beings, as well as magical traps and dangerous terrain, but the following characters will usually be found at Bonny's Tavern itself, the start of the game.

Some such as Ffod or Fe Hamma can be recruited, or persuaded to help. They will react according to their characteristics. Others such as Creepio may join you voluntarily, or obstruct a quest.

Bonny the Barmaid - Part-owner of the tavern, half-sister to Robyn. Her Tavern has strong magical protection gifted by a mysterious customer, possibly another part-owner.

Bullseye - His slim build, seamed and lined dark brown skin, and phenomenal upper-body strength, are unlike any known race. A superb non-magical bowman, using arrows etched with symbols that can pierce most armour, Bullseye can test and even defeat some magical shields. Despite his rounded ears, rumours persist that he must be at least part-Elven, while the malicious suggest part-dryad.

He is armed and armoured like a medieval longbowman, a fierce but agile melee fighter who prefers enchanted mail to heavy plate.

Cackle the Crone - A very old, experienced witch, using bound shades to animate a pack of small dead creatures such as rats, crows and foxes. She allegedly preys on children, but is more likely to pick on rich merchants. If she joins your quest, watch out for her pilfering your magical artefacts. You may give her one of them, in gratitude if her charms and potions heal

438

your wound-rot.

Cackle knows many small but obscure spells to improve love life, remove warts, or cause a septic ear. Her usual income is from selling charms and curses for healing, and protection for houses, to local villagers. She visits Bonny's tavern to sell personal protection and healing charms to fighters such as Roughly Hewn, Rusty Smallz and Bullseye.

Champ - The Tavern Bouncer, an ex-pugilist, heavily muscled and very good at dealing with rowdy customers. He has a cudgel for the tougher ones.

Chard Tsinda - A fire sorcerer, so his cloak ripples with what may really be flames. They can burn any shade of red, orange or blue, sometimes almost white, because he is a master of both fire and ice. His skin is jet black, with faint pale blue and scarlet veining, and his touch can turn unprotected humans to ash.

Creepio Mysterio - A church investigator and possible assassin. He is sneaky, dangerous, and magically powerful. Do not cheat or threaten him, or your body may never be found. Take care if Creepio offers to join your party. He can call on terrifying allies, but they may consider your safety irrelevant. Creepio might betray you for what he sees as a higher cause.

Duel - New character, not yet properly named, a notorious duellist with blade, pistol and magic. Arrogant, ruthless and handsome, he cuts a fine figure in his skin-tight duelling whites, but it isn't all show, he is highly skilled. Duel can be hired as a bodyguard, so check your opponent's companions before issuing a challenge!

Fe Hamma (element joke - Fe = iron) - A muscular, gnarled hunchback, allegedly a troll/dwarf hybrid, Fe is a master weaponsmith. His weapons are made of the finest steel, embedded with spells and gems to store magic and enhance their power, and well worth their extravagant prices. For a truly excessive price, Fe will enhance your personal weaponry without leaving any visible trace.

Ferryl Shayde - A half-cat sorceress. A powerful and skilled user of spells, she knows many intricate symbols well enough to throw them from memory. Her origin is shrouded in mystery, but her mere name can terrify lesser creatures.

Ffod the Hunter - A magical creature, never fully seen, Ffod sometimes takes the form of an ethereal leopard, wolf, eagle or, allegedly, an ogre, though few believe the last. Never fully aligned, Ffod might join a group if they can catch its attention, providing an almost invisible scout or night guard without needing magic. A strong magic user, Ffod can also kill or snare an unwary victim using only stealth. Unexplained deaths, those which don't leave a mark, are often ascribed to Ffod. (Only a select few know the origin of Ffod's name, though there are many legends of a hunter on the wind)

K'liss Windcatcher - A tall, slim sorceress who wears a pale blue robe, unlike the usual sorceress black and red. She is an absolute mistress of all air symbols, and an adept at mixing them with other spells to enhance the effect. Despite her gentle appearance, K'liss has a legendary temper if roused.

K'ress Bloodclaw - A tall, slim sorceress dressed entirely in tight, magically-enhanced black leather under a crimson cloak. Vicious, brutal and ruthless, she reputedly uses forbidden blood magic to raise and command the undead. Malicious rumours claim she is related to K'liss, possibly a twin.

Nikk Smartish - A Far Eastern warlock who fled to the West, changed his name and turned to crime. He uses skill, a personalised toolset, and magic to circumvent magical and mundane defences, either to steal or for hire. He casts mostly defensive hexes, but carries enchanted knives, poison darts, throwing stars and a miniature crossbow with charmed bolts. A good ally on quests needing guile, but make sure your own valuables are safely locked away.

Robyn D'Ritche - female mercenary, a scruffy inebriate, Bonny's half-sister and part-owner of the Tavern. She dresses in a frock-coat over a cuirass and tights, with tall boots, and a wide hat with a plume or braid. An expert with sword and knife, Robyn also carries a crossbow, and has a spear, shield, javelins and axes hung on her tough, shaggy horse. She supports and protects Bonny's Tavern, her base, where she recruits for fighting contracts or sells loot.

Rock'n Rolla - An earth sorcerer who can shape rock to form shields and armour, or command the earth itself to bury an enemy. Although a very difficult skill to master, using large amounts of magic, earth-wrought constructs are very resistant to both physical attacks and magic symbols. He wields a dwarven mace inscribed with powerful magic.

Roughly Hewn - A Barbarian adventurer with bluish-tinted skin - perhaps he has some ice giant blood. His favoured weapons are clubs or heavy swords, which may be enchanted. A brute force fighter, all muscle and rage, his body is naturally immune to minor spells and can tolerate serious injury in the heat of battle. He buys medallions inscribed with spell symbols or charms to provide extra protection, and help him heal.

Rusty Smallz - A mercenary footman wearing a mix of plate and chain armour. He is armed with a motley collection of weapons, from a double-handed axe and a long spear or pike, and a shield, down to hatchets and a punch dagger. Rusty carries all his spare weapons, tent and gear on a donkey, guarded by a bad-tempered mutt.

Saint Georgeous (pronounced Jorjeous as in George) - A Paladin, severe, androgynous, and beautiful. He/she is heavily armoured, with innate magical defences, and his/her weapons are inscribed with mysterious and powerful magical symbols. Saint Georgeous rides a white unicorn, which, despite wearing heavy armour, can run down the fleetest foe.

Shayde Warrior - Ferryl's bodyguard and apprentice, a fighter-mage trained in both magic and weapons, a difficult skillset to master. Shayde Warrior fights with ninja-style weapons, such as throwing stars and a staff, combined with martial arts. Beware, he can mix in a magical attack without any warning.

Spenz F'Lorinze - A foppish rake, the disgraced, disowned fourth son of a noble, Spenz is smitten, besotted with Bonny but often unfaithful. He has an allowance, on condition he never comes home, so he can afford the best magical protection. Rumours persist that he paid a fortune to have his ordinary-looking rapier enhanced by Fe Hamma himself.

Dressed in his broad-brimmed hat with a big feather, frilled shirt, striped tights, high boots and a rapier, Spenz tries to impress the ladies by joining quests. Luckily, he really can use the rapier, one of the few lessons he paid attention to. That, and his wealth, are both good reasons to include him in a quest, because a man with gold can open doors where magic and brawn fail.

Verdant Bounty - An archetypal fertility goddess in the making, Verdant has mastered the control of all plants. She is a natural ally of dryads, even if they sometimes clash over the magic in trees. A small act of kindness to a passing stranger can lead to your garden blossoming, literally, because Verdant Bounty likes to roam the world. She may be benevolent, but footpads beware. Even grass, braided as it grows, can crush a less than perfect shield, while roots can crumble rock.

Wind Chaser - A small, skinny, sprite trapper, Wind may have dwarf or some other non-human blood, but is sensitive about it. He looks innocuous, but catches and tames sprites as guards or hunters, which takes considerable magical skill and knowledge. For a price you may buy one, taking control of their magical tether, but none will be as strong as his own personal bodyguard, a very powerful wind sprite.

Usually a loner, Wind is invaluable as a scout or magical fighter if he/she can be recruited. Jesters like to link him romantically to Verdant Bounty, K'liss, K'ress, and if they really want a laugh, Ferryl Shayde.

Woods and Green - The magical solicitors with a small shack next to Bonny's Tavern, convenient for signing quest contracts. Contracts between players will include penalties for not fulfilling the quest, or lying about skill levels and abilities (these are not automatically revealed to other players). Players can earn or lose reliability points by their actions during a quest. Stealing the loot will make it harder to get another contract, but proof of charitable work on Low Earth (aka the real world, where we live) will increase health points.

Choose your character and your companions wisely, and let the game begin!

Rules of the Magical Tavern

Any Taverner is considered equal to any other Taverner regardless of race, creed, or magical ability. Progression in learning glyphs will be strictly by ability, assessed by the most adept. At any time Abel, advised by Zephyr, can prevent a Taverner moving on to the next glyph if he believes they are not ready.

All Taverners are voluntary. They can leave, but will no longer have access to training, Tavern premises, or extra Tavern magic.

Aims:

All Taverners must keep to the Accord.

The Tavern, the magical side of Bonny's Tavern, will be a force for good. As in the gameplay, the magical Taverners will help the weak and helpless in areas that are not covered by the magical community or a church. In return for the free magic and tuition provided by the Master of Castle House and Pendragon, and the sorceresses Ferryl Shayde and Zephyr, Taverners will provide free magical protection for the disadvantaged. Any pay for magical work will be passed to Pendragon Enterprises and used by the Tavern to extend their protection and train new recruits.

Taverners will not seek to take unfair advantage of their skills when dealing with non-magical humans. Taverners still in education will discourage bullying, theft and discrimination, and protect their schools with hexes. Older Taverners will try to alleviate similar problems where they find them, but will not usurp the role of the legitimate forces of Law and Order without the explicit approval of the Tavern adepts.

Penalties for Transgressions:

Minor transgressions will be punished with deprivation of magic and shunning for limited periods depending on the severity of the crime. The more serious crimes may warrant expulsion from the Tavern. The expelled culprit will be magically marked to warn all others, and will be permanently shunned by the Tavern.

Premeditated treachery leading to the death or tethering of a Taverner, or premeditated murder, will be punished by tethering or death. The death will be clean, and the culprit's choice.

Apprentices captured in battle will be tethered by the church, if they choose, or by the Tavern. The captive has the option of a clean death. Tavern tethering will not necessarily be permanent, and the captive may be allowed to train in the interim.

Sorcerers or sorceresses captured in battle will accept a Tavern tether, for life, or will be killed.

The Master of Castle House and Pendragon will be the final arbitrator in disputes. He administers High and Low Justice in his demesne, under the Accord, and the Tavern is under his protection.

Review

If you enjoyed this book, please share a short review with us on Amazon, Goodreads or the platform of your choice. Help other readers discover new authors.

Vance reads each and every comment you post and loves to hear from his readers.

Want more? Check out all of Vance Huxley's titles - from dystopian to military science fiction, there's something for everyone.

VANCE HUXLEY

Vance Huxley lives out in the countryside in Lincolnshire, England. He has spent a busy life working in many different fields – including the building and rail industries, as a workshop manager, trouble-shooter for an engineering firm, accountancy, cafe proprietor, and graphic artist. He also spent time in other jobs, and is proud of never being dismissed, and only once made redundant.

Eventually he found his Noeline, but unfortunately she died much too young. To help with the aftermath, Vance tried writing though without any real structure. As an editor and beta readers explained the difference between words and books, he tried again.

Now he tries to type as often as possible in spite of the assistance of his cats, since his legs no longer work well enough to allow anything more strenuous. An avid reader of sci-fi, fantasy and adventure novels, his writing tends towards those genres.